MW00883194

DRAGONBLADE

A MEDIEVAL ROMANCE
BOOK ONE IN THE DRAGONBLADE TRILOGY

BY KATHRYN LE VEQUE

© Copyright 2010, 2014 by Kathryn Le Veque
Print Edition

All rights reserved. No part of this book may be used or reproduced in any manner whatsoever without written permission, except in the case of brief quotations embodied in critical articles or reviews.

Printed by Dragonblade Publishing in the United States of America

Text copyright 2010, 2014 by Kathryn Le Veque
Cover copyright 2010, 2014 by Kathryn Le Veque

Library of Congress Control Number 2014-012
ISBN 1494229595

KATHRYN LE VEQUE NOVELS

Medieval Romance:

The de Russe Legacy:
The White Lord of Wellesbourne
The Dark One: Dark Knight
Beast
Lord of War: Black Angel
The Falls of Erith

The de Lohr Dynasty:
While Angels Slept (Lords of East Anglia)
Rise of the Defender
Spectre of the Sword
Unending Love
Archangel
Steelheart

Great Lords of le Bec:
Great Protector
To the Lady Born (House of de Royans)

Lords of Eire:
The Darkland (Master Knights of
Connaught)
Black Sword
Echoes of Ancient Dreams (time travel)

De Wolfe Pack Series:
The Wolfe
Serpent
Scorpion (Saxon Lords of Hage – Also related
to The Questing)
Walls of Babylon
The Lion of the North
Dark Destroyer

Ancient Kings of Anglecynn:
The Whispering Night
Netherworld

Battle Lords of de Velt:
The Dark Lord

Devil's Dominion

Reign of the House of de Winter:
Lespada
Swords and Shields (also related to The
Questing, While Angels Slept)

De Reyne Domination:
Guardian of Darkness
The Fallen One (part of Dragonblade Series)

Unrelated characters or family groups:
The Gorgon (Also related to Lords of
Thunder)
The Warrior Poet (St. John and de Gare)
Tender is the Knight (House of d'Vant)
Lord of Light
The Questing (related to The Dark Lord,
Scorpion)
The Legend (House of Summerlin)

**The Dragonblade Series: (Great Marcher
Lords of de Lara)**
Dragonblade
Island of Glass (House of St. Hever)
The Savage Curtain (Lords of Pembury)
The Fallen One (De Reyne Domination)
Fragments of Grace (House of St. Hever)
Lord of the Shadows
Queen of Lost Stars (House of St. Hever)

**Lords of Thunder: The de Shera
Brotherhood Trilogy**
The Thunder Lord
The Thunder Warrior
The Thunder Knight

Time Travel Romance: (Saxon Lords of
Hage)
The Crusader
Kingdom Come

Contemporary Romance:

Kathlyn Trent/Marcus Burton Series:
Valley of the Shadow
The Eden Factor
Canyon of the Sphinx

The American Heroes Series:
Resurrection
Fires of Autumn
Evenshade

Sea of Dreams
Purgatory

Other Contemporary Romance:
Lady of Heaven
Darkling, I Listen

Multi-author Collections/Anthologies:
With Dreams Only of You (USA Today bestseller)
Sirens of the Northern Seas (Viking romance)

Note: All Kathryn's novels are designed to be read as stand-alones, although many have cross-over characters or cross-over family groups. Novels that are grouped together have related characters or family groups.

Series are clearly marked. All series contain the same characters or family groups except the American Heroes Series, which is an anthology with unrelated characters.

There is NO particular chronological order for any of the novels because they can all be read as stand-alones, even the series.

For more information, find it in **A Reader's Guide to the Medieval World of Le Veque.**

TABLE OF CONTENTS

CHAPTER ONE

The Month of January
Year of our Lord 1326
Cartingdon Parrish; Northumbria, England

THE TIME OF year dictated that the landscape would be an eternal shade of twilight, no matter what the time of day. Gray colored the sky, the earth and the mood of the people.

The town of Cartingdon was no exception. The people were pale with the limited nutrition of winter, their woolen clothes barely adequate for the freezing temperatures that the north winds brought. More than the grayness of the air and people, there was something else this day that darkened the land. Everyone could feel it and they were edgy.

There were whispers floating about like the many snow crystals in the air. Word had spread through the markets that morning after Matins, moving to the avenue of the Smiths and finally to the street of the Jews, telling everyone of the meeting that would be held at Vespers. The purpose was to discuss the most recent rumor regarding England's king. These were turbulent times in a turbulent land.

The sun hovered on the horizon and the church-bells chimed the onset of Vespers, calling the masses to the meeting. The townsfolk flocked to the stone church that they had built with their own hands. Fanged gargoyles imported from France hung on the eaves, lending ambience to the disquiet. Once the people filled the church, they stood in angry, hissing clusters.

The priests had lit a few large tapers, giving the sanctuary a haunting glow as they prepared for the meeting and subsequent mass. Several aldermen were having an intense discussion near the great altar; their deliberation raged for some time until the tall man in the center of the discussion silenced the group and called forth the crowds that had gathered. What they had to say would affect them all.

The mayor of the town was Balin Cartingdon. He was a farmer of noble descent who had flourished, turning a small sharecropping plot into a vast agricultural plantation. He had been a very young man when he sank his first barley seed into the ground, when the settlement of Cartingdon had been an assembly of huts called Snitter Crag. Twenty-two years later, his barley production was the largest in Northumbria and he had added wool and sheep to his empire. The tiny town had exploded due to his farming and was renamed Cartingdon in his honor.

"Good people," Balin's voice rang above the fickle buzz. "Thank you for coming. We have called this meeting to discuss the needs of our king and country."

"You mean the needs of Mortimer!" someone from the crowd shouted.

As the others agreed angrily, Balin shook his head. "Roger Mortimer is not our king. I speak of young Edward."

The grumbling grew louder. At the rear of the church, a small figure suddenly entered. It was apparent that the form was a woman from the drape of the cloak she wore, a soft green-blue garment that clung to her shapely body. A few of the village folk recognized her, moving out of her way as she pushed through the crowd. By the time she reached the front of the church, she had removed her hood, revealing cascades of golden-brown hair and almond-shaped eyes that were a brilliant shade of hazel. She had the face of an angel, but beneath the sweet façade lay an iron will. In the township of Cartingdon, the first daughter of Mayor Balin was more feared and respected than her father.

"Mortimer rules the country with Queen Isabella." The woman

spoke loudly, addressing both her father and the assembly. "If rebellion is in the air and we support it, his hammer will fall on all of us. Everything we have built, and all that we have, will be confiscated. I personally do not want to see everything that my father has worked so hard for taken away in the blink of an eye."

"It is doubtful it will be taken away," Balin said patiently, displeased that his daughter had chosen not to remain silent. He had gone so far as to ask Toby not to attend the meeting, but alas, that was too much to hope for. If there was an opinion to be had, she was usually in the middle of it. "Our liege, Tate Crewys de Lara, also supports the rightful king. We have no choice but to support the crown if those who hold our fate have such loyalties."

"But what of the Queen?" the crowd spoke again. "She has the support of the King of France. He is her brother. What if she calls on him to quell the rebellion? What if the French overrun Northumbria and destroy our town?"

"They will kill us all!" another shouted.

The crowd surged unsteadily and Balin held up his hands. "You forget that young Edward has the Scottish king's support," he replied calmly, hoping to soothe the mob. "He will protect us. But we must help our king and that is why we are here today. It is our duty. Every man must decide for himself if he is willing to sacrifice for a greater cause."

"The king is a child," Toby pointed out. "His mother and Roger Mortimer rule on his behalf. Never forget that they did England a tremendous service by deposing young Edward's father, King Edward the Second. He was a vile infection that drained this country of all that was good and righteous. They subsequently rid England of the Despencers, the father and son who vied for the throne, thereby eliminating the last links of Edward's contemptible reign. For the past three years under Isabella and Mortimer, England has known a measure of peace. Do we truly want to feed the beast of rebellion again and perhaps create a tempest that will destroy us all?"

It was a brilliant summation of the recent past of England's monarchy, given by a woman who should have, respectably, known nothing of the matter. The crowd roared as she finished; some in approval, some in disapproval. Toby looked at her father, sorry she had not completely supported his stance, but in the same breath, hoping it would cause him to deliberate the potential consequences. She didn't want to see her people die for a futile cause. There had been too many of them over the past several years.

"Toby," her father had to raise his voice over the commotion of the crowd. "Please go home. You do not help this situation."

Toby was genuinely contrite. "I am sorry to appear as if I oppose you, but I do not believe you have clearly considered this subject. It is greater than you think."

"I am well aware of how critical it is. But these are simple folk; I cannot outline the detailed politics of England's situation. I should not have even outlined them to you, but I did for reasons that no longer seem valid. I should have known you would find a way to contradict me."

"I did not mean to. I simply meant to give you my opinion."

"I know well enough your opinion. I know it, I think, even before you do."

"I am simply asking that you think about what you are saying."

Balin rolled his eyes. "With you around, I can do nothing *but* think. Now be still before the crowd turns against us."

As Toby and her father exchanged opinions, back against the wall something was stirring. Several men stood in a unit, draped in dark cloaks as they listened to the spirited debate. The first man tossed back his hood; he had a face of classic male beauty, a granite jaw and full lips. His hair was dark like a raven's wing, shorn up the back yet long enough in the front so that it swept across eyes the color of storm clouds. He was a striking example of perfection, completely out of place among the worn, colorless peasants. He watched everything around him like a hawk, not missing a movement or a word. It was apparent that he was absorbing everything in his element until he had enough information to make a reasonable judgment.

The man moved forward through the crowd, taking his entourage of five with him. People moved out his way instinctively, not wanting to be trampled by the man who was a head taller than even the tallest man in the church. He approached Balin and Toby and softly cleared his throat.

"Forgive me, my lord," the man's voice was deep and rich. "I realize this is a town meeting exclusively for the residents of Cartingdon but I wonder if I may speak to the throng."

Balin and Toby looked at the man. Balin's reaction was far less than Toby's; the moment their eyes met, she felt a strange buzzing sensation in her head. It was enough to cause her to pull her gaze away, looking to her father to see if he was having the same odd reaction. He seemed unaffected.

"Who would you be, my lord?" Balin asked.

"I am Tate Crewys de Lara."

As if on cue, the group escorting Tate threw back their hoods and cloaks, exposing enough armor and weapons to handle a small battle quite efficiently. Two of the men were enormous; they were knights of the highest order, clad in expensive metal protection. Two shorter, stockier men-at-arms supported them, dressed in leather protection and sporting fine Welsh crossbows. The last member of the entourage was the squire, of lad of fourteen or fifteen years. He was tall, thin, and fair-haired.

"My... my lord de Lara," Balin was clearly shocked. "Although we have corresponded on the occasion of taxation and audits for your lands, this is the first we have met. I am indeed honored, my lord."

Tate heard his words, but his focus was on Toby. Now that he was closer and could see her more clearly, she was indeed worth a second look. "I have spent the majority of my life in London or in France, with the wars, and have hardly spent time in this land for which I hold title," his gaze lingered on Toby. "Harbottle Castle is a garrison I have seen three times in my life."

Balin could see where Tate's focus was and indicated his child. "May I present my eldest daughter, Mistress Elizabetha Aleanora de Tobins Cartingdon. She is the one who has seen to your requests with regard to revenue from the parish."

"Mistress, I thank you for your service."

"My pleasure, my lord."

Tate's gaze was like an immovable object. He tried not to be obvious about it, but the lady was quite lovely. Such beauty was very rare. He did not, however, like the bold nature he had seen come forth from her since their arrival. Were it not for that flaw, he might have considered speaking further with her.

"Please, my lord," Balin put his hands up to quiet the crowd. "Speak to our people. Tell them of England's need."

When Tate looked away from her, Toby felt as if she had been jolted. He had held her in such an odd trance that his sudden departure startled her. Still, she retained enough of her wits to remain attuned to the subject at hand.

"My lord, if I may," she said carefully. "These are simple people with simple lives. Things like war frighten them, not inspire them. I am afraid a thunderous address will only further alarm them."

Tate looked at her. "Mistress... Elizabetha, was it?"

His tone bordered on contempt. Toby struggled to retain her courage. "I have not gone by Elizabetha since my birth. I am known as Toby, my lord."

"Toby? That is a strange name. A man's name."

"It is a nickname, my lord, given to me by my grandsire."

"Why?"

"His family name was de Tobins. My mother gave it to me as a middle name. Everyone called my grandsire Toby and he called me the same."

Tate's reply was to give her one more look, a once-over, and turn back to the crowd. Toby took the opportunity to study the man; the Lord of Harbottle, the title for the Harbottle Commons lordship he held, was an exceptionally tall man with arms the size of tree branches and enormous hands. Though he wore no armor, merely layers of heavy tunics, breeches and massive boots, Toby could tell by the width of his shoulders that he was, quite simply, a very big man. She backed off, unwilling to provoke Cartingdon's liege, but she didn't leave completely. To do so, if he was going to war-monger, would have been to do a great injustice to the populace of Cartingdon. She felt as if she had to protect them.

Tate saw that she wasn't leaving and he tried not to let it affect him as he addressed the uncertain throng. He wasn't sure why she was so distracting, but she was.

"Good people of Cartingdon, I am Sir Tate Crewys de Lara, Lord of Harbottle. As your liege, it is a privilege to speak with you this day."

The crowd had simmered, but they were still uneasy. Tate continued in an even voice.

"I have listened to your mayor speak on young Edward's behalf," he said. "I am here to tell you that the king is ready, willing and able to assume the mantle left by his father. Those who are not the rightful rulers have assumed his throne. Most of England's nobles understand this and to them I have made my plea. I have spent many years in the service of the young king and I can personally vouch for his abilities. He is wise, thoughtful, and fair as much as his young age will allow. With the proper advisors, the rest will come with time." Tate raked his fingers through his short, dark hair as he collected his thoughts. "I sent word to Mayor Cartingdon days ago requesting men and money for the king's cause. My men and I have been in town for two days, observing the people and countryside. It is by sheer fortune that we are here for the meeting that will decide the aid you will provide Edward the King. I could easily tax you to death or simply take what, by all rights, belongs to me. But I choose not to do so. I would like the support from Cartingdon to be genuine, for the young king and his cause. I believe he will establish a stable monarchy from which we may all benefit. Therefore, I ask you to please decide favorably upon him. England is

Edward, and Edward needs your help."

By the time he finished, the entire church was silent. The townsfolk looked at Balin, Toby, each other, attempting to determine if what their liege said was true. He sounded convincing. Toby, too, was almost convinced of the young king's cause after his speech; she stood slightly behind Tate and to the right, able to see his strong profile. There was something about him that conveyed truth. She looked at the knights standing well behind him; they, too, seemed strong and virtuous. Even the squire seemed honorable. One of the villagers broke the silence.

"I am a ferrier, m'lord," the older man said hesitantly. "I canna provide ye with gold or coin, but I can provide ye with meself. If Edward the Younger is in need, then we must help."

Toby knew the man who spoke. He was kind but not intelligent. She could see most of the other townsmen talking quietly to one another, no doubt discussing their prowess with a sword and crossbow. Some of the men had already seen battle, called into action a few years earlier with the removal of King Edward and the Despencers. There were some men, however, that had left to aid the crown and had not returned.

"What of the opposition, my lord?" Toby could not keep silent; she hated to see men's lives wasted. "Can you please tell them of the opposition they will face?"

Tate looked at her, her beautiful face strong and her expression intense. He didn't sense hostility from her, merely concern.

"The opposition is Queen Isabella and her lover, Roger Mortimer, Earl of March," he said, glancing over the crowd. "Mortimer has a large army at his disposal, as does the queen. The king's troops, however, are loyal to young Edward; that much we have ascertained. The Queen's strength will come from France and her brother, the king's army. But once we have begun our campaign to reclaim the throne, summoning France's troops will take time. It is my belief that we will have enough time to subdue Isabella and Mortimer before support arrives."

"But what of the nobles?" Toby asked.

Tate's gaze fixed on her again; he seemed incapable of staying away for long. "There are many in support of the king."

"Who?"

"Alnwick, Warkworth and York in the north. Arundel in the south."

He had named some of the most powerful nobles in England. Their armed support collectively was staggering. Toby felt her questions had been answered and was reluctant to press him further, although she was still opposed to the general idea of war. Still, any more questions would have made her appear belligerent, which normally would not have concerned her, but she did not want to shame her father. Balin, sensing she had come to the end of her queries, thank the Lord, stepped in.

"I am sure that each man can find it within his conscience to lend what support he can, my lord," he said. "All men interested in committing themselves to the young king's army will assemble at the church tomorrow at noon for further instructions. For my part, I will supply a herd of my finest sheep to sell at market and donate the proceeds."

Toby's jaw dropped. "Father...."

Balin cast his daughter a withering glare. "My daughter, as she is most knowledgeable in the accounting of my livestock, will be glad to show you the prize herd north at Lorbottle."

Toby was speechless. It was the largest herd of sheep they had, nearly ready to be sheared. The money they would bring would be enormous. Astounded, she grappled with the concept as her father called an end to the gathering and the townspeople began to disband. She was so stupefied that she didn't realize when Tate came and stood next to her.

"If it would not take you away from any pressing duties, I would see the sheep this day," he said. "I would also like a full accounting."

Jolted from her thoughts, Toby looked up at him. From the corner of her eye, she could see that her father was about to make a hasty retreat from the church. "Excuse me a moment, my lord."

She raced to her father, cutting off his exit. Balin held up his hands.

"Not a word," he hissed at her. "You have my orders. Follow them."

"Father, do you realize what you have done?" she hissed in return. "To donate five hundred head of sheep, with the price of wool today, will cost us a fortune in lost money. We still have to pay the wages of our farm, our taxes, and eat on top of everything else. We need that money."

"It will not do us any good if England goes to the dogs under Isabella and Mortimer," he said flatly. "We have suffered so much under Edward's rule. Can you not understand that the young king is our best, brightest hope?"

"I understand that you have apparently lost your mind."

"There are many things in this world that I will tolerate and many things that I learn to accept," Tate was standing behind Toby, listening to everything that had been said. "But the one thing I refuse to accept is a daughter's disrespect to her father. You, Mistress Toby, have an appalling lack of manners. I have seen such display from the moment I first entered this church."

Toby was ashamed and defensive at the same time. "If honesty is a sin, then I am indeed guilty, my lord."

"It is not a sin. But your lack of control is."

Toby wisely refrained from an opinionated retort. She wasn't a fool and calmed herself with effort. "May I speak frankly, my lord?"

The corner of Tate's mouth twitched. It was difficult for him not to smile at what was surely to come. "By all means."

Toby took a deep breath, hoping he wasn't about to slap her for her insolence. "My father became prosperous by hard work and good luck, but only by harder work and even more good fortune have we maintained it. My mother used to maintain the business when I was very small, but that duty passed to me several years ago after she became ill. Since that time, we have seen our prosperity grow many times over. Were it not for me, however, my father would have given everything away and we would be living in poverty. He is generous beyond compare and does not know when to stop."

"And you believe that donating to the king's cause is an example of how your father does not know when to stop?"

"Not necessarily. But we were counting on that harvest of wool to pay wages to our farmhands for the next year. Many people depend on us for their livelihood."

Tate cocked his head thoughtfully. "Then your opposition is not against the king himself."

"Of course not." For the first time, Toby's tone softened. "I simply cannot believe that the king would want aid for his cause at the expense of starving out many of his loyal subjects."

"It is that serious?"

"It could be. Winter is not yet over and harvest will not come again until next fall. Our people must have something to live on, my lord."

Tate was quiet a moment; he glanced at the two massive knights who had accompanied him. One man was a giant, with short brown hair and cornflower blue eyes. The second man wasn't as tall but he was enormously wide with white-blond eyebrows. The pair of them gazed back at Tate and he knew either one of them would have gladly taken the lady over their knee at that moment. His focus moved to the squire, the skinny lad who accompanied him everywhere. The boy had a somewhat submissive expression. So far, none of those expressions helped Tate sort through the situation.

After a moment's deliberation, he turned back to Toby. "What would you suggest, mistress? I will leave it to your good judgment."

Toby was surprised at the question. She had expected far more of a battle, ending in her defeat. She thought quickly, hoping to come up with a solution that would placate him and not send her family to the poor house.

"There is a herd of older sheep that we were considering sending to the slaughter simply because their wool has become so tough," she said. "It is only around two hundred head, but the wool could be sheared one last time and sold for market value, and then the herd could be slaughtered for meat. It would bring you nearly as much given the proper market and negotiations."

"Of which you would so kindly provide me."

Toby nodded, feeling a good deal of relief. "It would be my pleasure, my lord."

"I would see the herd."

"You will dine with us first, my lord," Balin insisted. "Toby can take you to the herd at first light."

He wondered what adventures in indigestion he would discover during the course of dining with the opinionated Mistress Toby Cartingdon. If the woman was formidable in the public arena, he could only imagine her stance in a private setting. He was loathe to admit it to himself, but he was more than curious to find out.

🕉

"AN INTERESTING MEETING," the blond knight said as they made their way to their chargers, tethered at the livery near the church. Sir Kenneth St. Héver had served under Tate de Lara for many years and had, consequently, experienced many things with him. But the latest experience in the church was a curious one. "An interesting town."

His counterpart, Sir Stephen of Pembury, was the larger, darker knight. He was the more congenial of the two. "What kind of town can it possibly be that allows itself to be run by a female?" he said what they were all thinking. "A strong man could do wonders here."

Tate had notice an inn across the street and, collecting his destrier, began moving in that direction. "It seems to me that she has done wonders without the aid of a man. No matter how distasteful her manner, we are nonetheless fortunate to have received a sizable donation from her father."

Pembury snorted. "She is a beautiful woman. Too bad she has the disposition of a wild boar."

St. Héver glanced at him. "Do you have aspirations for her, then?"

"Me? Never."

"You could marry her and run the town."

"Somehow, I doubt it. She is accustomed to being in charge. Could you not see that?"

St. Héver merely lifted his white-blond eyebrows in agreement. The very thought was appalling, but Tate wasn't paying any attention to their chagrin. He was focused on the tavern and obtaining some much needed food and drink. Leaving the horses, they made their way inside the smelly hovel and found a table in the corner where a round woman brought them ale, bread and cheese. The young squire with them shoved half a loaf in his mouth before the knights had finished pouring their drink.

"Slow down, lad," Tate admonished lightly. "There is more bread to be had. No need to choke yourself."

The youth grinned and slowed to chew. The two men at arms that constantly shadowed the group of four took position against the wall opposite the table. They were the first line of defense against any potential happening, which was a fairly normal occurrence. England, and the world in general, was a dangerous place.

With the squire no longer in danger of choking and the knights settled with their ale, Stephen put his thoughts into focus.

"Did anyone notice if we were followed?"

Tate shook his head. "I do not think so. I've not seen evidence in a couple of days."

Kenneth took a deep drag of his ale. "We lost them in Rothbury," he said. "If nothing else, Mortimer's men are easy to spot. They follow us out in the open."

"He doesn't have to keep them to the shadows because he governs the entire country," Stephen snorted. "What does he have to fear?"

Tate regarded the ale in his cup. "He has to fear a young man on the cusp of adulthood who holds the throne he so dearly wants," he muttered, more to himself than to the others. He glanced up at the knights. "She asked valid questions, you know."

Pembury looked up from his bread. "Who?"

"Mistress Elizabetha."

"What questions do you mean?"

"About the opposition."

"You were truthful in your answer."

Tate lifted a resigned eyebrow. "Aye, but minimally; I did not mention that Isabella and Mortimer hold all of Windsor Castle and her wealth. That is the heart of the kingdom. And if we are to oust them, we must strike at the heart."

"I thought that was what we were doing."

The squire's soft voice entered the conversation. Tate looked at the youth, breadcrumbs on his fuzzy face.

"The more I go to these little towns, the more I realize that a rebellion must encompass far less than armies and knights intent on destroying each other," he explained to the lad. "We must take control of Mortimer and Isabella on a much smaller scale. Balin Cartingdon's outspoken daughter was correct in some aspects."

"Which ones?"

A distant look crossed Tate's face. "By feeding the beast of rebellion, we could destroy everything. Sometimes a larger operation is not the better tactic than a small, precisely planned one."

"Will we go back to London and re-think our strategy?"

The squire's question was posed with curiosity more than anxiety. Tate passed a glance at the knights before answering. "What would you suggest?"

"We still need support. And we need money."

"True enough; which is why my inclination is to stay the eve in Cartingdon, negotiate for the sale of the sheep with Balin's daughter, and then make our way back to London. I worry being gone overlong. Much can change in a short amount of time."

"That is a wise decision," Pembury said. "Without you in London, Mortimer lulls himself into a false sense of security. I never thought it was particularly prudent for us to have left the city in the first place."

Tate looked at his squire, reading the boy's concerned expression. He downplayed his knight's comment. "It was necessary," he said simply. "But for now, let us eat and enjoy this moment of peace."

The squire went back to eating only when the knights did. A group of minstrels struck up a lively song and soon the entire tavern was bouncing. It was a good moment of relaxation for them to remember; the future, Tate suspected, would hold few.

CHAPTER TWO

"THEY CALL HIM Dragonblade," Ailsa Catherine Cartingdon danced around the table in the large hall of Forestburn Manor, the Cartingdon home. "Have you heard, Toby? Dragonblade!"

Ailsa was ten years of age, a frail girl with golden curls. She had an energetic mind, sharp and inquisitive, but a weak body that kept her in bed a good deal of the time. She was always ill with something. It had started at her birth when her mother suffered a stroke whilst in labor; Ailsa was born blue and Judith Cartingdon had nearly died. Only by God's grace did either of them live through it.

"Aye, you little devil, I have heard it," Toby said. "But you must not say anything to him. Perhaps he does not like the name."

Ailsa stopped her excited dance. "Why not?"

Toby shrugged, putting the last touch on the mulled wine. "It does not sound very flattering."

Ailsa resumed her dance, ending up lying on top of the table. "And do you know what else I have heard?"

"I am afraid to know."

"I have heard that Tate de Lara is the son of King Edward the First. They say that he was saved from his savage Welsh mother by the Marcher lords of de Lara, who then raised him as their own. He is the half-brother of King Edward the Second and was there when the king was murdered. And some say that Queen Isabella asked him to marry her, but he refused, so she took Roger Mortimer as her lover instead."

"Where do you hear such nonsense?" Toby lifted her sister off the table.

"From Rachel Comstock's mother. She knows everything."

Toby made a face. "Rachel Comstock's mother thinks that she is God's blessing to all of Mankind and constantly reminds us of how she was a lady in waiting for King Edward's mother's sister's cousin by marriage. Truth be told, she was probably just the privy attendant."

Ailsa giggled. "She says that Tate should be king, not young Edward."

Toby paused long enough to ponder that. It seemed like such an immense prospect although she had heard the same thing from her father, once, a long time ago. The fact that Tate de Lara was Edward Longshanks' bastard son was generally accepted. He had the height and strength of the Plantagenets but the dark features of the Welsh princes. The more she thought on his royal lineage, the more unsettled she became. The man she would soon be supping with had a royal heritage on both sides that was centuries old.

"Not a word of this at supper, do you hear?" she said to her sister. "You have no idea the seriousness of your words."

Ailsa pouted. Her sister shoved some rushes into her hand, indicating she spread them, to keep her busy.

"But why must I keep silent? I want to know what it is like to live in London and I want to know of King Edward. Do you suppose he will marry some day?"

"I suppose so. He must, as the king."

"Could he marry me?"

Toby put her hands on her hips, smiling at her sister in spite of herself. "No, little chicken, he could not. He needs a woman of royal blood, not a farmer's daughter."

Ailsa was back to pouting. "But father says we have noble blood in us."

Toby spread the last of the fresh rushes before the hearth. "The best we can do is claim relation to the barons of Northumberland. The last baron, Ives de Vesci, was our father's grandsire."

"And mother is descended from a Viking king named Red Thor."

"So Grandsire Toby has told us."

"Do you not believe him?"

Toby just smiled. She had a beautiful smile; it changed her face dramatically. She could get her father to agree to anything when she smiled.

"Help me see to supper, little chicken."

Ailsa forgot about Northumberland and the Viking king. She skipped after her sister, who was more a mother to her than her real one. Judith Cartingdon had been bedridden since Ailsa's birth, unable to walk, barely able to speak. The care of the infant girl had fallen upon twelve-year-old Toby. As a result, the girls were inordinately close.

Supper was mutton, boiled and sauced, marrow pie, a pudding of currants and nuts, and bread made from precious white flour. Ailsa kept trying to steal pieces of bread and Toby would shoo her away. The cook was an elderly woman who had been Toby's wet-nurse years ago. The kitchen of Forestburn was low-ceilinged to keep in the heat and mostly constructed of stone; therefore, on a cold day, it was the very best place to be. But on a day like today, with the added stress of an important visitor, Toby was sweating rivers.

"Suppertime is near," Ailsa could always judge by the rising of the bread. It happened at the same time, every day, without fail. "Do you suppose Dragonblade will be here soon?"

Toby put the last touch on the finished marrow pie and wiped the beads of perspiration on her forehead. "I told you not to call him that," she told her sister. "And, aye, he will be here soon. I must go and change my clothes."

Ailsa followed her to the second floor of the manor. Her father had received license several years ago from the barons of Northumberland to build a fortified house to protect his family and farm. It was a stone structure with battlements, but no protecting walls other than the heavy wooden hedge fence that surrounded the immediate area of the home. There was a great hall, a solar, and the kitchen on the ground floor, while the upper floor held three large rooms and another smaller room used for bathing and dressing. Ailsa and Toby shared a room, their mother had one room, and their father another.

A servant helped Toby strip off her clothes. While Ailsa lay upon the bed and continued her musings about their alleged royal relations, Toby went to the smaller adjoining room and stood inside the great iron tub as the servant poured buckets of warm water over her body to rinse off the sweat. Scraping off the excess water, she then doused herself in rosewater before drying off and dressing in a surcoat of emerald damask, set with a scoop-necked collar of white satin and embroidered in gold thread. Her luscious hair was braided, left to drape over one shoulder. Ailsa got off the bed and danced around her as the servant put the finishing touches on her hair.

"Do you suppose Dragonblade will marry?" she asked.

Toby sighed heavily. "Ailsa, if you call him that one more time...."

Ailsa kissed her cheek and hugged her neck, careful not to ruin the hair. "Sir Tate, I mean. Would it not be fancy if he married you? You could live at Harbottle Castle."

"He will not marry me. He was married, once, so I was told."

"Where is his wife?"

"I heard that she died."

Ailsa looked sad as only a child can. "He must miss her, do you suppose?" From downstairs, they heard the front door bang open, a signal that their father had returned home. Multiple voices indicated guests and Ailsa began to jump up and down. "They are here, they are here!"

"I shall greet them," Toby leapt off the stool with the servant still fussing with her hair. "Go and see to Mother, Ailsa. Make sure she is tended to before you join our guests."

Ailsa protested. Toby took her by the hand and led her to the door of her mother's bower. The old woman, hearing their voices, called out.

"Toby!"

It was a bellow, a barely recognizable word. Toby, knowing by the tone that her mother's mood was not good, bade Ailsa to stay outside. It would not have been healthy for the child to go in. With a breath for courage, she ventured into the dark, musty bower.

It was like a chamber of horrors, a dusty, smelly, cluttered mess. Rats hid beneath the bed, waiting for the scraps of food that the invalid woman would drop. Judith Cartingdon had been a lovely woman once. But ten years of bad health, the inability to walk and the near-inability to speak, had turned her into a caricature of her former self. When Toby came near the bed, Judith picked up her good arm and hit her daughter in the shoulder.

"Where have you been?" she slurred. "I have been calling for you. Why did you not answer me?"

"We have guests for dinner, mother," Toby didn't rub her shoulder; she would not let her mother see that she had hurt her. "I had to see to supper."

Judith slapped her hand on the bed, drool running down the left side her face. "Supper for me, do you hear? Bring it to me now!"

Toby didn't argue with her; she didn't want to be near her mother, much less engaged in a futile conversation with her. She turned around to leave the room when Judith picked up a small pewter bowl and threw it at her, striking her on the top of her left shoulder. It stung deeply, but still, Toby didn't let on. She continued out of the room.

Ailsa was standing by the door, wide-eyed. "Bring her supper," Toby finally took the time, out of her mother's sight, to rub her back. "Make sure all of the plates are removed this time. And do not get too close. Her mood is foul this eve."

"She hit you again?"

Toby didn't answer her; the back-rubbing was enough. Smoothing her dress and saying a silent prayer that the meal downstairs progressed without incident, she descended the stairs into the hall below.

Sparks from the hearth had caught some of the rushes in the hall on fire; consequently, the hall was smokier than usual. Toby entered the room, curtsying to the men whose attention turned to her.

"Good eve, Father," she said. Then she looked at Tate. "My lord."

"Ah, Toby," her father greeted her, his normal chalice of wine in hand. "I was showing Sir Tate our humble farm."

Tate stood near the fire; there had been a slight mist outside and he raked his fingers through his hair to dry it in the heat. His eyes lingered on Toby in her emerald surcoat.

"This farm is anything but humble," he said. "The size and structure is impressive."

"You may thank me for the size and my daughter for the structure," Balin said. "Were it not for Toby, this would still be but a mediocre working farm, struggling to support a village."

More wine and ale were brought to the table. Tate had been accompanied by his entourage of men; the knights stood and drank their ale while the men at arms stood on either side of the front door in a defensive position. The squire sat on a small stool near the hearth, drying his thin body out.

"It is good to see a community that can support itself," Tate said. "There is so much poverty in the north that the peasants resort to stealing and begging to live. I have had a good deal of trouble with it on my lands."

Toby moved to pour herself some mulled wine. "Do you also not think, my lord, that the wars of the crown have created such poverty?"

"They do."

"Yet still you support another uprising."

Tate knew this moment would come; he just did not think it would come so soon. He turned fully to Toby, a radiant vision in the ambient light of the fire. The sight of her caused the harsh response on his tongue to ease. It was difficult to become angry with such beauty.

"I would not consider Edward's right an uprising, mistress," his voice was steady. "Do you deny the rightful king his entitlement?"

"Of course not. But is there not a more peaceful way?"

"If you have any suggestions, you have my full attention."

Toby wasn't a military expert by any means. Her gaze trailed to the two enormous knights standing near the hearth; their expressions were harsh and she did not like the feeling radiating from them. The men at arms were far enough away that they probably had not heard the conversation, but the squire was looking at her as if he had something to say to all of it. She almost wished she hadn't spoken out; too many times she would speak before thinking. This was one of those times.

"It would seem to me that the Queen would willingly relinquish the right to rule to her son," she said. "He is the king, after all. Unless the Earl of March has poisoned her against her own son, what mother would not want to see her child achieve his claim?"

"Power has a strange way of blinding those it serves," Tate said. "The king has attempted negotiating with the Queen. She does not believe him ready to assume the full mantle."

"And you believe that he is, my lord?"

Tate's dark eyes were intense. "I would stake my life on it."

There was something in his sincerity that Toby dare not question. Thankfully, the meal was brought at that moment, precluding the discussion from burgeoning into something uncomfortable. Her father, however, made sure to corner her privately as the guests took their seats.

"If I have ever asked one thing of you, now is the time. Behave tonight, if not for yourself, then for me. Please."

There was heavy alcohol on his breath. That was a usual occurrence, but Toby would have none of it tonight. "If you promise not to get drunk and fly out of control as you do, I shall promise to behave."

Balin's expression turned cold. "Mind yourself, daughter. And do as I ask."

With reluctance, Toby silently agreed and went to take her seat. She ended up seated at Tate's right hand; the knights were across from her, the squire on her right, and her father at the end of the table.

She was mildly uncomfortable seated so close to Tate. His hand was near hers and she put her hand in her lap. He lapsed into a quiet discussion with his knights while Toby silently attended her meal.

When the knights laughed at something and she looked up to see what the joke was about, Tate apologized.

"I do not believe I have made formal introductions to you, my lady." He indicated the two armored men across the table. "These are my trusted friends, Sir Stephen of Pembury and Sir Kenneth St. Héver. They have informed me that I have been most rude by way of presentation."

Toby looked at the men, suspecting they said nothing to Tate about his rudeness. More than likely, the laugh had been at her expense. She simply nodded at them as Tate indicated the young man sitting at her right.

"And this is my squire, John of Hainault." The lad looked mortified as all eyes turned to him. His mouth was full of food and it was a struggle for him to chew and not choke. "Careful not to get close to him, else he might bite. He eats everything within arm's length these days."

"He is a growing boy," Balin said. "Though I have no sons, I was a lad once. 'Tis a pleasure to see a young man with a healthy appetite."

Ailsa made her grand entrance at that moment. Not strangely, she singled out the squire and planted herself firmly between the young lad and her father. She had a tendency to like older boys. Her big green eyes were fixed on him, his clothing, his hair, even the way he held his spoon.

"Gentlemen, my youngest child, Mistress Ailsa Cartingdon," Balin said. "I hope you do not mind that I have allowed her to join us."

Tate passed a cursory glance at the child, who had eyes only for his squire. The knights barely looked up from their meal. The squire, however, seemed clearly uncomfortable.

"Hello," Ailsa said to him.

The young man swallowed hard. He cast the girl a quick glance. "Hello."

Ailsa watched with interest as he practically buried his face in his food in an attempt to avoid talking to her. "What is your name?" she asked.

"J-John," the boy replied.

"How old are you, John?"

"Fourteen years."

"Are you a knight yet?"

John glanced at the men seated around him, silently begging for help. Tate took pity on him. "He is not yet, mistress."

Ailsa fixed her attention on Tate. "Are you Sir Tate?"

"Ailsa," Balin hissed at her, shaking his head.

Tate responded. "A natural question to a strange man sitting at her table. Yes, mistress, I am."

"Why do they call you Dragonblade?"

Toby nearly choked; in fact, only a large gulp of wine helped the clot of mutton slide down her throat. "Ailsa, behave yourself."

"But I just want to know."

"Now is *not* the time." Toby turned to Tate. "Forgive her, my lord. She is young and without tact."

"That seems to be a family trait."

Her cheeks burned at his dig as she remembered her vow to behave. "As you say, my lord."

From what he had seen that afternoon, it was not like her to submit so easily. He found himself alternately pleased and strangely disappointed that she had not reacted. He cast both sisters a final look before returning to his food. "Bad manners aside, I will also say that beauty must be a family trait. It is too bad that one characteristic negates the other."

Ailsa's attention had returned to the squire by this time and Toby merely continued to eat. Balin, fearful that Tate would push his daughter to forget her promise to behave, poured himself more wine and changed the focus altogether with talk of the pear orchard he had planted two years ago on the southern edge of town.

Tate listened to the old man talk, largely saying nothing in return. The more Balin drank, the more he talked. Tate eventually discovered that Balin had nothing more vital to say other than discussing agriculture and that his political knowledge was limited to very basic elements. His argumentative daughter seemed far more intelligent, at least enough to keep Tate's interest. All the while as Balin spoke and drank, Tate was acutely aware of Toby seated next to him, silently eating her pudding. In fact, he was hardly aware of what Balin was saying at all. He kept hearing the soft music of Toby's voice instead, echoes from their earlier conversation.

Dinner was over, but not before Tate was nearly bored out of his mind by Balin's drunken chatter. The knights had eaten their fill and were given a room in the *garçonnaire*, a small two-room house next to the main house. Its sole purpose was to house traveling guests, usually male. With Tate's approval, they retired for the eve and took the stuffed, dozing squire with them. The men-at-arms, who had remained by the door for the duration of the meal, were given some food and moved into the warm kitchens.

Balin, sensing that perhaps their liege wished some time to himself in front of the fire, excused himself and the girls. A word from Tate stopped him.

"I would have a word with Mistress Elizabetha, if I may."

Balin wasn't sure if he should allow his daughter to be alone with him. She had restrained herself admirably throughout the meal, but there was no knowing how long the restraint would last. Balin would hate to wake up in the morning and discover that his liege had confiscated his lands in a fit of anger. Taking the jug of wine still left upon the table and convincing himself he needed it to sustain his courage, he left Toby alone with the great Lord of Harbottle.

Tate was still seated, watching Toby as her gaze moved to everything else in the room but him. He studied her profile, the way her cheeks curved, the soft pout of her lips. He thought perhaps that he should gouge his eyes out because he was growing more enchanted with the woman by the moment. It was purely based on her appearance and he had no time to waste with such foolishness. Thank God they would be leaving on the morrow and he would be done with this stupidity.

"I will only take a moment of your time, mistress," his voice was quiet. "Will you please sit?"

Toby sat down on the bench opposite him. There was something in her manner that suggested she had something better to do than sit with him. He eyed her, sensing her displeasure. An entirely different subject suddenly came to mind. "How old are you?" he asked.

She looked at him, surprised. "I have seen twenty-one years, my lord."

His dark eyebrows lifted. "And you are not yet married?"

She gave him such a look that he nearly burst out laughing. "My father needs me."

"One has nothing to do with the other."

"You will forgive me, but I do not see how that is any of your affair."

"It is not. It was simply a question."

"Is that what you wanted to speak to me about?"

Tate scratched his chin; the more agitated she became, the more humorous he found it. "Not really, but now you have peaked my interest. You are a beautiful woman and your father is wealthy. I cannot imagine that you have not had men falling over themselves to vie for your hand."

She sighed harshly. "I suspect you will not stop asking these questions until you have had a satisfactory answer."

"That is possibly correct."

"Then I will tell you, succinctly. I have not married because there is not a man in England who would want to marry me."

"That is an extremely broad reason. Why would you say that?"

She lifted a well-shaped eyebrow. "Do you find me agreeable? Compliant? Following you about like a stupid sheep?"

"Hardly."

"Nor shall you. Men do not like a woman who knows her own mind."

He couldn't help the smile on the corner of his lips. She saw it and it inflamed her.

"If you are done laughing at me, I shall bid you a good evening and go about my business."

She bolted up, but Tate was quicker and grasped her arms before she could get away. He yanked her harder than he had intended and nearly pulled her across the table. As it was, she ended up inches from his face.

"You are not leaving until I am finished," he found his face strangely warm to have her so near. "And I was not laughing at you, not in the least. I simply find your manner intriguing and your answer honest."

If Tate was warm, Toby was on fire. Her breath was coming in strange little gasps. "You find my manner horrid," she breathed. "You have said so."

"I never said horrid. I believe what I said is that you have an appalling lack of manners."

"Then you have answered your own question as to why I have never married."

"You realize that you have condemned yourself."

"I would rather be myself than pretend to be someone I am not. Woe to any man who cannot accept me as I am."

He stared into her eyes with that strange hypnotic sensation that Toby had experienced once before. She could feel his warm breath on her face. Just as quickly as he grabbed her, he released her. Toby caught herself before she fell, like a fool, on the table. Shaken, she resumed her seat.

Tate collected his own seat. He took a long drink of wine because he needed it. There were too many strange thoughts floating about in his mind regarding the woman across the table. Angry with himself, he focused on his reason for speaking with her.

"I will expect you to show us the herd at dawn," he said. "I have much to do tomorrow and do not want to be held up at Cartingdon."

"Aye, my lord."

"Can you give me an estimate of the worth of the sheep?"

Her brow furrowed as she struggled to focus on his question, not the heat from his stare. "The top of the market would be six silver florens a head. The wool will sell for twice that for a bale. In all, I would estimate you could gain a thousand gold marks for the entire herd when everything is sold. Leeds would be the best market. They have a huge export industry."

It was a pleasing number. Tate gazed at her a few moments longer before nodding his head. "I thank you, mistress. I know you are anxious to get about your duties so that you may retire."

"I will make sure a meal is prepared and sent with you on your journey tomorrow."

"That is kind of you."

She cocked an eyebrow. "Contrary to what you apparently believe of me, I do have moments of kindness and obedience, my lord."

He gave her no indication of what he thought of her comment. Toby begged his leave and stood up, feeling his eyes on her, wondering why it disturbed her so. She was to the door when she heard his voice again, soft yet commanding.

"Hold, mistress."

She stopped. By the time she turned, he was already standing behind her. His steps had been so silent and swift that she had never heard him approach. Toby's breath caught in her throat as he reached for her neck; for a moment, she thought he was going to throttle her and put an end to her atrocious behavior. Given their first meeting, she probably deserved it. But his hands forewent her throat and grasped her shoulders instead, turning her so that she was once again facing away from him. She felt a warm finger brush the upper part of her shoulder, as gently as a butterfly's wing. It was more than an improper touch and she should have scolded him. Instead, she couldn't stop the shudder than ran down her spine.

"What is this?" he asked quietly.

She was still trying to catch her breath, but she craned her neck around and was barely able to see the angry red welt left by her mother's bowl. Two choices raced through her head; either the truth or a plausible lie. She settled for both.

"I was in my mother's room and accidentally bumped my shoulder," she said.

Tate's face was expressionless. "You should be more cautious."

"I know. I am clumsy at times."

He didn't reply, but there was something in his gaze that suggested he did not believe her. Later, when she climbed into bed beside the sleeping Ailsa, visions of Tate Crewys de Lara danced in her head.

CHAPTER THREE

A T DAWN IT was dark, foggy and wet. Toby rose after a weary night of light sleeping and donned a garment of heavy gray wool with a matching cape. It was an elegant dress meant for travel and she wore layers of soft woolen undergarments to guard against the freezing temperatures. She was still struggling to awaken as her servant brushed and plaited her long hair, catching it up in a heavy net so that it would not get wet in the disagreeable weather.

The corridor was dark as she tiptoed towards the stairs. It smelt of soot. Her father would be up soon in spite of his usual night-long drinking binge, but her mother would sleep until noon. As she passed her mother's door, she heard the recognizable groaning. Feeling the familiar anxiety rise in her chest, anxiety she had felt since childhood, she paused and the groaning ceased. But the moment she tried to move again, her mother called out. How she wished she could simply keep walking. Resigned, Toby went into her room.

It was nearly pitch black, stinking to the rafters of feces. Toby knew her mother had soiled herself and she called softly for her mother's servant, an older woman who was deaf in one ear. The woman woke from her pallet in the corner of the room and went to get some water at Toby's request.

Judith was loud and miserable. "So you would leave me here to rot, would you? Where are you going?"

"I am going to conduct father's business."

"You are running away!"

Toby tried to keep her quiet. "Mother, I have business to attend to. I shall return shortly, I promise. Hegeltha will see to your needs this morning."

The old servant came back into the dank chamber and Judith eyed her. "I do not want that old witch near me. She bites."

"Nay, she does not."

"She does, I tell you!"

Toby's patience was waning. "She does not bite you. She is kind to you and you would do well to appreciate her." She turned away from her mother, looking at the serving woman. "Clean her up as best you can. See that she takes some nourishment this morning."

The woman nodded. Judith extended her good hand to her daughter. "Please," she rasped. "Please do not leave me."

Toby paused to look at her mother. The woman was pathetic, but still, Toby could not summon the emotion to feel pity for her. That had been taken advantage of long ago.

"I must. I shall see you when I return."

"Nay, please. *Please!*"

Judith's hand was reaching out for her, begging for contact. Against her better judgment, Toby took the outstretched fingers and was rewarded by Judith digging her jagged fingernails into her flesh.

"Do not leave me!" she hissed.

The nails drew blood immediately. Toby yanked her hand free, examining the four crescent-shaped wounds on her wrist. Judith began to twitch and cry, as close as she could come to a tantrum, as swiftly Toby vacated the room. Shutting the door to the chamber behind her so that her mother would not wake the house, she re-examined the bloody cuts in her soft flesh. They were swelling already and they were painful. Wincing, she pulled on the glove for that hand so that no one would see what her mother had done. To Toby, her mother's abuse was normal, but she was ashamed to let anyone else see her misery.

Toby had left orders the night before to have her horse and a light meal ready before daybreak. The meal was waiting as she descended the stairs and entered the great hall. A fire had been started, but the room was still very chilly and smelled of old rushes. She found Tate and his party milling about the room, having already eaten some of the food laid upon the well-scrubbed table. The squire was huddled near the fire while the knights, heavily dressed and armed, stood off in the darkness. Toby heard their low voices, ceasing altogether as she entered.

As her eyes adjusted to the dim light, she found Tate. He was standing with Stephen near the hearth, his large physique outlined by the backdrop of the blaze.

"Good morn to you, my lord," she said.

He dipped his head in response to her greeting. "We are ready to depart, mistress."

It was a rather clipped greeting but she didn't care. Much to her horror, she realized that she was glad to see him. She had no idea why. It was a terrible realization and she struggled to shake off the unfamiliar feelings.

"I am ready," she said. "Did you get enough to eat?"

"We did," he said. "Perhaps you should take something with you."

She took a small wedge of cheese, trying to delicately shove it into her mouth as they vacated the hall and moved out into the misty morning. Everything was soaking wet, including the horses. A couple of the dogs came sniffing around, recognizing her as she mounted her leggy warmblood. They yipped at the knights but kept a distance, especially when Tate threw a well-aimed rock at one of them. When the party moved out, they followed.

The group took the road to the northwest. The field where the herd grazed was three miles out of town. It was cold and sodden and silent but for the noise from the horses as they made their way along the rocky path. Toby was slightly in front of the rest of them, trying to keep her mind from wandering to Tate. Though she couldn't see him, she knew he was watching her. She fidgeted with her reins; anything to keep from looking back at him.

"Do you ever have trouble from raiders?"

Tate's voice came from slightly behind her. Startled, she glanced over to see that he had reined his horse close to her. He seemed to have a habit of sneaking up on her. She had been concentrating so hard on ignoring him that she hadn't heard the obvious.

"Sometimes," she replied. "Mostly border Scots who come to steal our sheep. Father had a long-running problem with the Elliot clan near Jedburgh but he solved that by donating ten head of sheep to them every fall. They have a sizable herd now."

Tate nodded in understanding, his gaze moving off across the land. Instead of lightening with the rising of the sun, it seemed that everything was growing darker.

"I will apologize for forcing you to endure this weather," he said. "Hopefully this will not take long and you can return to a warm fire."

She shook her head. "I love this weather."

He cast her a long glance. "Why is that?"

"Because there is peace to it. It is soothing. Sometimes with the sun there is such bustle and chaos. Everyone is out and about. With the fog and rain, no one is out. It is quiet and soft."

"Is your life so harrowed that you find bad weather comforting?"

"I take comfort where I can find it." The reply had slipped out before she had thought about it. Uncomfortable, she made a rapid attempt to change the subject. "You mentioned that you have not spent much time in your lordship. Do you like traveling so much?'

"I do not," he said. "I would much rather settle down in one place and live a peaceful life."

"Your life is not peaceful?"

He shrugged, his big shoulders lifting. "I am a warrior. I reckon that my life is not meant to be peaceful by virtue of my profession. That does not stop me from wishing, however."

Toby glanced at the knights riding behind them, massive men on massive horses. "And your companions," she said. "Do they travel everywhere with you?"

"They have for many years."

"I have never been out of Cartingdon," Toby said. "Someday I would like to travel to the places that you have perhaps been."

"Where would you go?"

She thought a moment, visions of exotic cities in far off lands filling her mind. Some days, when her father drank himself into oblivion and her mother was out of control, she would sit and dream about being somewhere else. It was a game she sometimes played to keep her sanity.

"I would like to see Paris someday. But I have a stronger desire to see Rome."

"I have been to Paris many times but never Rome."

"If you ever go, will you come back and tell me about it?"

There was something wistful in her tone that made Tate take a closer look at her. "Do you think you will never go? Perhaps your husband shall take you someday. Surely he would do this for you."

She gave him an ironic smirk. "I thought I clearly established that I will never marry. If I go, I shall have to go alone."

"Unacceptable. If it comes to that, I shall take you myself."

She laughed, a gesture that lit up the sky. "My lord, although your offer is most gracious, I will not hold you to it. You could barely stand to be near me for an evening. How on earth could you stand it for months on end?"

Tate was completely entranced by her smile; it was the most beautiful thing he had ever seen. "If you laugh like that more often, I should easily stand it."

His tone was quiet, sincere. It made Toby's heart leap. She looked at him, amazed he would say such a thing, uncertain why he would. Not knowing how to respond, her cheeks burned brightly. It was a delicious spot of color amongst the gray of the morning mist, not lost on Tate.

"Is Wales like this?" she asked.

The change in subject was blindingly swift. Tate nearly had his head ripped off at the rapidity of it and he had to turn away lest she see him grin. "Beg pardon?"

"Wales. I hear that is where you were born. Is it like Northumberland?"

"In a sense; Wales is more mountainous."

"I hear that it is a wild place."

"No wilder than the borders of Scotland." He rubbed his chin with a gauntlet-clad hand. "What were we just speaking? Oh, yes. Laughing. I would suspect you do not do it nearly enough. Perhaps if you did, it would ease your brutish manner. It might make you more attractive to a husband."

She raised her eyebrows at him. "How did I graduate from an appalling manner to a brutish one?"

He was struggling not to smile at her, but he couldn't help it. He had a devilishly attractive smile, his teeth straight and white. "Forgive me for moving you up the ranks so swiftly."

"At least have the courtesy not to do so until I have done something to warrant it."

"Of course, mistress. My most genuine apologies."

"Accepted."

Much to his surprise, she was showing a delightful sense of humor. He would never have guessed. "Thank you," he covered his heart with one hand sincerely. "Now, tell me; why do you not laugh more often than you apparently do?"

"How often do you know I laugh? You have known me for less than a day."

"I can see it in your expression. It is as if your entire face is surprised to show a measure of delight."

She looked away peevishly, but it was in jest. "I have no idea what you are talking about."

"Is your life so bad that you have no reason to laugh?"

"The sheep should be up this road about a mile and a half. If we pick up the pace, we will be there in well less than an hour."

"I do not want to pick up the pace and neither do you."

"I do not?"

"Nay. But you do want to answer my question."

She gave him a sidelong glance. "I see a pattern in you. Last night, you bullied me about marriage. Today, it is laughter. You talk more than any man I have ever met."

"Not really."

The conversation had been flowing easily until that moment. Suddenly, Tate seemed to quiet and Toby found herself sorry she had shut him up. She truly hadn't meant to; she had been enjoying the conversation very much. With every step the horses took, the silence grew more and more deafening.

"I smile as much as I am able, I suppose," she finally said. "It seems as if there is not much reason to at times. I rise in the morning and take care of my invalid mother before I go and assist my father in conducting business with his farm. My father rises early in the morning and is usually drunk by noon and cares little for the daily operations of our farm. He did, once, but no longer. By the time I am finished handling his affairs, I must tend my mother again and my younger sister and see to the management of Forestburn. If my manner seems appalling to you at times, it is perhaps because it has to be. There is no one but me to see to the care of my family and this business my father has worked so hard to achieve. I am strong because I have to be."

By the time she had finished, Tate was gazing at her intently. The mist had turned to freezing rain, dripping off of his dark lashes. He spurred his charger up a few paces until he was next to her, looking down at her from a gray warhorse that was a head taller than her mount.

"If I offended you with my comments on your demeanor, then I am truly sorry," he said quietly. "I can see now that my observations were incorrect."

"Not necessarily. I can be quite aggressive at times."

"It seems to me that you have had much responsibility laid upon you and instead of allowing it to crush you, you became strong with it. I would not call that aggressive. I would call that survival."

She was coming to feel foolish for telling him everything about her when they hardly knew each other. Moreover, the man was her liege, not a peer, and the realization made her feel increasingly awkward. But she didn't have any friends to speak of, at least no one she could confide in, and the words had just tumbled out. There was far too much familiarity with Tate. Self-preservation swept her when she realized his last statement sounded too much like pity.

"Forgive me for explaining too much," she sounded crisp. "I was not complaining and my apologies if I sounded as such. My life is truly nothing to be sorry for. We are better off than most people."

Where Tate had seen vulnerability moments earlier, it was swiftly replaced by the guarded woman he had come to associate her with. He liked the vulnerability much better.

"I never thought you were complaining, mistress. You were simply answering my question."

He didn't think she would reply to his statement and he was correct. She pointed a glove hand down the road.

"The village of Lorbottle is north of here," she said. "I can have the sheep brought to market there, as they have a rather large livestock grounds. It is popular with the border Scots."

"That sounds reasonable."

"Where shall I send the money?"

"That depends. How long do you think it will take to sell everything?"

"Within a day with the proper buyer. I would say at this time of year, we will find the proper buyer within a week. This is the middle of the season, and most sheep are not shorn until spring."

"Then send the money to Harbottle Castle. I have other business to conduct in the region and will expect it there."

"As you say, my lord."

He watched her from the corner of his eye, wanting to say something more to her but not sure he should. He hardly knew the woman, yet he felt an inexplicable draw towards her. He recalled yesterday how he had thought her beautiful, but lacking in other fine qualities. After their conversation today, he wasn't so sure that was true. She had great strength of character and a sharp sense of humor. But she was also too stubborn for her own good. The woman was a paradox.

They drew near the field where the sheep were kept, a vast foggy land with a hint of green where the grass lay. Toby reined her horse to a stop along the stone wall that fenced in the herd.

"They are out there, somewhere," she indicated the field that disappeared into the mist. "In this weather, however, they will blend in with the fog and we will never find them."

Shrouded in the clouds, they could hear bleating. It was one or two of the sheep at first, followed by several responses. Toby dismounted her horse, followed by Tate and the others. Deftly, she jumped on to the top of the rock wall and slid down the other side into the wet grass. She knew this field well and it seemed oddly quiet to her.

"We have three men that tend the herd," she looked around. "I do not see them. I will go and call for them."

Gathering her skirts as much as possible to keep them out of the wet, she walked out into the misty field. Tate and his men fanned out slightly, their eyes ever-watchful.

"Gordon?" she called out. "Emmit? Can you hear me?"

There was no answer. The sheep suddenly started bleating wildly. Concerned, Toby picked up the pace in the direction she thought the sound was coming from. Soon, she was running, unaware that Tate and his men were keeping pace behind her. The mist was denser the further she ran into the field. Something suddenly flew past her ear and she yelped, startled. As she tripped and fell to her knees, she bumped into a mass on the ground. A shepherd lay there with an arrow through his neck. Before a scream could bubble to the surface, a warm body fell atop her and she was buried underneath it, sandwiched between the wet earth and a pile of armor.

Tate had thrown himself on her when he realized arrows were flying. His arms were around her head lest an arrow come flying in that direction. Toby could hear the zinging sound of the projectiles sailing over them.

"Bandits!" she gasped.

Tate could not disagree. But their situation was precarious. They were in the mist, shielding their enemy from them, with nowhere to hide. Their survival now would depend on a combination of skill and luck. He called out to his men.

"Stephen?" he hissed. "Kenneth?"

They answered affirmative in rapid succession. "Where is John?" Tate asked.

"I am here," the squire was several feet away, on the ground.

"Are you well?"

"Well enough," the lad sounded frightened. "Where are the arrows coming from?"

Tate could not have guessed at the moment. They seemed to be coming from every direction. "Stay down," he commanded. "Do not move until I can see something in this soup."

Tate would have reconnoitered himself, but he couldn't. He didn't want to move and possibly draw their attention to himself and, consequently, to Toby. That last thing he wanted was for the arrows to come flying at her unprotected body. He shifted his weight slightly, more closely against her, and heard her grunt beneath him.

"Sorry," he whispered, knowing he must be quashing her.

"'Tis all right," she grunted. "But your knee...."

He shifted again, removing his right knee from what was surely the back of her thigh. When he had come down on her, much of his weight had come down on the right side of her body. He hoped he hadn't broken any bones.

"Better?" he muttered.

"Aye."

"I did not hurt you, did I?"

"Not at all."

He was quiet after that. He didn't need to give his adversaries a homing beacon with his voice. His biggest priority at the moment was to put Stephen and Kenneth on the move to scout the source of the arrows. As he turned his head to call to the knights, the dogs that had been following them since Forestburn suddenly ripped past them on a dead run. All teeth and a blur of legs, the dogs disappeared into the mist and there was a chorus of snarls, growls and various other unidentifiable cries. Tate listened to the grunts of men being bitten by the dogs and singled out at least three different voices. The dogs' snarling faded, the yipping rolling off into the distance. Then, it was eerily quiet.

Still, he didn't move. He was a warm, protective cocoon over Toby and he wasn't about to leave his position. Besides, he rather liked being this close to her in spite of the deadly circumstances. When one of the dogs suddenly emerged from the fog and went up to Toby, licking her forehead, Tate knew that all was well. He whispered a prayer of thanks for the dogs, sorry he had thrown the rock back at Forestburn. The animals had served a valuable purpose.

Still, he was cautious. Dogs or no, he wasn't comfortable in an open field covered with mist. Standing up, he pulled Toby to her feet. She was soaking from having lain on the grass.

"You are wet," he observed. "We should return you home immediately."

Her face was pinched from the chill. "I need to see what has happened to our shepherds," she said. "I only saw… Emmit."

She wouldn't look at the body, a few feet away. Tate muttered something to Stephen, who was the closest, and the knights disappeared into the gloom. The men at arms came to stand near Tate and Toby, crossbows drawn and cocked. The squire walked up, wiping the mud from his face.

"Did anyone see them?" he asked. "Were they Scots?"

Tate shook his head, resisting the urge to throw another rock at the dog sniffing at his leg. "I never saw them. They were clever to blend with the mist."

"The sheep," Toby said quietly.

"What about them?"

"I do not hear them."

Tate cocked an ear, but there was nothing in the air. It was quiet but for an occasional bird. "We will not go look for them now," he said. "Better to wait for the fog to lift."

Toby didn't argue. She followed Tate, the squire and the men at arms back to the road where the horses were tethered. Shortly, the knights returned and reported to Tate. The two other shepherds had been found, murdered. Deeply disturbed, Toby mounted her horse with Tate's assistance. Tate, however, remained on the ground.

"John, I will leave it to you and Oscar to escort the lady back to Forestburn," Tate indicated one of the men at arms, heavily armed with his crossbow. "Remain there. I shall come for you when I can."

Toby was surprised, concerned. "You are not returning with us?"

"Nay, mistress."

"Where do you go, then?"

Tate swung his big body aboard his charger. "To find whoever launched the attack." He looked over his shoulder to his knights. "Stephen, ride to Harbottle Castle and collect thirty men to form a search party. Kenneth, Morley, you ride with me. We shall see if we can find a trail while it is still fresh."

"My lord, if I may," Toby interrupted. "The raiders are most likely border Scots. They shall disappear into the land as quickly as they sprang from it. You will not find them."

His expression was dark. "Mistress," he said quietly. "Stephen and Kenneth examined the arrows that killed your men. They are not the arrows of border Scots."

A bolt of fear ran through her. "Then to whom do they belong?"

Tate's response was to turn her horse around and bark orders to John and the man-at-arms to move with all due haste. Toby's last sight of Tate was as he and his gray charger disappeared into the fog like phantoms.

CB

IT HAD BEEN a long night. Morning dawned and still they had not returned. Toby sat by the hearth in the great hall well after the meal was finished, wondering if something terrible had befallen Tate and his men. She wasn't feeling particularly well this morning perhaps as a result of the chill she had received yesterday; she was warm to the touch and generally exhausted. She could not even summon the strength to answer the cries from her mother. Not guilt or God could have motivated her to respond this day. She had sent Ailsa to see to the woman's needs instead, instructing her to stay out of arm's length.

The squire and the man-at-arms had remained in the *garçonnaire* since their return yesterday. She had seen them only twice, for the evening and morning meal. At this late stage of the morning, it was quiet with Ailsa taking her usual nap and her mother at least silent for the moment. Her father had gone into the village to drink and discuss town affairs with the aldermen and Toby was weary of sitting about, wondering what had become of the lord of Harbottle. There were accounting matters waiting for her in her father's solar that she had put off long enough.

Rising from the chair, she accidentally brushed her hand against the arm of the chair and winced painfully; the scratches her mother had given her were becoming angry red wounds. Examining it more closely, she saw that the entire area was swollen and painful. She knew she should have tended them yesterday when they were fresh but she had other things on her mind.

Arrowroot flowers grew wild in an open area near the village. Toby sent a servant out to gather some so that she could tend her wounds with them. By the time the servant returned with the flowers, Toby's entire body was hot, tired and throbbing. Sitting at her father's desk doing an accounting of their winter fruit supply was difficult; her eyes were hot and it was difficult to keep them open. In fact, she wanted very much to sleep. She gratefully set the quill down to turn her attention to the healing powers of the tender arrowroot. She promised herself a rest after tending the cuts.

The flowers were mashed into a paste against softened linen, allowing the juices from the petals to seep into the material. Toby packed some of the mashed petals against the red gashes and then wrapped the remaining petals and linen tightly around them. She was securing the edges of the linen so that the bandage would stay firm when she heard horses at a distance. Her weariness fled for the moment as she bolted to the window.

Tate had returned and he had a horde of men with him. Toby tried to play ignorant to the fact that her heart had leapt at the sounds of him returning. She almost ran for the door but stopped herself. In fact, it was best if she went back to her accounting and pretended she hadn't heard the horses at all. Moving for the desk, she sat calmly and resumed her bookkeeping with the exception of not truly looking at the count before her. She looked at the parchment but saw nothing. Her mind, vision and hearing were attuned to the entry door in the hall.

Her wait was a long, excruciating one. It took forever for the door to finally creak open. She had almost broken her quill with nervous fingers. She struggled to concentrate on her count as bootfalls crossed the hall, paused, and then moved for the solar. Only then did she very casually look up.

Tate was dressed to the hilt in armor and weapons. He looked every inch the feared warrior of the Dragonblade epithet. But he also looked weary, as if he had been up all night. His storm cloud eyes fixed on her.

"Mistress," he sounded weary, too.

She rose from her chair, feeling strangely light-headed. "My lord," she returned his salutation. "I hope all went well."

"It did not, but that should not concern you. Suffice it to say that your father is released from his pledge of the herd for young Edward's cause."

"I do not understand. Is something wrong?"

"I am returning to London and do not have time to wait for the collection."

His manner was clipped. Toby took a step in his direction, concerned that something was gravely amiss. "My lord, if we have done something to offend you, then I…."

He shook his head, forcing himself to soften. Having spent the past day and night in warfare mode, it was difficult to separate the man from the professional warrior.

"You have done nothing, mistress, I assure you," he said, his tone more settled. "I did not mean to suggest that you had. It is simply that business has arisen that requires my presence elsewhere. I have not time to wait for the money from the herd your father has pledged to me."

"Did you not find the sheep?"

"I did not look for them."

"Did you at least find the men you were searching for?"

"I found them."

He didn't say more than that and Toby didn't press him. He obviously did not wish to speak of it and it truthfully wasn't any of her concern. She didn't know why she suddenly felt so awful. Disappointment filled her and she struggled to graciously bid him farewell. It was horrible to realize that she did not want him to go.

"I would wish you a good journey, then, and good fortune wherever you may go," she said as sincerely as she could. "Should you ever go to Rome, perhaps you will honor me with the tale of your adventure someday."

He just looked at her, his expression softening, the dark eyes full of something she did not understand. Much to her surprise, he reached out and took her hand and led her over to the chair near the window. He indicated for her to sit and she did so, her heart thumping loudly against her ribs. There was no way with his bulk that he could sit, so he took a knee beside her to bring himself to her level. Toby could not help but notice that he never let go of her hand the entire time. The thrill of it caused her cheeks to flush warm and warmer still until she could hardly breathe.

"There is much I wish I could tell you, mistress, but alas I cannot," he said after a moment's deliberation. "Suffice it to say that I do not want to go but I must. It is safer for you and your family if I do."

"Safer?" she repeated. "What do you mean?"

"Just that. You need not be involved in matters that do not concern you."

She gazed at him, long and hard. The more she looked upon him, the more handsome he seemed to become. His face was so perfectly formed that it was difficult to find any flaw with it. She became so upswept in his male beauty that she nearly forgot her train of thought.

"May I ask you something?" she asked.

"You may."

"Are you running from someone?"

He almost looked amused. "Why would you ask that?"

"Because when you first came to the church in Cartingdon, you were wearing heavy cloaks to conceal your identity. You did not want anyone to notice you."

His gaze gave her a hint of what he might be thinking. "You are correct in that assumption, but that is merely prudence. Knights that go about announcing themselves are inviting trouble. I would rather not invite it. I have enough."

"Then you are not running?"

"Nay, mistress. I do not run from anything."

"I did not mean to suggest that you do."

He smiled at her, releasing her hand so that he could remove his gauntlets. "I know you did not." He ran his fingers through his hair, a gesture of fatigue, before reclaiming her fingers, this time flesh against flesh. Instantly, his brow furrowed. "Good Christ, your hand is searing."

Before Toby could reply, he put a hand to her forehead. "You are burning with fever. Did you not realize this?"

She hadn't, really. All she knew was that she hadn't felt very well. "I have not felt my best this morning," she admitted.

Tate put a hand on her cheek for good measure. It was soft, like baby's skin, and was quite warm. Inadvertently, he touched the bandage on her wrist and his focus was drawn to it.

"What is this?" he demanded.

He was unwrapping it before she could answer. "It… it was an accident," she stammered.

He ripped away the linen and was faced with the four festering crescent-shaped incisions. He stared at them a moment, and his manner cooled dramatically.

"Who did this to you?"

His voice was a growl. Toby looked at him, her eyes full of fear. "It was an accident," she repeated.

His jaw ticked. He reached to her neckline, pulling back the garment to expose a portion of the bruise he had seen the day before. "And this? Was this an accident, too?"

She tried to move away from him. "It was."

He grabbed both of her hands, refusing to let her leave the chair. "You will tell me who did this to you. Was it your father?"

She shook her head. "Nay, of course not. He would never lay a hand on me."

"Then who?"

"It was an accident, I tell you. You need not concern yourself. Moreover, I do not see how it is any of your affair."

He stared at her. Then he dropped her hands and stood up. "You are right, of course," he said coldly. "Forgive my impudence for asking."

He stood up and turned on his heel. He was nearly to the door when she called out to him.

"My lord?"

He paused, not saying a word, but turned to face her. Ill, uncomfortable, Toby stood up and fought to swallow her pride. She didn't want to tell him and wasn't even sure where to start, but he was the first person in her entire life that had ever shown any concern for her. She felt that she should explain so he didn't think her unkind.

"This has gone on so long that I do not think of it anymore," her voice was a whisper. "It is simply something that happens now and again. Please understand that my father, no matter how much he drinks, has never laid a hand upon me. Nor has my baby sister. What happens... what you have seen... cannot be helped."

He came back into the room. "What do you mean it cannot be helped?"

"Simply that."

"You do not do this to yourself, do you?"

She looked as if he had just asked her something deeply painful. "Of course not," she breathed. "It is just that my mother...."

"Your mother does this to you?"

He raised his voice and she put her hands up to quiet him. "She cannot help it, my lord. She is ill and confined and does not know what she is doing. After suffering an attack during the birth of Ailsa, she has never been the same. The lovely woman I once knew as my mother has become something wicked and frightful. She is out of her mind with disease and does not realize the pain she inflicts."

"On you."

She hesitated. "Aye."

He didn't know what to say but his expression eventually softened to one of sorrow. Reaching out, he gently took her swollen hand and re-examined the wounds. "What she does is wrong, mistress. You endure too much."

"I endure what I must."

Still holding her hand, he took his other hand and felt her forehead once again. It was a gentle gesture, something she was unused to. Much to her horror, tears sprang to her eyes and spilled onto her cheeks. No one had ever shown her such compassion. Before she could turn away to wipe her face, he swept away her tears with his thumbs.

"No tears, Elizabetha," he murmured, a gentle smile on his face.

"I am called Toby," she sniffled.

His smile grew. "To me, you are Elizabetha. I am the only one permitted to use that name."

She did not understand what he meant but she instinctively knew that it could not be bad. Moreover, she liked the way he said her Christian name; *Elizabay-tha*. He rolled it off his tongue in a marvelous way she'd never heard before.

He gently moved her back towards the chair. "Come and sit. Stephen was a Hospitaller knight and has knowledge of healing. He will give you a brew to abate the fever."

She allowed him to sit her down. "You are most kind, my lord."

"You deserve nothing less."

Stephen of Pembury seemed far more congenial with their second official meeting. He concocted a brew of willow bark for the fever and added something to make her sleep. Exhausted, ill, she fell asleep in the chair in her father's solar with Tate and Stephen standing vigilant guard beside her.

CHAPTER FOUR

"HOW LONG ARE we to remain here?" the squire asked. "I thought we were leaving for London immediately."

Tate and Stephen had entered the *garçonnaire* for a much-needed break. It was dark and foggy outside, the air filled with smoke from the early-morning fires. They had been with Toby all night, finally moving her to the chamber she shared with Ailsa towards dawn so that she could sleep more comfortably. Having fallen asleep in the chair was not the best place for her to rest, but she had resisted every time they had tried to move her.

"Mistress Toby is ill with fever," Tate said, removing portions of his armor and letting them fall to the floor. "Feeling somewhat responsible for her health since it was at my behest that she showed us the donated herd yesterday morning, I feel compelled to see to her well-being. There is no better healer in all of England than Stephen."

The squire had yet to learn the true virtue of patience. "But there are more pressing matters. There are assassins about. Does this not concern you?"

Tate looked at the tall, fair-haired lad with the deep brown eyes. "Your Highness, it does indeed. But we are safer here at Forestburn than out on the open road. Furthermore, the thirty men-at-arms that Stephen brought from Harbottle are camped outside the walls of this place, so I am confident that you are well protected."

It was rare that Tate addressed the lad formally. In fact, there were times that young Edward forgot who he really was. Traveling with Tate de Lara as his squire was a perfect cover. In this capacity, he was able to see and experience things in his realm that he would not have normally tasted. Additionally, he was away from his mother's court where Roger Mortimer was determined to see him dead. Tate had been mother, father, protector and savior to him in this very troubled time. He would have been dead without him.

"Those assassins yesterday morning were not aiming for you or the lady with the sheep," Edward said. "They were aiming for me."

"I am well aware of that."

"They followed us from Rothbury. But how did they find us? How did they know where we were going?"

Tate glanced at Kenneth; the big blond knight was cleaning his blade with a soft cloth, removing the blood that had spilt on it earlier.

"We did not get a chance to ask," Tate replied, his gaze still on Kenneth as if the two shared more information than they were willing to divulge. "They decided that dying in a skirmish would be better than being captured."

"Perhaps there were spies at the church yesterday, hearing all that was said," Kenneth suggested. "It would not have been difficult to get information from the locals to put them a step ahead of us."

Edward's jaw ticked as he paced around, having not yet learned that worrying was a useless endeavor. "So you tracked them and followed them to the town of Burnfoot to the north."

"Aye, "Tate said.

"How many were there?"

"The group that we saw in Rothbury had split. We only found seven."

"Did you kill all seven?"

"We had no choice. They drew the first sword."

Edward stopped pacing. "The rest will find us. If we do not leave this place, it is only a matter of time before they track us down."

Tate was used to Edward's concerns. He was young and spirited, concerned for himself and his country. His passions ran deep, and sometimes, so did his foolishness.

"As I said, we are safer here than almost anywhere at the moment," he said steadily. "It is my suspicion that the rest of Mortimer's assassins are in the vicinity of York, thinking we may be in that area. It will take them time to realize that we are not. By that time, we will be half way to London. They will not be able to catch us."

"But it is three hundred miles to London," Edward pointed out. "It will take us weeks to get there at a hard ride."

"It will not matter if we leave tomorrow or the next day."

Edward cocked an eyebrow, the Plantagenet stubbornness apparent. "No offense to the Mistress of the house, but I would think you would put my priorities over hers. I frankly do not care if she is ill or not."

Tate had the Plantagenet stubbornness, too, with the added benefit of age to bolster it. "Your priorities are, and ever have been, my greatest concern. If you are questioning my loyalty, perhaps you should find someone else to lead your cause."

"Perhaps I should."

Tate snorted; it was a bluff and they all knew it. "No one else would put up with your constant whining. By virtue of the fact that I am your uncle, I must."

Edward quieted somewhat. He wandered over to where Tate sat, pulling up a stool from the hearth and appearing somewhat forlorn. "It should be you on the throne, not me," he muttered. "Had things been different...."

"Had things been different, your grandfather would have married my mother and I would be the king. But things are not different. They are as they are. I accepted that long ago and so should you."

"I am afraid that I will not be an effective ruler, Tate."

Tate smiled at the youth, putting a big hand on his blond head. "You will be the best ruler England has yet to see. I see my father's strength in you. Trust in yourself, Edward. We do."

"Sometimes I wonder. There is so much at stake."

Tate had heard these words before, many times. When Edward wasn't doubting himself, he could be a responsible, decisive young man. But he was young and circumstances beyond his control had the tendency to frighten him.

"There is much at stake; that is true," Tate agreed. "But the rewards far outweigh the risks, do they not?"

The lad gave his uncle a reluctant grin. Tate gave the boy's hair one last shake and returned to the task of removing the last of his armor. He hadn't realized how exhausted he was until he sat down. Now, he was thinking seriously about a few hours of much deserved sleep. Stephen was already snoring in the corner. Tate had barely laid his head down when there was a knock at the door.

Morley, the man-at-arms, was the first to the door. He threw it open, sword in hand, to reveal Ailsa standing at the door. The sun was rising, giving her an unearthly glow as the rays filtered through the early morning fog.

"I am sorry to come," she stammered. "But my sister... she is worse."

Tate was up and so was Stephen. They crowded Morley away from the door, filling it with their bulk.

"What is wrong?" Tate asked.

Ailsa's face was pale beneath her blue hood. The frail child looked like a porcelain doll, able to crack at any moment. "Her fever has worsened. She does not answer when I speak to her."

Stephen was already out of the door, heading for the manor. Tate was close behind him with Ailsa bringing up the rear.

"Is she going to die?" Ailsa asked anyone who would answer her.

"She is not going to die," Tate replied.

Ailsa ran until she was beside him as he walked and still, she had to run to keep pace. It was exhausting work.

"How do you know?"

"I just do."

Ailsa was losing speed, breathing heavily. In the midst of his concern, Tate could see that the child was unused to physical exertion. He paused long enough to pick her up and resumed his stride. The last thing he wanted was for the younger sister to catch her death running about in the dank air.

Stephen was the first one up the stairs followed closely by Tate and Ailsa. It sounded like a thundering herd against the wooden steps. When they reached the top of the dimly lit stair hall, Tate could hear groaning coming from one of the rooms. He ignored the moans, trailing Stephen into the chamber that he had left Toby in. When they finally reached her, she was lying upon the sheets, her damp skin as pale as the linen.

Her eyes were closed. Stephen put a large hand on her forehead and shook his head. "She is on fire," he muttered. "We need to cool her down immediately. Have the servants bring a tub in here and fill it with tepid water."

Ailsa fled the room with all the grace of a headless chicken. The knights could hear the scuttling of feet as the servants were roused in the house. Stephen saw a rag and a bowl of water beside the bed; Ailsa had been using it in a vain attempt to keep her sister cool. He picked up the rag, dipped it in the water, and wrung it out.

"Pull the bed covers off of her," he told Tate. "We will have to cool her as best we can until the tub arrives."

Tate swung back the coverlet, exposing her to the chilly room. Stephen took her left arm, pushed up the sleeve of her shift, and swabbed water on her tender skin. "I need to get my bag."

Tate had felt helpless until this point. He took the rag from Stephen. "I will do this. Go get your medicaments and be quick about it."

Stephen quit the chamber. Tate looked down at Toby a moment, her pale sweating face, feeling his heart lurch strangely. Taking her right arm, he exposed the flesh and was faced with the bandaged wrist. It abruptly occurred to him why she was so ill. With a muttered curse, he unwrapped it.

The wounds were horribly red and swollen. Yellow pus seeped from two of them. Anger filled Tate; he knew with certainty that the source of her fever was not the chill from yesterday's exposure. It was the poison racing through her veins from the cuts her mother had inflicted on her.

He swabbed the cool water against her flesh, avoiding the cuts. When he ran the rag over her forehead and cheeks, she seemed to come around a bit and slapped at his hand. The gesture made him smile; even in her current state, the woman was a fighter. She would need all of her strength to battle this toxin. He swabbed her cheek again just to see her reaction and was rewarded when she slapped at him again.

"So you do not like that, do you?" he whispered. "Good. Perhaps if I do it enough, you will wake from the unpleasant state."

He ran the cloth over her neck, unconsciously inspecting her as he did so. She had a beautiful neck and shoulders. The shift was relatively modest, so there was no glimpse of the swell of her bosom, but he could only imagine that it was as delicious as the rest of her.

He put the cloth back into the water and squeezed it out. Sitting down carefully on the side of the bed, he gently lifted her head up with one hand and put the cloth on the back of her neck with the other. The cold sensation received more of a reaction than he had expected; her eyes flew open.

"To the devil with you," she gasped. "Why must you torment me so?"

She wasn't in her right mind; the words were coming out slurred, dreamlike, and her eyes closed once again. He removed the cloth and lay her head down on the pillow, all the while thinking how soft her hair had been. His thoughts were misplaced and he knew it, feeling rather caddish. The woman was gravely ill and all he could think of was how beautiful her hair was.

Ailsa came running back into the room, sliding to an unsteady stop. "Is she dead yet?" she panted.

Tate calmly swabbed Toby's left arm. "Nay, she is not. I told you that she is not going to die."

Ailsa slowed down and approached the bed, her little face full of fear. "But she looks so ill."

"She is," Tate said. "But Sir Stephen is great healer. He shall pull her through this."

Ailsa's eyes were big as she watched Tate methodically bathe her sister's face. Her gaze trailed to Tate, studying his strong features, wondering if she should believe him when he said that Toby was not going to die. As with all children, however, her attention span was finite and thoughts completely disassociated from her sister began to roll through her head.

"Are you married?"

Tate paused in his duties to look at her. She was innocent, and it was an innocent question. He'd long since gotten over the pain the question had once provoked.

"I was once."

"What happened?"

"She passed away giving birth to my daughter."

"Oh. Did your daughter die, too?"

"Aye."

Ailsa began to toy with the bed linens, her sister's limp hand. "My mother nearly died giving birth to me, too. I do not think I shall ever have any children."

He smiled faintly. "Why not?"

"Because it will kill me."

"Not always. As with anything else, one's fate is in the hands of God."

"Did God kill your wife and daughter, then?"

He shook his head slowly. "He did not, little one."

"But why does He allow bad things to happen?"

"I do not know. I have often asked myself that question. I would suppose that everything happens for a reason, though we do not know what that reason might be at the time."

Ailsa chewed her lip as she thought about it. He made sense and little made sense in her life; a distant father, an invalid mother, and a sister who was haunted by enormous responsibility. Tate seemed strong and certain.

"May I ask another question?"

He lifted an eyebrow at her. "I suspect you will no matter what I say."

"Is it wrong to ask why you are called Dragonblade?"

His eyes twinkled. "I suppose not."

"Then why?"

He lay down the arm he had been swabbing and picked up the other. "Your question will be answered when you see the hilt of my sword."

She tried to picture what he meant. "Is there a dragon on it?"

"When you see it, you shall know."

The thoughts were whirling in Ailsa's mind. Tate could almost see them. She was a lovely child and seemed sweet. He didn't mind talking to her.

A pair of men ushered through the door with a large copper tub between them. A female servant, an old woman with white hair piled atop her head, directed them to set it down. She had the voice of a crow, screeching at the horse dung that one of the men had tracked on the floor. Behind her, several house servants followed with great buckets of water and began emptying them in the tub with great splashes.

Tate continued to swab Toby's arms as Ailsa stood out of the way while the tub was filled. Stephen returned after a short time, leather satchel in hand, and ordered the fire in the hearth stoked. When he began to pull out his medicines, Ailsa could not resist standing next to him and watching curiously. It would seem she was intensely curious about everything.

Stephen ignored her for the most part but inevitably she began asking questions and he was obliged to respond. She wanted to know about everything and he patiently explained the willow bark, the crushed poppy, the foxglove extract and so forth. Soon, there was a fine brew rising in the small iron pot hanging deep in the hearth. With his ingredients cooking, Stephen went over to his patient.

"She is still burning," Tate murmured so that Ailsa would not hear.

Stephen ran his hands across her forehead and opened each eye in turn. "She will not survive much longer at this temperature," he said quietly. "We must get her into the water now."

The tub was half-full with water that was barely warm. Tate put the rag aside and took Toby into his arms, picking her limp body off the bed. She was hot, sweating and overwhelmingly delicious. He silently cursed himself for his perverse thoughts as he took her over to the tub. The servants were filling it furiously.

"Get her into the water," Stephen directed. "Hold on to her so that she does not slide under."

"We will lose our grip on her in the water," Tate didn't want to have to hold her by her hair as she slipped around in the tub. "Like so much dead weight."

"Have a better idea?"

Tate's solution was to step into the tub, fully clothed, and sit down in the water. Stephen helped him adjust Toby so that she was lying on top of him and he had a good grip around her waist. The servants continued to pour water and with the next cold dousing, Toby went rigid and a hoarse cry escaped her lips.

"My God," she rasped. "They are trying to kill me."

Tate's mouth was against her right ear. "Nay, mistress," he said softly. "We are trying to help you. Your fever is out of control and we must get you cool."

She was semi-lucid, unsure of what was happening to her. She looked at Stephen, unrecognizing, and began to panic.

"Let me out," she struggled against Tate's iron grip. "Let me out!"

Stephen gently but firmly pushed her back. Getting a good grip around her waist, Tate put a hand over her forehead and held her back against his shoulder.

"Calm, Elizabetha," he murmured against her ear. "No one is going to harm you, I swear it."

Ailsa ran up to the tub, putting her little hands on her sister's shoulders. "Be quiet, Toby. You must not be upset!"

Toby focused on Ailsa, the only face she recognized. "Wha… what devilry is this?" she panted.

Ailsa shook her head. "You are ill. The knights are trying to help you."

Toby grasped the front of Ailsa's gown with one hand as if the little girl would save her, but her struggles eventually eased and her grip relaxed. Breathing quickly, like a dog panting on a hot summer day, she closed her eyes and surrendered against Tate's powerful body. The strength to fight was leaving her.

Tate felt her go limp. He and Stephen passed concerned glances as the servants continued to fill the tub. Stephen had a grip on her wrist, feeling her fast, weak pulse. He didn't like it. As the tub filled and her blood continued to race, he shook his head.

"This is not a good sign," he murmured. "She is not calming."

"What about your brew?" Tate was genuinely concerned. Stephen did not raise an alarm for no reason.

"Another minute or so for full potency."

Tate fell silent but it was apparent that he was searching quickly for a solution. His mind was never idle nor was he familiar with surrender.

It was deathly quiet in the room but for the pouring of water. Then, Ailsa thought she was hearing things. There was a low hum in the air that would rise and fall in rhythm. She was so concerned with her sister that it took her a few moments to realize that Tate was singing. His lips were pressed against Toby's right ear, his soft baritone filtering through her fever-hazed mind. It was a miraculous sound and Ailsa was entranced; her sweet little face lit with a smile as the air was filled with the gentle sound of Tate's voice.

To the sky, my sweet babe;
The night is alive, my sweet babe.

Your dreams are filled with raindrops from heaven;
Sleep, my sweet babe, and cry no more.

It was a lullaby, sung from mother to child. Ailsa had heard Toby sing it before, though it hadn't sounded nearly as beautiful as when Tate sang it. Tate glanced up at Ailsa when he had finished the verse and, seeing her smile, gave forth the second stanza.

Your heart is light, my sweet babe;
Your slumber is divine, my sweet babe.
The angels hold you, my arms enfold you;
Be at rest, my love, for you are ever mine.

A peaceful hush had settled over the room. Like an attempt to quiet a fussy baby, there was a fragile spell in the air. Ailsa's voice shattered it.

"Sing the fairy song!" she cried.

Startled, the knights shushed her in unison. Justifiably contrite, it did not deter her enthusiasm. She whispered loudly this time. "Sing the fairy song!"

Tate gave her a reproving look. The singing excited Ailsa and thankfully seemed to soothe Toby. He launched into the old folk ballad, normally a lively dance. He wasn't surprised when Ailsa dropped her sister's hand and began to leap around the floor.

Dilly, dilly, lady fairy, how shall you fly? Long to the day as slumber
grows nigh;
On gossamer wings, you touch the stars.
On the wings of angels, you steal our hearts.
Come touch my heart, O fairy dove,
And take me from the world above.

Ailsa stopped her jig and clapped happily. The knights quieted her in unison again. *"Hush!"*

Ailsa's mouth formed an "O" and she put her hand to her lips in a silence gesture. She looked at Toby, fearful that she had disturbed her, but Toby was sleeping as peacefully as she could be given the circumstances. Tate began to sing another song, a calming lullaby, as Stephen went to take his brew off of the fire. He poured a good amount in a pewter cup and came back over to the tub.

"It should cool so she does not scald herself trying to drink it," he said quietly. "But your singing has accomplished wonders; she is calm now."

"Calm, aye, but she is still as hot as the sun," Tate said. "I can feel it through my clothes."

The last bucket of water went in to the tub. It was nearly to the brim with tepid water that would help stabilize Toby's temperature. But it also made her shift transparent, something Tate could not see and Stephen tried not to notice. When Toby started to shiver and her nipples hardened, Tate's attention was drawn to the tantalizing peaks shrouded in wet linen. So was Ailsa's; noticing her sister's state, she flew into a frenzy and ripped the coverlet off the bed. She tried to tuck it in around her sister, causing water to splash all over the floor.

The knights would have scolded her had they not realized what she was doing. Stephen went so far as to help her. The drink was cooled sufficiently at that point and the former Hospitaller knight held Toby's head up with one hand, administering the cup with the other.

The first spill of the warm brew into her mouth was a jolt. Toby sputtered and coughed, but Stephen managed to get an adequate amount of the foul-smelling liquid into her stomach. When he finally set the cup aside, Tate reached under the wet linens and lifted Toby's wounded wrist above the water.

"Now," his voice was a growl. "Tend this. I believe this is the source of her fever."

Stephen inspected the wounds closely. "What manner of demon did this?"

Tate was reluctant to say with Ailsa present. He simply shook his head and Stephen saw that he either did not know or would not answer.

He drew some powder from his satchel and mixed it with water, making a paste. Applying the paste to the wounds, he wrapped it with a strip of dry cloth.

"This should draw the poison out," he said. "Keep it out of the water as best you can."

Tate nodded silently. Toby was quivering against him in reaction to her prolonged submersion in the water, but she didn't seem as hot as she had been. He put a hand on her forehead again, feeling the warmth but confirming that his suspicions were correct; her fever was lessened. Feeling somewhat reassured that she would survive, he settled back in the tub, his big hand holding her head against his shoulder and the other arm wrapped around her waist, and began to sing again. It was soft and gentle, like a father singing to a sick child. Somewhere in the singing, he tightened his grip, certain he could out-wrestle Death if it came to claim her. The last time he had held a dying woman in his arms, Death had won. Now it was the principle of the matter. Death would not best him again.

Eventually, they moved Toby out of the tub and onto the bed. She was calm and the fever seemed to be abating. There was nothing left to do but wait.

൫

ARROWS DID AWAY with the some of the dogs that had attacked them the day before. The troops from Harbottle were settled on the eastern side of the enclosure and the party of eleven men bearing the seal of Roger Mortimer, Earl of March, entered from the west. One of them had been witness to the slaughter yesterday of seven colleagues and had unknowingly escaped from young King Edward's men. He'd gone in search of the other Mortimer men that he knew to be in the area and found them south of Cartingdon, searching the village of Warton.

Merchants in Cartingdon loved to gossip. It wasn't difficult to discover that Tate de Lara was at Forestburn Manor, a guest of the mayor. With that information, they wasted no time.

It was a brazen daylight attack. They killed the dogs and made their way across the vast enclosure and gardens, five of them heading for the house and six of them moving to the *garçonnaire*. The two windows of the small house proved to be convenient points of entry, but also deadly ones. The knight inside was as fast as he was large, and deftly killed two of their number in swift succession. But others were able to break in, doing battle with the two men-at-arms that were also inside. The young king managed to throw himself out of one of the broken windows and race for the manor at the far end of the enclosure.

Unbeknownst to the occupants of the manor, three of Mortimer's men had made it inside the large house by way of the kitchen. The cook was killed and two servants beat unconscious. They were waiting for the king when he flew into the house, yelling for the man that Mortimer knew as Dragonblade. The lad was in a panic and was nearly hit by a sword that came flying at his head. He managed to avoid being decapitated and raced into the great hall, pulling a sword down from the hearth and defending himself admirably. All of this happened in quick succession, but the fiercest battle was yet to come.

Two massive knights came hurling off the stairs, racing into the great hall to join the melee. Tate and Stephen were without armor or weapons and at a distinct disadvantage; Stephen grabbed the long, slender iron pole that was used to stoke the hearth and drove the dirty end into one man's neck. Tate picked up the nearest stool, used it to block a strike against him, then swung about and used it as a weapon to disarm his adversary. It was a smooth move, accomplished in a matter of seconds. An additional move took his foe's legs out from underneath him and he collected the man's sword before it hit the ground. In a deadly turn, he used it against him.

There was still another attacker in the room, going after young Edward. Stephen did away with the man, putting the fire pole between his ribs. As the man fell, the knight caught his sword. Now, at least they were armed. Their odds were increasing.

Edward was exhilarated and terrified. "In the *garçonnaire!*" he yelled. "There are more!"

"Go help Kenneth," Tate ordered Stephen. He looked at the young king. "Up the stairs, now."

The tone of command left no room for debate. Stephen left for the *garçonnaire*, but Edward had yet to move.

"I can fight," he insisted.

"It was not a request," Tate replied. "Get up the stairs to the mistress' chamber and lock the door."

Edward was about to argue further but he suddenly paused. "I smell smoke."

Tate smelled it, too. He suspected what was happening and his plan of attack shifted. Before he could say anything further, a body abruptly stepped from the shadows and hit him squarely across the back of the head. Without his helm, Tate went down like a stone. Edward's eyes widened as the figure came into the weak light.

"De Roche," he gasped. "What... what are you doing here?"

Hamlin de Roche was big, dark and ugly. His armor was of the finest grade and his demeanor gave him the ambience of the devil. He grinned at Edward, evil and death bleeding from every pore of his body. He stepped over Tate's supine form.

"My king," he greeted in a deep, raspy voice. "As Mortimer's finest servant, the earl does not pay me for my good looks or pleasant nature. I have come for a reason."

Edward was backing up as de Roche moved towards him. "Stay away from me, you bastard. You will not lay a hand on me."

"I do not intend to lay a hand on you," de Roche said calmly. "I intend to take you with me for Mortimer's pleasure."

Edward was to the stairs, backing his way up the steps and unaware that he was about to corner himself. He had a sword in his hand but dared not strike out at de Roche; as deadly as Tate de Lara was, de Roche had nearly the same reputation. He was a powerful warrior, Roger Mortimer's most valuable knight. Catching Tate unaware had been a first; Tate had gotten the better of de Roche many times.

"Stay away, de Roche," Edward raised the sword in a weak threat. "I will kill you if you come any closer, I swear it."

De Roche laughed low in his throat. "You are brave, sire. You have grown since last we spoke."

Edward was nearly to the top of the stairs and increasingly fearful of his fate. He was at a disadvantage and he knew it. But unexpectedly, a wet figure pushed past him, a blur of hair and ashen flesh. Toby suddenly wedged herself between Edward and the dark knight, causing Edward to trip and fall back on the steps. Truthfully, he was so startled to see her that he had fallen over his own feet.

Toby was pale and shaken, her nightshift damp from the bath she had taken to save her life. She had awoken on her bed, hearing urgent voices in the hall and wondering why she was all wet. Ailsa was asleep beside her and she had not the strength to wake her sister and ask what had transpired. When the voices drew closer, men she did not recognize, she was curious more than she sensed danger. But a terrified young man's voice told her something was amiss. Rising from the bed, which was no easy feat, she had stumbled to the door in time to see Tate's squire heading off with an enormous knight.

The lad was frightened, that much was evident. The big knight looked as if he was about to do the youth serious harm. Having no idea who the man was, she instinctively took a defensive stance. She was enraged that someone would violate the sanctity of her home, no matter what the circumstances. Staggering over to the hearth, she grabbed the fire poker, the only weapon-like instrument in the room.

De Roche was soon aware of a poker staring him in the face.

"How dare you enter my home without permission," Toby hissed. "Leave this boy alone. Get out of here."

De Roche's gaze drifted over her in a way that made Toby feel dirty and exposed. "Lady, this matter does not concern you. I shall leave your home gladly as soon as young Edward lets go his sword and comes with me."

Toby's mind was fogged with illness and she did not comprehend that the man had called the squire by a different name. She lowered the poker as if she meant to attack him.

"Get out. I will not tell you again."

"And I will not tell you again that I am not ready to."

She swung the poker at his head. He easily sidestepped the blow, grabbed the poker from her, and tossed it over the side of the stairs. Toby heard it clatter on the floor below. Keeping Edward behind her, she made sure to stay between the boy and the knight as they slowly backed away.

"You would make this far easier for yourself if you would simply move out of the way," de Roche told her.

"I am not moving," Toby replied, firm but frightened. "Why would you want to harm this boy?"

"I already told you: I do not want to harm him. I have simply been sent to retrieve him."

"He does not want to go with you; can you not see that?"

They had reached the top of the steps. De Roche was finished debating with her and reached out to move her aside. He truthfully had no intention of hurting her. But the moment he laid his hands on her, Toby turned into a wildcat and began kicking and biting. She nipped de Roche on the hand and he grunted, shifting his grip so she could not reach him with her sharp teeth.

He was about to toss her aside when he suddenly lurched forward. It was a violent move that pitched him onto the floor. He let go of Toby somewhere in the process and she stumbled back. Only the terrified king had saved her from falling completely. The two of them looked at the knight on the ground, dumbfounded. But the large body standing where de Roche had once been ended their confusion.

Tate stood on the top of the steps holding the poker he had picked up off the floor down below. His expression was grave as he inspected the man on the floor. Unlike de Roche's handiwork, Tate knew Hamlin would not be regaining lucidity any time soon. The whack to his head had been for damage. For his part, Tate had a slight headache but was none the worse for wear. He rubbed the back of his skull as he looked at Toby.

"Are you all right?"

She nodded, though in truth, she wasn't. She was horribly weak and still very ill. When she tried to speak, she suddenly felt very faint and would have collapsed but for Edward. He broke her fall and Tate picked her up.

"Edward, rouse the family," he ordered. "The manor is afire and there is little time to waste. Tell them to gather what they can and get out."

"My mother," Toby breathed, struggling weakly to remove herself from Tate's hold. "She cannot move by herself. She will need help."

"Then I will send a man up for her," Tate said. "We need to get you out of here."

While Edward disappeared into one of the rooms, Tate carried Toby back into her chamber. Ailsa, awoken by the commotion, sat up on the bed and rubbed her eyes.

"What is happening?" she asked. She saw Toby as her vision cleared. "Toby! What is wrong with her?"

Tate sat Toby very gently on the end of the bed. "Bravery is exhausting," he said simply, but there was no time for idle chatter. "Ailsa, we need to leave right away. Where are your traveling cases?"

Ailsa blinked as if she did not understand the question. Then she pointed to the wardrobe against the wall. Tate went to the bureau and quickly pulled out two large leather trunks. He started throwing clothes in them at random.

Ailsa ran over to him. "Why do we have to leave? What is the matter?"

She was verging on tears. Tate paused, putting his hands on her slender shoulders. "You must be brave, little one. I need your help."

Her lip was trembling. "Aye?"

"Help me pack. Quickly."

"Why are we hurrying?"

He threw the green damask gown that Toby had worn the eve they supped together into the trunk. "Because some men have come. They have set fire to the manor. We must get out of here. Do you understand?"

Her eyes were full of fear but, to his surprise, she did not panic. She began flying around the room, collecting items and throwing them into the second trunk. With the next gown he grabbed, Tate went over to Toby, still sitting on the bed.

"Put this on," he said gently. "Do you need my help to do so?"

Toby shook her head and, with quivering hands, began to pull at her night shift. Tate turned away, back to the packing. It seemed as if any doubt he had ever had about her had fled the moment he saw her standing at the top of the steps, defending Edward against a man three times her size. He had no idea how she had managed it, but her courage and strength astonished him.

The trunks were full in short order and he sealed them both. Then he turned to see how Toby was faring. She was still sitting on the bed, pale and sickly, but had managed to somehow pull her wet shift off and put on a linen shift and heavy brown broadcloth garment. Ailsa had found a pair of woolen hose and was trying to pull them on her sister's feet. Edward and Balin came into the chamber, both wide-eyed at what was happening around them, and Tate put them to work.

"Take these trunks out of here," he directed the king. "Balin, take Ailsa out. Do not let her out of your sight."

"But... my home," Balin gasped. "These men... dead in my hall. What is happening?"

Tate took the hose from Ailsa and threw propriety to the wind; he deftly rolled a stocking on to one of Toby's legs. "I fear that my visit has brought you bad fortune," he said quietly. "Get your wife and get out of this place. Be quick about it."

"This place is all that I have!" Balin wailed. "I will not go, I tell you!"

"You must or it will burn down over your head."

"Then let it burn. I will not leave!"

He ran off and they heard a door slam. Ailsa, confused and frightened, began crying. Tate rolled the other stocking onto Toby's leg, trying not to think of how soft and shapely it was. "Ailsa, sweetheart, find your sister's shoes," he commanded softly. "We must hurry."

She did as she was asked, sobbing. In little time, they had Toby dressed and Tate collected her in his arms once more. The three of them moved down the smoky stairs; de Roche still lay upon the landing and they stepped over him. On the first floor, the great hall was filled with heavy smoke and some flame. The fire was gaining. Tate carried Toby out into the yard.

The Harbottle troops that had been encamped on the eastern side of the manor house were trying to douse the fire that had consumed most of the northern section of the house; the kitchens and solar were completely engulfed. Toby, only semi-conscious, nonetheless realized what was happening.

"My father," she whispered. "Where are my father and mother?"

Stephen and Kenneth met Tate in the yard. All of Mortimer's men had been either subdued or killed and were no longer a threat. The men-at-arms had taken young Edward back to the *garçonnaire*, which was still standing. Mortimer's men hadn't tried to burn it. With all of the men running about trying to put out the fire, the environment was chaotic.

"I must go after the father and mother," Tate deposited Toby into Stephen's big arms. "Ask me later how she stood up against de Roche."

"I already heard," Stephen replied. "Edward told us. Where is de Roche?"

"Lying unconscious at the top of the stairs." Tate motioned to Kenneth to follow him but he gave Stephen a pointed look. "Take care of her."

"With all that I possess, I swear it."

By the time they returned to the manor, the majority of the structure was completely engulfed. The troops from Harbottle had given up trying to douse the flames and were simply standing around, watching it burn.

Tate was about to enter the front door when the roof collapsed, crushing everything beneath it in a horror of ash and flame. The force of the collapse blew out the doors and windows, nearly scalding Tate and Kenneth as they attempted to gain access.

Sparks and smoke flew into the late morning sky until all that was left of Forestburn Manor was cinders and sorrow.

CHAPTER FIVE

RIDING AT NIGHT wasn't the smartest thing to do, but Tate felt that they had been given little choice. The sooner they reach Harbottle, the better for them all. Mortimer's men were after them and Tate was anxious to put young Edward behind the massive walls of his castle.

Tate was in full armor, something he'd sorely missed earlier in the day with Mortimer's men running about. The tempered steel breastplate had been forged in Rouen, as had the sword at his side. His gloved hand stroked the dragonhead of the hilt, a carved masterpiece of metalwork. Though the road was quiet, still, he was preparing to draw it at any moment. He and his knights were silent, their senses attuned to their surroundings.

"Mortimer's days are numbered," Edward said quietly, attempting to fortify his courage. "He killed my father and he is trying to kill me."

"He has been trying to kill you since you were a small child," Tate replied evenly. "He is simply being more obvious about it now."

The youth hung his head. Edward was still very sensitive. Tate knew what he was thinking without the lad speaking his mind.

"As I have always told you, I am sure your mother knows nothing," he spoke with quiet assurance. "Mortimer is clever. There is much he can hide from her."

"But you told her what he was doing," Edward said. "She did not believe you."

"She refused to believe ill of him. He freed her from the tyranny of your father and she is blinded by that."

Edward sighed heavily, tightening the reins on his blond steed. "She will believe when I take my rightful place and throw Mortimer to the executioner."

Tate didn't reply. Like so many conversations with the lad, they had traversed this one before, too. He glanced at Stephen, astride his big black stallion, and at Kenneth, who was watching the surrounding trees like a hawk. It had been a long night for all of them and they were all exhausted, yet their exhaustion would have to wait. They were in the open and vulnerable and had to reach safety.

"It is my suggestion that we stay vigilant until we reach Harbottle," Tate said. "We will all be thinking more clearly once we are within the safety of her walls."

"What about Mistress Toby?" Edward wanted to know. "We must still go to London; our stay at Harbottle is not permanent. Do we leave the women at Harbottle to fend for themselves?"

Tate thought about the sisters, asleep in the wagon that they had taken from the stables of Forestburn. Toby had been too ill to react to her father and mother's gruesome death, but Ailsa had been inconsolable. He felt a good deal of guilt at the thought of heading off to London and leaving them behind in a strange castle. Like a vicious storm he had moved in, destroying everything in his path, and then left those caught in the maelstrom to deal with the aftermath.

"Only the manor burned," Kenneth cut into Tate's thoughts. "The farm is still functional. 'Tis not as if they have lost everything. They can rebuild."

Kenneth made it sounds as if the women were not destitute but they all knew it was more than that. Edward sighed heavily; after Toby had defended him, he, too, was feeling guilty about everything. She had risked her life to protect him and, because of him, men had burned down her home and killed her parents. All of that aside, however, he was anxious to return to Harbottle and, subsequently, London.

"Can we leave for London as soon as the women are settled, then?" he asked.

"We can."

"But what are you going to do with them?"

"They will enjoy the hospitality of Harbottle until such time as it is no longer necessary."

Edward didn't push. He could tell by the tone of Tate's voice that now was not the time. There were other things on his mind.

The night seemed to drag on forever. A fog had settled, collecting from the moist grass and rising as a thick mist. It was very damp and the chill was evident. Not even the moon could break through the fog, although there was a small amount of light from the shrouded full moon. Tate rode at the head of the group, his attention moving back to Stephen now and again. The Hospitaller was riding beside the wagon.

They had been on the road for a few hours when Tate put Kenneth at point and reined his charger back beside Stephen. He could see two figures resting in the wagon, covered by blankets they had managed to collect from the *garçonnaire*. In fact, everything the Cartingdon sisters owned that had not been burned now lay piled in the wagon. Tate peered at the still forms in the wagon bed.

"How is Mistress Toby faring?" he asked Stephen.

Stephen's cornflower blue eyes drifted to his patient. "She is sleeping heavily. She has had quite a night of it."

Tate lifted an ironic eyebrow. "No doubt. We should see Harbottle by dawn; a warm bed should do her wonders."

Stephen nodded his head though his focus remained on the lady. "So tell me how she stood against de Roche. We heard Edward's version in which she rose out of her deathbed and wielded the poker like the sword of Archangel Michael. What was the truth of it?"

Tate gave him a half-grin. "He was not far wrong," his smile faded as his gaze fell on her again. "She may be aggressive and outspoken but she has courage that men would envy. She is a brave and noble woman."

There was something in his tone that caused Stephen to look closely at him. He had suspected that Tate felt something more than polite interest since yesterday but couldn't honestly believe it until this moment. The Tate de Lara he knew was focused on young Edward's cause singularly. Stephen was frankly astonished to hear a tone comprised of awe and appreciation. He was also strangely jealous.

"Noble indeed," he agreed quietly.

Tate didn't notice the knight's soft tone or the distant look to his eye. He was focused on the bundles sleeping in the wagon bed. Then his gaze moved to their surroundings; it was a soft, damp and eerie blanket that covered the land. Even with thirty men from Harbottle, he was vastly uncomfortable traveling on the open road in the dead of night. It was as quiet as a tomb as they plodded along, hoping to make it to safety in relative peace.

Until Ailsa's cry suddenly pierced the air. The little girl sat bolt upright, wailing and rubbing her eyes. Startled, both Tate and Stephen reined their chargers near the wagon.

"Ailsa?" Tate was closer to her. "What is wrong?"

Ailsa sobbed and wiped the tears from her eyes. "My belly aches," she sobbed. "I want to go home!"

Tate pulled one of the blankets from the wagon onto his lap. He held out his hand to the girl. "Come here, sweetheart," he said. "Ride with me. You will feel better."

She sobbed and sputtered, waking Toby in the process. The older sister was very groggy as she struggled to sit up against the bumping of the wagon.

"Ailsa," she murmured hoarsely. "What is wrong?"

Ailsa sobbed and coughed. Suddenly, she vomited all over the front of her garment as Toby tried to catch the liquid with a section of the blanket. It turned into a mess. When she was finished gagging, Ailsa cried harder.

"I want to go home!" she wailed.

With a curt command from Tate, the wagon lurched to a halt and Stephen bailed from his charger, going in search of his medicament bag. Toby tried to clean up her sister.

"There, there," she whispered softly. "You will be all right now."

Tate had come to a halt next to the wagon, his storm cloud eyes watching Toby as she gently tended her sister. He hadn't sufficient experience in matters of the heart to realize that he was seeing the woman through entirely different eyes; now, everything about her was completely different. He almost couldn't remember that curt, aggressive woman he had first met at the church in Cartingdon. All he could see was the brave, compassionate soul.

Stephen approached with water and some manner of powder from his mysterious bag and together he and Toby managed to both calm and clean Ailsa. Stephen's potion did wonders to soothe her stomach and her sister's tender embrace soothed her tears.

With her sister calming, Toby looked up at Tate, still seated astride his charger and watching them closely. She smiled weakly.

"I fear we have caused you some delay," she said quietly. "She has never been a good traveler."

Tate waved her off. "We are nearly to Harbottle. 'Tis just over the hill and we shall have both you and your sister into a warm bed in little time."

Toby's smile faded, her eyes turning as if she could see the distant castle. "That would be welcome," she murmured.

Tate watched her intently as she returned to comforting her sister. "How are *you* feeling?" he asked softly.

It took Toby a moment to realize he was asking the question of her. She lifted her shoulders. "Exhausted," she admitted. "But well enough to…."

She trailed off. Tate peered more closely at her.

"Well enough to what?" he encouraged.

She looked at her sister, her hands, anywhere but Tate's probing eyes. "Nothing, my lord."

"My lord, is it?" Tate grunted. "You have not called me 'my lord' for two days."

"I have not been conscious for two days."

He grunted again, a smile playing on his lips. "You will call me by my name. Now tell me what you were going to say."

She looked up at him and he could see embers of the old fire within her brilliant hazel eyes, the Toby he had first met in Cartingdon. He knew that illness and devastation could not erase this woman's spirit. She was too strong.

"I was going to say that I am well enough to return to Forestburn," she said with more conviction. "I must see to the state of affairs if we are going to have any hope of regrouping."

He had known all along that it would have been her desire; he just didn't think she would voice it so soon. "Forestburn is ashes," he said quietly. "Give yourself time to recover before entertaining a return home."

Toby's lovely features tightened; he could see it even in the dark of the fog. "Forestburn may be ashes but my father's farm still exists. There are still sheep to be shorn and harvests to be brought in. Simply because the manor burned does not mean the empire no longer exists. Too many people depend on us. They must know that all is not lost, that they have not been deserted."

He expected nothing less from her but was not prepared to enter into what would undoubtedly be something of an argument. "Well," he said after a moment, scratching beneath his hauberk where it chaffed. "Nothing will be settled this night. We are nearly to Harbottle and from there you can plot your next move. But for now, I would strongly suggest we make all due haste to reach my fortress and see what the morrow brings."

"I *am* returning home."

"I know."

She eyed him as if daring him to challenge her. When she realized he had no intention of contradicting her, she backed down somewhat and refocused on her sister. Above her head, Tate and Stephen exchanged knowing glances; trying to keep her still long enough to recover her strength was going to be something of a chore.

Truth be told, Tate knew he did not have the heart to deny her. After what he had witnessed at the top of the stairs at Forestburn, he realized he would never be able to deny her anything ever again. Any woman that brave, that strong, deserved his undying support and loyalty. But it was more than that; beyond admiration and respect, he felt something more. He wasn't sure what it was yet, but it was lingering in the recesses of his mind just waiting for the moment to be unleashed. Every time he looked at her, he could feel himself drawing closer and closer to unhinging it.

Ailsa fell back into a fitful sleep. As exhausted as she was, Toby was holding her limp sister protectively to ensure the child's comfort. Tate ordered the wagon to move forward and it did, as carefully as it could manage. Stephen, still beside the wagon, rolled up a blanket and propped it behind Toby's back. She was able to lean back on it and she smiled her thanks at Stephen. He dipped his head gallantly and remounted his charger.

The party traveled deep into the night, eventually to come upon Harbottle Castle just as dawn began to break. As the sun rose and the fog turned from dark mist to puffy silver clouds, the pale gray stones of Harbottle Castle took on a cold and harsh countenance.

Toby was still awake, still with the sleeping Ailsa in her arms, as her gaze beheld the seat of the Harbottle Common lordship. In all of her years at Forestburn, she'd never once traveled far enough to see the castle. She'd never had any reason to. Now, as they passed through the small village and the castle loomed into view, she thought it looked very uninviting. It was a massive place with at least three stone towers that she could count, probably more, and a keep that stretched into the fog. She couldn't even see the top. It occurred to her that it would now be her residence until such time as she returned to Forestburn.

She did not get a good feeling from the place.

CB

WALLACE WORTHINGTON MAGNUSSON had been a priest many years

ago. But he had committed the unspeakable sin of falling in love with a woman and the Jesuits exiled him. Before he had been a priest, however, he had been a knight, and a very good one. So he had returned to the knighthood only to realize that he did not have the stomach for killing any longer. Then, whilst drowning his sorrows one night at a tavern, he managed to save the life of a young knight named Tate de Lara and from that moment on, the two had been unquestionably linked.

So the dishonored priest was given the job of majordomo at young de Lara's Harbottle holding and it was this hairy bear of a man who greeted the party from Cartingdon Parrish. Standing on the steps of the keep, he looked like a wild-man who lived in the forest and ate bark and berries to survive. His mass of shocking white hair was the first thing Toby noticed. It was hard to miss. As the party drew into the bailey and the massive portcullis was slammed shut behind them, she was coming to feel uneasy and disoriented.

Tate bailed from his charger as they neared the keep and made his way back to the wagon. Kenneth and young John were barking orders to disburse the men and Stephen was already at the wagon by the time Tate arrived. The Hospitaller had his arms around Ailsa, lifting her out of the wagon as Toby weakly fussed with the blanket her sister was wrapped in. She wanted to make sure her sister was warm enough and Stephen assured her that the child was indeed quite warm.

Toby looked a little lost as the tall knight walked off with Ailsa, watching as the two of them mounted the stairs to the towering keep. She wasn't sure she wanted her sister out of her sight in this foreign place, not even for a moment. The big man with the wild hair greeted Stephen at the top of the stairs and said something to Ailsa, to which the little girl began crying. Startled, Toby was about to climb from the wagon herself to see what the matter was when a soft voice distracted her.

"Elizabetha," Tate was standing at the end of the wagon bed, patting the boards with a mailed hand. "Slide down here, sweetheart. I will take you inside."

"Why is Ailsa crying?" she demanded weakly. "And who is that man? What did he say to her?"

Tate gave her a lopsided grin and motioned her in his direction. Dutifully, and slowly, she slid to the edge of the wagon bed. Tate already had a heavy woolen traveling blanket in hand and he tossed it over her shoulders, wrapping her up tightly. When he was satisfied that she was properly covered, he scooped her into his massive arms and walked towards the keep.

"That man is Wallace," he said, eyeing the bulk of a man as he began to descend the steps towards them. "He has run Harbottle quite ably for many years. However, he is not used to being around women and, I am sure, unused to tact or pleasant conversation. He simply does not know any better so you should not be upset by anything he says."

He turned to look at Toby as he finished, his storm cloud-colored eyes meeting with her brilliant hazel. There was a strange pull to the moment and a strange feeling of warmth that settled in his veins. He remembered feeling such a thing once, years ago, but not nearly with this intensity. The heat was so strong that it made his palms sweat, although it was not unpleasant. In fact, he rather liked it.

"I will not tolerate him causing my sister tears," Toby told him with quiet firmness. "If he lacks manners, then I shall be happy to teach him for the duration of my stay."

Tate grinned, studying her face, thinking he'd never in his life seen such a lovely creature. "I have no doubt that you will," he snorted softly. "I fear Wallace is in for a harsh lesson."

Before Toby could reply, the hairy beast of a man was upon them. He bowed swiftly to Tate and a horrendous smell of sweat and smoke billowed up from the layers of dirty robes he wore. Toby had to repress the urge to pinch her nose shut as his head came up and small brown eyes focused on her. There was something intense in the deep depths. Then he looked at Tate.

"My lord," Wallace greeted in a very deep, very gravelly voice. "We are honored with your arrival."

Tate walked past the man, continuing up the stairs. "What chamber did you tell Stephen to put the little girl in?"

"I did not tell him any chamber," Wallace followed. "We have no accommodations for womenfolk."

Tate paused at the top of the stairs, lifting an eyebrow at him. "Then make some. Clean up my chamber and put them in it."

"But, my lord...," Wallace began to protest.

"Do it now," Tate commanded. "Clean linen on the bed, a warm fire and a hot bath."

Tate sharply turned his back on him and headed into the dark, dank depths of the keep. It was a creepy place, smelling of must and spooks. Toby's grip around Tate's neck instinctively tightened as he took her into the unfamiliar bowels. He could feel her tensing in his arms.

Behind him, Wallace was grumbling and growling as he followed. It seemed the man wasn't finished voicing his opinion yet about women in Harbottle.

"My lord, we have no clean linen," he said pointedly. "What we have cannot be considered fitting for females."

Tate sighed heavily and came to a halt. He turned to face the man. "God's Blood, man, then go and wash some. Hang them out to dry before a blazing fire and put some water on to boil. If I have to command this again I swear I will throw you out on your arse and you can find yourself another liege."

Wallace scowled at him but wisely held his tongue. His grizzled gaze moved between his lord and the lady in his arms. Tate could read the man's disgruntled thoughts and suppressed the urge to smile; Wallace was a complainer but he would get the job done. He was just being old and stubborn and difficult. Tate's gaze moved to Toby's beautiful face, a light of magnificence in this dark and dreary place.

"This is Mistress Elizabetha Cartingdon," he told his majordomo. "Mistress, meet Wallace, the majordomo of Harbottle. He is at your disposal."

Before Toby could acknowledge the introduction, Tate turned for the great hall off to his left, a huge cavernous room that was dark but for the fire that Stephen was attempting to coax from a hearth that was taller than he was. Ailsa sat on a bench nearby, shrouded by the dark and wrapped in her blanket as she watched Stephen try to get a blaze going. Her little face turned towards the doorway as Tate and Toby entered.

"I do not like this place," she announced, hopping off the bench and running to her sister. "It frightens me. I want to go home!"

Tate gently put Toby down and the two sisters embraced tightly.

"Our home is here for now," Toby said softly, feeling distaste for the place even as she said it. "I will return to Forestburn in a few days and we shall see what is left. We can rebuild."

Ailsa buried her face in Toby's stomach. "But I want to go home now."

Toby soothed her weary, frightened little sister. "We cannot go home now. You must accept this. For today, we will have food and a little rest and things will look better."

"I want my father!"

Toby shushed her. "He is gone, little chicken. You must accept this also."

Ailsa began to sob softly and Toby steered her sister over to the bench. The two of them sat and comforted each other, the soft sounds of the child's weeping filling the air. Tate watched them a moment, feeling his guilt return. But he also realized one thing very quickly; he liked having Toby within these walls. He liked having her with him. And having Ailsa around was like having a daughter at his feet like the one lost those years ago. It was a warm, fulfilling sensation, something he'd never before experienced. It was also dangerous for he could imagine quite easily forgetting everything of import except for the two small women before him.

To his left, Stephen managed to get the fire going. A soft, warm light radiated from the hearth, growing brighter by the moment. The big knight stood up and brushed soot off his hands.

"That will do for now," he said to Tate, eyeing the two sisters as they consoled each other. "We must prepare a chamber for them. Both ladies need much rest."

As Tate nodded, Wallace scowled a few feet away. "This is no comfort-palace, Lord Tate," he said frankly. "There are only men at Harbottle and ever have been. Women do not belong in this place."

Tate eyed him. "Be that as it may, women are here and you will make them comfortable. I will hear no more of your complaints. Is that clear?"

Rather than challenge him, for he had already pushed his lord farther than he should have, Wallace merely shrugged and turned away to presumably go about his duties. Tate and Stephen watched the old man shuffle away, muttering to himself, and Tate finally shook his head.

"Go and see if there is something in the kitchens for the ladies to eat," Tate asked Stephen quietly. "I shall go and check on the state of my chamber to see what needs to be done in order to make it livable."

Stephen departed for the kitchens that were outside of the keep, situated to the west against the fortress walls. As he moved into the dawn, Tate turned back to the women only to see that Toby was nearly upon him.

"Go and sit by the fire," he put his hands on her shoulders to turn her around. "I will go and see to your chamber."

Toby tried to shake him off. "I cannot sit and do nothing," she said. "You must let me help. Where is Stephen going? Perhaps I can help him."

Tate was trying not to be harsh with her. "I want you to sit and rest. The past few days have been very traumatic for you. Moreover, Ailsa needs you. She is very upset right now. I shall see to your chamber and you stay here where it is warm and bright."

Toby managed to plant her feet so that he wasn't shoving her back towards the bench. Brushing stray hair from her eyes, she faced him.

"Please," she begged softly. "Please let me help you. I feel so useless right now. I feel as if I must be doing… something."

He knew that she was a woman used to being very busy. And he also knew she was feeling weak and disoriented; she was still very pale and not at all recovered from her bout with illness. Before he could stop himself, he kissed her on the forehead and turned her back for the bench.

"Go and sit with your sister," he instructed softly. "Warm yourself and I shall return shortly."

His lips on her forehead had left a searing brand. Toby was still feeling it. "But…."

He cut her off and gave her another gentle shove to the bench. "Elizabetha, please," he insisted softly. "I will feel better knowing you are safe and warm right where I left you. I shall return as quickly as I can."

Toby didn't argue further; she watched him fade into the dimness of the hall and into the stair hall beyond. He had a confident, stalking gate that she'd noticed before but never gave a tremendous amount of thought to until this moment. There was something about it that made her heart swell strangely. And the kiss… she touched her forehead as if she could still feel his lips there. Behind her, she heard Ailsa's soft voice.

"Why did he kiss you?" she asked, curious. "I saw him do it. Why did he do it?"

Toby's fingers lingered on her forehead a moment before dropping to her side. "I do not know," she turned back to her sister, noting that the fire was gaining in strength and she scooted the bench towards it. "Perhaps he feels sorry for us. Perhaps he was just showing pity."

Ailsa frowned. "He would kiss you to show pity?"

Toby's thoughts lingered on the kiss before she looked at her sister, returning the frown. "Stop asking so many questions. Take off that blanket and move closer to the fire."

Ailsa stuck her tongue out at her sister before shrugging the blanket off and lifting her hands to the delicious warmth of the fire. All manner of thoughts were rolling through her little mind as she watched the flames jump. She cast her sister a long look.

"Do you suppose that you shall become Lady Dragonblade?" she asked innocently.

With a scowl, Toby smacked her sister on the behind and Ailsa yelped. "No more talk of that," she hissed. "I am in no mood for it."

Ailsa made all sorts of faces at her sister, who soundly ignored her. When Ailsa realized that her sister was not reacting, she turned back to the fire. It was warm and wonderful on her face and she began to perk up. Her bright eyes moved about the hall, inspecting it, her curiosity now outweighing her disorientation.

The sounds of boots suddenly smacked in the keep entry. Both Ailsa and Toby turned to see Kenneth and the young squire entering the keep. Kenneth was removing his helm and peeling back his hauberk as Edward began sneezing. Ailsa left her post by the fire and ran to the squire.

"Are you ill?" she asked eagerly. "My father told me that wine cures all illness. Perhaps you should drink."

Edward took on the familiar petrified look as Ailsa focused her attention on him. He veered away from her, moving to the opposite side of the great table, but Ailsa followed him. When he sat, she sat. Edward sneezed again, trying not to sneeze on Ailsa as she sat right next to him.

"Do you feel ill?" she pressed.

Edward shook his head, trying to discreetly scoot away from her. "Nay, I am fine. Just dust in my nose."

Ailsa saw that he moved away from her and she closed the gap. "It is good that you are not ill. Toby is only now feeling better; is that not so, Toby?"

Toby turned to look at her sister as she pursued the terrified squire across the bench. Edward would scoot and Ailsa would scoot right after him. She motioned to her sister.

"Ailsa, come over here to the fire," she was attempting to help the lad out. "'Tis too cold over there."

Ailsa wouldn't even look at her sister; she was gazing adoringly up at the pale-faced squire. "Where were you born?" she asked him.

Edward looked at her with the same fear that one would have when gazing upon a man-eating beast. "I… I was born in London."

Ailsa batted her big green eyes at him. "I have never been to London. I hope to go someday. Do you suppose you will ever go back?"

Edward was starting to grow red around the ears. "I hope to."

"Ailsa," Toby hissed firmly. "Come over by the fire. If I have to get up to retrieve you, you will be very sorry."

Ailsa noticed her sister, then. Threats always made her notice, mostly because she knew that Toby wasn't bluffing. But she wouldn't give up so easily; she grabbed Edward by the hand and began climbing off the bench.

"Come over by the fire," she urged him. "It is warmer there. You can tell me more about London."

Edward didn't want to yank his hand away but he was truly terrified of the young girl. He followed her dumbly until they got within range of Toby, who mercifully reached out and disengaged her sister's grip on the young man.

"Leave him alone," she told her sister quietly. "He has duties to attend to."

Ailsa looked outraged, then disappointed. She gazed up at the tall young man. "Do you really have duties to attend to?"

Edward nodded feebly. "I… I must bed the horses."

"Go, then," Toby said, smiling encouragingly at him when he didn't move. "If you do not, then Ailsa will talk your ear off."

Edward nodded, his gaze moving between Toby and Ailsa, before fleeing the hall. Toby watched him go until a large obstacle was suddenly in her line of sight. Kenneth had moved up to the fire, his big body blocking out half the hall from where he stood. As Ailsa moved away to pout, Toby shook her head and returned her attention to the blaze.

"Your squire is going to have to learn to stand up for himself," she muttered to Kenneth. "Ailsa will take over his will to live if he is not careful."

Much to her surprise, Kenneth actually snorted. "He has more courage than he displays," he replied, holding up his big hands to warm them. "I would not worry about him."

Toby lifted an eyebrow as if she didn't believe him. "How old is he?"

"Fourteen years," Kenneth replied.

Again, Toby shook her head. "And Ailsa is ten. She will soon be asking if he is betrothed. She is desperate, even at her age, to find a mate. I do believe she has little friends telling her that she must be wed by the time she is fourteen or she will become a spinster like me."

Kenneth did look at her, then. "As for the squire, tell your sister to set her sights on someone else as he is already betrothed," he told her. "As for you being a spinster, I suspect that will not be true forever."

Toby's head jerked in his direction, her hazel eyes wide with surprise. "Why in the world would you say that?"

"Because you are beautiful and wealthy. You are a fine prize."

Stunned, Toby lowered her gaze and looked back to the fire. The big blond knight had barely said two words to her since their introduction and suddenly he was telling her that she was beautiful. She didn't know what to say.

Fortunately, Stephen saved her from further bewilderment. He entered the hall with loaves of bread in his hands, followed by an old male servant with spindly legs and long, stringy white hair. The old man carried a tray with food laden upon it. Just as Stephen reached the table, Ailsa suddenly forgot her pouting and she rushed to the big knight as he put the bread down. In fact, she grabbed a loaf right out of his hand.

"It is brown," she declared flatly. "I do not like brown bread. I want white."

"You will take what you are offered and be grateful for it," Toby said sharply, quietly. "Now sit and eat. Stop making a nuisance of yourself."

More pouting from Ailsa. The old man who had accompanied Stephen pulled back the cloth that covered the tray he had carried. He picked up a small earthenware jar and held it timidly in Ailsa's direction.

"Do you like honey, my lady?" he asked gently. "A little honey on the bread will make you think that angels themselves eat it."

Ailsa eyed the jar. "I… I like honey."

The old man smiled at her and put the jar down, taking a hunk of the brown bread and slathering some white butter upon it. Then he poured honey all over it and handed the sticky-sweet mess to Ailsa.

She grinned and took it gladly, chewing into it and getting honey on her face. Then she looked at the tray, inspecting the contents.

"What else did you bring?" she put her dirty fingers on the white cheese. "Is this all? No meat?"

Toby rolled her eyes. "Good Lord, Ailsa," she breathed. "Can you not be grateful for the hospitality you are shown? One more ungracious word from you and you can go stay with the pigs. That is where you belong if you cannot show more manners."

Ailsa took another big bite of bread and ignored her sister. She moved away from the table and wandered around the room, inspecting the walls, the floor, and anything else she could find. Somewhere along the line she began humming a tune; the fairy tune that Tate had sung the day before at Forestburn. Before long she was twirling about, bread on one hand and the edge of her surcoat in the other, dancing with unseen fairies or perhaps pale young men.

Toby watched her sister prance around the room, thankful that she was at least in better spirits. With the events of the past day, she wasn't at all sure how Ailsa would recover. But it would seem that she was showing a good deal of resilience.

"You must eat also, mistress," Stephen's deep voice was low as he placed a hunk of bread before her. "You must regain your strength."

Toby eyed the bread before gazing up at the enormous knight. "I thank you for your concern," she said, "but I am not hungry. Perhaps something later."

Stephen didn't push. He sat down at the table a few feet away from her while Kenneth took position on the opposite side. Toby continued to watch her sister flit around the room as Kenneth and Stephen silently consumed the food on the tray.

"She seems to show few ill effects," Stephen commented quietly.

Toby turned to look at him, watching him nod his head in Ailsa's direction. She, too, refocused on her dancing sister. "I know," she replied softly. "It is quite surprising, actually. She has never been particularly healthy and she has rarely been away from Forestburn. I was afraid that traveling all night in the cold air might have affected her health but she seems well enough."

"Has she said anything more about your parents?" Stephen asked as he took another bite of bread.

Toby looked away from her frolicking sister. "Not much," she picked at the bread that Stephen had put before her. After a moment, she dared to look up at the men around her. "I have not yet asked but I suppose I should. Did... did you search for my parents?"

Stephen's cornflower blue eyes were steady. "We found them in the rubble of the collapsed manor."

Toby drew in a long breath. "I see," she murmured, looking at the bread again. "May I ask what you did with them?"

"We left some men behind to bury them as we departed for Harbottle," Kenneth answered her before Stephen could.

She looked at the very blond knight. "Where did you instruct that they should be buried?"

"We did not instruct. We left it to the judgment of the men."

"So you do not know where my parents are buried?"

Kenneth looked at Stephen and the big knight cleared his throat softly. "I would suspect they are somewhere on the grounds of Forestburn," Stephen said. "I will find out for certain if it will please you."

Toby nodded faintly, looking back to her bread. She started to pick at it again but suddenly felt very much like taking in some fresh air. She needed it. Stiffly, she left the table, leaving Stephen and Kenneth behind in silence as her sister continued her dance around the room. The knights watched her go, knowing she would not go far in her condition. Kenneth returned to his food before Stephen did; the big knight watched the lady moved towards the entry to the keep, still gazing at the doorway even after she was gone.

It was cold outside as the deepening dawn struggled to lift the fog, strangely bright as the sunlight reflected off the mist. Still clad in the heavy broadcloth surcoat she had traveled in, Toby took the stairs slowly and ended up in the bailey. It wasn't particularly busy but there were a few people about. As weak and exhausted as she was, it actually felt good to walk so she moved across the bailey in an aimless path. It was slow going. Thoughts of her parents rolled through her head, people who hadn't been particularly kind to her for the duration of her life but people she was fond of. They were her parents, after all. But now they were gone.

The reality of their deaths began to sink in. She had been too ill to care yesterday but at the moment, she found that she cared a great deal. She traced the progression leading up to their deaths only to realize that she had been very ill for the past several days and recalled very little. The most she remembered was waking up to hear the young squire fighting off a monster of a man. She had tried to defend him. She remembered the man calling the squire young Edward, something that had no meaning until this moment. The intruder had seemed very certain that the squire's name was Edward and not John as she had been told. Then Tate had brained the man before he could do any further damage.

As the fog lifted from the ground, the fog in her mind seemed to do the same. Pacing back along the stables, her mind was wrapped up in the chaos of the past two days as she recollected. Men had burned her house down and Tate seemed to know who they were. He didn't seem surprised at all. In fact, it was almost as if he had expected it. Just as he had not been surprised that men had attacked them in the mist the day they went to visit the sheep herd. He had been gone for hours trying to locate the attackers. Then he had returned and she had become ill.

Toby came to a pause at the corner of the stable block that faced the kitchen yard. There was a rough-hewn bench there with some farm implements on it and she shoved the tools to the ground and wearily took a seat. As she watched a puppy chase chickens around the kitchen yard, her thoughts inevitably turned to Tate.

He was a man of wealth, skill and supreme power. Long had she heard the rumor that he was Edward Longshank's bastard. It was an accepted fact. It was also an accepted fact that he had served Longshank's son, Edward, until he had been imprisoned by Isabella and Mortimer. She thought of the man and his undeniable status, visions of his storm cloud colored eyes filling her mind and his handsome face invading her senses. For the first time since she had met the man, she admitted to herself that she found him wildly attractive. But he clearly had little use for her; at least, she thought so until he had kissed her on the forehead. The kiss had made her heart leap crazily, but it had been a wonderful sort of crazy. Yet she could not get her hopes up about the man. He was unreachable; especially to her. He was of royal blood and she was a farmer's daughter. That was the reality of things.

She hung her head moodily, eventually distracted by a noise off to her left. She turned to see the young squire quit the stables and head towards the keep. He was a tall lad, blond, and seemed nice enough. As she watched him avoid a pile of horse dung, she remembered what the intruder back at Forestburn had called him; *young Edward*. He said that he had been sent to retrieve him. Toby remembered asking Tate once if he was running from someone and he assured her that he was not. But he had come to Cartingdon Parrish to raise money for young King Edward's cause, a boy crowned while still quite young and now being hunted by his mother's lover.

And that's when it hit her. *King Edward*. Toby nearly fell off of the bench as the realization struck. There could be no other explanation; John of Hainault could be no other than Edward the Third. Traveling in the company of his Uncle Tate, the only man capable of protecting him from his mother and her vicious lover, the young king was disguised as a squire. What else would explain de Lara, two massive knights and a contingent of heavily armed men-at-arms around the boy? It made perfect sense. The more she thought on the awareness, the more stunned she became. And the more frightened.

She rose on shaking legs. The men who had destroyed Forestburn had obviously been hunting for the young king. They must have been Mortimer's men and the Cartingdon family had been unknowingly caught in the crossfire. Terrified, furious, Toby could only think of one thing; she had to get out of Harbottle. She had to take Ailsa and flee far from the young king and the murderers who pursued him. She had to get away to save them both; otherwise, surely they would end up as their parents had.

It was difficult to walk across the bailey on shaking legs. She made it to the stairs, pulling herself up until she reached the entry to the keep. Her fatigue was growing worse but she ignored it, determined to retrieve her sister. As she moved inside, she could see that Kenneth and Stephen were still sitting at the table, only this time they were joined by the squire. Ailsa was still dancing around the room. Toby staggered into the hall as fast as her weak legs would take her and went straight to her sister.

Ailsa took issue with being grabbed. She glared up at her sister until she saw the look on her face.

"What is wrong, Toby?" she asked.

Toby had her arm around Ailsa, eyeing the knights at the table. "Keep your voice down," she hissed. "We must leave this place right away."

Ailsa frowned. "Leave? We just got here."

Toby had a grip on her sister's arm. "You must trust me. We must leave this very moment and I do not want you to argue with me. Just come."

"But I do not want to leave," Ailsa said loudly. "Stop grabbing my arm. You are hurting me."

By this time, Stephen and Kenneth had heard pieces of the conversation. Toby tensed when Stephen rose to his feet.

"Leave?" he repeated. "Who is leaving?"

Toby was exhausted and frightened. She couldn't even look at Edward, stuffing his face with bread. At this point, it would do no good to lie about her reasons or intentions. She had never been one to mince words.

"We are," she announced, trying to pull Ailsa with her. "We are leaving this place and you will not stop us."

Stephen's gaze was steady. "Why are you leaving?"

Toby was backing up with Ailsa in her grip. Her hazel eyes moved rapidly between Stephen and Kenneth as if waiting for them to leap up and grab her.

"Because we must," she said firmly. "We must return to Forestburn."

"Forestburn is ashes."

"No thanks to you," she snapped; her quaking legs had spread to her body, making it difficult to remain balanced. "Those who burned my home were after you. I suppose I knew it all along but my illness has affected my thought processes. Now I know that my sister and I must leave if we are to survive. It was a mistake to come here with you."

By this time, Kenneth was on his feet. "Mistress, perhaps you should sit," he suggested. "You have been ill and...."

"I do not want to sit," Toby exploded, losing her grip on Ailsa. She stumbled backwards and in a reversal of roles, Ailsa was now the one with a firm grip on her arm. "I want to leave. I must leave. I do not want to be here when Mortimer's men burn this place down around our ears. I want to go home to Cartingdon where I belong."

"Toby, what is wrong?" Ailsa was starting to tear up. "Why are you so angry?"

Toby was losing ground fast. She struggled to stay on her feet as she looked at her sister. "I am not angry," she insisted hoarsely. "I am terrified; terrified because de Lara and his men have lied to us since the beginning. Those men who burned Forestburn and killed Mother and Father were sent by Roger Mortimer. They are looking for the king and we were caught in their path."

Ailsa's eyebrows lifted in disbelief. "The *king*? But...?"

Toby threw an arm in the direction of the table. "That squire, Ailsa. He is not a squire at all. He is King Edward the Third. They had come to kill him but killed our parents instead."

Astonished, Ailsa's head snapped in the direction of the table. Not surprisingly, Edward was no longer eating. He was staring wide-eyed at Toby, his expression one of a mouse caught in a trap.

Toby's pale face was clouded with loathing as she met his stare. "It would have been the decent thing to tell us who you really were rather than carry on a lie that would cost us everything," she directed her venom at the boy. "At least if we had known, we could have made an effort to protect ourselves. But you left us open and vulnerable without regard for our safety. Is that the kind of king you really are? Do you care nothing for your subjects?"

Slowly, Edward rose to his feet, swallowing what was left in his mouth. He wiped at his lips with the back of his hand.

"How did you know who I was?" he asked with surprising firmness.

Toby sighed heavily, her weakness growing. Lamely, she lifted an arm and let it slip back down to her side. "I did not for certain until this very moment," she realized that she felt overwhelming sadness more than anything. "We have lost everything because of you. Why did you have to come to Cartingdon in the first place? Why could you not have simply left us alone?"

"Because Cartingdon is my holding and I serve the king."

Tate emerged from the stair hall, his storm cloud eyes riveted to Toby. His progression into the room was slow, deliberate, the expression on his face unreadable. He had heard most of her rant as he came down the stairs, not surprised that she had figured out who the young squire was. She was a very smart woman. He found himself oddly torn as he faced off against her; torn between remorse and duty. He was sorry she had been put through such trauma but it had been, in fact, in the line of duty. And he was not going to apologize for his sense of duty.

Toby watched him as he moved towards her, his stalking gait and powerful form. The terror she had initially felt was fading, being replaced by a strange numbness. Her body was shaking with fatigue and emotion and it was increasingly difficult to hold a thought.

"You should have told me who he was," her voice was quivering. "Out of trust and generosity, we showed you hospitality and you allowed harm to come to my family. If this is the kind of king that Edward plans to be then I will side with Mortimer before I trust him again. He has allowed us to come to devastation."

She was so pale that she was gray; Tate knew she wasn't feeling well but he was having difficulty keeping his temper down. He was extremely protective of Edward, even against an ill young woman who had every right to be angry.

"In the first place, Mistress Elizabetha, it is not your right to know the business of the king," he said steadily. "In the second place, you have no choice in who you trust or support during this dark time. I am your liege and you will support whom I dictate."

"My parents are dead because you withheld the truth," she fired back with more strength than she felt. "My home is burned and my life devastated. You are no better than Mortimer's men sneaking around in the mist except that you deliver your deception under the guise of virtue."

"There was no deception."

"We trusted you!"

The last exchanged was rapid-fire, overlapping, Tate's calm voice against Toby's agitated one. They stared at each other, feeling more emotion than they should have. Toby was filled with sorrow for reasons she could not begin to understand while Tate resisted the urge to beg her forgiveness. He did not like to see her so upset, especially when he knew she was right. He had tried to leave Forestburn before things got too dangerous, but the threat had come too quickly. It had been upon them before they realized it and had been the cause of the destruction of her home. But he would not surrender.

"You are overwrought," he said, his voice quieter as he tried to calm the situation. "Let me take you to rest. You will feel better when you have had some sleep."

She shook her head and turned away from him, almost falling for the weakness in her legs. "Nay," she whispered. "I… I want to go home. I must leave this place."

"Why?"

She whirled to him and ended up stumbling against the wall. "Because whatever poison follows that boy will come here and destroy us all. I do not want to be here when it comes. I do not want my sister to fall victim to it. If you will not protect us, then I will."

Tate could feel himself softening. "So the true reason is revealed," he murmured, taking slow steps in her direction. "You do not feel that I will protect you."

On the verge of collapse, tears welled in Toby's hazel eyes. "You did not protect my parents."

He was almost upon her as she slumped against the wall, his storm cloud eyes gentle as he gazed into her pale, lovely face. "Had I known what harm was to come, I would have most certainly done my best to protect you," he said quietly. "But I swear to you now, upon my oath, that I will protect you with my life; you and your sister. No harm will come to you as long as I have breath in my body, Elizabetha. Please believe me."

She stared up at him with her almond-shaped eyes, so beautiful yet so sorrowful. When she finally blinked, fat tears splashed onto her cheeks. Tate moved in closely; so close, in fact, that his torso brushed against hers. His voice was low, soothing.

"Do not blame the boy," he murmured. "He has sorrow enough with his mother and her lover attempting to destroy him. We never meant that your family should fall to destruction."

She sobbed softly, unable to continue with the conversation. Without another word, Tate swept her into his arms, feeling more relief that he would admit when her arms went around his neck and she wept quietly against his shoulder. He wanted nothing more than to soothe away her fears. His gaze found Ailsa, a few feet away, and he smiled weakly at her.

"Come along, sweetheart," he said quietly. "You and your sister are off to bed."

Ailsa trotted after him as he quit the hall. The chamber on the third floor was dusty but passable. Tate put Toby on the bed and covered her with the cleanest blanket he could find, a dusty old thing that had been tossed into a corner. Ailsa climbed in next to her and Toby wound her arms around her sister, holding her tight. Tate pulled the blanket over Ailsa as well and tucked them both in very tightly, like a father tending his children. But Toby was still weeping softly and he just couldn't leave her in that state. He felt responsible. After a moment's deliberation, he lay down against Toby and pulled both ladies into his arms.

"Go to sleep," he kissed the back of Toby's head as he felt Ailsa squirm around to get comfortable. "Nothing will happen to you, I swear it. You may sleep peacefully."

Toby didn't even protest, nor did she say a word. She simply lay there, a hiccup now and again as her tears faded. She could feel him against her and rather than fight it, she accepted the comfort it gave her. Through all of the illness and turmoil over the past few days, Tate had proven himself to be a rock. At the moment, she needed the rock, no matter how unattainable he was. For the moment, she would pretend otherwise.

Tate lay with his chest against her back, feeling her soft body against him and thinking there was surely nothing more wonderful in the world. His thoughts began to drift to the day he first saw her and how beautiful he thought she was in spite of her boorish demeanor. But that opinion had quickly fled; she wasn't boorish at all. She was simply strong, opinionated and intelligent. As his mind began to reflect on the days past and the moments when he saw her smile, Ailsa's head suddenly popped up.

"Sing the baby song!" she demanded in a loud whisper.

Tate frowned at her. "Hush," he hissed sternly. "I will not sing anything if you do not lay still."

Ailsa stuck her lip out but obediently lay back down. When all was still and quiet in the room and Ailsa stopped fidgeting, Tate's pure baritone filled the stale air as gently as the brush of a butterfly's wing.

To the sky, my sweet babe;
The night is alive, my sweet babe.
Your dreams are filled with raindrops from heaven;
Sleep, my sweet babe, and cry no more

The words faded and he began to hum the tune, his lips against Toby's head and his arms tightly about her. He swore he felt her snuggle against him, sighing contentedly with slumber, and Ailsa wrapped a little hand around his enormous fingers as she drifted off to sleep. When he should have been seeing to his men and the threat of Mortimer's assassins, he found himself content to daydream away the morning with Toby and her little sister.

It was a joy he had been denied once, those years ago when his wife and child perished in childbirth. He would not be denied it again.

CHAPTER SIX

T HE ROOM WAS dark with dusk as soft sounds from the bailey wafted in through the lancet window. The old door to the chamber creaked open and someone entered the room quietly. Tate wasn't asleep; he'd heard the door open even though his back was to it. And he recognized Stephen's footfalls by the hollow sound of the boot.

"What is it?" he asked softly, his mouth muffled against Toby's head.

"Our sentries have seen movement about a half mile to the south," Stephen whispered. "You are needed, my lord."

Tate looked up over his shoulder, seeing Stephen's face looming in the dim room. "Is the fortress locked down?"

"Wallace has it sealed up tightly."

"Then I shall be down in a moment. You and Kenneth assemble in the solar and wait for me."

There was something in Stephen's lingering gaze that peaked Tate's curiosity. It was no more than a flicker before he turned away to do his liege's bidding, but in that flicker was something alien. Tate had known Stephen for years and wasn't sure what he just saw in the man's reflection. But he made a mental note to ask him about it later.

When the door to the chamber shut softly, Tate tried to very carefully disengage himself from Toby and Ailsa. But Toby had a grip on his arm and Ailsa still held his hand. He managed to get free of Ailsa but when it came to gently disengaging Toby's grasp, he woke her before he could complete the task. When she rolled onto her back to look sleepily at him, he smiled.

"Go back to sleep," he whispered, placing her arm beneath the blanket and tucking it in around her. "I will be back."

She yawned. "Where are you going?"

"Not far. I promise I will return shortly."

He gently touched her forehead and moved away from the bed. But she reached out to grab his hand before he could move away completely. There was a strange look of anxiety to her eyes and he kissed the hand that held onto him.

"I shall return, I promise," he kissed her hand again and put it back under the blanket. "Go back to sleep."

That seemed to satisfy her and she drifted off again. Quietly, Tate quit the chamber and went downstairs.

Kenneth, Stephen, Edward and Wallace were in the solar when he arrived. The room was lit by a bright fire, almost too hot in the small closeness of the room. Tate focused on Stephen.

"What is our status?" he asked.

"As I said, we have tracked movement about a half mile to the south," Stephen responded. "I have sent out a small scout party. We should be receiving a report from them shortly."

Tate nodded, raking his fingers through his dark hair and spying a pitcher and a few cups on a table near the door. He went to it, pouring himself a cup of strong ale.

"Then we wait," he said as he lifted the cup to his lips. "I have no doubt who they are. The question is how long it will take Mortimer to raise a large enough army to lay siege to Harbottle."

"Then we should leave," Edward said firmly. "We must get out of here."

Tate cocked an eyebrow at him. "And go where? I would suspect that there are far more of them than of us. I fear they are heavily onto our scent, enough so they have had time to gather reinforcements. I fear that if we leave the safety of Harbottle, it will leave us open and vulnerable on the road. We would do better to stay here where we are safe for the moment."

"Then send to Alnwick for reinforcements," Edward said with mounting irritation.

Tate's gaze was steady. "What makes you think that I have not already?" When Edward looked surprised, Tate took another drink of ale and turned away, pacing casually towards the windows. "When Stephen returned to Harbottle three days ago to gather more troops, he sent additional dispatches to reinforce Harbottle. I requested four hundred men from Alnwick, but I also sent a request to John de Clavering of Warkworth Castle. We should be seeing either army any day now."

The young king was embarrassed that he had challenged him. Tate was wise in all things and he should have trusted him. As Edward hung his young and agitated head, Stephen moved to take his own cup of ale. Kenneth moved up on the other side of him and the three of them began to make short work of the alcohol.

"I doubt the movement we saw to the south was Warkworth's men," Stephen said, cup in hand. "They would not be skulking just inside the tree line."

Kenneth took a long drink and poured himself more. "I am concerned that it is an advance party for Mortimer. The man is heavily allied with the Howards of Cumbria and we could very well be facing an approach from Howard's army from the west and Warkworth's from the east. We would be caught in the crossfire."

Tate looked at Kenneth, the quieter of his companions but definitely the more cunning. "What would you suggest?"

Kenneth looked at him with his ice-blue eyes. "Remove Edward from this place. Return him to London and put him under the protection of the Crown troops."

"Mortimer is at Windsor."

"But he is not at the Tower; the Tower is still held for the king. That was our original destination once we raised funds for the king's cause, was it not?"

Tate nodded slowly, thoughtfully. "And I am not varying from our plans. But with Mortimer so close on our scent over the past two days, I am very concerned about moving Edward on the open road. If we are caught...."

Kenneth lifted his hand in agreement, turning back to his ale. "I know," he muttered, taking another drink. "They will take Edward and kill us. Although I do not particularly relish the thought of my own death, I do not relish the thought of Edward's more."

"He is safer here at Harbottle than anywhere else until Warkworth or troops from Alnwick arrive."

"Agreed."

Stephen had been listening to their conversation. "What if neither castle received our missive?" he asked quietly. "Mortimer's men were closer than we realized when we sent messengers. What if they were captured?"

Tate's gaze moved to the tall, thin youth who was now gazing into the fire. "We will know in a day or two if troops do not arrive," he said quietly. "Then we will have to rethink our strategy."

The knights stood silently a moment, drinking their ale, pondering the course of the next two days. Tate finally broke from the pack and went to Wallace, standing near a lancet window and watching the activity in the bailey. It was developing into a quiet dusk, the sounds of night birds singing in the distance.

"Given the men we currently hold, how long can the castle withstand a siege?" Tate asked the old man.

Wallace looked thoughtful. "It would depend on the size of the attacking force."

"You know the size of the attacking force."

The old man grunted. "A month at most." He turned to Tate. "My lord, if you are going to remove the young king, then it must be now. You cannot delay."

"I have no plans to remove him."

Wallace shook his head in disagreement. "Give him to me," he said with quiet urgency. "I can spirit him to Scotland. My cousin is a monk at Kelso Abbey. Mortimer could not get him there."

Tate lifted an eyebrow. "If the Scots did not get you first," he slapped the man on the shoulder. "A noble offering, but I believe his safety is best served here at Harbottle."

Wallace's gaze moved to the young king, standing near the flames, and then back to Tate. "Then what of the womenfolk?" he asked pointedly. "Would you imprison them at a castle under siege?"

Tate's humor fled; the mere thought of Toby being separated from him made his blood surge. He knew that Wallace was correct in his suggestion but he was having difficulty with the rightness of it.

"They will be safer here than back at Cartingdon or worse, out on the open road," he said tersely. "You have been trying to be rid of those women since they arrived. What is your aversion to them?"

Wallace shook his head. "No aversion, my lord. But Harbottle is a man's fortress. Women do not belong here nor are they safe here."

"Safe?" Tate's eyebrows rose. "What do you mean?"

"I mean that soldiers sometimes lack control. Being that there are no women at Harbottle, their presence is something of an anomaly. They could easily make sport of one of them."

Tate's eyes turned stormy. "I will make this clear so that you, in turn, will make it clear to every man at Harbottle. If either of those ladies are touched, molested or otherwise annoyed in any way, my wrath upon the perpetrator shall be swift and deadly. Is that in any way incomprehensible?"

Wallace watched Tate's expression as he spoke; the man meant every word he said. He shook his head slowly. "It is quite clear, my lord."

"Good. Then I suggest you spread the word."

"I will. But I still advocate that they be removed if there is to be a battle."

"They will not be removed. Be on your way."

Wallace left the solar without another word. Tate lingered on the doorway where the man had disappeared for a moment, lost to his thoughts. He knew Wallace was more than likely correct about Toby and Ailsa leaving Harbottle, but in truth, there was nowhere for them to go. It was his way of rationalizing the fact that he did not want Toby away from him. The more time passed, the more attached he was becoming to her and he still wasn't quite sure how to feel about it. His emotions were muddy, like waters that had been stirred and had not yet settled. He had to wait for the silt to settle.

Night was upon them and the sky was brilliant with its blanket of stars sweeping across the heavens. It was a sharp contrast from the fog of the morning. Those in the solar had moved from war talk to small talk, imbibing more pitchers of ale as the fire burned and smoke huddled against the ceiling. Smells of roasting meat drifted in through the lancet windows and young Edward perpetually asserted how hungry he was. Tate finally sent a servant for bread and cheese to keep the boy happy as they ate and drank in comfortable conversation.

Kenneth had stopped drinking some time ago and sat with a pumice stone and his sword, wetting the stone and running it along the blade to sharpen it. He and Stephen were having a disagreement about the country that produced the finest wines; Stephen was sure it was Italy while Kenneth was an advocate of France. Tate sat with ale in hand, grinning at their argument until Stephen rattled the hilt of Kenneth's sword and almost caused the man to lose a finger. Kenneth lashed out a massive boot and kicked the chair legs out from underneath Stephen, sending the chair to the floor. But Stephen was quick and managed to leap out of the chair before it hit the ground.

Stephen and Tate roared with laughter; even Kenneth, who was not the laughing kind, snorted at the fun. When Stephen righted his chair, he managed to move it out of Kenneth's range and resume the conversation. But by then, food was being served in the great hall and Wallace came to summon them.

Tate left Stephen, Kenneth and Edward in the great hall as he mounted the stairs for the upper chambers. It was his intention to wake the ladies and escort them down to the meal. Quietly, he opened the chamber door, fully expecting to see that they were both still in bed, and was surprised when he realized they were both very much awake.

Ailsa had a broom in her hands that was as tall as she was, carefully sweeping the debris on the floor into a pile. Toby was on her knees before the hearth, a flint stone in hand as she attempted to light some kindling. When they heard the door open, two sets of lovely eyes turned to look at Tate.

He stood in the doorway, his massive hands resting on narrow hips as he surveyed the room. "I left you two sleeping," he said with mock sternness. "Whose bright idea was it to rise and go to work?"

He was looking directly at Toby. With a sheepish grin, she brushed the hair off her forehead and stood up.

"It would do no good to refute you so I must therefore confess," she said as she moved towards him, flint still in her fingers. "I am the slave master. Ailsa is accustomed to it."

Tate's lips twitched as he focused on her lovely face; she appeared much better than she had earlier in the day. In fact, there was even a bit of color to her cheeks. She was starting to look like the woman he had first met at Forestburn, beautiful and composed and strong. He realized, as he looked at her, that his heart was doing strange things against his ribs.

"You have a brutal streak in you, mistress," he winked at her as he looked at Ailsa. "And you, young woman; I suppose that you are hungry?"

Ailsa nodded eagerly. "I am famished."

"And your cruel sister is working a starving girl?"

Ailsa grinned, looking at Toby as she spoke. "She does it all of the time."

Tate cocked an eyebrow as Ailsa giggled and put the broom aside. "We will have no more of that," he told Toby in a quiet growl, all the while his gaze raking over her lovely face. "Supper is served in the great hall and I insist you allow your sister to eat before you drive her into service."

Toby coyly shrugged, moving back to the hearth to set the flint stone back where she found it. "If you insist," she said, setting the stone aside and brushing her hands off on her surcoat. "Am I permitted to eat also?"

"Only if you swear to never again abuse your power."

"I cannot swear it."

Ailsa giggled again and went to take Tate's hand. She held it tightly as Tate had eyes only for her sister.

"I can force you to swear it, you know," he told Toby.

"You can try, my lord. But I do not surrender easily."

Tate tried to hold back the smile but found he could not. Teeth flashing, he shook his head in submission. "I believe that. God help me, I believe it implicitly." He held out his free arm to her. "Would you come with me, then, and we may discuss it further over supper?"

Toby took the offered elbow. "My surrender is non-negotiable."

"We shall see about that."

Ailsa was the first one through the door, still clutching Tate's hand tightly, but Tate and Toby were sharing a private glance between them. It was an enchanted moment; the mood was lighter than it had been in days. With Ailsa still tugging on him, Tate leaned into Toby so he could speak softly and not be overheard by little ears.

"To be truthful, I do not wish to discuss your surrender," he said quietly. "Could we not speak on more pleasant things?"

He was very near and Toby was having difficulty breathing. "Like what?" she asked breathlessly.

"Like Paris in the spring and our future trip to Rome."

Toby smiled broadly, remembering those subjects from their very first in-depth conversation. "So you still intend to escort me to those places, I take it?" she asked.

"I told you that I would."

"You said you would do it only if I did not find a husband to take me."

"That is what we will discuss."

Toby's smile faded and she stared at him, her eyes wide with surprise. He gave her a bold wink, lifting the hand that gripped his elbow and kissing her fingers sweetly. Toby was so upswept in his last statement and subsequent kiss that she could hardly form a coherent thought. Was it possible he meant what she thought he meant? Or was she simply reading too much into his kindness?

As Toby and Tate lost themselves in each other's eyes, Ailsa let go of Tate's hand as they neared the narrow stairs. She skipped around, telling her sister to mind the stairs that were narrow and treacherous. But she apparently did not listen to her own advice; before Tate could grab her, Ailsa slipped on the top step and fell, screaming, down the entire shaft.

And then... silence.

CHAPTER SEVEN

"HER SKULL WAS smashed by the fall, Tate," Stephen said grimly. "There was nothing I could do. Even I cannot bring back the dead."

"I know," Tate raked his fingers through his dark hair. "I did not mean to question your skills. All I want to know is if there was ever a chance to save her."

Stephen shook his head wearily. "Nay," he said hoarsely. "She was dead by the time she reached the bottom of the stairs. There was never any hope."

Tate's expression was taut with grief as he stood with Stephen in the hall outside of the master's chamber. Kenneth stood slightly behind him and Edward was near the chamber door, his brown eyes swimming with tears as he gazed into the dimly lit room.

The four of them were entrenched in the unexpected tragedy, the shock of a little life cut short. The three knights, having been trained to control their emotions, were nonetheless having a difficult time concealing what they felt. Young Edward was positively beside himself. They had all been fond of little Ailsa, like a breath of fresh air in the midst of their hellish mission, and her accidental death was a dark and cutting thing.

By the door, Edward wiped furiously at the tears in his eyes. "Mistress Toby is just sitting there, holding her and crying," he said painfully. "Is there nothing to be done?"

The three knights looked at the young lad. "What would you have us do?" Stephen asked quietly. "Ailsa is dead. We cannot bring her back."

"Can you at least give Mistress Toby something to make her feel better?"

Stephen sighed heavily, moving to peek inside the half-open door. Toby was where he had left her, holding her sister's corpse fiercely and weeping her heart out. In fact, she'd not let go of the body since Tate had brought her sister up from where she had landed at the bottom of the stairs over an hour ago. Stephen could hardly examine the little girl; Toby refused to let go. But a full examination was not needed to know that she was quite dead.

"I have something to make her sleep," he said, looking to Tate after a moment. "It is not going to be easy separating her from her sister's body."

Tate could see Toby and Ailsa from where he stood. His own eyes were stinging and he realized it was because tears were close to the surface. He hadn't cried since that dark day four years ago when his wife had perished while giving birth. Then he'd turned into a stone. Now the stone was cracking. The emotions were starting to come forth once again. He didn't like it, but he knew there was no way he could stop it.

"Give her time," he finally said, fighting off pangs of grief as he turned to Kenneth. "We will need a coffin for Ailsa. Will you see to that?"

Kenneth nodded slowly, his ice-blue eyes beholding the scene through the crack in the doorway. But he tore his eyes away as if he did not want to witness such pain. He was about to reply when a low voice came from the darkened stairwell.

"I told you that womenfolk did not belong at Harbottle."

No one had seen Wallace come up the stairs. He stood several steps down from the landing, hidden by the shadows. Tate, Stephen, Kenneth and Edward turned to look at the man, looking dark and grim as he hovered just out of the light. Tate found that his patience with the man's grumbling was vanished. Now he was brittle, poised to strike at a wrong word.

"The child's fall down the stairs had nothing to do with whether or not she belonged here," he growled. "If I hear another dark word come out of your mouth about this incident, I will cut your tongue out and throw it to the birds. I have had enough of your grumbling; go with Kenneth and help him find a suitable coffin for the girl. Stay out of my sight until my anger has cooled."

Kenneth had never heard Tate issue such a threat; the man was perpetually calm in all things. He could only surmise it was the force of his emotion talking. The big blond knight moved to the stairs, grabbing Wallace by the arm and forcing him back down from whence he came.

Tate's angry gaze lingered on the darkened stairs long after they had gone as he struggled to collect himself. He realized very quickly that his unchecked emotions were manifesting into sharp commands and zero tolerance. He should have been embarrassed but found that, in truth, he was not. He was feeling something for the death of Ailsa and was not ashamed about it. With a heavy sigh, he turned back to the half-open door.

"Get your potion prepared," he said softly, pushing the door open slightly in preparation for entering. "I have a feeling we are in for a long and difficult night."

Stephen nodded faintly, following Tate into the room where his medicament bag lay open near the hearth. As Stephen went for the bag, Tate went for the bed. The closer he drew, the more his heart ached for what he saw.

Toby was cradling Ailsa against her chest, the child's head lying upon her breast. Toby had been weeping painful, steady tears for over an hour. Her left arm was wrapped around the body, her right hand pressed against Ailsa's head. Tears, saliva and mucus rained onto Ailsa as Toby expended her grief. Tate stood a moment, watching her slender body shake with sobs, wondering if there was anything in the world he could say to ease her sorrow but knowing in the same breath that there was not.

"Elizabetha," he murmured, leaning over and gently putting his hands on her arms. "Can Stephen have Ailsa for a while? Just for a short while so that you may rest."

Toby's reply was to weep harder and hold on tighter. Tate sat down on the bed behind her, his big torso pressed up against her back and his massive arms winding around hers until he, too, was holding Ailsa. He just held them both a moment, rocking them gently.

"I promise that Stephen will take good care of her," he murmured into Toby's hair. "But you must rest a while. Just a short while, I promise. Will you trust him to take care of her?"

Toby was in a haze of grief. She couldn't think of anything other than the tragedy that had befallen her and she held her sister's cooling corpse tightly, trying to infuse some warmth into it. It hadn't sunk in yet that her sister would never rise again. This was the child she had raised since infancy so in a sense, not only had she lost her sister but she had lost her child as well.

On the heels of Forestburn's destruction and her parents' death, the horrific accident was too much for her to take and she held on tightly for fear that if she let go, she would lose everything. At least if she continued to hold Ailsa, she'd not lost her entire family. Irrational thoughts, but at the moment, she was quite irrational. She was spiraling.

"Nay," she sobbed into Ailsa's hair. "You cannot have her."

By this time, Stephen was standing next to the bed, a cup in his hand that contained the sleeping elixir. He bent over, touching Toby's hand gently.

"I promise I will take great care of her," he said soothingly. "But I should like for you to rest a while. Ailsa would not want you to become ill again. It would displease her."

Toby tightened her grip, feeling threatened with one knight in back of her and another standing over her. She was sure they were going to snatch Ailsa away and she would not let them have her.

"Go away," she hissed. "Go away and leave us alone."

Stephen caressed Toby's hand comfortingly. "Please, Toby," he moved beyond the formalities. "Please let me take care of her for a while. You need to rest and I must tend to Ailsa. I cannot do that if you are holding her."

"You cannot have her," Toby sobbed.

"Why not?"

"Because she is mine."

"Of course she is yours. I do not wish to keep her. I only want to have her for a little while as you rest."

Toby gazed down at the ashen face of her little sister, who looked as if she was merely sleeping. No gore, no blood; just peace. Toby's face crumpled and tears fell like rain.

"Why did you do that?" she begged the child mournfully. "Why did you fall on those stairs? You know you should have been more careful. Why did you fall?"

Stephen continued to rub at Toby's hand, trying to offer what comfort he could. "It was an accident," he said gently. "You cannot blame her. She simply fell."

"Stupid!" Toby suddenly burst, shaking Ailsa angrily. "It was stupid! You should not have been running! I should have... I should have...." Her face went slack as if a horrible thought had just occurred to her. "I should have held your hand. I should have grabbed you before you got too close. I should have...."

Toby was bordering on temporary insanity as she babbled; Stephen's brow was furrowed as he and Tate passed concerned glances. "It was not your fault," Stephen said with more firmness. "It was an accident. Please let me take Ailsa while you rest; I promise I shall give her back."

Toby shook her head, recoiling from Stephen, realizing that Tate was behind her and trying to recoil from him, too. She ended up struggling to her feet, holding her limp sister and trying to get away from the knights. But she wasn't strong enough to lift Ailsa entirely and she ended up dragging her sister several feet across the floor. It was pathetic and harrowing. Tate rose slowly from the bed, watching Toby struggle to get away from them. There was tremendous pain in his eyes, knowing very well what she was feeling. He had felt it once, too.

But Toby was too weak with grief and recent illness and ended up falling before she could get too far away. Huddled on the floor, she held her sister's torso and head tightly while Ailsa's legs lay splayed across the floor. It was clear that she was not balanced. Tate didn't look at Stephen as he spoke to the knight; his eyes were riveted to Toby.

"I will take Toby," he whispered. "Be prepared to grab Ailsa and take her out of here."

Stephen nodded, heading off to his right while Tate moved to his left. They were stalking Toby, like predators, only these were predators of mercy. Toby would never gain her wits so long as she held a death-grip on her sister's body. Tate walked up behind her, crouching down and putting his big hands on her upper arms.

"Elizabetha, sweetheart," he tightened his grip as he spoke, his hands moving down her arms to her wrists. "Please let us have Ailsa. I promise we will be very careful with her."

Toby wept and sputtered. "Nay," she gasped. "She is all that I have left. She cannot… she cannot be dead."

"She is, sweet," Tate crooned softly, his cheek against the right side of her head. "I am so sorry for your loss. Believe me; I know what you are feeling. I have been there. But you must let us take Ailsa to prepare her for burial."

Toby howled. "Nay!" she cried. "You cannot bury her!"

Tate's grip around her was getting tighter as he prepared to pull her arms away from her sister's body. "We must, love," he had a good grasp on her wrists, making sure Stephen was prepared to strike from his position next to Ailsa. "Let Stephen take Ailsa. He will be kind to her."

Toby shook her head and Tate decided it was time to act. Grabbing her wrists, he pulled her arms away from Ailsa's corpse. Stephen was swift and grabbed the little girl, moving for the door in one keen motion. Realizing she had been tricked, Toby turned into a wildcat; she kicked and screamed and beat at Tate even as he lifted her off the floor and carried her to the bed. As Stephen slipped from the room, Tate and Toby fell onto the bed in a writhing, howling mass of grief.

Toby was screaming at the top of her lungs. Tate had both arms wrapped firmly around her so she could not get away from him; he was afraid that if she was able to get a hand free, he would find himself missing an eye. So he held her tightly, riding out the storm, knowing eventually she would exhaust herself. There was nothing more he could do. Toby twisted and cursed, showing surprising strength in her slender body, but eventually her energy left her and she ended up a quivering mass of warmth and hair in his arms.

Toby didn't have the strength to cry any longer. She simply lay in his arms, gasping for every breath. Tate took a chance on loosening his grip and he stroked her hair, her face, whispering soothingly in her ear and telling her that all would be well. But Toby didn't hear him; at some point, she gave a heaving gasp and suddenly lay still. Concerned, Tate felt for her pulse; it was fast but strong. And she was still breathing regularly. Realizing she had fainted, he welcomed the peace from her pain.

"Sleep well, sweetheart," he whispered, kissing her on the temple. "You have earned it."

Propped up on an elbow, he gazed at her for a very long time, feeling such sorrow for the woman as he could not begin to describe. She had been through so much in her life; a drunk father, an invalid mother, but she had not only survived, she had thrived. Then he came along and within days destroyed everything she had worked so hard to achieve. He had destroyed her world. Now her sister was dead. If he'd never come to Cartingdon, none of this would have happened. But, then again, he would have never met Toby.

He stroked her hair again, soft strands beneath his calloused hand. He kissed her baby-soft cheek, allowing his lips to linger on the flesh. Her lips were near and he was drawn to them, gently kissing her mouth for the first time and realizing she was as sweet as he had known she would be. He kissed her lips again, once more, before very slowly rising from the bed. Although she was unconscious, he did not want to disturb her. Taking the dusty old blanket, he tucked her in carefully.

"Sleep well," he touched her face one last time.

The room was growing dark and cold so he moved to the hearth and deftly started a small fire with the flint and kindling that was still there. Looking around, he realized there wasn't much fuel for the fire so he put what he could on the blaze. He stood up as the flames fired up, watching Toby's still form, fighting off a myriad of emotions swirling through his chest.

Leaving Toby to sleep, he shut the door softly behind him.

CB

THE FULL MOON was creating a brilliant gray landscape just after midnight. Night birds sang and nocturnal creatures foraged in the fields below the great bastion of Harbottle. All was peaceful and still, a world away from the turmoil that had gripped them over the past few days.

Kenneth was on the battlements of Harbottle, his ice-blue eyes watching the landscape for a hint of threat. He had taken charge of the defenses with Tate and Stephen distracted with Mistress Toby and her dead sister, removing himself from emotion that was difficult for him to digest. Moreover, it was distracting them from the king's mission. One of them had to remain focused and Kenneth decided it would be him. With Edward asleep inside the keep, Kenneth maintained vigilance for them all.

As he gazed out over the landscape, he heard footfalls down below in the bailey. A ladder that was ten feet away began to move slightly; he could see the wood shifting back and forth. As he watched, Tate mounted the last rung of the ladder and climbed onto the wall walk. He was without his armor, clearly not prepared for sentry duty. Kenneth remained silent as Tate walked up next to him and began scanning the silver landscape.

"No movement?" he asked quietly.

Kenneth shook his head. "Nothing, my lord. All is quiet."

Tate nodded faintly, his storm cloud eyes still moving across the scenery. "Were you able to locate a suitable coffin for Ailsa?"

Kenneth crossed his big arms, his gaze scanning the landscape just as Tate was. It was a habit with them, always vigilant and aware of their surroundings. "Nothing that I would consider suitable so Wallace is building one," he replied.

Tate lifted an eyebrow and looked at him. "He's building one?"

"Aye. The man can do anything, you know. Even build a coffin. Perhaps he is doing it because he feels badly about the girl's death."

Tate pursed his lips. "Perhaps he is doing it to get back into my good graces. When will this receptacle be ready?"

"He said that he would work on it all night. It may not be the nicest coffin you have ever seen, but it will be well-made."

Tate was silent a moment, pondering how in the world they were going to bury Ailsa without her sister going mad. "We'll have to put her in Harbottle's chapel for now," he said quietly. "It is a tiny place. I have not surveyed it yet to determine if there is space."

"I have," Kenneth replied. "There is a length of ground in the corner near the altar. It should be suitable."

"Very well," Tate looked at Kenneth. "Thank you for your foresight in planning this arrangement. I have been else occupied."

Kenneth nodded slowly, his ice-blue eyes fixed on Tate; he was the most stoic of the knights, rarely smiling and rarely voicing his opinion unless asked. He had a stronger sense of duty than most and had known Tate for many years. He had been present when Tate's wife had passed away and remembered how the event nearly toppled the man. Although Kenneth made a habit of not forming friendships, his relationship with Tate was a rare exception. He greatly respected de Lara, the man who should have been king.

"It has been my pleasure, my lord," Kenneth finally said after a moment. "And if I have not yet expressed my sympathies on the passing of Mistress Ailsa, then allow me to do so. Her death is a sorrowful thing."

Tate nodded pensively. "I feel as if we have brought great doom upon Mistress Elizabetha's head. I feel responsible for all of this somehow."

Kenneth was used to Tate expressing his emotions; the man was in touch, and usually in control, with them. It was not an outlandish occurrence for Tate to speak what was in his heart or mind.

"It is not your fault," Kenneth said frankly. "We could not have known what tragedies our association with Mistress Toby and her family would have brought."

Tate drew in a long breath, pondering his words, knowing he was correct in theory. But it did not stop him from feeling the guilt. After a moment, he scratched his head and turned back for the ladder.

"I am going to check on Mistress Toby and then I am going to sleep for a couple of hours. Wake me before dawn; sooner if you need me."

"I would not worry about Mistress Toby," Kenneth told him. "Stephen is with her."

Tate paused on the first rung of the ladder. "How do you know?"

"He was here a little while ago. As he left, he told me that he was going to check on her."

"He is supposed to be with Ailsa."

"There is nothing he can do for Ailsa."

Tate took the first two rungs of the ladder before pausing. He looked up at Kenneth. "Tell me something, St. Héver, and be truthful."

"I have never lied to you, my lord."

"I did not mean that. I meant be truthful in your opinion."

"Opinion of what?"

"Why would Stephen be so solicitous of Mistress Toby?"

Kenneth shrugged, not sure what Tate was driving at. "Because she is stricken with grief, I am sure. He is a healer and she, at the moment, is in need of help. Why else?"

"It could not be because he is interested in her, could it?"

"Interested in her in what way?"

"As a man is interested in a woman."

Kenneth understood then. For the first time, he seemed to lose some of his stoic demeanor. "Why would you ask?"

Tate shrugged. "I am not sure. Something in his expression at times. I have never known the man to show interest in any woman. What do you know of it?"

Kenneth shook his head. "You will have to ask him."

"I am asking you. He is close to you. Has he said anything?"

"Said anything? Nay, he has not."

"But you believe there is something more to it."

Kenneth sighed reluctantly. It was clear that he did not want to say what was on his mind but he knew that Tate would pester him until he did. So he confessed.

"His manner suggests that perhaps he shows more concern than normal towards her." He lifted an eyebrow at Tate. "Then again, so does yours."

Tate digested the statement and descended the ladder without another word. Leaving Kenneth on the wall walk, he was halfway across the bailey when a shout suddenly went up from the sentries on the eastern wall. Jolted into action, Tate barreled up the ladder to the battlements, thundering along the stone walkway just behind Kenneth as they made their way to the eastern wall. And there they saw it.

There was a line of torches and men that stretched a quarter of a mile in length. It was ominous in the silver moon glow, like a black tide of ants on the march. Tate knew without a word spoken that it could not be a good sign; any army that would approach by torchlight in a massive front was not there on a social call. He felt the familiar fire of battle fill his veins, rousing the warrior instincts.

"Rouse the men," he growled at Kenneth. "Everyone to battle."

Kenneth was gone to do his bidding. Tate remained on the wall, watching the army approach, knowing they were in for a siege. He could only pray that Harbottle's old walls held and Warkworth had indeed received his call for reinforcements.

Mortimer was upon them.

CHAPTER EIGHT

TOBY WASN'T SURE how long she had been awake, staring at half of a pillow with the other side of her face buried in it. Only one eye was able to open. She blinked, having no idea where she was and finally lifting her head to look about. Still, she did not recognize the place. It was a larger chamber, dusty, with a broom and a pile of debris in one corner. The fire in the hearth was faded to hot cinder, radiating some heat into the room. As Toby looked around, disoriented, her mind became more lucid and her memory unmercifully returned.

Ailsa. The remembrance of her sister's name hit her in the chest like a hammer and she visibly winced, tears springing to her eyes and a sob to her lips. Everything tumbled upon her and she remembered the day before, the fall, the horrific grief when she saw her sister lying still at the bottom of the stairs. She wept as she remembered Tate picking the child up reverently, his expression stricken with shock. She remembered him bringing her sister back to this very chamber, to lay to rest in this very bed. Weeping softly, Toby touched the coverlet that her sister had been laid upon. She could still see her there, lifeless and pale.

It was a crushing grief, not like the same sorrow she felt for her mother and father. This was different. It went beyond sadness to physical pain. She remembered, clearly, when Tate and Stephen had separated her from Ailsa but little after that. She knew, in hindsight, they had done what was best for her. Ailsa needed to be put in the ground and if Toby had any say in it, she would still be holding her dead sister's corpse. The knights had known better. She wasn't angry at them; she was too caught up in sorrow to spare the energy.

Wiping at her eyes, she struggled to compose herself. She wasn't weak by nature but the past few days had repeatedly crushed her. She was laboring to get hold of herself. She had to find out what the knights had done with her sister and make arrangements from there.

Someone had brought her things up during the night; she noticed two large trunks and a variety of loose items stacked neatly against the wall. Wiping at her eyes again, she made her way to the trunks with the intention of finding something to bury her sister in. But she passed by the lancet window on her way to the trunks and a waft of smoke caught her attention.

A glance out of the window caused her to do a double-take; from her perch on the third floor of the keep, which was situated on a motte, or large hill, in the center of the bailey, she was several dozen feet above ground level. From there, she could see the walls of Harbottle and the green fields beyond. Only the fields were covered with men and as she watched in shock, she could see two large siege towers being rolled towards the walls. Dozens of men were towing them. Arrows flew over the walls, some flaming, some not, and the men upon the walls of Harbottle were doing their best to fight off the siege. But she could see that the siege towers being rolled into position would soon change all of that.

Toby forced her grief aside in favor of the current situation. She was, frankly, terrified, but she managed to keep her wits as she went in search of her shoes. Her long hair was hanging limp and uncombed and she grabbed a scarf from one of her trunks, tying her hair back and out of her way. Yanking on her shoes, she bailed from the chamber.

The deadly stairs were tricky to navigate but she did so ably. Once on the second floor, the great hall loomed to her left and she stopped in horror at what she was witnessing; more than two dozen men were strewn about across the floor with a myriad of battle wounds. Some were screaming; some were simply lying still. Toby swallowed the bile in her throat as she witnessed the rivers of blood on the floor, pieces of limbs and flesh strewn about. It was ghastly. She could see the major-domo and an old male servant struggling to render aid, but it was clear they were overwhelmed. Although Toby had never worked on an injured man in her life, she knew she was about to have her first taste of it. She could not simply stand by while people suffered; all else in her mind, her own grief and suffering, would have to wait.

Toby walked up to the majordomo as he hacked at a man's nearly-severed limb in an attempt to amputate it. When the limb broke free, he caught a glimpse of Toby's shoes and looked up to her with a start.

"Lady," he barked. "What are you doing here?"

Toby was struggling not to become ill at the sight of so much gore. "I am here to help. Tell me what I can do."

Wallace shook his head. "Go back to your room. This is no place for you."

"If you will not tell me what I can do then I will just figure it out for myself," she snapped. "I can just as easily walk to the next man and do what I can."

Wallace glared at her. "Battle is not for womenfolk."

Toby growled with exasperation. "Good lord, man, I shall not be the first woman who has ever tended battle wounded. You have more than you can handle. Why must you argue with me?"

The old man's glare intensified and he stood up, hoping to scowl her to death. But Toby stood her ground. She wasn't one to be bullied. Finally, Wallace indicated the man whose arm he had just amputated above the elbow.

"I assume you can sew?" he asked irritably.

"Of course I can."

"Then sew up this arm so the man will not bleed to death," he gestured to a dirty length of gut and big bone needle on the ground. "Get to work."

Toby was sickened by the suggestion but she was not going to shy away; she had asked to help and he was going to give her a very dirty chore in punishment. Yet there was no way she would admit she could not do it. Without another word, she sat next to the unconscious man, collected the gut, and went to work.

Wallace pretended that he wasn't watching her but he really was. He could see her out of the corner of his eye, struggling with the bleeding flesh and he felt wicked pleasure in making her suffer. He knew she would not be able to handle it and he took fiendish satisfaction in knowing that she would more than likely give up. Then he would send her back to her chamber and be rid of her. But as he waited for the inevitable to occur, a funny thing happened.

Toby didn't give up. She struggled with the hacked limb but managed to sew up the end moderately well. The old servant, taking some pity on her, brought wine for her to clean the wounds with and all of the extra rags he could find. There wasn't much by way of medicine but he brought her what he could. It took Toby some time to realize that it was the same old servant that had given Ailsa bread with honey. The next time the old man brought her some boiled rags, she smiled gratefully at him.

Toby didn't even ask Wallace what more she could do; there were so many wounded in the hall that she simply moved to the next man and began working. It became easier with time to forget her squeamishness, but still, with each new gory injury, she had to steel herself again and again. She began to wonder where Stephen was, given that he was a Hospitaller, but she suspected his fighting abilities were needed more than his healing. It was evident, as time passed and more wounded were brought in, that the battle was intensifying.

Toby lost count of the men she had worked on. Some had nothing more than a big gash that needed sewing, but some came in with their torsos split open and guts falling out. Those were the worst. Wallace usually tended those as they came in the door, sparing Toby the horror of it, so she focused on the men she thought she might be able to help. The blood on her hands turned black, staining her nails and coagulating on her surcoat, but still, she pressed on.

She was bent over a man with an arrow imbedded in his shoulder when she noticed a pair of massive boots standing very close to her. She glanced over; from the boots to the legs to the heavy mail and armor, to finally the head. Kenneth was standing over her, an enormous man in full battle protection. Toby sat back on her heels, brushing stray hair from her eyes with the back of her hand.

"Sir Kenneth," she said. "Are you injured? Do you require help?"

He shook his head, his ice-blue eyes fixed on her. "I brought in an injured man," he regarded her a moment. "Why are you here?"

She stood up to face him. "Because there is a battle going on and these men need help."

Kenneth's gaze lingered on her for a moment before turning away. But Toby reached out a hand to stop him. "Where are Tate and Stephen and the king?"

"In the heat of battle."

"Is everyone all right?"

"So far."

"But I saw towers from my window being moved towards the walls. Has the fortress been breached?"

"We managed to burn down the first one that came close enough," he replied. "The second tower is still a threat."

She didn't know what else to say. As she turned back to her patient, Kenneth started back across the hall when the entry door suddenly burst open and a soldier raced in.

"The wall has been breached!" he shouted.

Kenneth swiftly turned to Wallace, who was several feet away. "Drop what you are doing and get your weapon," he commanded. As the wild man raced to do his bidding, Kenneth swung in Toby's direction. "Bolt this door after we leave. We will burn the stairs in our wake so they enemy cannot breach the keep. But bolt the damn door and do not open it for anyone. Do you understand?"

Toby realized she was shaking as she nodded her head firmly. Dropping what was in her hands, she raced to the entry as Kenneth, and eventually Wallace, ran through it. The old servant was beside her and together, they managed to get the heavy wooden bar across the doorway to secure it. They dropped in the iron pin to lock it. Panting, and terrified, Toby turned to the little old man.

"What is your name?" she asked.

"Althel, my lady," he replied.

She nodded in acknowledgement. "Althel, we must do all we can to secure this floor. Will you help me?"

He nodded eagerly. "The only windows are in the solar. The rest of them are high in the gallery or on the top floor."

"Is there any way to secure the windows in the solar?"

Althel nodded. "There are shutters."

"Then we must close them."

She followed Althel into the solar where there were indeed shutters that flanked the two small lancet windows that opened onto the bailey. Before they secured the first window, Toby dared to look out at the chaos in the bailey; men were pouring over the wall from the siege tower they had managed to prop against it. There was heavy fighting upon the battlements and she could hear violent clashes of sword against sword. Off to the right, high on the wall near the gate tower, she could see a big knight in combat with several soldiers and assumed it was Stephen. But her eyes were searching for Tate.

She didn't have long to search; she spied him on the wall right where the siege engine was lodged, battling the men who were pouring in from the tower. She could tell it was him because she recognized the armor. As she watched, he deftly threw men off the wall or used his skill to cut them down and cast them aside. Tate fought as if he would never tire; his dragon-hilted broadsword was both a weapon and a battering ram as he either shoved or gored the men coming at him. The longer she watched, the more she understood why the man was called Dragonblade; he fought with power rarely seen in mortal man. The only way to describe it was magical.

"My lady," Althel was hovering at her side. "We must close this shutter."

Toby nodded, though her eyes were still riveted to Tate. But smoke was starting to drift in the window and she knew it was because Kenneth had set fire to the stairs leading into the keep. With a final look at Tate battling valiantly on the wall, she slammed the shutters closed and Althel slid the bolt into place.

The two of them made their way back into the hall to continue tending the wounded, but not before Toby laid out a hasty plan for their situation. It would seem that with Wallace outside fighting, she was suddenly in charge.

"Where are the stores kept?" she asked the old servant.

The man motioned her over to a small alcove just off the great hall. There was a trap door which he opened, pointing down into the musty depths.

"Down there," he said. "There is no way in there except for this door. The well is down there, too."

Toby nodded shortly. "Good," she said. "We will need to finish tending these men and then see what we can do about feeding them. Do you know what is down there?"

Althel nodded. "Two barrels of flour, six wheels of cheese, some dried apples and some other dried stores. Late summer harvests, mostly."

"It will be put to use. Are there any weapons about?"

"Weapons, my lady?"

"Aye; in case the keep is breached."

"Wallace keeps some weapons in the small room upstairs, next to the master's chamber. He does not trust them in the armory. He says they disappear."

Toby nodded, her gaze roaming the room, trying to think if there was anything she had left out. For the moment, they had weapons, fire and food. She knew they could survive for a little while at any rate.

"Then let us get about helping these men," she said quietly, turning to look at the crowd in the room. "The rest is up to Sir Tate."

Althel nodded as he and Toby parted company; she went to start on the men near the entry door while Althel went to the group positioned near the hearth. The smell of smoke was growing heavier in the hall as the wooden stairs outside the entry door were fully engulfed, but inside the hall, Toby felt relatively safe. She tried not to worry for Tate, doing battle in the bailey. She'd already lost so much in the past few days; to lose him, too, would only diminish her more. She wasn't sure if she could take another death. She couldn't even think about it.

All they could do now was wait.

⬥

THE BATTLE WENT on well into the day. Dusk approached and still, the battle raged on. Toby knew that because she could still hear the fighting outside the solar windows. So far, no one had made a move to breach the keep but she was terrified to look outside, terrified to see what was going on. Terrified that she would see dead knights and terrified that one of them would be Tate.

Eventually, all of the men in the hall were tended. Some of them had died along the way. The dead had been grouped into a bunch tucked into a corner, far from the hearth and its radiant heat. Toby wasn't sure how long they would be shut up with the bodies and she didn't want the heat hastening the rotting process.

It had been dirty, hard work. Toby was exhausted but strangely, feeling stronger than she had in days. Her body seemed to be recovering from her bout with illness and the crescent shaped wounds on her wrist that her mother had given her were healing nicely. When she looked at the scabs, it seemed as if they had happened years ago. So much had taken place since then.

Since there were no women at Harbottle, the male servants had learned to do the cooking long ago. Althel had prepared a thin soup of boiled rabbit bones, some beans and dried carrots that he and Toby had been feeding to the men who were conscious. Toby noticed, as she moved from man to man, how young many of them were. All were vassals of Tate, most having been born on his lands. A few of the older men were retainers sworn to Tate from other parts of England, seasoned men that trained the younger. Toby finished feeding Tate's men, her mind lingering increasingly on Tate and his progress outside.

When dusk finally settled into night and the hall grew dark except for the fire in the hearth, Toby moved to the darkened solar and listened to the sounds of the battle outside. It was an eerie sensation listening to the sounds of fighting intermingled with the cries of the wounded. She had never even been remotely close to a battle, living a simple and uncomplicated life at Forestburn. This had been a swift education in the realities of life. Toby huddled on the floor against the wall, her legs drawn up against her chest and her arms wrapped around her knees for warmth as she listened to the sounds of the struggle.

As time passed and she continued to sit, it seemed as if the sounds of battle were drawing nearer. She could hear shouts, cries, and clangs as metal met metal. The sounds drew closer still. Afraid that somehow the enemy had found a way to breach the keep, she moved quickly from the solar and up the treacherous stairs, finding the smaller chamber that Althel had told her was used for weapons storage. A pile of staffs lay upon the ground, some with broken tips and some with very sharp tips. Two large swords sat propped against a wall. As she fingered through the pile of staffs, she suddenly heard a loud crash on the floor below.

Startled, she grabbed a staff with a very sharp point and hastened down the stairs. By the time she reached the bottom, she could see a man in mail climbing through a solar window. The shutters lay in pieces on the ground, having been shattered by the morning star that the soldier was carrying in one hand. Without delay, Toby leveled the staff and charged at the man with all her might.

The soldier wasn't quite through the window and unable to defend himself as she rammed the spear tip into his shoulder. He screamed and lost his grip on the windowsill, tumbling two stories to the bailey below. Terrified, Toby jammed the staff at the next man on the ladder and stabbed him in the eye. He fell back on his comrades and the entire line of soldiers climbing the ladder tumbled to the ground.

Toby was in survival mode; nothing mattered but preserving her life and the lives of the men inside the keep. She grabbed the edge of the ladder and struggled to push it away, only to notice that below her, Tate had a hold of the ladder and yanked so hard that he almost pulled her from the window. The ladder crashed and splintered. Toby looked down at Tate just as he looked up at her. Their eyes met and Toby felt a strong sense of joy at seeing him alive.

"Are you all right?" she yelled down at him.

He gazed up at her, the visor of his helm lifted, and smiled wearily. "Now that I have seen you, I can move mountains," he called up to her. "Are you well?"

Exhausted but elated, she met his smile. Her cheeks were flushed with fear, giving her a delightfully rosy appearance. "I am fine," she replied. "Are we winning this battle, then?"

He gestured towards the gates, now breached and burning. "Warkworth has been sighted on the horizon. We should be done with this in short time."

Toby felt a distinct sense of relief at the news. "Where is your squire?" she wanted to know.

"Safe," was all he said. Then he blew a kiss at her. "Go back inside. It should not be long now."

She nodded, but not before saying what was foremost on her mind. "Please take care."

He winked at her and trudged off, slugging a man in the face that came at him. Toby watched him slog off across the bailey, now muddy with blood from all of the wounded men. It was a grim and horrible sight. She watched him until he disappeared behind a group of fighting men before pulling herself inside and settling, once more, against the solar wall. But the staff was in her hand, waiting for the next fool to try and breach her sanctuary. She wasn't going to let it go without a fight.

CHAPTER NINE

HAMLIN DE ROCHE'S forces had been forced to regroup when reinforcements from Warkworth arrived. De Roche recognized the colors and knew that they were outnumbered by the fresh army. His men had been fighting almost a full day and night. He may have been a ruthless man, but he was not stupid. He knew when to quit. As soon as Warkworth drew near, he gave the order to retreat and his men fled to the south.

Warkworth gave chase for several miles, managing to kill a good many of them as they fled. The fresh army simply overwhelmed them. But soon enough, they drew back as de Roche's army continued on. After several more miles of running, they finally regrouped near the small town of Hesleyside.

Baron Keilder from Keilder Castle had been the one to supply troops to de Roche so he could move on Harbottle. Many of Keilder's men trickled back home, but about one hundred remained encamped with de Roche and his generals. Fires had been lit and tents pitched. Hamlin and his men took rest and food in a larger tent, reviewing the battle and plotting their next move. As the wind blew and a rain storm moved through the area, the men around the crackling fire conspired.

"Now that we know where the king is, we can assemble an even larger force and attack," an old general who had served Warwick was resolute. "Harbottle was greatly compromised during the siege."

Hamlin chewed on his bread wearily, gazing into the flicker of the fire. "They will move him," he replied. "Dragonblade is no fool. If we return to Harbottle, Edward will not be there. They will take him someplace far more fortified."

"Then we must strike again," the general asserted, "before they can move the boy."

"With Warkworth's troops occupying the place?" Hamlin shook his head. "It would be foolish. We do not have the strength of numbers now. But we will."

The men around the fire looked curiously at Hamlin; they were all seasoned men, having served kings and kingmakers in their time. Many of them had served Longshanks and viewed his grandson with the same fear that they had felt for Edward the Second. Like father, like son.

"Be plain," one man, a balding advisor, demanded softly. "What do you mean?"

Hamlin swallowed his bread. "Mortimer is on the march," he said quietly. He looked to the men, noting their confusion, and proceeded to explain. "When it was clear we were on young Edward's trail, I sent word to him. He has known our every move for quite some time. We used Keilder's men to attempt to breach Harbottle because it was the fastest solution at the time. I did not want to lose the opportunity. Even as we speak, Mortimer himself rides from Wigmore. He is determined to capture the king once and for all."

"But de Lara has other plans," the old general spoke again. "The man is cunning and powerful. I do not take opposition to him lightly."

De Roche nodded slowly. "He is his father's son," he muttered. "And, no doubt, he has more reinforcements arriving to Harbottle. Antony Bec's thousands from Alnwick Castle cannot be far behind Baron Warkworth's troops."

"So what do we do?" the old general demanded.

Hamlin was staring into the flames, thinking of how close he had come to young Edward at the manse back in Cartingdon. All that had stood between him and victory was a lovely lady. He cursed the woman for her bravery, furious and admiring it at the same time. He vowed not to make the same mistake twice; next time he had Edward in his grasp, he was going to snatch him.

"We will continue to watch de Lara," he said. "We wait and we watch. There will be another opportunity to capture Edward. But brute force is not the answer right now. Until Mortimer arrives, we will plan something more... cunning."

"Against de Lara?" the general snorted. "Best of luck, my friend."

Hamlin lifted an eyebrow at the man, seeing his humor. "We may call him Dragonblade, but the truth is that de Lara is human with human weaknesses," Hamlin looked back to the fire. "All we need do is exploit his weakness and Edward will be ours."

"How do we find de Lara's weakness?"

Hamlin wasn't sure at the moment. But he was determined to find out.

☙

WARKWORTH'S ARMY MADE short work of the forces that Mortimer managed to assemble. They had given chase for several miles, finally allowing whatever remained of the force to continue running, before returning to the castle. Harbottle was burning and disheveled, but it the keep had held. Now it would be a matter of shoring up the main gates to re-secure the bailey.

Tate had decided that the men should rest the night before beginning reconstruction. Mortimer's forces had been decimated and he rightly assumed that they would not regroup for a second attack too soon. So Warkworth's army pitched camp in and around the walls of Harbottle while several of the men went to work rebuilding the stairs that had burned. Until they had the stairs reconstructed, the keep was cut off from the ward and Tate was anxious to get inside; visions of Toby filled him until he could hardly stand the thought of being kept from her. He had to get to her, to touch her, and make sure that she was indeed all right.

Kenneth and Wallace were among the men working on rebuilding the stairs. They were going for the simplest design at the moment, something that wouldn't take too long to build but would be sturdy enough. Tate could hear Wallace yelling at the soldiers building the steps, telling them that they weren't doing good enough work. Then he would jump in and hammer out the iron nails himself. In the meantime, Tate stood below the keep entry, watching the activity and pondering future plans. He was in the process of determining the best course of action when young Edward marched up to him.

The lad was furious, that much was clear. He stomped up to Tate and practically threw a ring of heavy iron keys at him. Tate caught it deftly, eyeing Edward and knowing why the lad was so angry. But he didn't particularly care.

"There," Edward snapped as he tossed the keys to Tate. "Keep your stupid keys. And next time, do not think I will surrender to you so easily."

Tate remained patient. "I told you many times that the safest place for you was to lock yourself up in the vault and keep the key," he said steadily. "I was correct, was I not? They made it into the vault but were unable to reach you because you held the key. There was no way for them to take down the iron bars."

The boy was livid. "I could have fought them."

"And you could have died."

He pursed his lips, unable to think of a reply that would be stronger than Tate's argument. Still, he wasn't finished with him. "I looked like a coward, hiding in the vault."

"It saved your life. What are you complaining about? I'm sure there will be other opportunities to prove your worth with a sword, Edward. But right now, you are going to have to trust me to keep you safe."

Edward huffed and fidgeted and made faces, indicative of his anger. But he knew, deep down, that his uncle was correct. Locking himself in the vault had saved his life. Whether by hook or by crook, that was what Tate had been attempting to do for the better part of two years. So far, he'd done a good job. Still, at fourteen, Edward thought himself quite the grown man and silently vowed that the next time he would determine what was best for himself. Not Tate. Well... maybe.

Attention was taken away from his temper tantrum when the door to the keep overhead shifted and creaked open. Tate and Edward looked up to see the panel opening wide to reveal Toby and Althel.

It had taken them a while to get the door open because the old iron pin locking the bolt had been jammed. With some grease, they had finally managed to get it off. Toby stood for a moment in the doorway, surveying the destruction below with some awe; everything was in ruins, shattered or burnt. The healthy men were moving the dead into a pile near the gate house while the wounded were being put near the kitchens. Stephen, no longer obligated to fight, had his hands full with all of the wounded.

As she looked about, her gaze came to rest directly below and she saw Tate gazing up at her. Their eyes locked and she couldn't help the smile that spread across her lips. It was relief, joy and comfort all rolled into one. As the night wind blew her hair across her face, she knelt down, her gaze riveted to Tate.

"I see that you are still in one piece," she said. "I had my doubts."

Tate just took a moment to drink in the sight of her. "Never doubt me," he told her. "You would be wrong."

She laughed softly, noticing that Edward was looking up at her as well. "I see that you survived, sire," she said. "I am pleased."

It was far different from the woman who had wept and ranted two days before. She looked composed and strong. Edward wasn't quite sure how to respond.

"Thank you," he replied hesitantly. "I... are... are you all right in there? I can come up to help if you need...?"

Toby shook her head. "We have made do," she said, then she looked over her shoulder briefly before turning back to the men below. "Althel has made some soup. He is trying to find some rope so that we can lower the pot down."

Tate was still looking at her as if unable to move his eyes off of her. "That was generous of you," he said. "Have you fed the wounded?"

"We have."

"What is the tally?"

Her smile faded somewhat. "Twenty nine injured and eleven dead. I should like to remove the dead as quickly as possible. They are beginning to smell."

Tate nodded, looking a few feet away to where they were reconstructing the stairs. "It should be an hour or so and we'll have access to do that. In the meanwhile...."

He suddenly began looking around as if hunting for something. Toby didn't know how he did it, but as she watched, he collected two pieces of a broken ladder, somehow put them together, and climbed his way up the side of the keep to the open door. Before she realized it, he was standing in front of her.

All Toby could do was stare at him, a smile on her lips and her hands trembling with the thrill of seeing him in the flesh before her. She was so very glad to see that he was unharmed; more than that, he looked positively healthy. Other than the fact he was covered in dirt and sweat, he looked wonderful. She didn't even see any wounds on him; not a nick.

She hadn't realized that she was backing away from him as he moved closer. As she bumped against a wall, she found herself riveted to his storm cloud eyes, seeing emotions reflected in the dark depths that were puzzling and new. Her heart was beating so fast that it ached.

"I... I am glad to see that you are unharmed," she managed to stammer.

He continued walking towards her until he was up against her body; Toby could feel his cold armor on her flesh, his face looming inches above her own.

"You said that," he growled gently.

"It... 'tis true."

The smile playing on his lips broadened. Toby's limbs went weak with a painful sort of tingle; she wanted to throw her arms around him but dare not make a move. She had no right to touch the man. The self-restraint was agonizing as her palms began to sweat.

"Elizabetha?" he asked softly.

Toby could hardly speak for the excitement bolting through her body. "Aye?"

"I must do something now but I want assurance that you will not be offended."

"Offended by what?"

"I do not want my eyes gouged out."

"I... I will not gouge your eyes out, I promise. But what are you going to do?"

His response was to cup her face between his enormous palms, his dark eyes boring into her as if to drill holes through to the other side. Toby gazed up into his handsome face, unable to think or breathe, as his lips very gently came down on hers. It was soft and warm and wonderful. Her eyes closed of their own accord, her focus on his tender lips as they suckled her gently. Having never been kissed by a man before, she had no idea what to expect. All she knew was this was more, and better, than she could have ever dreamed.

Her self-restraint vanished and she threw her arms around his neck about the time he wrapped her up in his enormous arms. Together, they enveloped each other in a tight embrace. Tate suckled her top lip, her lower lip, his tongue finally licking at her mouth, silently pleading to be admitted inside. Toby opened her mouth slightly and he invaded, gorging himself on her sweetness. He suckled her tongue, a delectable little morsel, kissing her more fiercely with each passing moment.

His arms were wrapped tightly around her slender body, his hands clutching at her. Toby responded to him as if she had been doing it all her life, so familiar with the desires of a man she had never even touched. She sensed his passion, matching her own, understanding in that brief contact just how powerful it was. The spark that had been kindled with the first tender kiss was exploding into a raging fire.

They lost all concept of time, fueled by the eruption of their first taste of one another. Tate ended up bumping Toby's head against the wall during his tender offensive, hearing the soft thud and immediately apologetic. But Toby just rubbed the back of her head and laughed.

"No harm done," she murmured, her lips swollen and red from his furious kisses. The hazel eyes focused on him, drinking in his glorious face. "I… I must confess, I have never… that is, I never expected to…."

He smiled, kissing her again just because he could. She was delicious to kiss. "I know," he murmured against her mouth. "I never expected to, either. But I am glad that I did."

She looked at him with amused curiosity. "Did what?"

He kissed her again, very tenderly. "That," he breathed. "May I have your permission to do it again sometime? Perhaps many sometimes?"

Toby was breathless. "I… I am not sure."

He looked surprised and disappointed. "Why not?"

"Because… well, it simply isn't proper. We should not have… that is to say, we are not betrothed or married and actions such as this are only appropriate between…."

He shushed her. "Do you think I would have kissed you like this if I did not have something more in mind? Really, Elizabetha; for an intelligent woman, you are rather dense."

The almond-shaped eyes widened. "W-what?"

He kissed her again and let her go. "Think about it," he said, turning for the great hall. "I would check on my men now."

"Wait," she found her voice, grabbing him by the wrist. "You will be plain, Sir Tate. What do you mean?"

He took her chin between his thumb and forefinger, turned her head slightly, and kissed her on a dirty cheek. "Must I really explain this to you?" he whispered in her ear.

Toby was left breathless again by his kiss. "You must. I insist."

He grinned; she could feel his teeth against her cheek. "Where do you want to go first? Paris or Rome?"

"You are going to escort me to those places?"

"As your husband, it would be my pleasure."

Toby thought she might faint. In fact, she had to swallow very hard and take a very deep breath. "Good Lord," she breathed. "Do you mean to say that you plan to…?"

"I have for quite some time."

"But…!" There were tears in her eyes. "But… what about everything you said about my horrid manners? You told me it was an appalling trait. Moreover, you are above my station. You are… my God, you are…you *cannot* marry me."

He was laughing; she could feel it as he continued to nuzzle her cheek and ear. "I can marry whomever I wish," he murmured. "I think we are a good match, you and I. Do you disagree?"

She closed her eyes at the realization of it and tears coursed down her cheeks. He felt the moisture and looked at her, concerned.

"What is the matter, sweetheart?" he asked gently.

She was trying not to weep from sheer joy. "What about my terrible disposition?"

His soft laughter returned. "Forgive me; I spoke before coming to know you. I know now that you are simply a woman who speaks her mind and I respect that."

"Are you sure?"

"Sure enough that I am delighted with the prospect of spending the rest of my life with you."

The most amazing expression filled her face as the tears began to magically vanish. "I simply cannot believe it. I would never dare to hope."

He was smiling sweetly at her. A big hand brushed hair from her face as he studied her very closely. "And I would never dare to hope to find a woman like you. You are a remarkable lady, Mistress Elizabetha. I think that I shall enjoy this marriage very much. At least, I hope so."

She returned his smile, timidly. "I do not know what to say to all of this."

"It is simple. Say that you will marry me."

Her smile faded as her eyes grew intense. "If you want me, then I most certainly will."

His hand tightened on her face and he brought her to his lips for another gentle kiss. Toby was breathing unsteadily as he moved from her mouth to her nose to her forehead. It was the sweetest gesture she had ever experienced and a magic moment in the making. After several long seconds of touching, of tasting, Tate finally let go of her face and gently took her hand.

"Come along now," he said. "I have wounded men that I would like to see."

Toby followed him into the hall and made his rounds with him, but her focus wasn't on the injured men. It was on a mountain of a man named Tate de Lara she suddenly found herself betrothed to.

CB

TATE HAD TRIED to make Toby go to bed as midnight approached, but she repeatedly refused his requests to the point of walking the other way when he would look at her. There were double the wounded in the hall now that the injured in the bailey had been brought in and, consequently, double the work. Toby would not shirk her duties and worked deep into the night with Stephen, Wallace and Althel to ease the men's suffering. Eventually, Tate gave up trying to force her to rest and went about his duties with Kenneth. But it didn't stop him from keeping an eye on Toby, making sure he knew where she was every second. Now, things were different and he felt very possessive and very protective of her. Already, she very much belonged to him.

Just after midnight, Tate and Kenneth huddled in the solar to make plans for morning repairs. Toby was in the great hall tending to a very young man who had a sucking chest wound. He was, in truth, no more than sixteen years of age and her heart hurt for him as he struggled to be brave against the pain. While the other wounded seemed to be in various stages of sleep, the young man was wide awake because of his difficulty in breathing. Stephen had already used a great deal of skill to stitch up the initial wound but the lad didn't seem to be much better.

So Toby sat with him, speaking to him quietly to keep his mind off his pain. As she sat with him, thoughts of Ailsa began to creep back into her mind but she fought them, knowing that she still had a job to do before she could tend to her sister's burial. In truth, she had been so swept up in the battle that she'd not given any thought to her baby sister, now dead for more than a day. She knew that if she gave over to those thoughts that she would be useless, so she tried to bank them. These men were alive and needed her help. She wanted to do what she could.

The boy with the chest wound seemed to be increasingly uncomfortable. Toby found herself trying to distract him with tales of the cats that used to hang around their stables.

"There was a white one, an orange one and a black one," she said as she held his hand. "The black cat ran from everyone while the orange one was always begging for food. And the white one would attack your feet as you walked by. We had several dogs, too, that were our protectors. Not one of them had a name; we simply called the lot of them 'the dogs'."

The boy grinned weakly, trying to focus on something other than his increasing inability to breathe. "I had a dog when I was small," he said. "It would eat at the table with us. My father would become angry but my mother would feed it."

Toby smiled, patting him on the hand. "Are your parents still alive?"

"Still. My father is a farmer."

"So was mine."

Before the boy could reply, Stephen suddenly appeared and kneeled beside him. Toby looked up at the man; he was unshaven and clearly exhausted, but the cornflower blue eyes were still bright. When he saw that Toby was looking at him, he smiled faintly.

"I came to check on your patient," he said quietly. "He seems to be the only one not sleeping."

"He is having difficulty breathing," Toby explained. "I am telling him stories about my cats."

Stephen's smile grew. "Cats, is it? I see I have come in the nick of time to save him from boredom."

The youth laughed silently as Toby scowled. With a lingering glance at Toby, Stephen proceeded to unwrap the bandages on the boy's chest and look underneath. All Toby could see was blood and ooze and she turned her head, not wanting to study that particular gore. She'd seen enough of it lately. After a moment, Stephen replaced the dressing.

"I will need to place fresh bandages on this," he told Toby. "I will return."

She nodded, watching him as he stood up. As she looked at him, walking through the darkness, she suddenly had visions of him taking Ailsa from her arms and whisking her little sister off into the darkness. It was an odd transition from comforting a wounded man to thinking of her sister, but as she watched Stephen walk away, the urge to find out about her sister's whereabouts suddenly became very strong. She had been fighting off thoughts of Ailsa for some time but found she could no longer do it. For her own peace of mind, she had to know. Now that the battle was diminished and the wounded seemed to be settled, she could no longer fight her sisterly instinct.

She reassured the boy that she would return before following Stephen's path across the floor. He had his medicaments set up on the large eating table, an entire corner confiscated. Everything was in ordered arrangement. Toby walked up behind him as he organized new wrappings.

"Is the boy going to die?" she asked softly.

Stephen turned to look at her, his gaze moving out of the darkened hall to the lad on the other side. "If poison does not claim him, the wound should heal," he replied.

Toby continued to watch as he drew forth phials of white powder. "Sir Stephen, I was wondering...," she swallowed, collecting her thoughts. "I mean to ask where you have taken my sister."

Stephen looked at her; she seemed calm and rational enough. Frankly, he had been expecting the question and was prepared. "She is in the store room," he said quietly. "I put her there because it is cool and I was not certain when we would be able to bury her."

As much as she was trying to be strong, tears sprang to Toby's eyes and she wiped at them furiously. "So she has been beneath me all the while," she murmured.

Stephen nodded, not unsympathetic. "Wallace built her a nice, sturdy coffin and Tate has found a place in the chapel to bury her."

Toby was quickly dissolving into tears. She put her hand on Stephen's arm. "Thank you," she whispered. "For showing my sister such concern, I thank you. I am sorry that I was so unreasonable yesterday when you came to take her."

She moved to pull her hand away but Stephen covered it with his own hand and Toby realized that he was gripping her fingers. "I am truly sorry for your loss, mistress," he said quietly. "If it had been in my power to save her, please know that I would have done so. I would have done anything to spare you such grief."

Toby felt there was more to his declaration than simple words and it made her uncomfortable. In the midst of her tears, she could only nod her head and gently, but firmly, remove her hand from his grasp. But Stephen wouldn't be so easily put aside.

"You really should rest," he grasped her by the upper arm as she tried to walk away. "Wallace and I can handle the wounded. There is no need for you to remain."

"I am not tired."

"A noble lie. I will give you something to help you sleep."

"Stephen, truly," she pulled herself from his grasp almost irritably. "I do not wish to sleep. I want to help."

He smiled faintly at her. "There is nothing more to do for now. You will be needed more when the sun rises and these men awaken."

She hadn't thought on it that way. She looked around the room uncertainly, wiping what was left of the tears on her face. "Are you sure?"

"I am sure. If anything arises, I will send for you. But for now, you must rest."

As she sighed indecisively and fidgeted around, Stephen took one of the powders from his bag and put it in a cup. Taking some of the wine that was still left on the table from their earlier meal, he poured it into the cup and swirled it around. He tapped her on the shoulder and extended the cup.

"Here," he said when she turned to him.

She eyed the cup. "What is that?"

"Nothing that will harm you; it will help you. Just drink it."

She stared at the cup before taking it out of his hand. Drinking the contents without stopping, she made a face as she handed the cup back to him.

"Whatever that was, it tastes awful," she wiped her mouth with the back of her hand.

He just smiled. "Go up to bed now."

She shook her head at him. "I want to bathe first. I am covered with dirt and gore."

"Then I shall have water sent up to you."

The situation was decided. Toby couldn't think of another argument so she nodded her head as she turned for the distant stairs. "Thank you for your kindness," she said as she passed him. "I shall not forget it."

Stephen watched her walk away, not saying what he was thinking. The more time he spent around her, the more enamored he became with her. He was not oblivious to the fact that Tate felt the same way. Turning back to his medicaments, he realized that he was going to have to do something about it if he was going to stake his claim before Tate did.

Stephen didn't simply send up water; he sent up a giant copper pot and two male servants, including Althel, to fill it with hot water. Stephen himself carried the pot into the room because it was beyond the strength of the servants. Stephen was an enormous man, taller than Tate by a head, with bulging arms to match his size. He set the pot down near the hearth as the servants went to work filling it.

He noticed that Toby had stripped the bed of the dusty coverlet and cast it into the corner along with the dust pile that Ailsa had created two days ago. Toby's trunks were open and linens that had covered the beds at the *garçonnaire* now covered the bed in the master's chamber. It was much cleaner than what had been there previously but the room was still grossly dusty. Still, Stephen suspected that would be remedied shortly. If he had learned one thing about Toby, it was that she wouldn't lie around when there was work to be done.

The fire in the hearth was burning brightly, radiating a good deal of heat into the room as Toby bustled back and forth between her open trunks, rummaging through what Tate and her sister had managed to pack. She managed to find several things that she was grateful for, including a luxurious sleeping shift that she had purchased on a trip to Leeds. It had been wadded up in a ball and she knew Ailsa had packed it that way. When she unrolled the ball, she hugged the shift to her, feeling her sister's touch. The tears came again, this time silently, but she forced herself to work through them.

Stephen and the servants were busy filling her bath, although she wasn't exactly sure why Stephen was still there. He had brought up the pot but lingered. Toby didn't give him too much thought as she continued to inventory the contents of both trunks, thankfully coming across some soap, a comb and other vanity items that Ailsa had apparently haphazardly thrown into the trunk. She inhaled deeply of the soap that smelled of lavender and lemon rind, thankful to have something to wash with. She was positive that the whole of Harbottle Castle had nothing even remotely useful for cleaning.

Stephen was loitering near the door as Althel picked up the last of the buckets and quit the chamber. He watched Toby stand over the pot and swirl her hand around in the water.

"Is it too hot?" he asked her.

She shook her head. "Not at all," she shook out her wet hand and looked at him. "Thank you for bringing this up to the room. I am very grateful."

Stephen took a step into the room, his cornflower eyes intense. "Will there be anything else, mistress?"

Toby was unnerved by the look in his eye; there was something strong and suggestive there. "Nay," she said. "I think I can do for myself."

"I shall be outside if you require anything."

"No need."

It wasn't Toby who had answered him; it was Tate, entering the room and gazing at his knight with an unreadable expression. Stephen turned to his liege and the two of them exchanged equally stony expressions. But there was no mistaking the tension that suddenly filled the room.

"You are needed in the hall," he said to Stephen. "I will take care of Mistress Toby."

Stephen almost opened his mouth to refute him but thought better of it. Tate was, in fact, his commander. And Stephen never disobeyed an order. Still, with a woman involved, there was something of an instinct to stand his ground. Casting a lingering glance at Toby, he quit the room in silence.

It had been an odd exit. Toby wasn't ignorant to the strain between Tate and Stephen and she was uncomfortable with it. She wasn't quite sure why things were so strained but she had a suspicion. When Stephen was gone, Toby smiled timidly at Tate.

"I did not want to bother you," she said, perhaps to explain the other knight's presence. "Stephen brought up a bath so that I could wash this dirt and blood away."

Tate gazed at her a moment; dirty and disheveled after the hellish past few days, she was still the most beautiful woman he had ever seen.

"I am glad to see you have decided to retire," he said. "I will therefore leave you to your bath and sleep. But I wanted to make sure you did not require anything further."

She shook her head at him, her eyes never leaving his. "All I require is to see you before I go to sleep," she said, lowering her eyes coyly as she did so. "Since you have shown yourself, I require nothing further."

It was a charming thing to say. Tate smiled as he moved towards her. "You just wanted to see me?"

She nodded sharply, averting her eyes. "Aye."

He stopped right in front of her, dipping his head down to look at her lowered face. "Nothing else?"

Her cheeks were turning a deep shade of pink as she avoided his probing gaze. "Nothing."

"Not even a kiss?"

She looked up at him, preparing to reply, when he suddenly pulled her into his arms and, with a wicked grin, kissed her deeply. Toby ended up weak and boneless as he sucked the strength right out of her. When his lips finally released her own, the storm cloud eyes gazed at her half-lidded.

"I was right."

"About what?" she asked breathlessly.

"It was as good as I remembered."

As she grinned, he kissed her again, so passionately that it made her head swim. He seemed to take great delight in suckling her tender lips before moving to her face, kissing her cheeks, nose and eyes gently. All the while, Toby simply held on to him and struggled not to fall. She had no sense of time or balance; she was lost in the man's embrace.

"As much as I would like to do this all night, it is important that you rest," he finally said, his voice husky. "I will therefore leave you to your bath and to sleep. I will leave a soldier out in the hall should you require anything."

Toby simply nodded her head, sighing raggedly when he kissed her soft lips again and released her. Taking both of her hands, he kissed them, too.

"Good sleep, sweetheart," he murmured.

Toby stood in the middle of the room where he had released her, watching him walk to the door. He smiled at her as he opened it, issuing another soft good night before closing it quietly. Still, she stood there like an idiot, hardly able to think much less move. But the smell of the soap reminded her that her bath waited and she began to remove her surcoat with unsteady hands. Without someone to help her unlace the stays, it took longer than usual but eventually she managed to get it off. The shift followed, as did the pantalets, hose and shoes. She untied the scarf around her head, allowing her dirty golden-brown hair to go free. Climbing into the pot, it was a tight fit but suited her wonderfully.

Picking up the lavender-lemon soap, she went to work.

CHAPTER TEN

T HE FOLLOWING DAY, they buried Ailsa.

Stephen made the recommendation to Tate at dawn; having just come from the coffin of the young girl, her body was rapidly deteriorating and it was important they get her it in the ground before she putrefy further. Stephen made the suggestion purely based on how Toby would react to her sister's decaying corpse and Tate was forced to agree.

The air between the two knights was strained but professional. Tate hadn't told Stephen that he and Toby were betrothed, mostly because it wasn't any of the man's business. Although he was certain of Stephen's interest in Toby, the man had yet to make any inappropriate moves. When, and if, it came to that, Tate was prepared to act. It was a bizarre situation that Tate could never have imagined they would face. Kenneth just tried to stay out of it.

Tate extricated a couple of men from the army of soldiers digging a mass grave for the victims of yesterday's battle and put them to digging a grave in the floor of Harbottle's small chapel. As the sun began to rise, he was reluctant to wake Toby with news that they had to bury her sister right away but he knew that he had little choice. Stephen and a few men were bringing the coffin up from the store room and the day was already busy. Shortly after sunrise, Tate went up to her chamber.

Knocking on the door softly, he was surprised when she immediately responded. The door was unlocked, too. Opening the door, he should not have been surprised to already find her awake and dressed. Clad in a muted red surcoat and off-white linen shift, she was clean and washed and looked positively radiant. She also had the room in complete disarray. She smiled at Tate as he entered the room.

"Good morn to you," she said. "I hope you slept well last night."

He couldn't help but smile in return; every time he saw the woman, he felt his heart soften just a little more.

"I was going to ask you the same question," he made his way towards her. "But my next question would be why you seem to be tearing the room apart."

Her smile broadened as she looked about. "Well," she began, "it seems to me that I will be spending some time in this chamber. It needs to be cleaned and I need to see what, exactly, you brought from Forestburn so I can begin to calculate what was saved against what was lost. There seems to be a good deal to do and I am at a loss as to where to start, so I thought I would begin here."

He was standing next to her, watching the way her mouth curved when she spoke. "This can wait, sweetheart. You do not have to do everything in one day."

"But I must see what I have lost so I will know what I must purchase to replace it."

He put his hands on her upper arms and pulled her head to his lips for a sweet kiss. "I will buy you whatever you need to replace what has been lost," he said. "You need not worry about money."

She closed her eyes as he kissed her temple again, relishing the feel of him and thrilled that everything that had transpired between them yesterday had not been a dream. When she had awoken this morning, she almost wasn't sure what was real.

"I am not worried about money," she said with a furrowed brow. "But I will be honest when I say that I am worried over many things."

"Like what?"

"The people of Cartingdon, for example. I really must return to Forestburn as soon as possible to ease their minds." She fidgeted with the edge of the bed. "And then there are my parents... and Ailsa...."

She hung her head, biting her lip to keep from bursting into tears. Tate could see the mood darkening and he collected her in his arms, taking her over to the bed and pulling her onto his enormous thighs as he sat. It was a tender moment, full of the warmth of discovery. She was soft and sweet upon him. He held her tightly, his face against the side of her head.

"We must speak of your sister," he murmured. "I realize how difficult this is for you, but we must bury Ailsa this morning. Stephen has already moved her coffin to the chapel in preparation for doing so."

The tears came then and she wiped at them, missing a few that fell silently to her lap. Tate gave her a squeeze, kissing her on the side of the head and wishing he could give her more comfort.

"I know she must be buried," she whispered. "But it is difficult to think of putting my little sister in the ground when she was alive and well only two days ago. I simply cannot believe that she has passed."

He kissed her cheek. "I know," he muttered, "for I have been in your shoes. I understand completely."

She looked up at him, the hazel eyes swimming with tears. "I heard whispers once that you lost your wife years ago," she said. "Cartingdon Parrish, if nothing else, is a fertile ground for gossip. If it is untrue, I apologize for repeating it."

He gazed into her eyes, remembering the pain he had suffered through four years ago. Strange how he didn't feel it as horrifically as he used to; true, it was still there, like a faded ache from long ago. Oddly enough, Toby seemed to do a great deal towards pushing it into the deep recesses of his memory where it was a moment of sadness and nothing more. It had been a time when he thought he had died inside. But Toby made him feel very much alive and he was willing to speak on the subject.

"It is true," he said. "She perished in childbirth. I lost my daughter as well."

Toby's grief shifted focus. "I am so terribly sorry for you," she said sincerely. "Losing a sister is bad enough, but to lose your wife and child… I surely cannot imagine the pain you experienced."

"I hope you never will. I will do my best to ensure that you do not."

Toby stared into his storm colored eyes, realizing she felt comforted by the fact that he had indeed experienced grief on her level. He understood. It gave her strength, somehow drawing them closer, and she wiped at her face in an effort to compose herself.

"Then we should not keep Ailsa waiting," she rose from his lap but continued to hold his hand. "I am ready."

He stood next to her, towering over her with his size and strength. Gently, he tucked her hand into the crook of his elbow as they moved towards the door.

"Your bravery, as always, is astonishing," he said softly, allowing her to pass first through the door.

She smiled weakly. "'Tis not bravery. 'Tis simply the way of things; it must be done and hysterics on my part will not change it."

"That is much more like the Elizabetha I first met at Forestburn."

"How do you mean?"

"Strong and decisive."

"And appalling?"

He grinned, hearing his words echoed. "You are never going to forgive me for that, are you?"

"Perhaps. But not today."

He kissed her hand as she descended the stairs, his gaze lingering on her golden brown head. As much as he had loved his wife, he couldn't ever remember feeling such strong emotion for her as he felt for Toby. There was something about the woman that already had her embedded deep into his heart and soul as if nothing else had existed before.

Together, they made their way to the tiny chapel of Harbottle. Toby felt moderately strong until she entered the chapel and saw her sister's coffin near the altar. Then, she faltered, her eyes brimming and her heart pounding. It was a struggle to remain strong. As Tate escorted her into the small chamber, Kenneth, Stephen and Edward were there to greet her. One of the most tender acts of compassion that Tate had ever seen was when the young king, unable to voice his sympathies, took Toby's hand and held it tightly. As she struggled not to cry, he struggled not to cry also. He just stood there and held her hand. The little girl that had so terrified him with her attention had nonetheless left her mark.

Wallace gave the liturgy that sent Ailsa's young soul to a better place. Instead of a hymn, Tate stood over the grave and sang the song that Ailsa had loved so well.

To the sky, my sweet babe;
The night is alive, my sweet babe.
Your dreams are filled with raindrops from heaven;
Sleep, my sweet babe, and cry no more.

The tenderness of it broke Toby's heart.

೮

JANUARY WAS A bitterly cold month and it was rare that the sun was able to break through the heavy covering of clouds at any given time. On the afternoon following Ailsa's burial, the sun, remarkably, was able to burst through the mist. In the master's chamber, organizing all of her worldly possessions, Toby took it as a sign from God. She thought perhaps he was happier now that he had Ailsa to keep him company and that thought, however foolish it seemed, kept her from the depths of grief. It was a comfort.

She stood for a moment in the lancet window, eyes closed, feeling the weak warmth on her face. Her emerald-colored surcoat was in her hands, as she had been fussing with a spot on the fabric. She knew it must have occurred the night Tate and his knights had come to sup at Forestburn. She remembered that day with some fondness, though it seemed like a terribly long time ago. In fact, everything at Forestburn seemed like it belonged to another time and another world. Now her world was Harbottle Castle and a future she could never have imagined.

A future that revolved around a man she was becoming increasingly attached to. As Toby kept busy in her chamber, Tate and his men were down in the bailey effecting repairs on the walls and front gates. The siege had left them burned and a small army of men were going into the forest that lay to the south of the castle and harvesting trees to rebuild the gates. Toby could see the men in the distance filtering in and out of the tree line. She didn't see Tate but she imagined he was among them.

Thoughts of the man brought a smile to her lips. For twenty-one years of her life, she had been relatively alone. She had never imagined she would ever wed, as she had firmly told Tate when they first met. Now she was betrothed to the man who had called her appalling. She giggled softly as she thought of his initial impression of her; not that he hadn't been correct, but at least now he saw her strong personality as a positive trait and not a negative one. She hoped, with time, he would see her as much more. She couldn't even hope that the man would love her; that was a fool's dream. A strong like was good enough for her.

A knock on the door roused her from her thoughts and she turned in the direction of the panel.

"Come," she called.

The door creaked open softly and Stephen stood there, his corn-flower blue eyes intense. "Good afternoon, mistress," he said in his deep, gentle voice. "I have brought you something."

Curious, Toby stepped away from the window and the glare of the weak January sun. Immediately, she spied something small and furry in the crook of Stephen's left arm. Two big cat-eyes looked back at her.

"My goodness," she said with a grin. "What in the world do you have, Sir Stephen?"

Stephen took a timid step into the room. "I seem to remember you boring one of my patients with tales of your cats," he indicated the little orange kitten in his grasp. "I brought you one."

Toby's smiled broadened with delight as she set the emerald garment aside. She held her hands out and Stephen deposited the warm, purring bundle into them. She hugged it tightly.

"He is so sweet," she crooned, laying her cheek against the furry head. "Wherever did you find him?"

"The stable is full of them," he told her. "They multiply like mad in there. This one, however, is small and seems to be left out of the food chain. I thought you could help him since you seem to like cats so much."

She cuddled her new pet, her hazel eyes full of gratitude. "Thank you," she stroked the little head and was rewarded with a healthy meow. "I love him already."

Stephen smiled, watching her embrace the kitten. It had worked the magic he hoped it would. In truth, while Tate was off repairing the castle, Stephen had finished with his rounds in the great hall and had set off to the stables in search of a cat. He'd seen them there before and as luck would have it, there were several for his choosing. He'd stood by and watched her say a very difficult farewell to her sister that morning and was hoping the cat would cheer her up.

"Well," he said, realizing his business was concluded and that he should probably leave. "I can see that the cat is in good hands."

Petting the kitten, Toby began looking around the room. "I fear that I have nothing to feed him. I should go down to the kitchen and find him something."

"Would you allow me to accompany you?"

A twinge of disquiet ran through Toby as she gazed up into his brilliant blue eyes. She was coming to sense that the man was interested in her on more than a mere acquaintance level; that was obvious when Tate and Stephen ran into each other in her chamber last night. She did not want to be cruel to the man but she did not want to encourage him, either.

"I am sure you have more important things to attend to," she insisted. "You do not need to worry about me. I can fend for myself."

"You are the last person I would worry over," he replied. "And I offer to escort you for purely selfish reasons."

"What might those be?"

"Because I want to."

A warning bell went off in Toby's head. The smiled faded from her lips as she gazed up at him, not at all wanting to hurt the man's feelings for he had been inordinately kind to her. But it was not fair to not tell him the truth of the matter; she wasn't interested in him and never would be so long as Tate was in her life. She cocked her head thoughtfully, trying to think of the correct way to phrase what she must say.

"Sir Stephen," she started off hesitantly. "May I... speak with you?"

His expression warmed. "Of course. What do you wish to speak of?"

The cat meowed again and she looked at the animal, rubbing its ears as she thought of way not to upset the big knight.

"You have been extremely kind to my sister and me," she began. "I want you to know how grateful I am. You have been compassionate and attentive and I will never forget your kindness."

"It has been my pleasure," he said before she could finish her train of thought. Then he wriggled his eyebrows. "Although when we were first introduced, I must admit I was not so sure our association would be pleasant."

Toby was caught off-guard by the statement. "What do you mean?"

Stephen laughed softly. "You were, shall we say, rather outspoken."

She lifted an eyebrow. "I see," she sighed with exasperation. "Did all of you think I was an appalling lout, then?"

He laughed again. "You were not a conventional lady, to be sure. I think we were caught off guard more than anything. It was apparent having only known you for a few minutes that you were the one who ran the town, not your father. We could see who truly held the power."

"And?"

"And a strong woman is a rare thing though, in this case, not entirely unpleasant."

She frowned in a way that made him laugh yet again. "I am so pleased to see that I have somehow redeemed myself."

"You have," his laughter faded as the cornflower eyes grew intense once more. "In fact, I would say that you are one of the more appealing ladies I have met. Very appealing, in fact."

They were back to his obvious interest and Toby swallowed hard at the look in his eye. She hugged the kitten closer as if the little animal would somehow protect her from him.

"Sir Stephen," she struggled her way through the sentence. "I cannot… that is to say, we cannot… if you are thinking of something more than friendship between you and I then I must very humbly decline. As flattered as I am, such a thing is not possible."

His eyebrows lifted but the amiability was still in his expression. "Is that so? Why not?"

"Because I am betrothed."

She watched the warmth go out of his face like water dousing a flame. The cornflower blue eyes turned hard and there was a very long pause before he replied.

"I see," there was no warmth in his tone, either. "I was not aware when we were introduced that you were already spoken for."

She shook her head. "I was not at the time," she said quietly. "But that situation has changed."

Stephen's eyes glittered at her, inspecting her, as if trying to ascertain what, exactly, she wasn't telling him. But he was not stupid; he could already guess. He'd been expecting it at some point. But Stephen believed he still had some time; Tate was not one to show unrestrained interest in a woman or act rashly. Neither was Stephen; yet, apparently, his sense of caution had worked against him. He'd waited too long. "Then allow me to say that Sir Tate is a fortunate man," he said in a low voice. "I suppose it is my fault for not declaring my intentions quickly enough."

He turned to leave but she impulsively put her hand on his arm. "I am sorry," she said earnestly. "And I am deeply flattered."

He gazed at her steadily, perhaps pondering things that were best left unsaid. But he couldn't help himself from speaking. "It is I who am sorry, mistress. More than you know."

Toby lowered her gaze, unsure what more she could say that would ease his disappointment. Anything more might sound trite or worse; she might sound as if she was mocking him. As he turned to quit the room, she stopped him.

"Do you want the cat back?" she offered timidly. "I would understand."

He shook his head, the cornflower blue eyes without the intensity they had once held. "Nay," he said quietly. "He is a gift."

"I am not sure if it is proper for me to keep him."

"It is just a cat," he lifted his big shoulders, moving through the door. "'Tis not as if I gifted you with rubies."

Toby watched him disappear down the stairwell. She felt sorry for the man; rejection was never an easy thing. Truth was, she was indeed very flattered. She had never really had a suitor and suddenly she had two of them, both very handsome and powerful men. But the reality was that she had eyes only for Tate. Stephen was a kind man, but there was no affection for him. His glances did not cause her to swoon nor did she think of him constantly. That privilege was reserved for de Lara.

CB

IT WAS VERY late. Toby had not seen Tate all day and now, at this late hour, she lay in bed by the light of the fire, petting her new kitten and waiting for sleep to claim her. The bailey was busy with the sounds of men working even at this late hour. It was a distraction because Toby knew that Tate was in the middle of it. She wanted to stand at the window and watch him all night but she knew he would probably become cross with her. So she took her new furry friend, George, to bed and the cat lay quite contentedly next to her. In fact, she didn't hear a sound out of the cat until suddenly, it let out a strangled cry.

Along with the meow came a hissed curse. Startled, Toby realized that she must have fallen asleep as her eyes focused on Tate's massive form in the darkness. She had never heard him enter. Instead of looking at her, however, he was peering at the cat.

"Where in the hell did that come from?" he demanded in a harsh whisper. "I nearly sat on the beast."

Toby struggled to sit up. "That is George," she told him. "He was a gift."

"A gift? From whom?"

"Sir Stephen," she cuddled the cat, soothing it. "He gave him to me."

Tate's expression cooled; Toby could see that even in the darkness. "And you accepted?"

She could hear the hazard in his tone and all of her sleepiness fled. "You need not worry," she said quietly. "He is under no false pretenses that my accepting the cat is in any way a prelude to courtship."

"What do you mean?"

She sighed with exasperation. "I told him that I was betrothed. I had to, Tate. He wanted to court me."

The storm cloud eyes flashed. "Did he tell you that?"

Toby could see where the conversation was leading. Tate was growing angry and she did not want a blood bath on her hands. Moving the kitten aside, she patted the bed next to her.

"Sit down," she commanded softly. "Please."

He paused a moment before acquiescing to her wishes. He sat very close to her as she lay propped up on an elbow, his storm cloud eyes reflecting the soft firelight. Toby smiled up at him, putting her hand on his thigh.

"You need not worry about Stephen," she said quietly. "He knows that you and I are betrothed. He understands that there is no chance for him. I asked him if he wanted the cat returned, but he said that it was a gift. There is no harm in keeping a kitten given to me by a man you have clearly triumphed over. 'Twould be right for you to be a gracious winner and allow me to keep it."

He just stared at her. Then, he gave her a lopsided smile and picked up the hand on his thigh, kissing it. "Well put," he said, somewhat reluctantly. "I knew that Stephen would assert himself sooner or later. I suppose it is best if the rejection comes from you and not me."

She regarded him closely, seeing something of disquiet on his brow. "You are concerned for him," she ventured.

He shrugged, lowering his gaze. "I have known Stephen for many years and consider him a friend," he toyed with her hand. "I realize that I was somewhat cold to him the other day when I found him up here with you, but I wanted him to understand that you are off limits."

"Perhaps you should have simply told him."

He nodded reluctantly. "Perhaps," he said softly. "I was hoping he would understand without a word spoken. Perhaps I just did not want to verbalize it. A woman has never come between us before."

"One still hasn't."

He cast her a sidelong glance, his grin broadening. "I hope not. I should regret it."

"Then perhaps you should speak to him as a friend and not a rival. A few words might ease whatever disappointment or animosity he is feeling."

He nodded slowly. "Wise words. I suppose I should have handled this situation differently from the beginning but it is something I have never experienced before."

She smiled at him. "I am glad."

"For what?"

"That you have never experienced a situation like this before."

He laughed softly, kissing her fingers. They fell silent a moment and he began toying with her digits, inspecting her lovely hand. She had the prettiest hands. Toby watched him as he rubbed the soft skin of her palm, a pensive expression on his face. She knew he was still thinking about Stephen and she, too, hoped no permanent damage would result from them both wanting to court the same woman.

"He says that you are a fortunate man, you know," she said softly.

"Who?"

"Stephen."

He kissed her hand again. "I agree completely." He wanted to shift the subject off of Stephen. "I regret not having seen you most of the day. I missed you a great deal."

She felt warmed, giddy, by his declaration. "You did? I missed you also. But I kept busy."

"Is that so?" he shifted so that his arms were braced on either side of her slender body. "What did you do all day?"

"Went through the trunks you brought from Forestburn."

"And?"

"And I am missing most of my winter clothing. No cloaks or warm things. With this weather, I am afraid that I shall freeze."

He nodded in understanding. "I apologize. I grabbed what I could find."

She reached up and touched his cheek. "I know that," she said. "I did not mean to criticize. It simply means that I must obtain some winter fabric very soon."

"Of course," he nodded. "We can go tomorrow."

"Go where?"

"Into the village. There are a few merchants there, or at least there were. Hopefully they did not run off when Mortimer's army invaded."

Toby nodded, not at all pressed to admit she was looking forward to a shopping trip with Tate. She watched him as he played with her fingers, inspecting the skin and acquainting himself with the texture. He seemed preoccupied and weary. Finally, she gaze a squeeze.

"Are you going to tell me why you came to see me?" her eyes were twinkling when he looked at her. "It was not simply to sit on my kitten, was it?"

He relaxed into an easy grin. "Nay," he said, seeming to hunt for the correct words. Finally he shrugged. "I suppose I simply wanted to see you. I cannot explain it, but you have been on my mind all day and I could think of nothing else but to see you."

She flushed sweetly. "I am honored," she said. "And, I will admit, surprised."

He put her hand against his lips as he spoke. "Why?"

She was having a difficult time concentrating on her train of thought as his lips gently nibbled her flesh. "Because it was only a few days ago that we were at Forestburn and things between us were quite different. A world of difference, in fact; I am still coming to grips with the fact that we are betrothed. And the offer came from a man who openly insulted me when we first met."

His mouth was still against her hand. "I did no such thing."

She nodded emphatically. "Aye, you did. You told me that beauty and bad manners were a family trait and that, unfortunately, one trait negates the other."

He just stared at her. Then he burst out laughing. "Do you memorize everything I say?"

"I have an astounding memory."

"No doubt," he sobered, shaking his head. "I shall have to watch what I say around you if you do not easily forget."

She was smiling in spite of herself, watching the expression on his face. "Nay, I do not forget," she said softly, her smile fading. "Would you mind, then, telling me what changed your mind about me?"

He cocked a dark eyebrow in mock exasperation. "Must you know everything?"

"I must."

He was amused. "Suffice it to say that your trait of beauty negated the trait of bad manners. And so did your traits of bravery, intelligence and compassion."

She watched him as he rubbed his cheek against the back of her hand. Now that they were communicating easily, there were many more questions she wanted to ask him. She was suddenly wildly curious to know more about him, this man who would be her husband. When she thought about it, they'd never had a moment to truly sit and come to know each other. Everything had been in passing or during a crisis. But now, there was time.

"Will you be truthful with me?" she asked timidly.

"I will always be truthful with you. Lying is not in my nature."

She was sobering, growing serious. "Will you please tell me if the rumors about you are true?"

"What rumors are those?"

"That you are Longshank's son?"

His smile faded, an odd look coming to his eye. "Does it matter?"

"It does not. But I would like to know the truth."

He sighed faintly, somehow moving closer to her in the process. There was a lengthy pause, during which time Toby watched his expression as he pondered her question. She held her breath, wondering if he was going to answer her. Finally, he opened his mouth.

"Since we are betrothed, I suppose it is your right to know," he said. "Aye, he was my father. I was his firstborn son, born exactly one month before his heir, Edward the Second."

Toby struggled not to openly react to what she had always been told. Still, to hear it from his lips was something of a revelation.

"And your mother? Was she really a Welsh princess?"

He nodded slowly. "From all accounts, she and my father were very much in love," he began stroking her shoulder, his hand trailing down her arm. "Her name was Dera. She was the youngest daughter of Dafydd ap Gruffydd and she met my father when Dafydd and Edward were briefly allied against Dafydd's brother, Llewelyn, Prince of Wales. Their love affair was brief, resulting in my conception, and when my mother perished in childbirth, Dafydd turned me over to my father for fear that Llewelyn would somehow harm me. My father gave me over to the great Marcher Lords of de Lara to raise when I was still an infant, hence the name I carry is de Lara."

"But you are a prince on both sides of your family, not simply a knight."

He shrugged. "I would be proud to be a mere knight, but by virtue of my birth, I am slightly more. The Harbottle Commons lordship is only the beginning."

She lifted an eyebrow. "The beginning? I do not understand."

He drew in a long, thoughtful breath. "Along with Harbottle, I hold title to the baronetcies of Workington and Consett as well as the title Viscount Whitehaven, Lord Protector of Cumbria. I am also the Earl of Carlisle."

Toby couldn't help it; her eyes widened. "You are an earl?"

"That is a recent title."

Her mouth flew open; she slapped a hand over it so she wouldn't look like an idiot. Tate acted as if it was truly nothing to be shocked over and took her hand back, just so he could kiss it again. The storm cloud colored eyes glittered.

"Now you will tell me about your linage, Mistress Elizabetha Cartingdon," he said. "And mind you leave nothing out."

She was still stunned, struggling to gather her wits. "I am certainly none of the peerage you speak of," she said. "The most I can do is claim relation to the barons of Northumberland. The last baron, Ives de Vesci, had several daughters. My father was a son of de Vesci's third daughter. And my mother's sire told me that we are descended from a Viking king named Red Thor."

He smiled knowingly. "I can see the beauty of Viking maidens in you," he said. "You clearly should bear the title of 'lady', not mistress."

She shook her head. "My father is only a farmer, a wealthy man through hard work. He is slightly above a peasant and slightly below the nobility."

"Nonsense," Tate said softly. "If you are relation to the barons of Northumberland, then you are clearly entitled to be called 'my lady'. And when you are my wife, you will be much more."

Toby just stared at him, her hazel eyes limpid with a doe-eyed expression. It was clear that she was still struggling to digest everything. "Will you tell me something more?" she asked softly.

He was moving closer to her, inspecting her, devouring her with his gaze. "Anything."

"Will you tell me about your wife?"

His dark eyes gazed at her with mild surprise. "What do you wish to know?"

She shrugged, averting her gaze. "I… I suppose I was just wondering who she was and how you met her." She looked up at him again, speaking quickly. "You do not have to tell me if you do not want to. I am only curious and nothing more. I would hold only the highest respect for her, I assure you."

He gazed at her a moment before a smile tugged at his lips. "I would never think otherwise," he said quietly. "And I suppose it is natural to be curious; therefore, her name was Catherine and she was a member of the de Broase family, close allies of the de Laras. We were pledged many years ago, in fact, when she was slightly more than a child. I was fifteen years older than her when we married; she was only sixteen."

Toby nodded every so often, listening to every word. "I take it that she did not have appalling manners like me," she quipped softly.

He laughed. "Nay, she did not," he replied. "She was a sweet little thing with big green eyes and a funny laugh. But she had never been in the best of health. When she conceived our daughter, the pregnancy was terrible. She was in bed for the duration. And when it came to deliver the child… well, suffice it to say that her body could not handle the strain. She passed away shortly after the stillborn birth."

Toby put her hand on his. "I am sincerely sorry," she said quietly. "It must have been devastating for you."

"It was," he agreed quietly. "Catherine and I were together less than a year, but in that year, she showed me something of love. It was a surprise."

Toby smiled faintly. "That she showed you how to love?"

"That I could feel love." He looked at Toby's face, moving an index finger along her cheek to her jaw line. There was something smoldering in his gaze that seduced and devoured her. "I never imagined I could experience the emotion. I thought it was impossible. Then when she died, I thought all of my ability to feel any emotion had died with her. And then I met you."

Toby's heart was pounding painfully against her ribs as his storm cloud eyes gazed at her intensely. His touch was hot, gentle, moving across her chin and down her neck, scorching her until she could hardly breathe.

"You felt nothing but frustration with me at first," she said in a ragged voice. "Of that, you were clear."

The corner of his mouth twitched and he shifted his body, moving closer still. His hands gripping her upper arms, trapping her. "Frustration then fascination," he said hoarsely. "From fascination to awe. And then from awe to…."

He didn't finish as his mouth suddenly clamped down over hers, his lips warm and soft and gentle. But a moment later, his enormous arms were wrapping around her slender body and he was pulling her fiercely against him. He kissed her as he had never kissed a woman before, unrestrained and potent. He kissed her as if he couldn't get enough of her fast enough. She was sweet and soft and his tongue demanded entry into her mouth, taking advantage of it when she opened timidly to him. He swooped in, licking her, tasting her, feeling his heart pound in his ears and his loins grow harder by the second.

As Tate dominated, Toby submitted. Normally aggressive by nature, it seemed to be her inherent reaction to surrender when being passionately dominated. Her arms were around his neck as he ravaged her, his mouth moving over her cheeks, lips, neck and to her shoulders. In the warm sleeping shift that Ailsa had packed, there was nothing between the garment and her naked flesh. Tate held her ferociously against his torso with his right hand while his left began to wander.

Toby was aware of his lips on her shoulder, his hand moving across her back to her forearm. She was muddle-headed, feeling each new sensation as if she were feeling repeated strikes of lightening. Everything made her quiver and shake. When his big hand moved to her abdomen, she shuddered, and when it finally moved up her torso to gently cup her right breast, she nearly bolted.

Tate held her fast, his mouth coming up from her shoulder. "I am sorry," he murmured. "I did not mean to frighten you."

She shook her head, her breathing coming in fast little pants. "You did not," she said, meeting his half-lidded gaze. "But you... you did startle me."

"If you do not want me to touch you there, I will not."

She blinked as if she did not understand the question. "As my betrothed, it is your right."

He smiled faintly. "I know what my rights are. But I do not want to make you uncomfortable."

Toby didn't know what to say. She looked at him, half in apprehension, half in passion, until he gently held her face between his two enormous hands and kissed her cheek.

"Here," he said softly. "Let me show you what I was about to do. If you decide you do not like it, then I will never do it again."

Toby nodded unsteadily, watching his reassuring wink. The shift was laced between her breasts; without a word, Tate began to carefully unlace the bindings. One by one, the holes were unlaced until the string was cast aside. The shift was now nearly open to her navel. As the fire snapped softly and the kitten purred at the other end of the bed, Tate very gently pulled her shift off her shoulders, exposing tantalizing flesh inch by inch, not saying a word as the lamb's wool garment fell away. He watched her breasts become more and more exposed to his hungry eyes until the edge of the fabric was just at nipple level. He could see her taut nipples straining against the fabric. Then he looked at her.

"May I?"

Toby was breathing so heavily that she could hardly speak. It was a terrifying experience for a virgin yet an extremely arousing, intimate one. He was undressing her inch by inch and her body was on fire for reasons she did not understand. When he asked the question, she merely nodded.

He smiled faintly, lowering his head and tenderly kissing the top of her breasts. It was a slow, warm, provocative gesture. When he finally gave a little tug, the right side of the shift pulled way and her entire right breast was exposed. The nipple hardened with the sudden movement. Tate was still kissing the top of her breasts but he moved to the right one, gently suckling on the flesh surrounding the nipple. He made no move to actually touch the puckered pellet. Toby let out a harsh exhale that was something between a gasp and a groan, feeling lightheaded with the flames he was stirring within her. For a moment, he stopped kissing altogether. Then, she felt something warm, wet and firm against her nipple.

Toby couldn't help the moan that escaped her lips. That primal noise was all Tate needed to unleash the lust that had been building in his veins for the past several minutes; he pulled her against him once more, tightly, and his mouth began to suckle her nipple furiously. Toby cried out as at the pleasure of it, her arms going around his head as if holding a starving child to her breast. The tighter she held his head, the harder he suckled and the more firmly he held her against him. They were engulfing each other.

For as gentle as he had been, Tate was very quickly deteriorating into mad oblivion. He'd never had anything so sweet and strong and delicious. The shift came off completely as he laid her back on the bed, his hands and mouth doing things to her that made Toby oblivious to all else. She was gasping for every breath as his mouth moved between her breasts, licking and suckling with a vengeance. His hands were on her thighs, moving up to cup her heart-shaped bottom with both hands as his passion overwhelmed him. She was soft and warm, and he was raging out of control.

Tate forgot himself as his mouth moved down her torso to her navel; he ran his tongue around it, listening to her gasp with pleasure. He was in a fog and vaguely remembered peeling off his own tunic and removing his breeches. He couldn't stop himself, not if God himself had appeared and demanded he cease. Everything about Toby was perfect and delectable and he was consumed with the feel and taste of her. He wouldn't stop; more than that, he couldn't.

He lifted himself back up so that he was face to face with her, his enormous body atop her slender one. His mouth fused with her lips, once again tasting the honeyed tongue that had driven him mad with desire. Toby grunted when his weight came down on her, instinctively parting her legs so that a good portion of his weight slipped onto the mattress below them. Tate felt her legs part for him and he was lost; he knew what he was about to do and he furthermore knew that he shouldn't. But what he felt for this woman overtook him until he could think of nothing else. He knew he was in love with her; he'd known that for a while. But he could not bring himself to verbalize it. He realized that his body was about to say it for him and he could not stop it. He did not want to stop it. He wanted her.

He pushed into her gently, swallowing her gasps of surprise with his amorous kisses. He withdrew and thrust again, pushing further into her tender body and feeling her tense beneath him. He kept his kisses warm and insistent, hoping to relax her as his arms wrapped tightly around her body. When he withdrew a third time and thrust once more, he slid into her wet folds with a great deal of ease. Another thrust and he was seated to the hilt. A ragged sigh came from his lips as he savored that moment, the joining of their flesh. The feel of her fed him like nothing he had ever known.

He withdrew fully and thrust again and he could hear Toby panting. But she was no longer tense; in fact, he could feel her sweet body relaxing beneath him. His hands began to move, roving her torso, into her hair, against her breast as he thrust again and again, gently at first but increasing in power and passion. He moved into her, against her, feeling her body as it began to respond to his onslaught. More thrusts, more friction, and Toby was moving with him, gasping softly with ecstasy. Her legs wrapped around his hips and he held her buttocks tightly, his pelvis against her, his thrusts powerful and measured, her hips responding in rhythm.

Tate's mind was consumed with a white sort of fire that seemed to be filled with Toby's light. He could see her nude outline in the weak light, the flare of her hips and the ripe swell of her breasts. His lips continued to kiss her passionately as his body thrust into her again and again, feeling himself approach complete fulfillment and not wanting to see the glory end so quickly. It was one of the most powerful emotional moments of his life, coupling with this woman that had quickly come to mean so very much to him. He thrust into her hard enough to rattle her teeth, grinding his pelvis against her Venus Mound and acutely aware when her slick walls began to tighten around him. He held her tightly as she experienced her first release, listening to her weep with joy as he took his own.

As fast as the storm rose, it banked swiftly but did not die completely. Tate continued to move within her long after their passionate climaxed, still wanting to be a part of the woman as he had never been a part of any other. When the gasping and heaving died away, she fell asleep in his embrace and he succumbed shortly after.

They slept deep into the night, the best night's sleep either one of them could ever recall.

CHAPTER ELEVEN

I T WAS JUST before dawn as Tate made his way out of the keep and headed towards the building that housed the knights; he was going with a particular purpose in mind. Having just left Toby sleeping soundly, he was determined to find Stephen and clear the air between them. But his thoughts inevitably kept drifting back to Toby, her delicious body in his arms and the myriad of emotions that continued to assault him.

It was true; he felt as if he was suffering a gentle onslaught of emotions that he never believed himself capable of. It was something terrifying and wonderful, something that caused him to lose control as if he was a weakling. Whatever power Toby had over him, it was stronger than all of the might he had ever faced. All she had to do was give him a word, a look, and he surrendered like a fool.

But he had to get a grip on himself as much as he was able to. The first step would be to straighten out whatever odd situation had evolved between him and Stephen. And the second would be to determine the next course of action with Mortimer on their heels. Still, thoughts of Toby filled his mind and it was an effort to concentrate on issues that he knew must be the priority.

The knight's quarters was a stone building built against the side of the outer wall. It was a badly lit structure with small, cell-like chambers. Tate entered the building and into a small common room with a muted fire burning in the hearth. He'd barely closed the door when one of the cell doors flew open and Kenneth appeared with a sword in his hand.

When he saw it was Tate, he lowered the weapon.

"'Tis you," he muttered.

"Aye, it's me," Tate replied. "Where's Stephen?"

Kenneth yawned, tossing the sword back onto his bed. "He relieved me upon the battlements about an hour ago."

Tate turned for the door but Kenneth stopped him. "Is something amiss?" he asked.

Tate paused after opening the panel. "Nay," he said after a moment. "I simply must speak with him."

Kenneth wisely kept his mouth shut, suspecting that whatever it was did not involve him. If it was a private conversation between Tate and Stephen, there was little doubt as to the subject. As Tate shut the door behind him, Kenneth wondered if he should follow to make sure there was no bloodshed with the undoubtedly volatile subject. On second thought, however, he decided to stay his course and simply remain an uninvolved bystander. With a woman involved, it was the safest course to take. Or so he believed.

Tate mounted the steep stairs to the battlements of the gatehouse, his trained gaze moving over the cold and dark landscape, searching for anything out of the ordinary. With a gaping hole where the main gates used to be, he was particularly on edge even though there were thirty soldiers patrolling the gap. A loop half-way around the wall walk brought him right to Stephen.

The big knight was on the west wall, in quiet conversation with one of the knight's from Warkworth. The bulk of their army had remained, at least until the gates were repaired, so several hundred soldiers and a few knights lingered. When Stephen saw Tate, he excused himself from the conversation and went to his liege.

"Nothing to report, my lord," he said. "All remains quiet."

Tate nodded, his dark gaze moving over the pre-dawn landscape once more. "Very well," he replied. Then he continued to stand there, gazing over the view but not really seeing it. Stephen stood beside him silently, vigilantly, as he always had. Tate finally crossed his arms and emitted a heavy sigh.

"Stephen, I must ask you something," he said.

"Of course, my lord."

"You and I have long been friends, have we not?"

Stephen nodded slowly. "It has been my honor."

"We have seen much of life and death together."

"Indeed we have."

"I consider you one of the finest men I have ever served with."

"A true privilege, my lord."

Tate turned to look at him. "I would not want anything to ruin that."

Stephen returned his gaze. "Nor would I."

Tate cleared his throat, a waiver in his confidence. "I find that I must be honest with you, Stephen. I suppose I should have been from the onset but I was unsure how to go about it."

"Speak your mind, my lord."

Tate lifted his eyebrows with some hesitation. "I am attempting to," he cleared his throat again. "You were with me when Catherine died."

Stephen's expression visibly eased. "Aye, my lord. I was there."

Tate was having difficulty looking at him. "I was positive that I would never recover from it. But it seems that I was wrong."

Stephen could see where this was leading; he'd known it from the start. It was only a matter of time before Tate confronted him about the situation with Toby. After the gift of the kitten earlier, it was expected. There was no point in dancing around the subject as Tate was doing so he cleared his throat, averting his gaze.

"In truth, my lord, I never had a chance," he said quietly. "She has eyes only for you."

Tate stopped fidgeting and looked at him. "What?"

Stephen's gaze moved to the landscape beyond the walls. "Mistress Toby," he clarified. "She has eyes only for you. I suppose it was my pride that caused me to see only what I wanted to see. I knew you were growing fond of her as I was. I thought I could win her over but I was wrong."

Tate stared at him. "I remember back in Cartingdon when Kenneth jested with you about marrying her and ruling the town. Do you recall?"

Stephen nodded "I do."

"You clearly showed no interest."

"I had none at the time."

"What changed your mind?"

"What changed yours?"

They gazed at each other for a moment before breaking into soft laughter. It was a welcome moment in a situation that could have quite easily gone the other way. As small as the gesture was, it was a relief, a moment between friends that signaled things were righting themselves. Tate finally shook his head.

"I have no idea," he muttered. "All I know is that day we ventured into the mist to inspect sheep, something inside me changed. The woman already has unearthly beauty but that day, I saw incredible strength in her as well. Beyond that, I cannot explain more. All I know is that I see a chance for happiness with her again and I will take it. The woman is coming to mean a great deal to me."

Stephen's cornflower blue gaze lingered on him a moment. "Do you love her?"

Tate looked at him as if surprised by the question. He was about to deny it but found, in his heart, that he could not. He averted his gaze as if suddenly defeated, unable to muster the strength to deny the obvious. "I believe that I do."

"Have you told her?"

"Nay."

"You should, you know. She loves you as well."

Tate looked at him again. "How would you know that?"

Stephen's eyes glimmered. "I do not for sure. But if she looked at me the way she looks at you, then I would know that she loves me."

Tate felt strangely empowered by that statement, as if his heart suddenly sprouted wings. It felt light, happy. "If that is true, then I am indeed blessed," he said, turning to look Stephen fully in the face. "But I am deeply sorry if my relationship with her affects our friendship."

Stephen's gaze lingered on him. "It does not," he said quietly. "It would take much more than that to destroy the trust that you and I have achieved over the years."

Tate puffed out his cheeks with relief. "I had hoped so but in truth I was not sure. When a woman is involved, things can go very badly."

"We are better than that, my lord."

"I hoped so."

"Besides that, we have more pressing matters to focus on."

"Indeed we do."

"There are the missing gates, the threat of a Mortimer counter-attack, and our imminent trip to London which has thus far been delayed."

Tate nodded faintly, thinking of the priorities that had faced him two days ago were now becoming sidelined by his growing involvement with Toby. But Stephen was correct; there were more pressing matters that must be the priority. It was a struggle for Tate to refocus on something other than Toby.

The silence between them settled, though not uncomfortable. Tate had said what he had meant to say and Stephen had conceded. More than that, there was a clear understanding now. They both felt relieved by it.

"Congratulations on your betrothal, by the way," Stephen finally said. "May you have much joy in this marriage."

"Thank you."

"There is one more thing, however."

"What is that?

Stephen turned to look at him, an intense look to his eye. "Should anything ever happen to you, know that I will take very good care of your widow."

Tate's eyes widened. Then, he burst out giggling like a fool. Stephen tried to hold back the chuckles but soon he was roaring with laughter. After a few moments of uncharacteristic snorting, Stephen sobered with dramatic speed and wiped the smile from his face.

"I am serious."

Tate abruptly stopped laughing and gawked at him in outrage. He balled up a fist and took a swing at Stephen's jaw, but in the process burst into more laughter and ended up almost falling over the parapet when Stephen side-stepped the blow. Hooting and snorting, the two of them made their way back towards the gatehouse as the sun began to rise in the distant east. But the laughter soon turned to conversation and by the time they hit the gatehouse, they were already discussing the priorities of the coming day. It was as if no contention had ever been.

In the bailey below, Kenneth heard the chortling. He stood below the wall walk, watching Tate and Stephen, hearing the laughter and saying a silent prayer that he wasn't picking up body parts. He had been standing there since Tate had left the knight's quarters, watching and waiting. With a woman involved, he had no way of knowing what turn the situation would take. He was glad it wasn't the wrong turn.

Without even trying, Toby could have done more damage than Mortimer's army could have ever dreamed of.

CB

TOBY AWOKE TO the sounds of shouts coming from the bailey. Every so often, a dog would bark or a bird would screech. She was lying on her back on the bed in the master's chamber, one arm over her head and the other clutching the coverlet to her naked chest. She lay there a moment, staring up at the ceiling and forgetting, for a split second, where she was. She didn't recognize the place. Then, remembrance dawned.

It all came tumbling upon her. She remembered Tate from the night before and her heart began to pound at the mere thought. She remembered everything, from the moment he had first touched her until she had fallen asleep in his powerful embrace. Warm delirium swept her as she thought on the power, the passion, and the excitement. She thought it might have been a dream until she lifted her hand and smelled Tate on her flesh. She lay there a moment, inhaling deeply, feeling her body tremble at his scent. She should have been shocked at her behavior, ashamed at the very least, but she found that she was neither. She felt a fulfillment in her soul that she'd never had before. But her warm thoughts faded as she looked around, noticing that she was quite alone in the bed and in the room.

She sat up, still holding the coverlet to her chest. The kitten suddenly leapt onto the bed and she petted the little beast absently. Her thoughts drifted to the night before once again and she thought of Tate's magical touch, the heat of his mouth, the gentle power of his body when he took her. She hadn't been prepared for that intimate action but had very quickly succumbed to his passion. It had been the most powerful physical and emotional event of her life, propelling her onto a plane that she had never known to exist. But now that she found herself alone in the bedchamber, embarrassment was beginning to join her puzzlement.

Perhaps Tate had left because he had been embarrassed, too. He had left without a word. Perhaps he left because he realized it had all been a horrible mistake. From the deeply personal memories of the night before to a creeping humiliation, she wrapped herself in the coverlet and went in search of her clothes. As she made her way to her neatly stacked trunks, she passed next to the hearth and made a startling discovery.

Someone had drawn a smiling face into the ashes. Toby stood there a moment, staring down at the two eyes and big smiling mouth. That had not been there the previous night. It occurred to her that Tate must have drawn the face when he had left that morning, not wanting to wake her but wanting to leave some mention of his passing. One corner of her mouth twitched and then the other; soon, she was laughing softly, laughing harder when the kitten walked through the face and left little paw prints all over it.

As she finally reached her trunks, she also noticed a basin of clean water on the nearby table. That hadn't been there last night, either; nor had the small wooden platter of cheese and bread. She felt awful that she had thought poorly of Tate, that he had abandoned her after their night of passion. Obviously, the man had put a good deal of thought into greeting her with a pleasant morning and she adored him for it. Her heart was swelling so with happiness that she was sure it would burst. With a huge smile, Toby dropped the coverlet and grabbed her cake of lavender and lemon rind soap.

When she finished washing with the soap and tepid water, she dried off with a linen sheet they had brought from Forestburn and proceeded to dress in pantalets, a linen shift and brown surcoat that emphasized her slender waist. She brushed her hair furiously and pulled it away from her face with a strip of cloth that wrapped all the way around her head, tying a bow just behind her right ear. It was a very flattering style for the heart-shape of her face.

As she pulled on her shoes, she threw bits of cheese to the kitten. When all of the bread and cheese were gone, and she and the kitten were fed, she collected the cat and quit the chamber with the intention of taking the kitten outside to relieve itself. But more importantly, she wanted to find Tate. The kitten was just a convenient excuse.

The keep was dark as she made her way down the deadly stairs. She hardly heard a sound. But as she neared the great hall, she could hear the men inside, mostly wounded, and she ventured into the cavernous room. It was dim and smelling of smoke from the fire in the hearth. The very first thing she saw was Stephen directly to her left, tending to one of his patients. He looked up and their eyes met. Startled to see him, Toby did the only thing she could do; she smiled timidly.

"Good morn to you, Sir Stephen," she said. "I fear I must have been more exhausted than I thought. I seem to have slept long into the morning."

Stephen's gaze lingered on her. "No harm done. You obviously needed the rest."

She shrugged faintly, looking around the room and petting the cat in her arms. "May I help you this morning?"

Stephen finished securing the bandage of the man he was working on and stood up. "There is not much to do," he followed her gaze around the room. "Most of the men seem to be healing steadily. The only thing you could possibly do is lift their spirits with a kind word."

"Perhaps they would like to pet my cat."

He looked at the animal and cracked a smile. "I fear that grown men aren't as attached to felines as women and children are."

She grinned, noticing that he did not seem tense or angry with her this morning. Perhaps Tate had taken her advice and spoken to him. She could only hope.

"I am going to find my young friend with the chest wound," she said pointedly. "I will wager that he would like to pet my cat."

Stephen's smiled faded. "He is not here."

"Oh? Where is he?"

He hesitated. "He passed away last night."

Her face fell. "Oh," she whispered, looking pained. "I had hoped... you said that you thought he would...."

Stephen moved towards her, wiping his hands off on a rag. "I said that he would survive provided that poison did not set in. Unfortunately, it did. It took him very quickly."

Toby nodded, realizing that she was blinking tears away. But she couldn't stop them. "He was so young," she wept softly. "He was only sixteen years old. He was just a boy."

Stephen stood next to her, wanting to comfort her but knowing that he should leave that to Tate. It had been made clear to him that Toby was the property of his liege. Still, she was upset and he put his big hand on her back in a comforting gesture.

"Do not weep for him," he said quietly. "He is no longer in agony. He is with God."

"But he was so young."

"I know," he patted her back and took his hand away. "But that is the way of war. It does not take young or old into consideration."

Toby wiped at her eyes and turned away, heading for the keep entry. Stephen watched her go, his cornflower eyes lingering on her slender beauty. He found himself once again regretting that he had not been successful in his wooing attempt. But he could not linger on regrets; if his discussion with Tate earlier that day was any indication, the man was in love with a woman he once thought dreadful. Stephen was glad that, at least, she was in good hands. Tate didn't view her as a contest won. With a final glance at her shapely backside, he turned back to his patients.

The weak morning sun was bright and Toby dried the last of her tears, shielding her eyes from the glare. The new keep stairs were braced up against the stone edifice and Toby took the stairs gingerly; they seemed to sway a bit, which made her nervous. When she reached the bottom, she looked back up the stairs to see just how precarious the stairs really were. Shaking her head at the rickety steps, she turned around and almost ran headlong into Wallace.

His hair was wild and he smelled like manure. Toby took a step back from the man just so she wouldn't be so close to him.

"Good day, my lady," he greeted. "I see that you are looking well this morn."

It was as much as the man had said to her since they had been introduced. She nodded. "It is a fine morning," she said. "Do you know where Sir Tate is?"

Wallace raised an eyebrow. "Ah, he is more than a 'sir', my lady," he corrected her. "He is an earl and addressed accordingly."

She nodded quickly. "Of course, I'd forgotten," she corrected herself. "Have you seen him this morning?"

"He is outside the walls, my lady. They are having trouble fitting the new gates and he is supervising the installation. I will take you to him if you wish."

Toby looked to the gaping hole in the wall where the great wooden gates use to be. "I do not wish to distract him," she said, although it wasn't the truth. She wanted to see him very much. "It can wait."

With her gaze lingering on the open gates and the activity surrounding it, she turned for the kitchens that were to the rear of the keep. It took her a moment to realize that Wallace was following her. She looked up at him, a mildly friendly-but-puzzled look on her face. He clasped his hands behind his back and pretended not to notice her curious stare.

"It is a fine day today," he said, looking up to the billowing clouds above. "A good day for rebuilding."

It was odd conversation from a man who had thus far gone out of his way to make her feel unwelcome. She was wary of his company.

"I am sure it is," she didn't know what else to say. In her arms, the kitten squirmed so she set him down and watched him hop away. "At least it is not raining."

"Ah, but it will," Wallace sniffled loudly and continued to look up at the sky. "Come the nooning hour, it will pour. It always does."

Toby simply nodded, unsure what to say to that. She was increasingly wondering why the man was tailing her. When she went to collect the kitten so he would not get trampled by some nearby horses, she noticed that Wallace continued to follow.

She stopped beating around the bush and faced him. "Is there something you wished to say to me?"

"Say to you? What do you mean?"

"I mean that you have not said more than five words to me since my arrival. Now you are making conversation so I assumed there was something more that you wished to say to me."

His bushy gray eyebrows lifted, as if surprised by the frankness of her statement. Then he shook his head. "I have nothing to say to you, lady," he said, but just as swiftly corrected himself. "But I suppose if I was going to say something, it would be to thank you."

"Thank me? For what?"

"For your help with the wounded during the siege the other day," he shrugged his big shoulders. "With the recent loss of your sister…

well, you surprised me with your courage. That is rare in a woman and I would congratulate you."

Toby stared at him. He seemed quite gruff with the praise and she couldn't decide if she was offended or flattered. So she nodded unsteadily and turned away, leaving Wallace standing there, watching her, with a puzzled expression on his face. After a moment, he shrugged again and walked back the way he had come. He still didn't understand women, not after all these years. He probably never would. He'd given the woman a compliment and she had not seemed pleased with it.

Toby kept on walking, petting the kitten and realizing that Wallace's statement, though he'd not meant to do so, had unearthed thoughts of Ailsa. As she gazed up into the blue sky and breathed the fresh air, she realized that she missed her sister very much. The loss was still shocking and painful. She was starting to feel some guilt that her growing relationship with Tate had given her momentary reprieve from her grief. She felt some remorse that she wasn't completely miserable day and night from the loss of Ailsa. The more thoughts of her sister haunted her, the more she found herself hurting for the life cut short.

Toby wandered around the circular keep, realizing when she was very nearly at the doorstep that she had come upon the chapel. She paused a moment, gazing at the rough-hewn door to the tiny sanctuary and feeling tears sting her eyes. Ailsa was in there and so was deep pain. But she had to face it. With the cat in one hand, she pushed open the door and entered the cool, dark room. It was barely big enough to hold more than a dozen people at any given time. Very small lancet slits cut into the outer wall allowed some light to enter, but it was still dark and eerie and smelling of the fresh dirt from Ailsa's burial. Setting the kitten down near the door, she made her way to the fresh grave near the altar.

As she stared down at the dirt, the tears came. They popped out of her eyes and onto the fresh earth. She knelt down, her hand on the grave, guts aching with grief.

"Oh, Ailsa," she wept softly. "I wish I could tell you all that has happened since you went away. There is so much to tell. So much you were right about."

The chapel remained still; no one answered her. Toby sat down next to Ailsa's grave, now both hands in the soft, cold dirt.

"You asked me once if Dragonblade could marry me," she whispered, tears coursing over her lips and falling to the floor. "Would you believe me if I told you that he could? I am to become Lady Dragonblade and I cannot even tell you that. I cannot even watch you rejoice about it and then scold you to keep quiet."

She thought of her sister, skipping around, cheering at the prospect of her sister marrying Tate. Toby closed her eyes miserably, sobbing as visions of a jubilant Ailsa filled her thoughts. Her head was lowered and her eyes closed so that she did not see the chapel door open slightly; a faint stream of sunlight trickling in as Tate entered silently and closed the door behind him. Toby did not hear him; all she could hear at the moment was her sorrow.

She sat next to the grave for quite some time, her fingers in the dirt, thinking of her sister and wondering how she was going to get along without her. She was expecting her to burst through the door at any moment or perhaps demand to know, yet again, why she could not marry young Edward. The thought brought a weepy smile to Toby's lips. She could only imagine her sister as a queen; what a young tyrant they would all have to deal with.

But she could not wallow in agony though she wanted to. She knew that she had to be strong and move forward. The tears were drying and she wiped at her face, removing the last remnants. The kitten meowed, reminding Toby that she had a very small charge that required her attention, and she brushed her hands off as she stood up. It was easier to forget her sorrow when she focused on something else; a little orange ball, at the moment, would have to suffice.

"Are you all right?"

Tate's soft voice floated upon the cool air and she started, whirling around to face the man who was lingering in the shadows. Their eyes met and he smiled timidly, stepping out into the light. For a moment, they just stared at each other, the air between them filled with unspoken emotion. Then Tate broke the silence.

"Forgive me," he said quietly. "I did not mean to startle you but I did not want to intrude until you were finished."

Toby's heart was thumping painfully against her ribs as he approached; gazing into his dark eyes, she was extremely glad to see him. Tate walked up to her and took her hand, kissing it gently. Toby remembered his kisses from last night and couldn't help the intimate thoughts that filled her head, inappropriate and wicked as they were.

"I am all right," she replied to his initial question. "How long have you been standing there?"

"Not long," his gaze devoured her. "Wallace said that you were looking for me."

She nodded. "I was," she said. "I just wanted to say good morn, I suppose."

His gaze was extraordinarily gentle upon her; his eyes moved over her face, her forehead, the delightful style of her hair. She looked exquisite this morning and his heart was swelling hugely at the sight of her.

"And a very good morning to you as well, my lady," he addressed her as he said he would; as a noble lady. Then he chuckled, losing some of his confidence. "I must say that I am rather surprised that you are speaking to me this morning. I half expected you to… well, I was not sure if you would look so kindly upon me this morn."

Her eyebrows rose. "Why not?"

He scratched his forehead, suddenly having difficulty looking at her. "For my lack of control last night." He squared his broad shoulders and forced himself to fix her in the eye. "I swear to you, I have never suffered such a complete lack of control ever in my life. What happened last night… Elizabetha, if I could apologize enough or make appropriate amends, please know that I would gladly do so. I do not know what came over me. All I know was that something filled me the likes of which I have never experienced. I should not have done what I did last night and I pray that you will forgive my impetuousness."

It was apparent, by his speech, that he had been giving much thought to the subject. Toby stared at him, her eyes wide and her mouth popping open. "Do you mean to say that you regret it, then?"

He almost nodded but saw, very quickly, that it would probably not be the best response. He put his hands on her upper arms, gripping her tightly. "No, sweetheart," he said evenly. "I do not regret it. But I should not have been so bold with you. I should not have forced myself upon you and for that, I am truly sorry. I should have been more considerate. It should not have been something so brashly taken and I am deeply sorry for that. But I could not help myself."

She gazed at him with her lovely almond-shaped eyes, her porcelain beauty so sweet and ethereal. She seemed to be mulling over his answer.

"If anyone should apologize, it should be me for allowing you to take such liberties," she said quietly. "But I realize that I am not sorry at all. God knows, I should be. I should be horrified and ashamed. But I am not because it seemed the most natural of things. You are to be my husband, are you not? Perhaps... perhaps I feel that you already are."

He smiled faintly. "If that is true, then I am an extremely fortunate man."

She met his smile. "It is true."

His grip on her tightened. "Then let us not wait. Let us see our marriage today."

Her eyes widened. "Today?"

He nodded firmly. "There is a church in Harbottle. A small one, but we can be married there today."

Toby was suddenly so giddy that she felt faint. All she could do was nod at the man. Tate kissed her swiftly and ushered her towards the door.

"Then go and dress," he instructed. "I will prepare an escort to take us into town."

Toby was in a daze, pausing a moment to pick up the kitten before she left the chapel.

"Are you sure?" she asked. "So soon, I mean? We only just became betrothed yesterday."

He paused as they stepped out into the sun, the excited expression on his face dampening somewhat. "There I go again," he muttered. "I am forcing myself upon you and not giving you any say in the matter."

She shook her head. "That is not what I meant," she said quickly. "'Tis simply that I do not want you to feel as if you must rush into this after what happened last…."

She couldn't even say it, lowering her gaze and looking away. Even though she did not regret what had happened, still, she was not yet brave enough to speak frankly of it. Strange, given her frank nature. Tate's dark eyes twinkled and he put his hands on her arms again, pulling her up against him. His forehead rested against the top of her lowered head.

"What happened to us last night only made me realize that I cannot wait any longer to call you wife," he murmured, kissing the top of her head. "The sooner we wed, the happier we will be."

She lifted her eyes, smiling shyly at him, and he laughed softly as he kissed her again, this time on her soft lips. He wanted to do more but dare not make a spectacle in public. At least, not until she was legally his. Putting his arm around her shoulders, he escorted her in the direction of the keep.

He couldn't even tell her what was truly on his mind after his conversation with Stephen that morning. They were headed to London as soon as the gates were repaired and he was loath to leave her behind. In fact, he couldn't even stomach the thought. At the moment, he simply wanted to feel his joy at becoming Toby's husband. The rest, he would deal with at the appropriate time.

CHAPTER TWELVE

"**H**E TOOK A wife," the general announced.

Hamlin's eyebrows rose. "Who did?"

"De Lara," the general said it as if he could hardly believe it. "One of our men trailed them from the castle into the town yesterday and saw them at the church. He married her yesterday."

Hamlin's surprise only increased. "Two days after a siege, he marries?" He looked at the men seated around him; they were still in the encampment in the woods where they had been for three days. It had been a relatively uneventful period until this shocking bit of news. De Roche was astounded. "De Lara must not have a care in the world if he is taking a wife at this time. A very strange move for a usually guarded man."

The general shrugged. "Who knows why men do what they do? All I know is that he has indeed married. A very beautiful woman from what I am told."

De Roche turned to his general, his mind working over the information. "And you trust the source?"

The general nodded. "The same man who tailed them to Cartingdon. In fact, he believes de Lara's wife to be the Cartingdon heiress but he cannot be sure."

For three days they had been mulling over their next move, sending out spies to see if they could gain headway on de Lara's movements. So far, they had received nothing useful. Harbottle had been swiftly repaired and Warkworth's army remained. There were reports that reinforcements were arriving from Alnwick, but so far, they'd seen no truth of that. The hope was that Mortimer's army would arrive from the Marches before Alnwick arrived to support Harbottle. In either case, the impending battle would prove to be explosive. At the moment, they were playing a waiting game.

"So de Lara marries," Hamlin stroked his chin and began to pace. He held up a finger. "This is good news, in fact. Here we sit, waiting for Mortimer's reinforcements, all the while looking to find a weakness we can use against de Lara. If we can exploit him, then a battle will be unnecessary. Lives will be saved. That is a good thing."

The general who had delivered the news sat next to the old vizier, trying to generate some heat back into his bones. The pouring rain outside had all of them wet and cold.

"So tell us why this is such good news?" he demanded as he took some wine for himself.

Hamlin smiled coldly. "A weakness," he said as if it was the most obvious thing in the world. "What motivates a man more than warfare?"

The others looked around like idiots, trying to glean an answer from vacant expressions. The old general finally spoke. "What?"

Hamlin looked at the fools around him and shook his head. "Love," he said obviously. "Love motivates a man more than warfare. We can lay siege to his castle, burn his troops, kill his friends and de Lara will not falter. But take his wife and the man will bargain."

The men in the tent continued to look at each other, some in understanding, some in disagreement. Hamlin threw the cup in his hand to the ground and tossed up his arms.

"Fools," he snapped. "We get the woman and de Lara will give us whatever we want. This entire war will be over."

The general finally shook his head. "There are no guarantees," he said. "Perhaps de Lara was forced to marry her. Perhaps he does not care for her in the least."

Hamlin put his hands on his hips. "He marries in the midst of a crisis? I would say this is more than a forced marriage. A man would only do such a thing in the middle of this hell only if he wanted to."

"So you are saying use the woman against him?"

Hamlin nodded as if the man was a simpleton. "De Lara's weakness. We have found it."

"How can you be so sure?"

"For the very reasons I mentioned."

"Then it will not be easy to get at her."

"Probably not. But we will take whatever opportunity we can." Hamlin reclaimed his cup and went for more wine, listening to the thunder outside. "Send out more men to hide in the shadows and watch de Lara. Watch Harbottle closely. I would wager there will be another opportunity, especially if he is bold enough to venture from the safe confines of the castle and into the village. If he does it again, perhaps we can catch them along the open road."

"He will travel with an army for protection."

"Or he will only travel with a few in order to not draw attention to himself," Hamlin shot back. "How many men did he take with him to the village yesterday? Did you ask?"

The general nodded. "Indeed I did. He took two knights and six men at arms."

Hamlin lifted his eyebrows. "You see? He only took a small contingent. Now he is overconfident. He believes he is not being watched at the moment."

"Never. De Lara is not that stupid."

"Nevertheless, you will put your best men on him. If an opportunity presents itself, we will take it. We will take *her*."

The general shook his head. "We cannot even get close to the king. What makes you think we can get close to de Lara's wife?"

Hamlin paused as he poured his wine. "Your men will have to be clever and swift. I care not how she is taken, but get her. If we hold her, we hold the kingdom."

The general cast him a long look but did as he was ordered. More men would need to be dispatched, more spies to watch de Lara's every move and wait for an opportunity. It wasn't going to be easy, if such a thing was even possible at all.

CB

"I DO NOT care if you and your entire fleet of servants are up all night," Toby said pointedly. "This keep will be clean by tomorrow morning."

She was facing off against a huffing, puffing Wallace. It was pouring rain outside, loud thunder and bright lightning. But the thunder in the sky was nothing compared to the storm brewing in the great hall of Harbottle. Lady de Lara was now chatelaine and Wallace was having a difficult time with the transition. It was unexpected; more than that, Wallace was offended. His insult against Toby's determination was a volatile combination.

"We have more important things to attend to, my lady," he was trying not to show disrespect to the woman his liege had recently married. "We are still repairing damage from the siege and I hardly think that scrubbing the keep is a priority."

"I will decide what the priorities are," she snapped. "I am in charge here. You will do as you are told."

Wallace's leathered face tightened with fury. "I take my orders from Lord Tate."

Toby lifted an eyebrow. "When you are inside this keep, you take them from me. This is now my domain and the sooner you understand that, the better we shall get along. This keep is an embarrassment and I intend to see it cleaned from top to bottom."

"There is no embarrassment to this place, my lady."

"Are you going to help me or not?"

"I have more important things to do."

"Then get out."

"What?"

"You heard me. Get out. And stay out."

Wallace opened his mouth in outrage but Toby was already moving towards the hearth. A long iron poker stood propped against the wall and she grabbed it, wielding it like a weapon.

"Did you hear me?" she barked. "If you are not going to do as you are told, then you will get out."

His brow furrowed and his teeth bared, preparing for a very sharp retort that would perhaps be not so polite. But Toby swung the poker at him and smacked him across the thigh, not hard enough to do damage but hard enough to sting.

"Out!" she yelled.

When Wallace didn't move fast enough, she took another swing and the old priest jumped out of the way, making his way very quickly towards the keep entry. Toby followed on his heels, swinging the poker again and catching him across the buttocks.

"Out!"

Wallace shot out through the entry door as if the devil himself was on his heels. He was half-way down the stairs when Toby appeared on the landing, leveling the poker in front of her.

"And stay out until you can learn to obey my wishes!"

Wallace ran across the bailey and disappeared somewhere in the vicinity of the knight's quarters. Upon the battlements near the gatehouse, Tate and Kenneth had been given a marvelous view of the last few seconds when Wallace ran from the keep with Toby chasing after him. They both watched Wallace scurry across the ward and out of sight as Toby stood on the entry landing, holding a very large fire poker and threatening him. After a few moments of stunned silence, Kenneth looked at Tate, whose storm cloud eyes were riveted to his wife. He seemed quite unconcerned about the entire incident.

"Hmmm," he muttered casually. "I was wondering how long it would take for Elizabetha and Wallace to come to blows. I see that I did not have long to wait."

He looked at Kenneth, whose head was lowered. Upon closer inspection, the man seemed to be shaking. Tate peered even closer and realized that Kenneth was far gone with laughter. The normally stoic and unflappable knight was red with mirth. Realizing that it was indeed a very comical scene, it was a struggle for Tate to keep a smile off his face.

"Stop laughing," he commanded quietly. "For I must go confront my wife and if I remember your laughter, it will be impossible for me to keep a straight face. Stop it, I say."

Kenneth took a deep breath and lifted his head, struggling to focus. "Of course," he said, though it was in an oddly strangled tone. "It was not the least bit humorous."

"Aye, it was, but I doubt Elizabetha will think so and I have no desire to feel a blow from that poker. You may see me running out of the keep with an angry woman on my heels."

Kenneth couldn't help it; he busted out into muffled guffaws and Tate slugged him weakly on the shoulder before making his way back down to the bailey. Crossing through the mud and rain, he mounted the steps to the keep and took refuge inside the dark, stale entry. Immediately, he spied Toby in the great hall ahead of him. She was without the poker and speaking with Althel and another old servant. Young Edward was also standing with her, listening intently. Tate walked upon the group.

"Greetings," he was focused on his wife, although Edward responded to his salutation. "I do not wish to interrupt, but may I have a word, madam?"

Althel and the old servant immediately stepped away. Edward was a little slower, not realizing Tate had meant a private word with Toby but understanding the matter quickly when Tate cast him a long look. The young king disappeared as Tate focused on his wife.

As he gazed at her, he could hardly believe they had been married an entire day. It seemed as if he had never been without her yet he could still hardly believe she belonged to him. He'd met the woman a week ago and already, she was indelibly a part of him. When she smiled he reached out and pulled her against him, kissing her gently.

"I have not seen you since dawn," he murmured, kissing the end of her nose. "I had to come and see you again."

Toby's entire body tingled with the thrill of his embrace, her heart swelling with joy at his words. She, too, was finding it difficult to believe that they were married, that this man who had abruptly transformed her life was now her husband. Last night had been another glorious night of exploration and lovemaking. It seemed like a dream but it was a dream she was glad never to awaken from. She never knew she could be so happy in spite of the highs and lows of the past several days. It was like walking on clouds, every minute of every day.

"I am glad that you could not stay away," she wound her arms around his neck. "It all seems quite empty without you."

He kissed her again, nuzzling her cheek. "I think you are doing well enough at keeping yourself occupied," he said, pulling back to look at her. "You are busy enough to chase Wallace from the keep. I have never seen the man so terrified."

She lifted an eyebrow at him. "He would not help me clean the keep. So I told him to get out and stay out until he could learn to obey my wishes. I refuse to live in squalor and that man seems content to."

Tate sighed. "He is used to running Harbottle his own way. You must give him time to become accustomed to you."

"He says he takes orders only from you."

"I will rectify that."

"Please understand that I am not trying to dominate the man, but he must learn to take orders from us both."

"Agreed." He leaned his forehead against her, closing his eyes a moment to relish the feel of her against him. "So you intend to clean this keep, do you? You have quite a task ahead of you."

"I know," she snuggled against him, delighting in his powerful warmth. She fell silent a moment before speaking again. "But there is another task that is far more important to me. Will you hear it?"

He opened his eyes and looked at her. "I believe I already know it."

She pursed her lips, toying with the ties on his tunic. "I must return, Tate. You know this. Every day I delay there is more chance of someone stealing our sheep or ransacking what is left of the manor. I do not want to lose what we have left. I must return to see what pieces I have to pick up."

He sighed again, rubbing his cheek against her forehead. Then he released her, taking her hand and leading her over to the massive table. Sitting her on the bench, he took a seat beside her, straddling the wooden plank. He took her hand, holding it warmly as he thought on what to say.

"And I have priorities as well," he said, studying her features in the firelight. "I was supposed to leave for London five days ago. But instead, I have seen a siege and a marriage that has me slightly off track. Every day I delay, Edward could be in jeopardy. I have a mission to complete. You have known this since the day we met."

She smiled weakly. "You came for money for Edward's cause. You ended up with a wife."

He grinned. "I will take the money, of course, but somehow that seems rather insignificant by comparison."

"What do you mean?"

"The wife was by far the better deal."

Her smile broadened and she lowered her gaze modestly; she was thrilled and flattered by his compliments. It was enough to make her feel giddy but she managed to keep her head.

"Then, may I ask, what seems to be the most pressing in your view?" she asked. "Of course I would say that my wants are most important to me, but I also realize that you have far larger issues at hand. I am only worried about a small parish in Northumberland while you are worried about an entire country. What will we do?"

He watched her as she spoke, noticing how her nose crinkled when she asked a question. She had the most amazing face and he was in danger of becoming swept away the longer he looked at her.

"Well," he grunted, shifting on the bench and pulling her between his legs. "I am destined to take Edward and head for London at some point; however, we are safe for the moment so I am not entirely inclined to move from this haven. Secondly, I suspect that when I do go, you will be no less determined to return to Forestburn and I do not want you returning there alone. In fact, I do not want you out of my sight. So I would imagine that we should take a day and ride to Forestburn so you can at least assess the damage and assure the town that all is as it should be and that you are still in charge. With your father's death, however, there is no more lord mayor of Cartingdon."

She lifted her eyebrows in agreement, trying not to think on the fact that she was both fatherless and motherless. It brought inherent sorrow. She tried to stay focused to the issue at hand.

"My father was mayor for many years," she said softly. "The people of Cartingdon will not soon forget him. For now, I think it wise that they see me and know that they have not been abandoned. I will secure a few of the local farmers to tend our sheep, mingling them with their own stock and splitting any increases in the herds, which will take care of the problem of our sheep for the time being. I will also need to scavenge the ruins of Forestburn for anything salvageable."

"Do you think you can accomplish this all in one day?"

"I do not know. Can you at least give me two?"

He nodded after a moment. "I suspect I can. We will go tomorrow."

She smiled gratefully. "Thank you."

He returned her grin, giving her a squeeze and kissing her cheek. "My pleasure, madam. Is there anything else we should discuss before I take my leave of you and return to the bailey?"

"One more thing."

"What is that?"

She looked at him, hesitantly. "When you leave for London, will I stay here?"

His smile faded as he gazed into her almond-shaped eyes. "You will be safe here."

She took a long, deep breath, lowering her gaze. "How… how long do you expect to be gone?"

"I do not know."

"Are you going into battle?"

"Aye."

She sat there, looking at her hands, before falling against him and burying her face in his shoulder. His big arms enveloped her, his face on the top of her head. As the flames in the hearth snapped and smoked, he rocked her gently in the weak light of the hall. He knew what she was feeling without benefit of words; mostly because he was feeling the same thing himself. There was already a longing for her in his heart that he could not begin to describe.

"I could not bear if it something happened to you," her voice was muffled against his shoulder. "I have lost my entire family. I could not survive if I lost you as well."

She could feel him sigh into the top of her head. "I am sorry to cause you such fear," he said quietly. "But I have a destiny to fulfill and so does young Edward. A man is ruling England who has no right to the throne. I must make sure that the rightful king takes his place and that the threat of Mortimer is vanquished."

She pulled her head from his shoulder and wiped at her face; he realized that she was crying and it touched him more than he could have imagined. Women had cried for him before, of course, but their tears had never meant anything to him. But Toby's mattered a great deal. Before she could wipe all of her tears away, he took her face in his hands, forcing her to look at him.

"Elizabetha," he whispered. "Look at me."

It took her a moment to lift her eyes to meet his; they were still full of tears. He smiled gently, caressing her soft cheeks with his thumbs. "I have been a warrior for many years and have yet, in all that time, to become grievously injured. I can only swear that I will do my best to continue that tradition. I will do my best to return to you."

"I could not bear it if I lost you," she murmured, blinking and spattering tears on his hand.

He pulled her face to his lips and kissed her tenderly. "I swear to you upon my oath that I will do all in my power to ensure that you do not. I want to return to you as badly as you want me to."

"But I am so frightened for you."

He lifted an eyebrow. "You? Frightened? I do not believe it. The woman I saw this morning with a poker in her hand is not the frightened type."

He was attempting to lighten the mood but she wanted no part of it. "Why can I not go with you to London? I swear that I will not be a burden."

He looked at her as if she was mad, dropping his hands from her face. "I am going into battle, sweetheart. You cannot go with me."

"I will bring my poker. I can fight alongside you."

He stared at her. Then he burst out laughing. He put his arms around her again and held her close, chuckling.

"You probably would," he said. "And I would be proud to have you. However, I would be more worried for you than for me and distraction in my profession can be deadly. I could not have you as a distraction, a lovely one though you may be."

She could see that he would not be swayed. Resignation and despair filled her. "Then I hope that God will not be so cruel as to take away everyone who is close to me at the same time," she said softly. "My father, my mother, then Ailsa... perhaps you. Do you suppose that I am being punished for all of those years I disagreed with my father at every turn or punished Ailsa when perhaps I should not have?"

He shook his head slowly, his dark eyes glittering. "I do not believe God to be a vengeful God," he said softly. "In fact, I see him as a kind and generous God. He brought us together, did he not?"

In spite of her fear, she smiled at him, her small hands on both of his cheeks. "I am grateful that He brought you to Cartingdon," she whispered. "I never knew it was possible to feel such things."

"Feel what things?"

Her smiled faded, her hands caressing his stubbled cheeks. After a moment, she shrugged. "Hope and joy," she stumbled through an explanation, not exactly sure how to put her thoughts into words. "I did not think you liked me very much at first. You were quite cold."

He snorted. "I was not."

"Aye, you were," she insisted. "But I do not blame you. I am quite difficult to tolerate sometimes. When we were ambushed in the fog near Lorbottle and you went off in search of our attackers, I was so glad to see you when you returned. But I could never tell you that. I was not even sure why I was happy to see you, but I was."

His smile warmed. "And I was glad to see you as well, but I was not going to tell you, either."

She cocked an eyebrow. "You did indeed tell me. You took my hand and spoke kindly to me. You told me that you did not want to leave but that you had to. Do you not recall this?"

He pretended to be very forgetful. "I said no such thing. It must have been another suitor that told you such silly things."

She pursed her lips irritably. "I have not had any other suitors."

"Hmmm," he scratched his cheek distractedly. "Well, then I suppose I must confess. And there is something else I must confess."

"What is that?"

He pushed a stray lock of hair from her cheek, his storm cloud eyes intense as he gazed at her. "When I returned from chasing assassins through the fog and saw you seated at your father's desk, it was at that precise moment that I realized I was feeling more than normal concern for you. It must have been shortly thereafter that I realized I loved you."

He said it so casually that it took her a moment to comprehend what he had said. Then Toby's eyes opened wide. "You... you *love* me?" she gasped.

He eyed her briefly as if she was mad for thinking otherwise before breaking down into a gentle smile. "Of course, you silly wench," he leaned forward to nuzzle her cheek. "How could you possibly think differently?"

She closed her eyes to his gentle kisses, throwing her arms around his neck and squeezing tightly. Of all things she imagined their relationship to be, love had not truly entered her thoughts until yesterday. Then the notion had crept up on her so subtly that she was not surprised or afraid; just as everything else with Tate, it had seemed the most natural of things. She could not remember when she had not loved the man.

"Oh, Tate," she murmured. "I love you, also. With all my heart, I do."

He laughed softly. They remained in their embrace for quite some time after the conversation died, simply content to hold one another and reflect on their unexpected confession. It had been difficult for Tate to spit out, but he was extremely glad he had; the last person he had confessed his love to had died and to feel adoration again, to admit it, had been a huge step for him to take.

Tate rocked her gently, his cheek against the top of her head and his gaze lingering on the fire. But his warm thoughts faded as his mind inevitably moved to the next few days and what he needed to accomplish. More than that, he knew he was dreading their separation more than she was and it was a distressing thought. If she had begged any longer to accompany him he might have very well brought her along, and that would not have been healthy for either of them.

He was saved by further debate and perhaps failure of his resolve by Kenneth entering the hall. Tate stood up as his knight approached.

"I have come into possession of some information you might find interesting," Kenneth told him. "I have sent for Stephen. He should hear this, too."

"What is wrong?" Tate demanded softly.

Kenneth passed a glance at Toby, who was now rising from the bench. Tate caught the implication and turned to his wife.

"Where are you off to now, sweetheart?" he asked casually.

Toby stepped over the bench and smoothed out her surcoat. "The store room," she said. "I need to see the state of our stores. I am sending Althel and his servants to the living chambers above to start cleaning out those rooms. Everything needs to be scrubbed."

"Aye, General."

She smirked at him and he kissed her on the forehead, sending her along her way. He watched her luscious figure as she went to the corner of the hall where the door was cut into the floor. She lifted the hatch and carefully disappeared down the ladder. When she was out of sight, Tate looked at Kenneth again.

"What in the hell is going on?" he asked in a low voice.

Kenneth lifted an eyebrow. "Our spies have located de Roche's army, camped about six miles to the south."

"And?"

"And they are entrenched into the site. They have even built temporary structures. Our spies seem to think that they are waiting for something."

It didn't take a genius to figure out what he meant. Tate cocked an eyebrow. "Reinforcements?"

Kenneth nodded. "Mortimer's army from Wigmore Castle, perhaps? It would be the most logical assumption. That is where he keeps the bulk of his army."

Tate's mind shuffled through all of the possibilities. As he turned back towards the fire, pensively, Stephen entered the keep and joined the huddle. Kenneth told Stephen what he had just told Tate and the two knights watched their liege closely for his reaction.

"If that is the case and they are truly waiting for reinforcements, then that puts us in a precarious position," Tate finally muttered. "Warkworth remains but I would suspect Mortimer would bring twice their numbers. Harbottle is marginally repaired but I do not believe it can withstand an onslaught from a thousand men, which means we either dig in or we flee." He turned to look at his men. "If Alnwick has not arrived by now, I suspect that they are not coming. Something must have happened to the messenger."

Stephen and Kenneth did not disagree. "What would you propose?" Kenneth asked.

Tate pursed his lips thoughtfully and began to pace. "We need to face the fact that Mortimer has located Edward," he said. "We no longer have the luxury of traveling incognito. With this threat upon us, we need to make it to a larger fortress that can handle such an assault. Harbottle is not strong enough at the moment."

"Where do we go?" Stephen asked.

"Alnwick. It is the closest and largest."

"When?" Stephen asked again.

"Now," Tate told them. "We will waste no more time here. And we take Warkworth's army with us for escort. Ken, you organize the wagons, supplies, weapons, and get Harbottle's army prepared to move out by dusk. Stephen, you have a plethora of wounded that you must mobilize. I suggest you decide your immediate course of action and get to it. I will deal directly with Warkworth and tell them our plans. By nightfall, this place will be empty."

The knights were on the move, a strong sense of urgency filling them. Tate went to the last place he saw his wife, preparing to tell her as gently as he could that their trip to Cartingdon was not to take place. He was dreading her reaction but it could not be helped. He could hear her voice as he descended the ladder into the storage basement.

It was dark and dank, smelling of dirt. Two torches burned against the south wall, sending black soot to the ceiling. Tate spied Toby standing several feet away, speaking with young Edward. The lad had apparently gone into the basement when Tate had chased him out of the hall and now stood with a large piece of cheese in his hand, his cheeks full to bursting. He looked like a chipmunk. Tate cocked an eyebrow as he walked upon the two, his gaze on the fat-cheeked youth.

"You are going to choke if you keep eating as you do," he told him.

Edward's answer was to take another bite. He grinned at Toby, who grinned back. Tate rolled his eyes.

"Enough foolery," he snapped without force. "Edward, go into the hall and wait for me. I have something very important to speak to you about. Do not wander away; I will be up in a few minutes."

Edward's brow furrowed. "You keep chasing me from room to room."

"And I shall be kicking you from room to room if you do not do as I say."

Edward made a face but dutifully did as he was told, grumbling all the way. When he was gone, Tate looked to Toby.

"Now," he said softly, "I must speak to you."

He looked serious and she grew concerned. "What is it?"

He sighed, trying to put it as delicately as possible. "It appears as if our situation has gone from bad to worse. We think that a massive siege may be imminent and I have ordered Kenneth and Stephen to prepare to move out. We are leaving for a more fortified haven."

Her eyes widened. "What has happened?"

"Nothing as of yet. But the army that attacked us two days ago has made encampment to the south and is just sitting there, waiting. The only reason they would not have disbursed is if they are planning another attack or perhaps waiting for reinforcements before doing so. We will presume it is the latter."

Her brow furrowed and she put her hand on his arm. "Where will we go?"

"To Alnwick," he replied, putting his hand over hers. "It is about twenty miles away. We can make it there in a few hours at a fast pace." He rubbed her hand gently. "I am sorry, sweetheart. I know I told you that we could go to Forestburn but I am afraid this latest information will prevent that for the time being. I must get Edward, and you, to safety. Harbottle cannot withstand another siege of large proportions."

She looked up at him, her big eyes glittering with a thousand unspoken words. He could read fear, confusion, disappointment, but most of all, she looked sad. The sorrow only increased until she finally lowered her head.

"I understand," she said quietly. "When do you think we will be able to return to Forestburn?"

"I have no way of knowing. As soon as we are able, I promise."

She nodded her head, still looking at the ground. Then her head came up slightly. "We...," she whispered, catching herself and then starting again. "We will have to leave Ailsa here, will we not?"

It was not a question he had expected. With all of his troubles, he had nearly forgotten about the little girl they had buried two days ago and guilt swept him. He should not have been so insensitive to Toby's feelings. With a gentle hiss, he pulled her into his big arms.

"She is safe in the chapel," he murmured. "No harm will come to her."

Toby broke down into more tears, still expelling grief over her little sister. Tate held her tightly.

"I am sorry," he murmured. "I have caused you nothing but grief since nearly the moment we met. I am sorry we have to leave your sister here. But it will not be forever."

"She will be all alone when we go," she murmured, knowing it was foolish even as she said it but it was her sorrow speaking.

"She is not alone," Tate corrected her gently. "She is in Heaven with your mother and father and, I suspect, a host of other relatives. Perhaps she is even now annoying Red Thor, your Viking forbearer, demanding that he sing the Fairy song."

That brought a smile to her lips and she looked up at him. "You are right, of course," she attempted to wipe her face clean and stop her tears. "I am sorry I am being so foolish. 'Tis just that... well, Ailsa and I have never been separated, not ever. This will be the first time."

He smiled down at her before kissing her on the forehead. "It will not be permanent, I promise," he said. "Now, I need for you to pack up everything we brought from Forestburn. Can you do that?"

She nodded, wiping daintily at her nose. "In truth, I have not yet unpacked completely. But I will take Althel with me and make sure everything is packed and ready to leave. What about the stores?"

"Kenneth has charge of supplies and will make sure the kitchen is cleaned out." He kissed her forehead. "When you are finished packing, then offer to help Stephen. He has a good deal of wounded to move and could probably use your assistance."

Toby nodded, eyeing him as she did so. "Did you talk to Stephen, then?" she asked hesitantly. "He seemed pleasant enough this morning."

Tate nodded, taking her elbow and leading her towards the ladder to the upper floor. "All is well."

He did not elaborate and she did not press him. He helped her gather her skirts as she headed back up the ladder. Once in the great hall, he took both hands, kissed them, and went on his way. Toby's gaze lingered on him as he quit the keep, still hardly believing she had married the man and wholly given to daydreaming when there was work to be done. But her daydreams consisted of Ailsa, of Forestburn, and of what the future held for her and Tate. So much in her life had changed over the past few days. She felt as if she was living someone else's life.

When Tate had left the keep and all was silent but for the sounds of the bailey coming in through the open door, Toby shook herself of her musings and went in search of Althel. They had work to do.

CHAPTER THIRTEEN

"**H**E IS MOVING his army. Our spies could see great wagons being loaded and the troops being mobilized." The general's gaze was on de Roche, hard and questioning. "If he moves his army, we lose the advantage of an attack against a weakened fortress."

Hamlin digested this latest information before responding. "What would you have me do? Our numbers are not sufficient to successfully attack again. We will destroy ourselves if we do."

"Then perhaps we have enough men to simply keep them on the defensive inside Harbottle," the general replied. "He cannot move his army if there is another laying siege. That would be suicide."

Hamlin shook his head, setting aside his cup of ale. It was his fifth cup in as many hours, whiling away the hours as the thunder above their heads rolled.

"It would be as if we were fleas attacking a dog," he said frankly. "We would be annoying but no threat. If he is moving his army, then we must follow him to see where he is going."

"Where else would he be going?" the general threw up his hands. "Alnwick is twenty miles from Harbottle. It is a massive fortress. Once he is sealed up in that place, we will never get to Edward."

De Roche drew in a long, thoughtful breath. After a pause, he began to pace about pensively. "Where are our spies to the south? Do they know how close Mortimer's army is?"

"The last we were told, Mortimer is due sometime on the morrow," the general replied. "De Lara's army will have departed long before then."

De Roche nodded slowly, still thinking. "Perhaps," he said meditatively. "But we could move to intercept the army as it moves towards Alnwick."

"We are not even sure that is the destination," the general reminded him.

"True enough," de Roche held up a finger. "However, where else would de Lara go? Warkworth is too far and he would not take the army to the seat of his earldom in Carlisle simply for the fact that is too far away over a good deal of treacherous country. So where else would the man go?"

He had a point. The generals and senior soldiers inside the warm, smelly tent looked to each other, conceding the logic. The old vizier popped and creaked as the tent fell silent. All eyes were on Hamlin as he decided his next calculated move.

"If de Lara takes the road to Alnwick, he must swing south for a distance before trekking out towards the sea," he said thoughtfully. "If we send word to Mortimer's army to move towards Alnwick instead of straight to Harbottle, there is a good chance we can intercept de Lara's army on the open road. That would be a far better scenario than laying siege to Harbottle again. The odds will be much more in our favor."

"You are sure?"

"Sure enough. We must send word to Mortimer immediately so that he knows to hurry."

The general was already calling for a messenger. Orders were relayed and memorized and soon, the man was along his way. Hamlin stood out of the chaos, watching his men make plans for the eventual battle. Unlike a siege, battle on open ground was something of a dance; it had to be carefully choreographed or one might end up attacking one's own men. De Lara was such a clever battle commander that he could quite possibly make it happen. They would have to be very astute in order to avoid the situation.

Hamlin would have to anticipate every move.

CB

"I FEAR I have made a gross tactical miscalculation."

It was mid-afternoon and most of Tate's army was ready to depart. Hundreds of men filled the bailey of Harbottle and spilled from the gates into the countryside beyond. It was a break in between storms and weak sun shown onto the bailey, struggling to dry up the prolific mud. The army was ready to move out but Tate's quietly uttered words caught the attention of both Stephen and Kenneth.

"What miscalculation?" Stephen asked.

Tate was in full armor, standing upon the battlements, watching his army mingle with Warkworth's forces. Stephen was already loaded with weapons, his helm atop his head, and Kenneth had enough armor and weapons strapped on to single-handedly conquer half of England. A wicked-looking crossbow lay slung across one of his enormous shoulders. All three men were ready to ride out but Tate's words gave them pause.

Tate didn't reply immediately to Stephen's query. It was obvious that he was pondering something serious. When he spoke, his focus remained on the bailey below.

"First of all," he said softly, "I would apologize for my short-sightedness."

Stephen shook his head, perplexed. "For what?"

Tate took a long breath before turning to his men. "For my mind not being where it should be," he said quietly. "I have been focused on other things when I should have been focused on our strategy. For every move Mortimer and de Roche make, I must be five steps ahead of them and I fear that I have failed to do that."

Kenneth unslung the crossbow from his shoulder and stepped closer, curiosity on his face. "What are you talking about, Tate?"

Tate's gaze moved to the army again and beyond that, the Northumberland landscape. He was facing south, studying the storm that was just leaving. Another was following on its heels and he glanced to the east, watching the dark horizon.

"As I stood here and watched the mobilization, it occurred to me that if we have sent spies out to assess the army to the south, then they most certainly have sent spies to assess our current status as well," he leaned forward on the parapet. "And, just as we have seen them camped several miles south, they have undoubtedly seen our army preparing to move out."

Stephen and Kenneth were following his train of thought, nodding in agreement as he reached the end of his sentence. But then he abruptly stopped and the knights looked at him expectantly.

"And?" Kenneth pressed.

Tate turned to look at them. "Think about it," he hissed. "If Mortimer's army approaches from the south to reinforce the troops that laid siege to Harbottle two days ago, then what would you, as the commander of Mortimer's forces, do if you knew that your enemy was about to leave the safe haven of a moderately fortified compound and head onto the open road?"

Kenneth stared at him. "I would move my army to intercept."

"Which is exactly what I suspect Mortimer will do if, in fact, he is close enough." Tate shook his head. "I should have realized this but I was so concerned with moving Edward and Toby out of a compromised fortress that it did not occur to me, until now, that Mortimer's army might be close enough to intercept us before we reach Alnwick. It was stupid and short-sighted of me."

"So what do you suggest?" Kenneth asked.

Tate's dark eyes were stormy. "We will continue along this path. But if Mortimer engages us on the open road, Edward has a greater chance than ever before of falling into his hands." He looked between his two knights. "It stands to reason, then, that Edward and the three of us will stay behind as the rest of the army moves to Alnwick."

Kenneth cocked an eyebrow as the light of understanding dawned. "A diversion?"

"A ruse," Tate confirmed. "Let Mortimer pursue the army while we remain at Harbottle. While Mortimer is distracted with our army, we will move west to Carlisle. I have eight hundred troops stationed there. We will be amply protected."

Stephen, listening to the entire exchange, emitted a low whistle. "I refuse to believe that this was not your scheme all along. It is a brilliant plan."

Tate gave him a lop-sided smile. "You are too kind, old friend. While I do not regret that I have had a new wife occupying my thoughts, I should have seen the situation clearly enough to realize the long-term implications of exposing our army."

Stephen scratched his forehead. "Not to have realized the folly would have been to allow it to proceed until Edward was compromised."

Tate merely lifted an eyebrow and moved to the ladder that led down to the bailey. There he would find the Warkworth commander and let the man in on their plans. And then they would remain at Harbottle and wait for the right moment to travel into the west.

It was, in fact, a brilliant scheme as Stephen had said. Tate only hoped it would work.

ᏏᎦ

ANOTHER STORM HAD rolled in by the time Tate's troops, mingled with Warkworth's, moved out of Harbottle. This time, however, the rain turned to snow. As the black clouds belched great waves of white powder, Tate, Stephen, Kenneth, Edward and Toby watched the army trickle from the bailey from their posts on the second and third floors of the keep. Tate deliberately had his soldiers remove any hint of de Lara colors so that any onlookers would not be able to identify de Lara men from Warkworth men. Warkworth knights rode up at the front of the column, specifically in groups of three. That was because Mortimer's men would be looking for de Lara plus St. Héver and Pembury. Groups of three knights would confuse them even more.

Wallace, Althel and four men at arms, including the seasoned Morley and Oscar, had also stayed behind. The men at arms were in the great hall below while the others made their way between floors, making sure to stay clear of the windows in case they were spotted by anyone who might be peering at the castle. For all intents and purposes, the castle must be deserted. Tate arranged to have a provision wagon and seven horses left about a mile north of the castle, to be collected by Tate and his party when they determined the time was right to flee the keep. Now they would wait for the cover of darkness.

Toby had been lingering in the master's chamber, sitting in a chair next to the hearth that they had let die. There was to be no smoke from the fires to give away their presence. Wrapped in the only cloak she had brought from Forestburn, she sat and listened to Tate converse quietly with Stephen. Kenneth was downstairs, watching the landscape from his post in the solar, and young Edward was with him. Dusk was upon them, made even darker with the storm.

At some point, Stephen left Tate to see to things downstairs. Tate remained by the window as the snow blew in, hitting him in the face as wind whipped it into whirlpools in the bailey below. He could see nothing in the fields beyond Harbottle and only a faint line in the distance as his army faded into the night. He knew they were being watched by enemy eyes and his senses were highly attuned.

As Tate watched the nightscape, Toby watched her husband. She inspected the broad lines of his body and felt the power that seemed to radiate from him. It was like the first time she had ever seen him, when the man was in pure battle mode. She was apprehensive but would not let him know; he was edgy enough and she kept her mouth shut, not wanting to distract him. So she amused herself with a stick, using the ashes in the hearth as a drawing board. She drew flowers and birds and animals with no distinct shape. When she tired of her drawings, she would erase them and start again. It was a process that had been going on for hours.

"What are you doing?" Tate looked away from the window. "I can hear scraping from where I am standing."

She smiled up at him, sheepishly. "Drawing."

He moved in her direction and took a knee beside her, his mail grating as he moved. He grinned at the half-erased bees and flowers. "You draw delightfully," he said. "I am sorry I do not have paint or parchment to offer you to stave off this boredom."

She leaned her head against his, resting the side of her head against his cheek. "I am not bored so long as you are near," she said. "I am sorry if my drawing bothers you."

He kissed her forehead and stood up. "It does not," he said, his mailed hand on her back affectionately. "'Tis I who am sorry that I cannot offer you a fire. But we cannot chance that the smoke will be seen."

She shook her head. "You need not apologize. I am quite warm in my cloak."

He touched her hair, her cheek gently, before returning to the window. Outside, the storm was lashing the sides of the keep and Toby rose from her chair, making her way to Tate as he stood next to the window. She pressed up against his back and he turned slightly, lifting an armored arm and putting it around her. Together, they stood and watched the driving snow.

"Do you really think we are being watched?" she asked softly.

He was standing to the side of the window so that he could not be easily seen by prying eyes. "More than likely."

"By the same men who burned Forestburn?"

He turned to look at her, reading her fear. "Some of the same," he turned her back towards the chair. "Sit down, sweetheart, and away from the snow. You shall be in it soon enough when we make our move."

She let him put her in the chair, watching him as he went back towards the window. "May I ask something?"

"Of course."

"When all of this is over with, where shall we live?"

He leaned against the wall, his gaze moving outside the window again. "Carlisle Castle, I suppose. Why? Where do you want to live?"

She shrugged, collecting her stick and resuming her drawing. "I have only lived at Forestburn. I never thought I would ever leave."

"And so you have," he winked at her when she turned to look at him. "I think you shall like Carlisle Castle. It is a big place and quite comfortable."

"Do you have other castles?"

He nodded. "Aside from Harbottle and Carlisle, I hold Grayson Castle, Whitehaven Castle and Kendal Castle, all of them in Cumbria."

"Are they beautiful?"

He shrugged. "Kendal is small, but Grayson and Whitehaven are large and prosperous. Whitehaven is particularly nice because it sits right on the sea. On a clear day, you can see all the way to Ireland."

She pursed her lips in disbelief. "You cannot."

His eyes twinkled. "I have been told that by the locals."

She shook her head to let him know what she thought of that tale and looked back to her drawings. "Do you think that Edward will let you rebuild Forestburn?"

His gaze lingered on her. "Is that where you wish to live?"

She shrugged, still drawing flowers. "Forestburn supports Cartingdon parish. I do not wish to see it left to rot. I would like to rebuild it."

He watched her lowered head. "Then we shall rebuild it," he said softly. "If that is your wish, I will move heaven and earth to grant it."

She looked up at him, a timid smile on her lips. "Truly?"

"Truly."

"And when all of this madness is finished, may we go to Paris and Rome?"

He laughed softly. "Anywhere you wish, sweetheart."

"I hear they have spectacles of fighting in Rome and women who pierce their ears and paint their faces."

"You can find that anywhere."

"Really?" she was genuinely surprised. "Have you seen this in other places?"

His grin broadened. "I cannot tell you what I have seen in other places because you are a delicate lady and such things are unseemly. Suffice it to say that the world is full of debauchery."

She formed an "O" with her lips, thinking on all of the wild things she'd not been privy to living her rather sheltered existence in Cartingdon. Tate snorted at her expression and turned back to the window.

"I was thinking something else," he ventured as a gust of wind blew snow into his face.

"What was that?"

"Well," he wiped snowflakes from his eyes. "I have a good deal of wealth and many holdings. It is difficult to maintain and difficult to keep track of, considering I am hardly in one place long enough to settle my accounts. I am thinking that you would be the perfect person to manage my estates."

She looked surprised. "Me?"

"Of course. You made Cartingdon what it is. I would have you do the same for my holdings. In fact, if you can do for me what you did for your father, I would say that our children will be extremely wealthy prospects to future mates."

The potential of managing Tate's holdings did not displease her. In fact, she found it rather exciting. "I would be honored," she replied. "But are you sure you want your wife managing your estates?"

"You and no other. You are the only person I would trust."

She dawdled in the ash, thinking. "We could build an empire supporting the people and the land." She looked up at him. "Tell me more about Whitehaven. I am interested in the castle that overlooks the sea."

He shifted on his big legs. "It sits on a cliff overlooking the ocean. I have only been there a few times; it is a rather large place and the gulls from the sea are constantly swarming over it. It holds about four hundred troops at any given time."

She smiled. "I asked about the castle, not its military might. How does it survive? Does it breed sheep?"

He shook his head. "Cattle," he replied. "Black and white herds; hundreds of them. The peasants make their living off of the cattle."

Her eyebrows lifted. "Truly?" she cocked her head thoughtfully. "I do not know much about cattle but I see that I shall have to learn. I think I might like to live at Whitehaven. I would like to live by the sea."

He just smiled at her, returning his attention to the snow storm outside. Suddenly, his smile vanished; his eyes narrowed as he spied something beyond the window, the expression on his face hardening in a flash. Toby still had her head lowered, paying attention to her drawings, and did not see his body tense or his countenance darken. When he suddenly moved away from the window and grasped her arm, she was startled.

"What is wrong?" she half-demanded, half-pleaded. "What are…?"

He put a finger to his lips. "Come with me. Hurry."

She dropped her stick and scurried with him to the chamber door. By the time he hit the landing outside, Kenneth was bolting up the stairs.

"Incoming riders," Kenneth said before Tate could say a word. "Looks like several."

Tate thrust Toby at Kenneth. "Take her," he commanded. "Get her out of the keep. There is nowhere to hide in here and I do not want her boxed in."

Kenneth took Toby's arm without another word, helping her quickly navigate the deadly stairs. Tate was right behind them.

"Where are you going?" Kenneth asked.

"To get Edward," Tate replied, his gaze lingering on his wife, a strangely pained expression in his eyes. "Kenneth will take good care of you, sweetheart. I must see to the king."

Toby nodded quickly. "I know," she shoved at him. "Go, hurry. You must get Edward."

He grasped her hand and kissed it swiftly, disappearing into the dark hall. Kenneth had hold of Toby's elbow, gently but firmly pulling her towards the entry.

"Come with me, Lady de Lara," he said, unslinging his crossbow as he opened the heavy oak panel. "Let us see if we cannot find a safe hiding place for you."

The snow was swirling outside and it was nearly as dark as pitch. When he deemed the coast to be clear, Kenneth took Toby down the rebuilt stairs and whisked her across the bailey. The snow was so heavy that it was blinding and Toby kept a tight grip on Kenneth as he led her through the maelstrom. When she finally opened her eyes, she realized they were at the chapel. It gave her a moment of pause and Kenneth felt her hesitation. When he looked at her and noted her reluctant expression, he actually smiled at her. It was a forced smile, but a smile nonetheless.

"Come along," he said, opening the panel into the black room. "We shall hide out in good company."

With a deep breath for courage, Toby stepped through. Kenneth followed and left the door half-opened behind them. He did not shut it at all.

It was, literally, as quiet as a tomb. It was also black and freezing. The only source of light was from three lancet windows cut high into the wall, barely giving any illumination to see by. But Kenneth would not risk a torch so he took Toby by the hand and felt his way along the wall until they reached Ailsa's fresh grave. He carefully steered Toby around it and took her towards the altar.

The one feature that the chapel had was that there was an alcove behind the altar for the priest. It was shielded by a partial wall carved from oak, and very old. A tiny door was cut into the alcove that led through the exterior wall of the fortress and into the stables. The theory was that the priest would arrive at the stables and pass through the hidden passage, unseen and protected, to the chapel. Since it had not been used in fifty years, the door that led into the stables was blocked off with hay and other stable implements. It was into this passage that Kenneth took Toby.

It was dark, dank and bitterly cold in the tunnel. There was no light at all except for the small door which Kenneth had cracked open. He crouched just inside the tunnel by the door, his ears peaked and his knightly senses attuned. Toby sat on the ground behind him, wrapped tightly in her cloak, and shivered.

"Why did you not shut the door chapel door?" she whispered.

His ice-blue eyes were riveted to the opening in the small doorway. "Because if they were to come upon a closed, bolted door, they would assume there was something inside to be protected," he whispered in return. "By leaving the door open, they will assume it is an abandoned room and not give it further thought."

She nodded in understanding, hunkering down beneath her cloak. It was bitterly cold and she was beginning to wonder where Tate, and everyone else, had gone. She was terribly worried about him and congratulated herself on being rather brave when they had been separated. It had all happened so fast. Now, reality was beginning to set in and her apprehension was growing.

It wasn't long before they heard voices in the bailey. Horses snorted and there were sounds of weapons moving about. Kenneth remained still as stone, listening to all that was transpiring and the voices of the men as they began moving about the bailey. Someone gave the command to search the keep. Toby's heart was pounding in her ears as she heard voices from the bailey draw nearer.

She buried her face in her cloak, praying that they would not be discovered. Kenneth was so quiet that she swore the man had turned to rock. She could not even hear him breathing. Long minutes passed and they heard voices now and again, very faint, as the intruders searched the grounds. Toby's apprehension was reaching splitting capacity and it was difficult to keep her breathing quiet. Her body was quivering with fear and cold.

Voices suddenly seemed to be coming from the stables; they could hear them off to their left. Kenneth finally moved from his stone-like position and slid past her, moving to the end of the passage that butted up against the stables. He could hear better there. From the sounds of it, it seemed as if they were on to something, or someone, in the stalls. Toby was terrified that it was Tate.

Her palms were sweating and her breathing began to come in pants. If they were to capture Tate, then Edward was surely with him and both of them would die. She had little doubt. She could not allow that to happen, not if she could possibly save them. It was an idiotic notion and she knew it. But her fear for Tate outweighed her sense of self-preservation, so she did the only thing she could think of.

Kenneth was too far away to grab her when she suddenly shot out of the passage. Toby raced through the chapel and exploded out into the snowy bailey. The trouble was, however, that most of the men were concentrating their search near the stables and kitchens. They were fairly far off and she could see their dark outlines through the white haze. Even though she had just bolted from the chapel, they had not seen her.

Several horses stood off to her right and their presence suddenly gave her an idea. Toby suddenly began screaming and waving her hands.

"Here!" she hollered, watching several helmed heads turned towards her. "Here I am! I am over here!"

Fed by panic, she raced to one of the horses and managed to scramble into the saddle. Gathering the reins, she dug her heels into the side of the beast and nearly lost her seat with then horse took off. Soon, she was racing from the bailey as at least a dozen soldiers ran to their horses in pursuit. Within seconds, an entire posse was roaring after her into the dark and snowy night.

Kenneth bolted from the chapel in time to run into two soldiers. He made quick work of them with his broadsword, all the while swearing under his breath at Lady de Lara. Suddenly, the stables came alive with the sounds of a sword fight and Kenneth raced into the dark, cold stable just as Tate and Edward put away three men. The dragonblade broadsword in Tate's hand dripped red with blood. Four more intruders were in the kitchens in a massive battle with Stephen and Wallace. Edward raced in the direction of the fight but Tate grabbed Kenneth before the man could follow.

"What in the hell happened?" he nearly shouted. "Where is Toby?"

Kenneth felt like he had failed by letting her get away from him; on the other hand, it was the bravest, most foolish thing he had ever seen. "She rode off on a stolen horse with about a dozen men in pursuit," he couldn't explain better than that. "She ran away from me before I could stop her."

"Why in God's name did she run?"

"Bait, I believe." He could think of no other reason.

Tate looked at him as if the man had lost his mind. "She... she lured those men out of the stables?"

Kenneth nodded. "She must have heard the commotion and thought to divert their attention. I, in fact, thought they had located you."

"They had," Tate growled, then ripped his helm off and tossed it to the ground in a fit of anger. "Damn her! She is going to get herself killed, the silly wench. I must go after her."

Kenneth stopped him. "Nay," he said firmly. "Take Edward and the rest of them and get to the horses north of the castle. Do not waste her sacrifice. She pulled those men off for a reason. I will go after her."

Tate had never been more torn in his life; his momentary anger at her actions suddenly gave way to terror. "My God," he breathed. "I said that she was brave but I had no idea just how brave she really was. Did she truly gain their attention to draw them away from Edward and me?"

"I can think of no other explanation," Kenneth replied. "She moved before I could stop her."

Tate swallowed hard as sounds of the swordfight near the kitchens died away and he turned in time to see Wallace dispatching the last soldier. Edward and Stephen were running in Tate's direction, swords up and in full battle mode, but all Tate could think of at the moment was Toby. He put his hand on Kenneth's shoulder, struggling with his emotions.

"She is all to me," he whispered. "Know this."

"I do, my lord. I shall not fail, I swear it."

Kenneth was off, racing for the horses that were still tethered in the bailey. Tate watched him thunder from the outer ward before turning to Stephen, Edward, and now Wallace. In the distance, he could see Althel and the men at arms approach. His heart was aching but he forced himself to focus. He would not waste her sacrifice, as much as it was paining him not to help her. He would have to trust Kenneth.

"We go," he growled, shoving Edward back in the direction of the kitchens where a postern gate lay lodged in the northern wall. "We have a very long night ahead of us to Carlisle."

Edward, however, had heard the entire conversation about Toby. He was pale with anxiety.

"Is it true?" he demanded as Tate shoved. "Did Toby really pull those men off so they would not discover us?"

Tate realized that he was very close to tears. His heart screamed to save his wife but his head demanded he follow his duty to Edward. It was a horrific struggle.

"It would seem so," he labored to stay on an even keel. "Kenneth is going to help her while I take you to safety."

"But we must all go and help her!" Edward insisted. "I cannot allow her to sacrifice herself!"

Tate grabbed him around the neck, so hard that Edward visibly flinched. His eyes were like daggers as he stared at the boy. "To allow yourself to be captured would be to shame the courage she has shown," he hissed. "We will honor that sacrifice. She has given us this gift and we will not waste it."

Edward nodded unsteadily as they continued on, rubbing his neck where Tate had grabbed him. Together they moved to the postern gate, unlatching the nearly-frozen bolt and shoving it open. The snow was beginning to pile up, making it difficult to move the gate. But they managed to get it open and spill out into the yard beyond.

De Roche was waiting for them.

CHAPTER FOURTEEN

TOBY WASN'T SURE how long she had been riding. With the snow and darkness, she had lost all sense of time. More than that, it was increasingly difficult to follow any given path. The snow was completely obliterating it. So she followed what she thought was the road as the snow built up and the horse began to tire. She had stopped looking behind her long ago, fearful of what she would see, and just kept riding. So far, she had remained free. She thought she might even escape. But all of that eventually came to an abrupt, painful end.

Something hit her from the side, so hard that the horse went down and her with it. She heard bones cracking in her torso and she groaned in pain as a large, armored body came crashing down on top of her. There was so much pain that she couldn't even fight back. All she could do was lay there and struggle to breathe.

The man pushed himself off of her, roughly reaching down to yank her to her feet. But Toby was in so much pain that she screamed the moment he tried to move her so he let go of her arm and stared down at her. She lay in the snow, gasping in agony. Soon, several more faces joined him.

"Who are you, girl?" one of the men asked.

Toby could hardly breathe; tears were stinging her eyes as she struggled. "To.. Toby Cartingdon."

"What were you doing at Harbottle?"

"V-visiting friends."

The man doing the questioning pursed his lips irritably. "Get her to her feet," he commanded. "Take her back to Mortimer."

The same man who had knocked her off her horse turned to his commander. "She is injured, m'lord," he told him.

"That is her fault. Get her on a horse."

The soldier turned his attention back to her and, obeying orders, grabbed Toby by the wrist and yanked her into a sitting position. Toby screamed again in agony and, upon being jostled a second time, succumbed to the welcome shroud of unconsciousness.

When she finally came to, she was in a dark, cold shelter that she did not recognize. She lay there a moment, eyeing her surroundings and having no idea where she was. But she did remember the chase, the fall, and her heart began to pound loudly in her ears. Wherever she was, it was no place friendly. She had no idea how long she had been unconscious or what had happened during that time. All she knew was that she was in a good deal of trouble. She could only hope that Tate and the others were able to get away.

She took a deep breath and pain shot through her torso. Agony returned full bore and she groaned softly, her hands against her ribs as if to hold in the pain. Tears ran down her temples as she wondered just how badly she was hurt. Any movement was torture.

"What is your name, lady?"

The voice was soft in the darkness. Startled, Toby tried to twist her head around to see where it came from. She could see a body off to her right, back behind an old vizier that was struggling to give off some heat. But the twist of her neck hurt her torso so she resumed her former position, lying still and staring up at the ceiling.

"Who is asking?" she replied breathlessly.

The man didn't say anything for a moment and Toby heard rustling, as if clothing was being shaken. Suddenly there were footfalls near her head and she closed her eyes, praying that the man wouldn't step on her skull. But the footfalls came to a halt and she could hear breathing as the man stood over her. He was silent for quite some time because, Toby was sure, he was inspecting her.

"You are a captive of Roger Mortimer," the man finally said. "I would suggest you cooperate so we can have your ribs attended to. I was told you were injured in a fall."

You are a captive of Roger Mortimer. More tears trickled down Toby's temples. She was terrified. While most of her refused to let the man know who she was, a small part of her was adamant that she tell him. If he did not know who she really was, he might think she was just another peasant girl and kill her. Worse than that, they might take her to sport. If they knew she was de Lara's wife, it might give her some amnesty. Frightened, injured, she had never even been in a battle until a few days ago and was naïve to the rules of engagement or captivity. She could only go with her instincts and her instincts, weakened by her pain, lessened her resolve to be a difficult prisoner. She was afraid of what would happen to her if she was less than cooperative.

"I was injured when one of your men threw me off my horse," she whispered, opening her eyes to look at the tall, thin man standing over her. "If you tell me your name, I will tell you mine."

The man's brown eyes glimmered in the weak light of the vizier as he crouched beside her. "My name is of no consequence. I was told you were discovered at Harbottle Castle."

"I was running from Harbottle Castle."

"Why were you running?"

"Because there were a dozen armed men in the bailey and I was frightened. What else was I supposed to do?"

"Why were you there?"

She paused, eyeing him in the weak light. "What you really wish to know is who I am. I told you; tell me your name and I will tell you mine."

The corner of the man's mouth twitched. "You drive a hard bargain, lady."

"I have been told that."

"You are also exquisitely beautiful so I would suspect that you are not a servant."

"Are all servant girls so ugly?"

"I have never seen a servant girl look like you. In fact, I have never seen any woman look like you."

Toby was feeling uncertain and uncomfortable. She didn't like the tone the man was using nor the way upon which he was looking at her. But she was in a very bad position to defend herself should he try to force himself upon her. Fear began to creep into her veins.

"Who are you?" she demanded in a harsh whisper.

The man cocked an eyebrow. "I told you. You are the prisoner of Roger Mortimer."

"Are you Mortimer, then?"

He nodded vaguely. "Now," he sat down on his buttocks next to her. "Have I earned your trust enough so that you would tell me your name?"

Roger Mortimer. Toby stared at the man, wide-eyed, hardly believing it was true. He had dark hair with flecks of silver in it and was rather long-jawed. For a man with such a powerful reputation, he didn't seem to fit the mold. The Roger Mortimer she had imagined was nine feet tall and breathed fire. Not this ordinary wisp of a man. He did not fit the ideal.

"Do you swear it?" she breathed.

"Upon my oath."

She continued to stare up at him, debating on whether or not he was telling her the truth. He didn't seem the lying type, but then again, the man could be prolific at it and she would never be wiser. Yet now was not the time to mistrust. She was a captive and she was injured and, as much as she loathed the idea, she would have to depend on others for assistance. She had no choice.

"What is it you want from me?" she finally asked. "I cannot tell you anything of value."

"You may tell me who you really are and why you were at Harbottle."

She shifted slightly, sending waves of pain through her body. With a sharp intake of breath, she waited for the pain to subside. Roger watched her intently.

"I have sent for my physic," he said quietly. "He will attend you once you have told me your name."

She opened her watery eyes, outraged. "So you withhold care until I have told you what you want to know? What kind of barbarian are you that you would treat a woman in this manner?"

"You were found leaving Harbottle Castle and, until I know otherwise, considered an enemy," he leaned towards her, his brown eyes intense. "You struck a bargain with me; my name for yours. So far, I have proven to be the only one trustworthy between the two of us."

She studied him a moment, realizing he was correct. Turning away from him, she closed her eyes as she spoke.

"I am the Lady Elizabetha Cartingdon de Lara," she whispered. "I was at Harbottle because it is my husband's holding."

Roger stared at her, already knowing the answer but struck to hear it from her lips. He could not have a more valuable captive if Edward himself was lying in front of him.

"So the rumor was true," he murmured. "Dragonblade's wife in the flesh."

Toby didn't reply; her eyes were still closed as if to ignore him. Roger's gaze lingered on her a moment before he spoke louder. "Where is your husband, my lady?"

She shook her head weakly. "I do not know. Hopefully he is well away from you."

"So he would leave his wife alone to suffer? That does not speak well for your husband."

Her eyes opened, the hazel orbs flashing. "You will not speak ill of him. He has a duty to Edward and, God willing, he is doing his duty."

Roger regarded her a moment, inspecting the lines of her lovely face, seeing great strength in her. He had been told how she led a dozen of his men on a wild goose chase and, frankly, expected no less from de Lara's wife. He actually found it amusing. Rising to his feet, he suddenly disappeared from the tent.

Toby continued to lay still, closing her eyes and feeling the warm tears trickle down her cheeks. She regretted that she told him her identity and was glad she had all in the same breath. Perhaps now he would send someone to help her. Either that or he would send someone to kill her. Lying still and pale upon the pallet, she awaited whatever sentence Mortimer was to bring upon her. She was at his mercy.

She did not have long to wait. She was almost asleep again when she heard the tent flap pull back and bodies enter the shelter. She was in so much pain that she did not bother looking.

"Here is your lady," she heard Roger say. "Her story is the same as yours. And because you have been truthful with me, I will permit you to stay with her for now. But have no doubt that you and I shall have another talk very soon."

Toby heard his words, struggling to open her eyes. Next she realized, a big hand was on her forehead and she opened her eyes only to look up into a familiar, well-beaten face.

Kenneth was gazing down at her, looking as if he had been beaten within an inch of his life. One eye was grossly swollen and his lip was split and bloodied. One look at him and Toby burst into soft sobs.

"Oh, Sir Kenneth," she wept. "What have they done to you?"

He shushed her softly. "It looks far worse than it is, my lady," he said quietly. "The bigger question is what have they done to you? I am told that you are injured."

Her eyes closed again as if to ward off the throbbing pain in her torso. "Someone knocked me off the horse," she murmured, tears spilling down her temples. "I think I broke something when I fell."

Kenneth's jaw ticked as his gaze moved down her torso. "Where does it hurt?"

"My ribs."

"A sharp pain?"

"Very sharp."

He grunted. "You probably broke a few. Can you breathe well

enough?"

"It hurts if I take a deep breath but for the most part, I can breathe."

"Good," he moved to peel her cloak away. "Hopefully nothing has been punctured. Although I am not Stephen, I have tended my share of wounds. Would you allow me examine you?"

She nodded faintly and he proceeded to pull the heavy woolen cloak away. A simple woolen surcoat and heavy linen shift lay beneath but he did not remove them; instead, he began to gently push on her torso until he reached a tender area and she gasped.

"I am sorry," he said sincerely. "But I must see if I can feel the bones moving."

She nodded, eyes closed, and turned her head as far away from him as it would go. Kenneth pushed a few times on the area in question, listening to her groan softly, knowing she was enduring excruciating pain. He'd had a few cracked ribs himself and knew how painful it could be. Finally, he removed his hands.

"Well," he said softly. "I do not believe anything has separated. I can feel the fractures but the bones are still intact. You will be all right once they heal."

Toby did nothing more but nod; she was exhausted and in extreme pain. She could feel Kenneth as he gently wrapped her back up in her cloak. Then he sat beside her in silence because she could feel the heat from his enormous body. For the longest time, neither one of them moved. They lingered in dim, uncertain silence.

"What are you doing here?" she finally asked, opening her eyes and turning to look at him. "Why did you not go with Tate?"

Kenneth cocked an eyebrow at her. "Because someone had to come after you to protect you from the hordes of Mortimer's men bent on capturing you," he said. Then he held up a finger. "And just so you and I are perfectly clear, if you do anything like that ever again, I will blister your backside, husband or no husband."

He wasn't serious and she knew it. Unwinding a hand from the cloak, she reached out and grasped his thick fingers. It was comforting.

Kenneth, the man made of stone, squeezed her hand tightly.

"But it was also one of the most courageous acts I have ever witnessed," his scolding softened considerably. "It was an honor to have been a part of it."

"How did they capture you?" she whispered.

He patted her hand. "They did not exactly capture me."

"What happened?"

He sighed, unsure how much to tell her. He opted for all of it for there was no point in keeping it secret. "I was too late to help you; by the time I came upon you and the men in pursuit, they had already captured you. At that point, I had a choice of either returning to Tate to tell him what had happened or offering myself as a hostage so that I could stay with you during your captivity. I chose the latter."

"Why on earth would you do that?"

"Because your husband made you my responsibility. You are caught up in something bigger than you can comprehend. I did not want you to face Mortimer alone."

She squeezed his hand again. "But they beat you."

He waved her off. "If you think I look bad, you should see the men who did this. Trust me when I say that at least eight of them are far worse off than I."

He sounded rather proud of himself and she peered more closely at him, thinking he seemed amused by it all. Kenneth was an enormously broad man and she had no doubt he could do a substantial amount of damage. But he was enjoying it. She sighed with disapproval.

"You should have returned to Tate," she told him. "He will not know what has happened to us."

Kenneth's amused expression faded. "He will know soon enough," he said quietly. "I am sure that Mortimer is even now sending word."

Toby stared up at him and Kenneth could see the thoughts rolling through her head. The tears were gone and she suddenly looked very serious.

"So Tate was correct," she said softly. "The remnants of the forces that attacked Harbottle two days ago were waiting for reinforcements."

Kenneth nodded slowly. "Tate is usually correct. But it did not take a great military genius to deduce that a larger, more substantial force was on its way to Harbottle. Once Edward had been located, it was just a matter of time. Mortimer has been trailing us for two years."

"So the man that spoke to me earlier really was Roger Mortimer?"

"Aye."

She fell silent a moment. "Sir Kenneth," she ventured hesitantly. "I am going to ask you a question and you must swear to be entirely truthful with me."

"Of course, my lady."

"I have made a mess of things, have I not?"

"What do you mean?"

"Mortimer is going to send word to Tate that he has me as a hostage. Tate will want me back."

Kenneth suspected what she was driving at. "He will undoubtedly negotiate for your return."

"There is nothing he can negotiate with except Edward. And he will not turn the king over to Mortimer, not even for me. I would not want him to."

Kenneth gazed at her a moment before averting his eyes, looking down at her hand as it held his. "It is possible that Mortimer will ask for Edward in exchange for you."

Toby's grip tightened and her hazel eyes were unnaturally hard. "This cannot happen, Kenneth. We must not put Tate in a position where he must choose between me and Edward."

"It may not come to that. Tate is very skilled at negotiating; we must wait and see what transpires. Do not give up hope."

She sighed heavily and looked away. The tears were returning and she closed her eyes tightly, trying to stave them off. "I should not have run from Harbottle," she whispered tightly. "I should have stayed where you told me to and I should not have moved. Perhaps we all would have gotten away safely had I not interfered."

Kenneth squeezed her hand again. "Lady, had you not fled when you did, Tate and Edward would have been discovered by two dozen men who would have quite eagerly speared Tate at the end of a broadsword and taken Edward a captive. What you did… you saved their lives. I believe you saved all of our lives. Do not question your bravery."

Her eyes opened and she turned to look at him. "Do you really think so?" she sniffed.

He nodded, the ice-blue eyes oddly warm. Kenneth was not the warm type. "I do indeed," he said quietly. "So you must not despair. We will all get through this. You must trust that Tate will do what is right."

"But I am afraid."

"I know. But do not give up hope."

The tent flap suddenly moved again, issuing forth a small man with thinning blond hair. Icy air blew in after him, rattling the tent. The man was clad in heavy robes and held a big satchel in one hand. Kenneth was on his feet, placing his massive body between Toby and the new entrant.

"What is your business here?" the knight demanded.

The man was diminutive and meek, quite intimidated by Kenneth's hulking presence. "I am the surgeon," he said in a soft, high-pitched voice. "My name is Timothy. I have been sent to help the lady."

Kenneth eyed him as if by sheer glare he could crush the man, but the little surgeon had yet to fade. Gradually, the knight moved aside to allow him access. The little man kept a close eye on Kenneth as he scooted to the lady's side, setting his heavy bag down.

"She has at least three broken ribs that I can assess," Kenneth said. "There is nothing to do but wrap her tightly so they will heal."

Timothy St. Maur had been Roger Mortimer's physic for three years. He was a former priest, as many of them were, who had a gift for healing. The fact that he was a consecrated priest had oft come in handy when giving last rites to patients he could not save. But the small lady lying before him didn't seem to be in need of that particular talent.

Toby opened her eyes when she felt the man beside her. He was small and pale. She watched him as he opened his bag and rummaged around in it. He pulled out a strange device that looked as if it was two wooden cones with some sort of leather string in between. She began to watch him more curiously as he rubbed at the cones.

"What is that?" she asked.

The young physic smiled. "This is my listening tube," he told her. When she looked worried, he held it up so she could examine it. "See? The cones magnify the sounds that travel through this leather tube. I will be able to hear many things from your body to determine your health."

She looked dubious. "What do you do with it?"

Timothy gestured to her torso. "May I?"

She frowned. "May you *what*?"

"Demonstrate, of course."

She looked up at Kenneth, who shrugged faintly. Toby reasoned that as long as Kenneth was standing nearby, no harm would come to her. Reluctantly, she nodded.

"Very well," she said. "Will this hurt?"

The physic shook his head, very carefully peeling back the edges of her cloak. "Not at all."

"What are you going to do?"

"Listen, my lady."

"Listen for what?"

The edges of her cloak fell away and he moved for the neckline of her shift. The moment he did so, he felt a very large hand grasp him around the neck. Not tight enough to cut off air, but the implication was obvious. Timothy put up his hands as if in surrender.

"I am going to listen to her breathing, I swear it," he said, his voice strangled by Kenneth's grasp. "Nothing improper will occur but I must be permitted to examine the lady if I am to help her."

Kenneth looked at Toby for permission, who nodded faintly. Kenneth released the man and Timothy coughed a couple of times, rubbing his neck, before resuming. He delicately pulled the neckline of Toby's shift down to just below her collar bone. Then he took one end of the strange contraption and put it against her flesh, the other end to his ear.

"Now," he told her. "Cough."

She gave forth a weak cough, groaning when it pained her. Timothy listened intently, moving his cone around to different positions before finally removing it.

"She sounds stable enough," he put the device back in his bag. "I hear nothing strange so I would assume nothing has been punctured."

As Kenneth hovered over him, Timothy proceeded with his examination, going so far as to examine her arms and legs. After he had thumped and poked enough, he finally returned to his big bag.

"She has three broken ribs and her entire right side is bruised, but she should heal," he announced, pulling forth a roll of linen. "I am going to have to wrap your ribs, my lady, and I cannot do it through your cloak and surcoat. We must remove your clothes down to your shift."

Toby wasn't particularly shocked by his statement. She had seen Stephen wrapping the ribs of men wounded in the siege and those men had been naked from the waist up. While Kenneth very gently helped her sit, she and Timothy managed to remove her cloak and surcoat. She was in so much pain that she could do nothing more than lean against Kenneth as Timothy tightly wrapped the linen around her torso. Although it hurt tremendously, it also felt strangely better. By the time the physic was finished, she was exhausted with stress and pain and Kenneth lay her gently back down on the pallet. Timothy helped her to drink a strong willow bark potion and quite soon, she drifted off into a heavy sleep.

Kenneth sat near her head as the physic packed his medicaments back into his big bag. "I will return in a short while," he said. "If she awakens, do not let her move around overly. She must be still for the next few days."

Kenneth nodded as Timothy quit the tent. When all was still and quiet, his gaze drifted to Toby and thoughts of Tate inevitably followed. He wondered if his liege had indeed made it to Carlisle Castle and how long it would be before the man was at Mortimer's doorstep. He knew for a fact that Tate would not let Toby's captivity go unanswered. But the method in which the man chose to respond was the question; knowing Tate and his connections, an army of unfathomable proportions was not out of the question and Mortimer might find himself seriously overwhelmed. Mortimer, however, held the advantage no matter how large of an army Tate assembled; he held Toby.

Kenneth lay down between Toby and the tent entry, thinking he should probably get some rest. But he spent the next hour staring up at the ceiling, wondering what course their lives would take in the next few days. He wondered if he would be strong enough to endure it.

❧

TATE HAD EDWARD and, at the moment, that was all he was concerned with. He didn't even bother trying to fight de Roche and his men when they surprised them just outside of the postern gate. All he could think of was getting clear of the skirmish. To stay and fight, when he was clearly outnumbered, was not the wiser choice. He had to run.

So they fled through the woods as de Roche and his men tried to pursue, being seriously hampered by Stephen, Wallace and the four men at arms. It was a blessing that the snow and trees slowed the pursuit, as Tate and Edward were on foot. It had been tricky to cross the frozen River Coquet, which bordered the northern edge of the castle, but they had used the old footbridge and then dislodged one end of it when they were across. As the bridge collapsed and floated away, they tore through the snowy foliage until they came to the horses and wagon that had been left for them. Each man had grabbed a horse and sped away.

Edward kept tight pace behind Tate as they tore through the forest. Since the bridge was gone, they did not expect pursuers but kept up a fast pace. Tate fleetingly wondered what would become of Stephen and the others, with no way across the river to their mounts, but he had to put that thought from his mind. Unless the man was dead or dying, Stephen would find his way to Carlisle Castle and Tate fully expected to see him there in a few days. He was too strong to fail.

The journey to Carlisle would be a difficult one. It would take them at least two days but with the snow and bad weather, perhaps longer. Tate's thoughts inevitably moved to Toby, wondering where she was and praying that she was well. He trusted Kenneth and knew the man would do all in his power to keep her safe, but he could not help himself from worrying to the point of being overwhelmed by it. Now that he and Edward were away and presumably safe, his mind was occupied with thoughts of his wife. Although he had only known the woman a week, he felt as if she had been with him his entire life. No greater bond nor love nor admiration could he have felt for her had he known her for a thousand years. He was desperate to see her safe, to hold her and to tell her how much he loved her. He could think of nothing else.

As the snowfall eased and the clouds began to clear, the moon soon emerged to bathe the land in its eerie white light. Tate and Edward pushed on into the night, determined to put as much distance as they could between them and de Roche, waiting for the day to dawn in the hopes that it would bring good news and a brighter outlook.

In hindsight, if he had known at that moment what he would later come to discover, he would have sent Edward on alone to Carlisle and turned his horse for Mortimer's camp. But when he and Edward finally reached Carlisle Castle on the morning of the third day and found themselves quite alone but for eight hundred troops, he spent two additional days not eating and not sleeping, waiting for any sign of Toby and Kenneth.

On the sixth day since leaving Harbottle, Stephen, Wallace and two men at arms, Morley and Oscar, arrived at Carlisle. They were exhausted and haggard but alive. The rest of their party, including Althel, had perished in the flight. Tate was glad to see them but they knew nothing of Toby or Kenneth. The despair he felt deepened tenfold.

It was then on the seventh day since fleeing Harbottle that an escort arrived at Carlisle Castle bearing a missive from the Earl of March. It came during the first meal Tate had eaten in four days. Fatigued and on edge, he knew what the missive said before he even read it. He just had a gut feeling. And even after he read the carefully scripted words, he continued to stare at the parchment as if hardly believing what he had read.

Young Edward's response to the message was to rage while Stephen stood in brooding silence, finally quieting the young king who was verging on a tantrum. All eyes were on the Earl of Carlisle as the missive in his hand eventually fell to the floor. As Tate walked away in stunned disbelief, the words on the parchment screamed forth from the dingy and dusty floor.

Your wife is my guest and St. Héver with her. The Lady was injured in her adventure and has required the constant attention of a physic. Should you wish to have her returned, you and I must come to terms at Wigmore Castle.

Tate made it out to the bailey before vomiting.

CHAPTER FIFTEEN

F OR SOMEONE WHO had never traveled out of Cartingdon, Toby was doing a lot of traveling as of late. Seven days as a guest of Roger Mortimer now saw her moving with his army for Wigmore Castle in the Welsh Marches. She was seeing more of England than she had ever seen in her life but she wasn't enjoying it in the least.

Her ribs were much better thanks to a good deal of rest and Timothy's skilled care. But she was still too uncomfortable to ride a horse so she sat in one of Mortimer's provisions wagons, tightly bundled up against the winter weather. Surrounded by a massive army of hundreds and hundreds of men, the troop movement was an impressive sight and a master scheme of tactical planning.

Kenneth rode beside her on a big Belgian warmblood that Mortimer had graciously loaned him. It was a young horse, mean and muzzled, but Kenneth handled him with skill. He had been allowed to regain his armor but not his weapons, including his beloved crossbow. Mortimer had taken that from him. But Kenneth was nonetheless allowed the dignity of his station as a knight, riding as if he had not been stripped of his broadsword and bow.

Toby would have been more at ease if Hamlin de Roche hadn't been so close to her. The dark, ugly knight rode just in front of the wagon. She had recognized him as the same man who had invaded Forestburn, remembering how he had tried to get his hands on Edward. He would turn around every so often, glance at her and then cast a challenging glare at Kenneth. But the big blond knight kept his eyes straight ahead or on Toby and ignored the man who was trying to bait him.

Seated on the wagon bench next to the soldier driving the team of horses, Toby eventually grew bored and motioned Kenneth towards her. He reined the big stallion next to her, struggling with the animal as it tossed its head and tried to fight him. Toby watched with a frown, trying not to get bumped.

"They could not have given you a more docile animal?" she wanted to know. "I do not believe this horse has ever been ridden."

Visor raised, the corner of Kenneth's mouth twitched. "He is as gentle as a kitten."

"A raging kitten, you mean."

Kenneth lost his struggle against the smile. "Did you call me over here to complain about my horse?"

She pursed her lips at him, shifting on the bench to a more comfortable position. "I did not," she snapped without force. "I called you over here to find out where we are."

Kenneth looked around, drawing in a thoughtful breath as he did so. "Somewhere to the west of Leeds, I believe," he said. "Given our rate of travel, that would be my best guess."

"How much further?"

Kenneth looked at her. "Another week or more. It is difficult to move this many men in this weather."

Toby looked around, at de Roche several paces up ahead, at Mortimer and his retainers far to the front, before turning back to Kenneth. "Do you think Tate knows where we are?" she asked softly.

Kenneth nodded thoughtfully. "He knows where we are headed. We know that Mortimer has sent him a missive to that effect."

"Will he be waiting for us at Wigmore Castle?"

"He will do what is necessary and right, my lady."

It wasn't much of an answer. She didn't realize until later that Kenneth had been purposely ambiguous in case anyone was close enough to hear his answer. Toby, however, was left feeling depressed and uncertain.

"What will happen to us once we get to Wigmore?" she asked.

Kenneth shook his head. "I honestly do not know."

"Are they going to throw me in the vault?"

"I would sincerely doubt it."

"Are they going to throw *you* in the vault?"

"That is a possibility."

Her eyes widened. "Truly?"

He could see that he had frightened her. He didn't want to tell her what he really thought, but upon reflection, it was better if he did so she was prepared. He did not want her to be startled when, and if, the situation took a distressing turn.

"It is a possibility but I doubt it," he lowered his voice. "But you must prepare yourself for the possibility that I will no longer be allowed to shadow you. Since your health is returning, I am not sure Mortimer would see any need for me to remain with you."

He had only succeeded in frightening her more. "Oh, Kenneth," she gasped. "He would not… they would not kill you, would they?"

He shook his head. "Nothing so drastic, I think. But he could very well send me elsewhere as a hostage."

Her eyes welled. "You cannot leave me," she whispered. "I will not allow it."

He sought to soothe her. "No need to fret. Nothing will happen for quite some time yet."

She sniffled, wiping her nose that was red with the cold. De Roche turned around at that point, noticed her distressed expression, and reined his horse back towards the wagon.

The man was big and ugly. Everything about him bled of evil. His muddy gaze moved between Toby and Kenneth as flakes of snow adhered themselves to the dirty beard exposed on his face.

"Is something amiss, Lady de Lara?" he asked. "Do you require something?"

Toby didn't like the man; that much was plain. She cocked an eyebrow at him. "Not from you."

De Roche smiled, his stained teeth ugly behind his thick lips. "Spoken like a true de Lara. Pride is never in short supply."

Toby looked away from him, having no desire to engage in any conversation. But de Roche wasn't finished with her yet; he'd not had much contact with the lady for the fact that she had been recuperating from cracked ribs. This was, in fact, the first time he'd been near her since his return from chasing her husband from Harbottle and he remembered what an exquisite woman she was from the day he had seen her at Forestburn. Aye, he remembered her well; he hadn't known she was de Lara's wife at the time, which was a pity. He might have paid more attention to her but he had been more concerned with capturing the young king at the time. Lady de Lara had prevented him from doing so and he never forgot it. He was a man with a grudge.

"Tell me something, St. Héver," he said casually, his gaze moving over their snowy and cold surroundings. "Do you stay so close to the lady because it is your intention to claim de Lara's widow? I can hardly blame you; she is a pretty little thing."

Toby's head snapped to the knight, her eyes wide. Before she could work up a righteous explosion, Kenneth reached out to touch her arm. She looked at him, eyes welling and accusing, but he shook his head at her calmly. She understood his silent implication and she bit her lip, lowering her head.

"I stay close to the lady to protect her from fools like you," Kenneth said steadily. "And as much as you would like to rattle her, you and I both know that Tate is alive and well. Do not let your bitterness show because the man has once again evaded you. He toys with you as a cat toys with a mouse."

De Roche turned towards Kenneth with a baleful eye. "I would not be so confident that de Lara is still alive. He was crossing a bridge when I saw it collapse. He fell into the frozen river and was swept away as I watched."

Kenneth waited for Toby to respond but, to her credit, she kept her head lowered. The knight knew that de Roche was trying to upset her and that fueled very uncharacteristic anger within him. His jaw ticked faintly.

"You should hear how we laugh at you, Hamlin," Kenneth's voice was seductive, gritty. "You have provided us hours of entertainment."

"It shall not last."

"I beg to differ; this mere woman bested you. Either that says a great deal for her skills or not very much for your own. You are a pathetic excuse for a knight."

"We shall see."

"I anxiously await the day."

The air was crackling with hazard. Toby's head came up and her big eyes focused on Kenneth. The knight, however, was wearing that oddly amused expression again, the same one he had held when he had told her of all of the knights he had thrashed upon his capture. *He is enjoying this*, she thought.

"Do not provoke him, Kenneth," she whispered sternly. "You are not carrying any weapons."

Kenneth glanced at her before returning his attention to de Roche. "I do not need any weapons against him," he said loud enough for Hamlin to hear.

"My mother could best you, St. Héver."

"And your mother was a tasty bit of flesh when I bedded her."

De Roche suddenly reined his horse around. With a roar, he charged at Kenneth but Toby suddenly stood up to defend him, throwing herself in front of Kenneth. She was half way across his lap when de Roche rushed at him, sword drawn. Only fast thinking by Kenneth saved Toby from being gored; he very swiftly reined his horse around so that his back was facing de Roche. The man's broadsword glanced off of his armor. But he was still furious and Kenneth was in a very bad position with Toby lying across his lap.

Quickly, Kenneth dropped Toby to the ground. She landed on her feet but stumbled backwards, her balance off with the pain in her torso. Any movement was difficult. As Toby watched in horror, de Roche charged Kenneth again with his sword but Kenneth managed to side step him, grabbing the hilt of the sword as de Roche's horse slipped in the snow. Suddenly, Kenneth had a weapon and he used the butt end to smash de Roche on the back of the neck. De Roche started to go down, but not before he unsheathed a dirk that was strapped against his leg. As he fell forward, he shoved the dirk into Kenneth's right thigh.

Toby screamed, bringing the entire army to a halt. From his position far forward, Mortimer began to charge back through the lines to see what the commotion was about. By the time he reached the middle of the column, Kenneth was dismounted and preparing to drive the broadsword into de Roche's chest.

"Stop!" Mortimer roared. "St. Héver, drop the sword or I will kill you where you stand."

Toby rushed to Kenneth's side. "No, my lord," she stood in front of Kenneth with her arms spread as if to shield him. "He was only protecting me."

Mortimer wasn't looking at her; he was still focused on Kenneth. "Drop the weapon, St. Héver. I will not tell you again."

Kenneth could see from his peripheral that there were at least two crossbows trained on him, probably more. The broadsword fell to the ground and he grasped the hilt of the dirk protruding from his leg, ripping it free and tossing it away. Blood poured down his leg as he stood there with Toby still in front of him. From the beginning of the fight until this very moment, his stone-like expression of calm had never changed.

Mortimer was still glaring at him, though his distaste seemed to be more focused on de Roche at the moment.

"What started this?" Mortimer demanded.

De Roche was picking himself up off the ground. "A disagreement, my lord."

"Obviously," Mortimer snapped. He eyed Kenneth, who kept his mouth shut, before looking to Toby. "My lady? Would you be truthful with me?"

Toby didn't want to get Kenneth in trouble. "I… I am not entirely sure, my lord," she said. "I was not paying attention to what was said. But de Roche was the one to make the first move."

Roger cocked an eyebrow at his knight. "Is this true?"

De Roche looked defiant and ashamed at the same time. "Aye, my lord."

Roger's dark eyes flashed and he leaned forward on his saddle. "You will cease this foolishness, both of you," he hissed. Then he looked at Toby. "My lady, since you are well enough to defend your husband's knight, then you are well enough to ride at the head of the column with me."

Toby shook her head. "My lord, I assure you, I am not well enough in the least. I would prefer to ride on the wagon."

"You will ride with me."

"I want to stay with Sir Kenneth."

"I am not giving you a choice."

Toby gazed steadily at the man, feeling her anger rise. "It is not your choice to give. I will choose my own company and I choose to stay with Sir Kenneth. Go ride with your retainers and soldiers for I want no part of you."

Mortimer looked at de Roche and tipped his head in the lady's direction, a silent command for the knight to force her into submission. De Roche moved towards Toby and Kenneth suddenly came alive, striking the man in the jaw with his head-sized fist and sending him reeling. Soldiers began to move towards Kenneth but Toby swooped down and picked up the heavy broadsword, swinging it at two of the soldiers and slicing through their tunics. She cut one man substantially in the stomach. Kenneth saw what she was doing and, not wanting her to injure her ribs further or find herself bound and gagged, took the broadsword away from her and tossed it out of range. But de Roche had recovered from Kenneth's strike and was moving towards the man with a nasty-looking dirk.

"Cease!" Mortimer roared.

De Roche came to a halt, though it was evident that he wished to follow through with his attack against Kenneth. Toby was plastered in front of Kenneth as if to protect the man while he had her around the shoulders, intending to shove her out of the way. But Mortimer's order brought the action to a grinding halt and all parties concerned, including the men at arms, looked at Mortimer as if expecting more sharp commands. Roger, for his part, was finished with pleasantries. His blood was beginning to boil at the very lovely, but very disobedient, Lady de Lara and he intended to gain a handle on her before she caused further chaos.

His dark brown eyes focused on her. "Now," he said, quietly now that the pandemonium had settled. "If you disobey me again, no matter what the issue, St. Héver will receive your punishment. If you so much as refuse a request, I will take it out on St. Héver's hide. Any infraction by you will result in severe punishment to him. Am I making myself clear?"

Toby's face was dark. "You bastard," she hissed. "How dare you threaten me."

Mortimer didn't reply; he nodded his head to one of the men at arms standing behind Toby and Kenneth. The man produced a sword and smashed the butt end of it across the back of Kenneth's neck. The man went down, taking Toby with him. As Toby screamed, de Roche swooped down and pulled her free. He wrestled her all the way over to where Mortimer sat astride his big warmblood. Toby fought like a wildcat.

"That is only a foretaste, my lady," Roger told her as she struggled against de Roche. "If you continue to fight, I will see to it that St. Héver is quite incapacitated."

Furious, terrified and bordering on tears, Toby looked over at Kenneth as he struggled to pick himself off the ground.

"You are a beast," she growled before she could stop herself. "You are the most hateful beast that...."

Another queue from Mortimer had the men at arms kicking Kenneth savagely as he lay on the ground. Toby knew that, this time, her opinions and fearless tongue would not be forgiven. Mortimer had shown her twice. She stopped struggling and looked up at him, tears on her cheeks.

"All right," she said quickly. "Please stop. Do not hurt him anymore. I will be cooperative, I swear it."

Roger lifted his hand and the kicking immediately stopped. He smiled thinly at Toby. "Very good, my lady," he said. "As I said, now that you are feeling better, I should like your company as we ride. Hamlin, find her a palfrey."

De Roche let her go and Toby instinctively moved towards Kenneth to help the man. But Roger stopped her.

"Nay, my lady," he said almost casually. "You will not go to him. You will come with me."

Toby could see that Kenneth was struggling to push himself up off the ground. Even though he was in armor, he had been pummeled mostly in the head because his helm had come off. His lips were bloodied and there was blood coursing out of his nose. But his ice-blue eyes were open, looking at her.

"I am well enough, my lady," he told her so that she would not disobey again; he wasn't concerned for himself but, at some point, they were going to start punishing her and he was fearful for that moment. "Go along. I will be all right."

Toby's face screwed into unhappy tears. "I am sorry," she mouthed to him.

He winked a bloodied eye at her, propping himself up on his left elbow. "Run along. I will see you later."

Wiping furiously at her eyes, she turned for Mortimer, who dismounted his steed. He held out a hand to her and without looking at him, she took it. Together, Toby and Mortimer walked towards the front of the column, awaiting the palfrey that de Roche was preparing.

Kenneth watched her go, the smile fading from his lips. *God help her*, he thought.

ॐ

FEBRUARY HAD BEEN a brutal month of heavy winter weather. Tate, Stephen, Wallace, Edward and a thousand troops had made the trip from Cumbria to London in just over two weeks. Tate had taken five hundred men from Carlisle and another five hundred split between his castles of Whitehaven and Grayson. It was an impressive sight, the Earl of Carlisle moving a thousand men down the throat of England and into London. But Tate had a purpose and had all intention to show his power. And there was still more to come; like a man possessed, he knew no boundaries.

The night before they arrived in London, they camped on the outskirts of the town in a giant encampment with great bonfires that lit up the sky. It had snowed for a week before their arrival to the area and the land was blanketed in white. But this night was clear and a full moon shone bright upon them, creating a silvery-gray landscape. Tate and his men sat outside his tent, spread around an enormous fire and eating one of the black and white cattle they had brought with them from Whitehaven. The air was full of the smell of roast beef and Edward was so full that he had promptly passed out before the flames.

Stephen sat next to the boy, pushing his booted feet closer and closer to the fire. When his feet grew hot enough to start smoking, Edward would awaken, sleepily wonder why his feet were in the fire, pull them out and then swiftly fall back asleep. Stephen did this three times before Edward realized what was going on and grumpily moved away from the snickering knight. Wallace and Stephen had a good laugh at Edward's expense.

But not Tate; he had remained relatively silent and emotionless, watching the comedy but not feeling light enough to laugh at Stephen's jokes. Normally Kenneth and Stephen would play the jokes together, but the absence of Kenneth was painfully obvious. If Stephen felt it, he did not let on. Still, there were times when a trained observer could tell that he missed his comrade. He missed the man's quiet reserve, his strength, his solid wisdom. He missed his friend.

But Tate was glad Kenneth was not there. He thanked God every day that the man had surrendered himself to Mortimer in order to play protector to Lady de Lara. A greater sacrifice Tate had never seen and as he prayed for his wife's safety, he also prayed for Kenneth. He was sure that Toby would be relatively safe in Mortimer's custody but Kenneth was another matter. As a knight sworn to the king, Mortimer would not look upon him kindly. For that, and so many other reasons, they were on the outskirts of London. Tate had a mission and even as Mortimer seemed to be holding all of the power, Tate would not let the man gain the upper hand. He would do all he could to undermine him.

"Will there be anything else tonight, my lord?" Wallace asked as he rose from the fire; the old priest was fatigued by the weeks of travel and it showed.

Tate shook his head. "Nay," he replied. "Be ready to ride before dawn."

"Aye, my lord."

Wallace moved to rouse young Edward but the king would not be stirred. After much shaking and a couple of gentle kicks, Wallace reached down and picked the lad up. When Edward realized he was being carried like an infant, pride alone woke him from his food coma and he irritably chastised Wallace for man-handling him. Tate and Stephen could hear Wallace laughing as the two disappeared into the night.

The fire crackled and spit, filling the silence in their wake. Stephen drained the last of his wine and set the cup down.

"I suppose I should get some sleep also," he said, looking at Tate. "Do you have any orders for me, my lord?"

Tate was staring at the fire as if hypnotized; the man that Stephen had known for fifteen years had not been himself since that fateful day at Harbottle. He was darker somehow, meaner even. Mortimer's actions had brought out the Devil in him and Tate was growing more ruthless by the second. It was in his words, his actions, the very air he breathed. But Stephen understood why.

"Make sure the men are ready to move before dawn," he told Stephen.

Stephen nodded, pausing as if waiting for more orders. When none were forthcoming, he spoke.

"Shall I send word ahead of our arrival?" he asked.

Tate drained his wine; it was the fifth cup he'd had that night. "I sent her one missive already," he replied. "She already knows that I am coming and God help her if she is not prepared."

Stephen still didn't leave; he was watching Tate's manner, the way his jaw ticked when he spoke. The man was tightly coiled.

"Mortimer has troops at Windsor," Stephen said quietly. "Do you have reason to believe that they are not lying in wait for us in the wake of your announcement that you are coming to visit the queen?"

Tate turned to look at him. "Isabella would not dare order them against me," he said. "She does not want to incur my wrath."

"What about Edward?"

"He stays with you while I speak with her. He is not allowed near his mother for any reason. Not even if he begs."

It was a hard statement but a necessary one. Stephen cleared his throat softly, his gaze moving to the clear sky above.

"Just so I am clear, my lord," he ventured. "We are to march on Windsor tomorrow and lay at her base. You have requested audience with Queen Isabella under a flag of truce."

Tate nodded slowly; the tick in his jaw was increasing. "She will understand that I am no longer tolerant of her lover's tactics. It is one thing to attempt to kill the king but it is purely another to hold my wife hostage." He turned to Stephen, the dark eyes wild with storm. "Even now, I have a thousand men from Henry of Lancaster bearing down on Wigmore Castle. From the Trinity Castles of Hyssington, Caradoc and Trelystan, all holdings of my brother, Liam, I have five thousand men also moving for Wigmore. I have even asked my brother for aid from his Welsh allies. Another two thousand Welsh should be marching upon Mortimer at Wigmore, awaiting my word to unleash hell. If

Isabella wants her lover to live to see another day, she will use her influence on him to release Toby."

Stephen had known he had sent word to the Earl of Lancaster and his de Lara kin for assistance but he had not known the extent. At the thought of eight thousand troops bearing down on Wigmore Castle, he lifted his eyebrows.

"What of the troops we sent to Warkworth?"

"They are Harbottle troops and already weary from a brutal siege," Tate answered. "I will leave them at Warkworth, as I will not call upon Alnwick at this time. They are too far to the north and Henry of Lancaster is a great supporter of our king. He is much closer to the Marches and more than willing to commit men to the cause."

Stephen nodded in agreement, finally emitting a pent-up sigh. "Dragonblade commands and men will follow," he breathed, trying not to sound too stunned. "Eight thousand men is quite a force. Are you not concerned that Mortimer might somehow hurt Toby if he feels threatened?"

Tate shook his head confidently. "The man has twelve children he must be concerned for. If he harms my wife, I cannot guarantee where my vengeance would stop."

"You would harm his children?"

"I would make it so he never saw them again."

Stephen believed every word. It was all part of the ruthlessness that had emerged in Tate over the past several days. There was no use in speaking to him about it because he was blinded by his fear for Toby and his determination to retrieve her. Nothing else mattered. Stephen scratched his head and stood up.

"Then I will beg your leave," he said. "I will make sure the army is ready to move out by dawn."

Tate didn't acknowledge the man as he disappeared into the darkness. He was staring into the fire, seeing Toby's face with every flicker of the flame and wondering what she was doing that night. He wondered if she was thinking of him every second of every day just as he was thinking of her. His desire to get her back moved beyond normal determination; it was in a state of desperation.

Woe to Isabella should she deny him his wants. He was finished being the hunted in this battle between Edward and Roger Mortimer. He had now become the hunter.

CHAPTER SIXTEEN

Windsor Castle

T HERE WAS NO structure in all of England as enormous as Windsor Castle. Towers were several stories tall, the blond and sometimes gray stones glistening starkly against the snow upon the ground. From its perch on a hill, the bastion could be seen for miles.

Tate and his army lay just outside the village that surrounded the castle. From a clear night to a cloudy day, it was bitterly cold. Astride his great bay charger, he left Stephen and his men in their base camp and made his way through the village towards the castle. Villeins and storekeepers came out to watch him pass, the great Tate de Lara with his blue, gold and silver crest of a great dragon on his tunic. Everyone knew the dragon emblem and the man associated with it. As the charger clopped up the incline that lead to the main entrance of the castle, the town was oddly silent.

As Tate knew, there was no waiting ambush for him. But he could see hundreds of men on the battlements, watching him approach. But he rode onward until he reached the great gates, coming to rest just shy of the drawbridge. He shouted up to the sentries on the wall.

"You will tell the Queen that the Earl of Carlisle has come seeking audience," he called. "Tell her I wait for her at the gates."

A great commotion followed; he could hear the soldiers shouting to each other; men were on the wall, off the wall, and yelling abound in the lower bailey. Tate wondered how long he would be forced to wait as word reached Isabella.

He remained in place for at least a half an hour. Snow was beginning to fall again, a light dusting blanketing his armor. His charger snorted nervously, dancing around impatiently. The clouds above his head darkened and birds scattered about seeking shelter. Still, Tate continued to wait patiently. But as the snow fell heavier and his patience began to wane, the great gates of Windsor began to slowly crank open.

Tate could see her just inside the gates. She was busily chatting with her ladies, who apparently wanted to accompany her. But he could see Isabella ordering them away, the gossipy and whorish French women that attended her. Tate had never liked them, although all of them, at least once, had tried to seduce him. He had to laugh at their boldness and ingenuity in doing so, although they were not the type of stories he could ever tell his wife. Maybe someday when they were old and gray and needed a good laugh, but not now. He didn't think she would appreciate the humor.

Isabella eventually headed towards him. Under the great gatehouse and across the drawbridge she came. She had been quite a beauty in her time, with dark hair and hazel eyes, but time and her trials had seen that beauty fade. She was only thirty-one years old but looked older.

Dressed resplendently in white fur and golden brocade, Isabella smiled at him as she made her way across the drawbridge. In spite of the reputation the woman had, Tate had always found her to be kind and honest. She was, however, extremely pliable to the will of men, which is how Mortimer had managed to enslave her. All the woman had ever wanted was the love of a man and would do anything to get it. It was unfortunate.

"Dragonblade," she greeted fondly in her heavy French accent. "My God, let me look at you. It has been far too long."

Tate dismounted his charger and went to her, taking her gloved hands to kiss them. "My Queen," he was as pleasant as he could be given the circumstances. "Time has been kind to you."

She rolled her eyes at him as if to disbelieve him. "You are very sweet," she said, her hazel eyes moving over his handsome, stubbled face. "I am so happy you have come to visit me."

"I wish it was a social call."

She cocked a dark eyebrow. "And it is not?" she clucked softly. "Whatever do you mean?"

Tate's gaze was steady on her; in his peripheral, he could see dozens of soldiers just inside the gates, knowing they were watching him like a cat watches a mouse. They were Mortimer's men. Tate took Isabella's hand and tucked it into the crook of his arm.

"Walk with me, Iz," he said softly.

Isabella immediately complied, like an eager puppy. She was bundled tightly against the weather and felt no cold as they began to walk down the slope from the main gates. In fact, she felt rather giddy in the company of a man she had once been wildly in love with.

"So you call me Iz, do you?" she snorted softly. "That cannot be a good sign."

The corner of his mouth twitched. "How would you know?"

"Because you only call me that when you are cross with me."

He did laugh, then. "You are imagining things."

She laid her cheek on his arm affectionately. "Nay, I am not," she said as they continued down the road. "Now, would you care to tell me why you have come if it is not a social visit?"

He nodded, putting his thoughts together. Although he had been over and over this conversation in his mind, still, he did not want to come across as too harsh at first. Yet it was difficult, especially with the subject matter.

"I have come with a problem that you can help me solve," he said softly.

"Problem? What problem?"

Tate paused as they came to a crossroads in the avenue that led from the castle; it was right at the edge of the village. He faced her as the snow fell between them.

"I was married a few weeks ago," he told her.

Isabella's eyes opened wide. "Married?" she gasped. Then she threw her arms around him. "Oh, Tate, that is marvelous. I am so happy to hear this."

"Thank you," he replied as he hugged her and then let her go. "I am also very happy. Happier than I have ever been in my life. But my happiness came to a brutal halt when Mortimer abducted my bride."

Isabella stared at him. Then, her eyes bugged again and she staggered as if hit. Her hand flew to her chest.

"Roger," she breathed. "What do you mean? What happened?"

Tate told her the entire story, from the time he visited Cartingdon until that very moment. He omitted the information about the armies of Henry of Lancaster and the Lords of de Lara for the moment, but for the most part, he told her the truth. He watched Isabella ride a wild sea of emotion; she was up, she was down, she was weeping, she was furious. She was also extremely insecure and extremely jealous. Tate knew this, which he was planning on using to his advantage. A jealous woman would be of tremendous help. He hoped it would be enough.

"My God," she gasped with the story was concluded. "Do you know where he has taken her?"

"In the missive he sent me, he told me to go to Wigmore Castle," Tate replied. "I would assume he has taken her there."

Isabella was pale with shock, her mind focused on her lover and the fact that he had Tate's wife in his company. It did not sit well with her. She rubbed her chin in thought, her gloved hand drifting over her cheeks as she pondered the situation. Then her hazel eyes fixed on him.

"So why have you come to me?" she asked, somewhat suspiciously. "What do you want me to do?"

Tate cocked an eyebrow at her. "You will do everything in your power to have my wife returned to me immediately," he told her in a tone she had rarely heard from him. "I will not tell you how you must achieve this. I believe you can figure it out."

Isabella looked uncomfortable, fiddling with her gloves. "He may not listen to me," she said softly. "He has a very strong will."

Tate would not be put off by a weak woman. He gazed steadily at her. "I have eight thousand men converging on Wigmore Castle as we speak," he told her in no uncertain terms. "If you do not convince Roger to release my wife, then I will lay siege to the castle and destroy it. And when it is breached, I will destroy Roger. Have no doubt that I can do this. And if my wife is harmed in any way, I will make sure that Roger's family suffers the consequences because my vengeance will know no limits. Is this in any way unclear? I am giving you the chance to save the man who saved you from your husband. If you fail, I will destroy him."

She looked at Tate with naked fear. "Please do not harm him. He may be foolish at times but he is not evil."

God, the woman is blind, Tate thought. "He is inherently evil, Iz," he said, more gently. "This man has been trying to kill your son for two years and you have done nothing to stop him. Why do you think I took the king with me? To protect him. We have been running from Roger for two long years but I will not run any longer. Roger has crossed the line and I will kill him if he does not release my wife unharmed."

Isabella's eyes were filling with tears. "Where is my son?"

Tate would not be shifted of the subject. "He is still with me, strong and healthy and alive," he put his hands on her upper arms, gripping her tightly. "Listen to me and listen well; when I leave here, I ride for Wigmore. You may ride with me to talk some sense into Mortimer when we arrive. If you do not ride with me, then know that I ride to kill him. The choice is yours."

She sniffled delicately into a lace handkerchief. "Is that why you have come? To threaten me?"

"I have come to seek your help in the release of my wife. That is all I care about."

She wept quietly into her hand for a few moments. Tate stood there and watched her, not at all sorry he had made her cry. The situation with her son was a perfect example of the fact that she lived in her own world of denial and he was not going to allow her to do it this time. He wanted her help and he was going to get it. More than the might of an army, Isabella would be the one to sway Mortimer. He would listen to her.

"Will you help me, Iz?" he asked softly, adding leadingly: "My wife is very beautiful. There is no telling how she has caught Mortimer's eye."

Isabella looked at him with her watery eyes, shocked. "Why do you say such things?"

"Because you know him as well as I do. He cannot control himself around a beautiful woman and neither you nor I would want to deal with the consequences of that."

She sobbed louder, muffled in her hand. "He would not do that to me."

"Aye, he would," Tate shook her gently. "Please help me, Iz. I want my wife back. I love her. Please help me."

She sniffled and sobbed a few moments longer before looking at him again with her red-rimmed eyes.

"All right, Tate," she whispered. "You win. But I want something as well."

"What is it?

"You must allow me to see my son."

Tate sighed heavily; she was shrewd when she wanted to be. Tate had kept Edward from her for two years because he was afraid any contact with his mother would lead to Mortimer getting ahold of the boy. This time, however, Tate would have to relent. At least for now.

"Agreed," he granted softly. "Get your women together and your escort. We leave for the Marches by noon."

He took Isabella back to the castle, handed her off to her women, and collected his charger. As he rode back to his base camp through the softly falling snow, all he could feel was a tremendous sense of anxiety. He wanted Toby back more desperately with each passing moment and was having a difficult time controlling his impatience. He knew that Roger would not harm her but he also knew the man was an opportunist and had an eye for beautiful women. And Toby was certainly beautiful. As he thought of Mortimer trying to seduce Toby, he began to grind his jaw. He trusted his wife but he also protected what was his. The more he thought of it, the more tightly he clenched his teeth. Eventually, he bit his tongue.

When he reached base camp, Stephen thought he had been in a fight for all of the blood that was coming out of his mouth.

ᘓ

Wigmore Castle, Herefordshire

IT WAS A shockingly clear day in February. The snow was heavy on the ground, several feet deep in some places, but the sky was blue and the sun shone weakly. The fair weather was all Roger needed to force everyone outside for some sport. He had selected archery as the game of choice and had the field north of Wigmore transformed into an archery range. Half the castle had turned outside to watch.

Toby had been forced outside as well; having been given access to Roger's wife's wardrobe upon her arrival to Wigmore, she was glorious this day in a heavy blue brocade with gray fox lining that was a little too snug for her. Roger's wife, Joan, was a tiny woman and Toby was a bit taller and a bit heavier, which made the gowns and shifts strain against her. Adding to this situation was the fact that all Toby had done for weeks was continuously eat, giving her a deliciously curvy figure. The woman was mouthwatering to look at with curvy hips and full breasts. Roger went into a pant every time he was around her.

It had been almost four weeks since her abduction and Toby had been at Wigmore a little over a week, during which time she had tried to behave herself to keep Kenneth out of harm's way and, so far, the only time he had been punished for her bad behavior was that day on the road. He'd recovered quickly and she had maintained her coopera- tive attitude. But she was suffering from increasingly unstable mood swings that, although not enough to warrant punishment, had Roger unsteady. It was safer to keep Kenneth at her side to absorb her mercurial moods and stoic, emotionless Kenneth had been on the receiving end of some serious disposition highs and lows. The only other man that could tolerate Toby's unpredictable behavior was Timothy. The small physic had developed quite an attachment to the lady and she to him. He was animated at times and he amused her. Kenneth, the stone-faced knight, seemed to tolerate the physic moderately well although he did not trust him completely. The man served Mortimer, after all. Kenneth was fairly sure that the man was a plant but said nothing to his mistress. She would not have taken it well.

On this freezing, bright day, Kenneth had escorted Toby out into the snowy field north of Wigmore to watch Roger and some of his retainers compete against each other in the sport of arrow slinging. Kenneth carried a chair out to the field for Toby and she planted herself in it, accepting the candied pumpkin that Kenneth had brought along. She chewed with boredom as Roger let fly arrow after arrow, watching with distaste as he applauded himself and made sure no one bested him. Kenneth stood silently beside Toby, declining the candied pumpkin she offered him until she grew insulted and he was forced to eat it. Then, deciding he liked it, he took the bag from her and ate all of it.

"I cannot see anything in this snow," Mortimer announced as he finished a volley of shooting. "And someone has moved the targets. They are further away than they used to be."

"They are exactly where they have always been, my lord," de Roche said as he loaded his bow. "Perhaps the snow is blinding you."

Hamlin sailed the arrow at the hay target and hit it dead on. Others congratulated him, including the generals who had served with him during the siege of Harbottle, as Roger scowled. While the men laughed and offered praise to de Roche, Roger suddenly launched an arrow that ended up very closely embedded to Hamlin's arrow. Roger threw his hands up in victory.

"You see?" he crowed. "Not even de Roche can best me."

Hamlin scratched his cheek, eyeing the distant target. "I believe mine is still closer, my lord."

Roger was back to scowling. "We will solve this issue once and for all," he turned to Toby, sitting several feet away with Kenneth and Timothy in attendance. He marched over to her, speaking as he moved. "Lady de Lara, it will be up to you to decide who is closer to the target. Will you be so gracious to judge?"

Toby had been trying to coerce Kenneth into finding her more candied pumpkin and was startled by the attention suddenly focused on her. Not wanting to play Mortimer's game, she also did not want to see Kenneth beat because of her refusal, so she rose to her feet obediently.

"Of course, my lord," she said.

It was clear that she was unhappy as she stomped off towards the targets with Kenneth and Timothy in tow. Mortimer and his retainers followed. Timothy caught up to walk beside her.

"He cannot see, you know," he muttered. "The man is as blind as a bat."

Toby looked at him in surprise. "Mortimer?"

Timothy nodded, making sure Mortimer was not close by. "Once, he thought his wife's gray cat was a cowl and tried to put it around his neck. Was he surprised!"

Toby burst out in giggles, slapping a hand over her mouth to stifle them. Mortimer, several feet away, heard her laughing.

"You seem to be in good humor today, Lady de Lara," he said loudly. "Would you care to share the source of your laughter?"

Toby tried to look innocent, her mind whirling as she tried to think of a plausible lie. She did not want to get Timothy in trouble with his liege.

"I am sure you would not find it so humorous, my lord," she said, refocusing on the targets that were looming a few feet ahead. "It looks to me as if...."

Mortimer cut her off. "What was so funny? Is it a secret?"

It was apparent he would not let the subject go. The group of them came to the targets and she turned to face Mortimer with some irritation.

"Nay, my lord, it is not a secret," she said with veiled impatience. "We were discussing cats. I had a cat that used to jump on unsuspecting people. Once it grabbed me around the neck and almost bit my ear off. That is all we were discussing – cats."

Mortimer lifted an eyebrow at her as if he did not believe her but he let it go. He returned to the targets.

"Look and see, Lady de Lara," he pointed to the giant bale of hay with arrows sticking out of it. "Is my arrow not closer than de Roche's?"

Toby was tired of the game, exhausted in general. Most of all, she hated being around Mortimer and his men. They were pompous, overbearing, conceited and powerful. She found it a stifling combination. All she wanted was to go home, wherever that may, be so long as Tate was there. She missed him more with every breath and the fact that he'd not yet made it to Wigmore to rescue her was beginning to weigh quite heavily on her. It was part of the reason for her severe moods.

"Aye, it is," she said shortly, turning to Kenneth. "My feet are wet. Carry me back to the castle, please. I am cold."

Kenneth didn't say a word as he bent over and scooped her into his enormous arms. Bundled against the cold as she was, she made an armful. As he walked away with Timothy beside him, Mortimer called after them.

"You will attend the nooning meal, Lady de Lara," he said in a tone that suggested she had no choice. "I have visitors I should like for you to entertain."

Kenneth glanced down and could see the storm brewing on her face. "Pleasantly, my lady," he whispered. "Pleasantly."

She looked up at him, scowling, but knew he was correct. By the time Kenneth came to a halt and turned around, Toby's scowl was gone.

"As you wish, my lord," she said.

"And wear something delicious. I should like to show you off."

"I am not yours to show off."

Mortimer cocked an eyebrow. "You are indeed my guest to display as I please."

Kenneth could feel Toby tensing in his arms again and he gave her a quick squeeze, silently telling her to behave. She was close to exploding. Still, she managed to keep a civil tongue.

"As you wish, my lord."

She said it through clenched teeth and Kenneth very quickly swept her towards the castle before she could say something more that would have them all in trouble. Just as they came to the muddy road leading into the big gatehouse, Toby pushed herself out of Kenneth's arms with a growl.

"Ooooo," she stomped her feet angrily. "I do not want to attend him at the nooning meal and I do not want to entertain his visitors. I hate him, I hate this place, and right now I hate you for stealing my candied pumpkin. I want to go home!"

She suddenly burst into tears, weeping angrily. Kenneth struggled to keep a straight face as he and Timothy moved forward to comfort her.

"You are simply exhausted, my lady," Kenneth said evenly, taking her elbow. "Let us go inside where you may rest."

"I do not want to rest!" she stomped her feet again, a full-blown tantrum quickly approaching. "I want to get out of here. I want my husband. Why has he not come for me yet?"

Kenneth had her by the arm as he led her under the gatehouse. She was pouting and weepy, angry one moment and sad the next. Timothy kept his head lowered lest she see his grin and Kenneth tried to focus on anything other than her comical ranting. He tried to think of battles, bloody wounds and ugly women. But he was losing the fight.

"Come along, Toby," Kenneth pushed aside the formalities as he had many times during their captivity. "Go inside and rest. I will go find you more candied pumpkin if it will make you happy."

She sobbed, stepping in a big mud puddle and wailing when she saw that she had completely mucked the bottom of the lovely surcoat. It was all Kenneth could do to keep a smile off his face; she was hysterically funny. With a patient sigh, he picked her up and carried her the rest of the way to the keep.

She sobbed and muttered as she made her way into the enormous keep of Wigmore. It was cloyingly warm as the result of several blazing fires; Mortimer did not like the cold and the keep was generally kept quite warm. It was also a vast and luxurious place as far as castles went; creature comforts were everywhere. Kenneth and Timothy escorted Toby to the third floor where her chamber was located. But she came to a halt just outside the elaborate bower door, yanking her arm from Kenneth's grip.

"I am hungry," she announced. "Go and get more pumpkin."

Kenneth just looked at her, his ice-blue eyes glimmering with humor. Nodding his head wearily, he turned for the stairs. But he apparently wasn't moving fast enough and Toby swatted him on the shoulder as he began to descend the stairs.

"'Tis your fault so you need not blame me," she told him. "You ate my pumpkin so now you must find me more. And if you see anything else that looks good, I want that, too."

"God give me strength," Kenneth muttered.

Toby heard him mumble. "What did you say?"

He turned to look at her, his normally stony expression oddly animated. "I said, I am going right away," he looked at the physic. "Take her inside and put her to bed. Sit on her if you have to. And give her something to improve her disposition, for God's sake. I am not sure how much more of this tyranny I can take."

Toby's face screwed up angrily. "Come back here, St. Héver. Come back and say that to my face!"

She was holding up a balled fist. Kenneth opened his mouth to calmly retort but he ended up breaking down into laughter. He couldn't help it; it was just too comical to believe. Toby was furious a moment longer before erupting into a grin; an angry grin, but a grin nonetheless.

"I hate you, Kenneth," she told him sincerely as he continued down the stairs. "I truly do."

"I know," he replied, dead-pan. "You hate me and my mother, my grandmother, my father and every ancestor before him, my horse, my...."

He faded off as he went. Toby, softened by his reaction to her temper, realized she sounded like a complete shrew. She stood at the top of the stairs and called down to him.

"I love you as if you were my own brother, Kenneth," she called after him.

"I know," his reply was very faint.

"Now bring me my pumpkin!" she screeched.

She swore she heard him laughing again. Turning for her bower, she almost forgot about Timothy standing there, grinning at the exchange between her and the knight. She walked up to him, eyeing him critically.

"Are you really going to sit on me?"

Timothy shook his head. "I am afraid you might do me serious bodily damage if I did," he said, taking her elbow as they passed through the open door. "But I will sit and talk to you."

She let him escort her into the room, which was warm with a blazing fire. Thick furs covered the floor and her bed was piled with lush and warm materials. Mortimer had been, if nothing else, lavish with his attention on her. There was absolutely nothing she could want for. Toby went to the fire, carefully removing the cloak that had mud on it. Timothy took it from her and cast it into the corner for the servants to clean. She stood for a moment, dragging her hand across her softly rounded belly.

"Timothy," she said after a moment. "There is something we can talk about."

He was at the elaborate sideboard against the wall, pouring them both a measure of wine from a lovely glass decanter. "What is that?"

"You have been a physic a long time, have you not?"

"I have, my lady."

Toby's gaze lingered on the flames before turning to him, her cheeks rosy from the warmth of the fire. "You must know a great deal about babies."

He nodded. "I believe so. What do you wish to know?"

Her hazel eyes twinkled as she told him.

Cʒ

FOR THE DURATION of the trip to the Marches, Edward had kept a distance from his mother. Strange, considering he had very much wanted to see her. For two years, he had begged Tate to take him home to see his mother. But Tate had refused and had given clear explanations as to why he had refused. Edward was therefore well aware why Tate kept him from his mother. For two years, he had understood that the woman who gave birth to him would not protect him from her lover. Isabella and Mortimer had ruled during that time as Regents to Edward since he was so young. But the queen was clearly more loyal to her lover than her son. It was a devastating understanding.

Isabella had wept at the first sight of her son in two years and had tried to embrace him. But Edward had run from her and even now, five days later, would not warm to her. He rode with Stephen as company, astride the big blond charger that Tate had given him for his fourteenth birthday and morose in his thoughts. He was not much company. Stephen and Tate simply left him alone, knowing he would come to terms with his mother's presence soon enough.

The snows had fallen heavy along the Marches this year. As the army plowed their way northwest through Gloucestershire, the snow became heavier and Edward felt his determination to stay away from his mother wavering. He missed her, in spite of everything that had happened. He just wished she loved him more than Mortimer. As he struggled to get up the nerve to speak with her, a messenger was sighted to the north. Distracted, he followed Stephen as the man spurred his charger out of formation to intercept the rider.

The man was a spy that had been sent out on many missions for de Lara. He was older, wily, and knew well his craft. He was also freezing, his horse thrashed, and he came to an unsteady halt as Stephen and Edward raced upon him. Stephen threw up the visor on his helm to gain a better look at the man. Snow flew off the visor when it snapped open.

"Well?" he demanded. "What do you have to report?"

The man wiped at his running nose, red with the cold. "Liam de Lara's men are just south of Croft Castle, m'lord," he said. "He has them hiding out in the woods, but it is difficult to hide so many. He awaits orders from his brother."

"How many would you estimate he has with him?"

"Several thousand."

Stephen's eyebrows lifted in response. "What about Lancaster?"

"He is encamped to the north by several miles. He has two thousand men with him."

Stephen absorbed the information. "How many men would you estimate are prepared to march on Wigmore?"

The spy's gaze moved out over the distant de Lara army before coming to rest on Stephen again. "With what you are bringing, there should be at least ten thousand. It is a mighty army, m'lord. You could raze Wigmore in a night."

Stephen nodded slowly, digesting everything he had been told. "Get some food," he finally told the man. "I will inform Lord Tate of the situation. Be prepared to answer more questions if he has any."

"Aye, m'lord."

Stephen and Edward raced off in Tate's direction, skirting the massive army and coming upon Tate about a half mile down the road. He was at the front of the column, riding alone as he so often did these days. Stephen and Edward charged upon him, flanking him on either side as he rode.

"My lord," Stephen reported smartly. "Our spies have returned from the vicinity of Wigmore. The aid you requested is already positioned and awaiting your command. Including the army we bring with us, it is estimated that ten thousand men await your orders."

Tate nodded faintly, not at all impressed with the numbers. He could have more if needed. But he was nonetheless pleased with the show of support.

"Send missives to the commanders of my allies," he instructed. "I will camp tonight to the east of Leominster. I will meet with my allies there."

Stephen nodded sharply, racing off to fulfill the command. But Edward remained, riding silently beside Tate as they moved through the snowy, slushy ground. After several minutes of silence, Tate finally turned to Edward.

"Did you have something more to say about all of this?" he asked quietly.

The young king shook his head. "Nay," he muttered. "Do you really plan to lay siege to Wigmore?"

"I plan to get my wife back."

The lad was silent a moment. "But what if Mortimer wants to deal? What... what if he wants me in exchange for Toby?"

Tate eyed him. "Where did you hear something like that?"

Edward shrugged, looking at his gloved hands. "Everyone is saying it. Everyone says that Mortimer will want to exchange Toby for me."

Tate's gaze lingered on him. "He cannot have either of you."

"But if you had to make a choice, what would you do?"

Tate had been wrestling with that thought for several weeks. There were two choices; the logical choice and the emotional choice. As much as it tore at him, he knew that only one choice was possible. He sighed heavily, looking away from the young king as he prepared his answer.

"Mortimer will not harm my wife, of that I am sure," he said quietly, with gritty resolve. "But he would kill you. I have spent fourteen years of your life protecting you as one would protect his own child. In protecting you, I am protecting England and protecting the future for my own children. It would therefore stand to reason that if given the choice, I would have to choose you. But I would find some way to free Toby, have no doubt. I would never give up. Even to the death."

Edward looked at him, surprise and sadness on his young face. "But...Toby...?"

"She would understand," Tate cut him off; it was too painful for him to think on it. "She would support my reasons. But she also knows I would stop at nothing to get her back."

Edward fell silent again as they rode along, the distant mountains of Wales beginning to come visible on the western horizon. They looked like great white mounds of flour. The more he thought about Tate's dilemma, the sadder he became.

"I remember when your wife died," he said softly, wondering if he should even say such a thing. "I remember seeing you cry. You didn't know I saw you, but I did. It was right after she perished and you were sitting alone, holding your dead daughter. I was supposed to be in the great hall but I had gone upstairs because... because I guess I was curious. I saw you sitting with the baby, weeping over her." His head suddenly came up and he focused on his uncle. "I will not see you cry again, Tate. I will not let you go through this again, not when you have found someone to love again."

It was a passionate speech from the young man. Somewhere over the past few weeks, Edward had begun to grow up and sense that his responsibilities were not only to his country, but also to his family and friends in spite of the example his mother had set. Tate looked at the young man, his stormy eyes glittering.

"I appreciate your concern," he reached out and gently cuffed the lad on the side of the head. "I do not believe it will come to that. But you are correct about one thing; I do love her. Very much."

Edward smiled weakly, feeling somewhat embarrassed by his out-burst. He didn't know what else to say and nervously fiddled with the reins. Tate snickered softly at his sudden case of nerves.

"Have no fear," he said. "I will do what needs to be done which means that, at this moment, I must speak with your mother."

Edward watched Tate rein his charger about and move back through the column. He lost sight of him as he reached the queen's escort, swallowed up by the banners and well-dressed soldiers. The young king focused his attention ahead, thinking on the battle that surely lay ahead. He knew he would fight it this time, not like at Harbottle when Tate had locked him away. And this time, Edward was sure, he had an arrow with Mortimer's name on it.

Meanwhile, Tate had reached Isabella's fine carriage. It was a smaller cab purely for the warmth it would provide and several ladies, including the queen, were stuffed into it. They were also covered by mounds of furs, doing their *petit poi* to pass the hours of travel. One of them was reciting her own poetry from memory. When Tate pulled up to the carriage, however, all movement stopped.

Isabella was wedged in between two of her women to keep warm, supported by layers of heavy furs. She smiled at Tate when he opened his visor to look at her.

"*A que dois-je le plaisir de votre visite?*" she asked sweetly.

He eyed the whores surrounding her and dismounted his charger. "*Partir vos femmes et marcher avec moi,*" he replied.

Leave those women and walk with me. It was rare when he spoke French but he wanted the ladies to understand that he wished to speak with the queen alone. They did not need followers. Isabella climbed out of the cab, no easy feat with the amount of furs and cloaks they had covering them, and took Tate's offered hand as her small feet hit the slushy road. When he realized that it would be difficult for her to maneuver the muddy road bed in her fine slippers, he lifted her up to sit upon his horse. Leading the animal, he walked several feet away from the army, paralleling the column as it proceeded.

"What did you wish to speak of?" she asked him.

"We are nearing Wigmore," he replied. "We should be upon it by this eve."

Isabella's smile faded. "I see," she said quietly, eyeing him a moment before speaking again. "And you are wondering how I will convince him to release your wife."

"It has crossed my mind."

Her smile returned, knowingly this time. "I have been thinking very heavily on this, Tate. I have thought of little else. It is my belief that you should let me go alone to speak with Mortimer."

He turned to look at her. "Alone?"

She nodded. "He should not know that an army is waiting to attack him if he does not turn your wife over; at least, not yet. It will be easier to deal with him if it is simply me. I am not a threat, you see; I have given him something he very much wants. I have given him power. I can take it away as well. I believe that will be a stronger influence over him than your army."

Tate brought the horse to a halt and faced her. "I have almost ten thousand men waiting to lay siege to Wigmore," he said frankly. "You do not believe he will respond to that?"

"He will respond," she said softly. "But it will only drive him to war. It will not drive him to negotiate."

Tate cocked an eyebrow. "I want my wife back. I will have her back tomorrow one way or another."

"I understand, *bien-aimé*," she said soothingly. "But your method will have you kill Mortimer in order to regain her. I do not want him harmed. I believe I have another idea that will gain us all what we wish."

Tate stared at her for a moment. "He cannot have Edward."

She shushed him. "I did not mean that. I mean another way."

"What other way?"

Tate found that he was willing to listen. Mid-way through her explanation, they both looked up to see Edward bearing down on them. Isabella stopped talking, looking at her son anxiously as the lad came to a halt. Tate watched him, waiting for him to say something to his mother, but the youth remained silent. He just stared at her. After pausing a few moments to see what would transpire, Tate finally motioned to him.

"Go and get Wallace," he told him. "I think you both need to hear what your mother is suggesting. And be quick about it."

With a lingering glance at Isabella, Edward galloped off in search of Wallace. He returned with the former priest in short order, whereupon Isabella resumed outlining her plans for Mortimer and Wigmore.

It was the first step towards a son opening communication with his mother and it was the first step in a mother perhaps redeeming herself to her son. Perhaps in helping Tate and Toby, they were helping each other as well.

CHAPTER SEVENTEEN

T HE NOONING MEAL commenced two hours after its normally
scheduled time. Toby had pouted and raged in her chamber about
the fact that she did not want to attend but she knew that she must.
Even the candied pumpkin Kenneth had managed to locate did not
improve her mood. So the knight was forced to give her a very stern
talk about her behavior and the necessity for cooperation. Toby had
thrown pumpkin at him. Kenneth had calmly picked it up off the floor
and ate it.

Pushing the limits, Toby waited until the last minute to dress for
the meal in another Joan Mortimer gown. Toby had fleetingly wondered about a woman who would allow her husband to so openly
cavort with another woman, even if it was the queen. She didn't
imagine the woman had a lot of self-respect or, more likely, a lot of
choice in the matter. Not that she particularly cared, but it was a
curious situation.

Toby dressed in a cream-colored lamb's wool with white ermine
lining. It was an exquisite gown that was both very soft and very warm.
The sleeves were long and belled, the neckline rounded and flattering.
A gold belt draped around her waist, giving her a very angelic appearance. She brushed her golden brown hair vigorously, securing it at the
nape of her neck in a delicately wrapped bun pattern. Mortimer's wife
had left a variety of hair ornaments and she secured her bun with an
ornate golden butterfly comb. It was extremely flattering.

Gazing back at her reflection in the polished bronze mirror, she found herself thinking on the whirlwind that had been her life for the past month. At the turn of the New Year, she had been Toby Cartingdon, the same as she had always been. Her days had been filled with managing her father's estate, tending to her invalid mother, and tending to her younger sister. While she had not been particularly happy, she had been moderately content. She had been resigned to her existence. Never in her wildest dreams could she have imagined the life she now led. To have married Tate de Lara had given her more joy than she could have imagined, but everything else that had happened during those few weeks still had her disoriented. She still expected to wake up and realize that it had all been a dream.

She smoothed the skirt of the surcoat, fingering the neckline and noticing how the cut emphasized her round breasts. They had filled out quite a bit over the past two weeks. Her waist was still slim but her breasts were lusciously full. It didn't look like her usual figure; she was delicious and round. But Timothy told her that the filling out of the body was normal in early pregnancy.

Toby grinned as she ran her hand across her belly, slightly rounded beneath the belt. *A baby.* She remembered when her mother had been pregnant with Ailsa and how ill the woman had been. Other than being ravenously hungry constantly, Toby felt fine. And, of course, the mood swings, but she wasn't particularly concerned about that. At the moment, her most predominant thought was the baby and somehow reuniting with Tate. She missed him so much that her heart literally ached and with each passing day that he did not appear, her anxiety was growing. Kenneth had told her to have faith but it was becoming increasingly difficult.

A knock on her chamber door roused her from her thoughts. She stepped away from the mirror, inviting the knocker to enter.

Kenneth entered the chamber, closing the door softly behind him. Mortimer had forbid him to wear his armor inside the keep so he was dressed in a dark tunic and leather breeches. He stood politely by the door, his big hands clasped behind his back. He was actually shaved and combed and looked rather gentlemanly. Toby had seen him that way many a time since their arrival to Wigmore and Kenneth always looked extremely uncomfortable. The man missed his armor as one would miss a lover.

"Are you ready, Lady de Lara?" he asked. "Mortimer has sent me to retrieve you."

She pursed her lips irritably, keeping her retort to herself when he lifted a rebuking eyebrow at her. Turning away from him, she went over to the vanity table with its vast array of powders and perfumes. Sitting down, she picked up a delicate cotton powder puff and began to powder her shoulders and décolletage with a very fine talc powder fragranced with rose oil.

"Why do you suppose Tate has not come yet?" she asked him quietly.

He watched her dust off her lovely shoulders. "He will be here, my lady."

She stopped dusting and looked at him. "As you have said many times, yet he has not appeared." She stared at him a long moment. "You... you do not suppose that de Roche was being truthful and he drown in the frozen river?"

Kenneth shook his head. "If he had, we would be hearing it from other sources by now. Yet de Roche is the only one who has mentioned it. Not even Mortimer has mentioned it." He watched her absorb the information, ripples of doubt and hope spreading across her face. "Are you ready to go?"

She put the puff down, giving a little sigh as she did so. "I do not suppose we could tell Mortimer that I am ill, could we?"

"Not a chance."

She made a face. "Who is his visitor, then?"

Kenneth shifted on his big legs. "The Earl of Suffolk, Robert de Ufford. He is a major supporter to Mortimer's cause."

"Why is he here?"

"I would like to know that myself."

Toby stared at herself in the mirror, seeing Kenneth's reflection also as he looked at her. Feelings of helplessness and restlessness swept her. She closed her eyes tightly and clenched her fists.

"I do not want to be here any longer," she hissed. "I want to go back to Harbottle or Forestburn or wherever Tate wants to live." She suddenly looked up, gazing at him in the reflection of the mirror. Her hazel eyes welled. "I just want to go home."

Kenneth nodded. "I know," he said gently. "But we cannot at the moment."

She turned to look at him beseeching. "When, Kenneth? When will he come for me?"

"I do not know, Toby. You must be patient. He will come."

Toby opened her mouth to reply but was interrupted by Timothy blowing into the room. He hadn't even knocked. Both Kenneth and Toby watched him as he went straight for Toby with a pewter chalice in his hand.

"Here, my lady," he thrust the cup at her. "Drink this. It will be very good for the baby."

Toby's eyes widened. So did perpetually stone-faced Kenneth's; his expression gradually morphed until he looked as if he was about to explode.

"What baby?" he demanded in an uncharacteristic burst.

Timothy looked at him with surprise. "She did not tell you?" he clucked softly. "Our lovely lady is pregnant, knight. You do not think that her outbursts and tantrums have been the mark of her normal disposition, do you? Lady de Lara is expecting. We must take great care of her now."

Kenneth looked at Toby, who gazed back at him somewhat fearfully. He just stared at her, a million thoughts rolling through his head. He began to look unsteady.

"Does Mortimer know?" he asked, his tone oddly tight.

Toby shook her head, wary of his reaction. "Of course not."

Kenneth did a very strange thing then; he exhaled loudly and sought the nearest chair as if all of his strength had suddenly left him. As he sat heavily, his ice-blue eyes fixed on her in shock.

"Toby, you have no idea...," he trailed off, regrouping his thoughts. He was, frankly, reeling. "God's Blood, are you sure?"

She sensed that he wasn't entirely happy to hear her news. If he wasn't happy, then perhaps Tate would not be happy. She suddenly felt awful about it and began to blink rapidly as her eyes started to well again.

"Fairly sure," she was beginning to sniffle, a prelude to bursting into tears. "Why? What's wrong? Why do you look so?"

Kenneth didn't want to frighten her but he was, in fact, frightened himself. *Tate's legacy.* Of course, he was thrilled for Tate but he was also terrified. If Mortimer knew of Lady de Lara's pregnancy, then he feared the dynamics of the situation would change dramatically. Not only would de Lara's wife be captive, but she could quite possibly have the child in captivity. Then Mortimer would have Tate's entire family to bargain with. Tate had already lost one wife and child; Kenneth knew, as he lived and breathed, that Tate would not lose another.

"I am sorry," he struggled to compose himself. "I did not mean to frighten you. But you must understand the seriousness of this situation. Mortimer must not know that you carry Tate's child."

She sniffled. "I did not plan to tell him."

He was glad she had not asked for more of an explanation; it would have frightened her further and he was trying very hard not to upset her. "Good," he sighed. "You must adhere to that vow. It is important."

"I will," she was giving him a pouting face. "But why?"

So much for not having to explain his reasons to her. "Because Mortimer will use the child against Tate just as he is using you," he tried not to sound too intense. "What man would not risk everything for his wife and child?"

Her face darkened, somewhere between guilt and anger. "He would not harm the baby, would he?"

"Nay. But Tate would risk his life for you both. The harm, if any, would come to Tate."

She looked as if she was about to cry again but steeled herself. Naïve as she was about war and politics, she was getting a very quick lesson on the brutality of warfare. Fortunately, she was a good student. She understood the seriousness of the situation.

"We must keep this secret very safe, then," she looked at Timothy, the earl's physic. "You will not tell him, of course."

Kenneth looked at Timothy, too; he was the only uncertain element in all of this and Kenneth still did not trust him. But at the moment, he had little choice.

Timothy, seeing that all eyes were upon him, nodded quickly. "He will not hear it from my lips, I swear it," he said, indicating the cup in Toby's hand. "Drink up, my lady. It is a nourishing brew."

Toby put the cup to her lips and drank. Kenneth watched her, softening, understanding now why she had been so volatile. Over his initial terror, he realized that he was quite happy for Tate. He knew that the man would be thrilled. Standing up, he went over to Toby and took her free hand.

"Let me be the first to offer my congratulations to you and Tate," he said sincerely. "I know he will be very pleased."

She licked her lips of the slightly sweet brew. "Do you really think so?"

Kenneth nodded fervently and released her hand. "I do."

A timid smile spread across her face. "I cannot wait to tell him."

Kenneth met her smile and, taking the cup from her grasp, set it upon the vanity. He held out an elbow to her. "Unfortunately, you will have to," he said. "But for now, Mortimer is waiting and we do not need to agitate the man. Come along."

She took his arm and he led her to the door. Kenneth opened the panel and allowed her to pass through first. Timothy was right behind them. Before the little physic left the room, however, Kenneth growled at him.

"Be sure you honor your word," he rumbled. "If you mention anything to Mortimer about this, they will never find your body, I swear it."

Timothy blanched, looking at Kenneth as if the Devil himself had just threatened him. But before he could reply, Kenneth quit the room and resumed his escort of Lady de Lara. Timothy stood there a moment, struggling to compose himself; he didn't doubt that the knight was sincere. The man had not liked nor trusted him from the onset of his association with Lady de Lara. But Timothy was becoming quite attached to the lady, far more attached than he was to Mortimer. Still, he was sworn to the Earl of March. It was where his loyalty was. But his friendship was rooted sentimentally to the lady.

Taking a deep breath for courage, Timothy followed.

C3

THE EARL OF Suffolk was a tall, thin man with a receding hairline and a beak-like nose. The moment Toby entered the room on Kenneth's arm, the earl and Roger vied for her attention like two smitten schoolboys. It infuriated the normally-calm Kenneth so much that Toby sent him to the opposite side of the room so he would not throttle them both. Kenneth did as he was told, lingering in the shadows and shooting daggers with his ice-blue gaze. Toby could feel his fury from the dais, hoping that Mortimer didn't feel it also.

She sat between Suffolk and Mortimer, feeling their hot, smelly breath on her cheek as they talked non-stop. Most of the chatter was pointless and boring and between themselves as they spoke over her, but several times they tried to engage her in conversation. Her answers were short and disinterested, much to Mortimer's displeasure. She seemed preoccupied with everything in the room but the two of them. The more she ignored him, the angrier Mortimer became.

When the meal was finished and the dogs were fighting over the bones, Toby continued to sit at the large dais, boxed in between Roger and de Ufford. She stared straight ahead as they chatted over the swell of her bosom; she could only imagine the heated stares she was getting from both men but she refused to acknowledge them. She could see Kenneth over near the hearth, lingering in the shadows, while Timothy sat at another table directly in front of her. He kept wriggling his eyebrows at her and Toby struggled not to smile at him.

De Roche entered the hall at one point and stood several feet away from Kenneth, watching the man as Kenneth watched the dais. It was the normal dynamics of their existence; being so close to each other had the seasoned knights highly attuned, ready to defend or attack at a moment's notice. De Roche wanted nothing more than to slip a dirk between Kenneth's ribs and Kenneth wanted nothing more than to murder Mortimer and de Roche, in that order. But they maintained their posts in silence until the relatively calm atmosphere of the room abruptly changed when Toby slapped de Ufford across the face.

It was the suggestive caress on her right thigh that set her off. Toby's instinctive reaction was to slap the man on her right as hard as she could and de Ufford was the recipient of a vicious whack to the face. As he fell back, Toby leapt to her feet and grabbed her half-eaten trencher, smashing it over his head. The man completely lost his balance and ended up sprawled on the floor. Before Toby could further attack him, Mortimer had her by the arms.

"Lady de Lara," he exclaimed. "You will behave yourself!"

She whirled on him furiously. "And you will control your associates, my lord," she yanked her arms out of his grip. "Teach them not to touch another man's wife and I will not have to teach them for you."

Mortimer was so angry that he was white. He grabbed her by both wrists and yanked her up against him. "Enough of this," he growled. "I told you what would happen if you did not cooperate."

"I will not allow any man to take liberties with me, including your lascivious friends."

"You will do whatever I wish. And it seems I must again teach you that lesson."

By this time, Kenneth was on the move. He was already at the dais by the time Mortimer issued his threat and Toby saw him from the corner of her eye. She knew that any backlash against her would fall on him and she was unwilling for the man to take the punishment for her outburst. She held out a hand to stop Kenneth's advance and labored to calm herself as she faced Roger.

"No further lessons are necessary, my lord," she said with more control than she felt. "But I will not permit another man to touch me. I do not consider that being uncooperative."

Suffolk was off the floor by this time and reached out, grabbing Toby by the hair. She screamed and swung around to strike him but Kenneth was already on the dais, grabbing Suffolk around the neck and driving his fist into his face. The earl went sprawling and Kenneth grabbed Toby from Mortimer's grasp, whisking her several feet away before Mortimer's guards were upon him. De Roche was suddenly in his path, blocking his exit, and he could advance no further. With Toby in his protective embrace, Kenneth was trapped. But he was fully prepared to fight to the death.

"Take St. Héver to the vault," Mortimer hollered at de Roche. "Remove the man from my sight."

Toby held on to Kenneth, terrified that if she let him go she would never see him again.

"Nay, my lord, please," she gasped at Mortimer. "He was only protecting me. You cannot punish the man for doing his duty."

"He struck the earl," Mortimer pointed out succinctly. "He must pay the price."

"I will pay the price," Toby let go of Kenneth and went to Mortimer, her hands clasped in front of her as if praying to the man. "I struck the earl first. Please, my lord; you must not punish Sir Kenneth. I beg that you punish me instead. I was the one who started it; he was only doing his duty."

Mortimer almost shouted at de Roche again to take St. Héver away, but a better thought occurred to him. When Suffolk staggered to his feet again and tried to take another charge at Kenneth, Roger motioned to a couple of his men to see the earl from the hall. As de Ufford was half-carried, half-escorted away, Mortimer turned back to Toby. His anger was beginning to cool as he saw a way to turn the situation to his advantage. He was, if nothing else, an opportunist.

"Very well, my lady," he said calmly, after some deliberation. "I will, in fact, take you up on your offer. Your compliance will buy St. Héver's life."

Toby wasn't stupid; she knew that Mortimer would extract a high price from her though she was not sure, exactly, what it would be. She was a little too unworldly to imagine how high the price could soar. In her mind, perhaps it would be supping with him nightly or entertaining him all day, every day. Perhaps it would be something distasteful but not horrific. She could not have been more wrong.

"I will comply," she agreed. "What are your terms?"

Mortimer took a step closer until he was literally breathing in her face. His dark eyes were deep and intense as he gazed into her almond-shaped eyes.

"One night with you," he growled seductively. "One night with you and I will release St. Héver. He will be free to go."

Toby stared at him, her eyes widening as she realized what he meant. She could hardly believe her ears and horror such as she had never known filled her breast. The mere thought made her want to vomit. She took a step back from him, her eyes bulging with disgust.

"Are you mad?" she hissed. "I am a married woman."

Mortimer cocked an eyebrow before turning to de Roche again. "Take St. Héver to the vault," he commanded. "He meets his death on the morrow."

"Death?" Toby shrieked. "You cannot kill him!"

"He struck the Earl of Suffolk."

"So did I. You must kill me also if that is your justice."

Mortimer's jaw flexed, grabbing her by the arm and whipping her against him. "One night and your knight goes free," he snarled. "Refuse and he dies. Those are the terms."

Toby was beyond horrified; she couldn't even imagine what type of man would make such a bargain. Her breathing began to come in heavy pants as she stared at him, finally turning to look at Kenneth. The knight was gazing steadily at her, his ice-blue eyes intense.

"The price is far too high, my lady," Kenneth told her emotionlessly. "I am not afraid to meet my death."

De Roche threw out a fist and struck him in the mouth to silence him. Kenneth's head snapped sideways but he did not lose his balance or his tense expression. Toby watched blood trickle from the corner of his mouth before turning back to Mortimer.

He was looking at her rather confidently, as if he knew he had her cornered. Toby met his stare, realizing that she could only make one choice. She could not let Kenneth die no matter what the terms of the bargain. She would therefore agree to the terms but there was no way she planned to go through with them. She wasn't sure how she was going to get around it, but she would think of something. She had to; too much was at stake.

"Very well," she almost choked on her words. "Your terms are accepted. But you will turn Sir Kenneth loose this very instant and I will watch him ride from this place. I would make sure he is well away before complying."

"Nay," Kenneth said through clenched teeth. "You will not do this."

Toby shushed him with a harsh hand gesture and he stilled immediately. Her eyes remained on Mortimer. "Do you accept my terms?"

Roger smiled victoriously. "Of course, my lady," he said, turning back to de Roche in a much more congenial fashion. "Retrieve St. Hével's mount and armor. And be quick about it; I am sure the man is eager to return to de Lara."

De Roche simply nodded his head and quit the hall, leaving Kenneth standing alone in stunned silence. Toby couldn't even look at him. As quickly as the storm had risen, it had died leaving devastation in its wake.

"Toby...," Kenneth whispered painfully.

She shut him off with a hand gesture. "Not a word, Kenneth."

"You *cannot* do this."

She spun to him, her eyes brimming. "And you cannot die."

For the first time since she had known the stone-faced knight, his face reflected something of his agony. The ice-blue eyes were glimmering with sorrow.

"I would rather die than see you do this."

"Your death would not prevent it in the long run. You know this. Eventually he will take what he wants."

Kenneth knew she was correct, knowing further argument would be futile. But the thought of her sacrifice was killing him; he could only imagine how Tate would react, how it would destroy the man. Tate had gone through too much destruction in his life and had lived to tell the tale, but something like this would likely topple him. Trouble was, Kenneth could not think of a way to stop it. For all of his knightly experience and cunning, he could not think of a way out of this unless he planned to throttle Mortimer at this very moment. He was close enough to do it but he wasn't sure he could complete the task before a dozen broadswords ended his life.

So he watched, helplessly, as Mortimer moved to take Toby's arm to presumably lead her back to the dais. Toby moved stiffly, as if all of the life had been sucked out of her. As she and Mortimer moved to take a seat, a sentry entered the hall and ran straight for Roger.

"My lord," he said, bowing swiftly. "The Queen is upon us. We have sighted her party about a mile out."

Mortimer's eyebrows lifted in astonishment. "The Queen?" he repeated. "But... how is that possible?"

"I do not know, my lord," the man said. "She will be here within the hour."

Roger's mouth popped open in shock, hardly believing what he was told. "Are you sure that is her?"

"Positive, my lord. A herald has arrived before her."

With that, the man bowed swiftly again and dashed away. Mortimer stood rooted to the spot, stunned, wondering why Isabella had come to

Wigmore. It was not like her to stray from the warm confines of Windsor during the winter and he had been planning on the woman keeping a distance for a few months. It would give him time to pursue his own interests away from her nervous energy; worse than his wife, she could be cloying and unsettled. Her approach did not set well with him; not well at all.

More than that, Isabella didn't even like Wigmore Castle; she said it smelled too much of Joan. Roger began to imagine all of the reasons she might have for coming and couldn't think of a truly solid one. Perhaps she was coming just to spy on him. He would have wagered money on it.

But he was no fool; it gradually occurred to him that the true reason for her visit was standing next to him. He knew that Isabella and Tate were very old, and very good, friends. And he knew how Isabella felt about Tate. She had asked the man to marry her once, something that had happened long ago in distant memory. But Tate was still around, still as strong as he ever was. Roger was suddenly angry at himself that it had never occurred to him that Tate would go straight to Isabella to tell her of her lover's folly. It was the surest way to force him to behave. *Damn the man!*

Slowly, he turned to Toby; she gazed back at him with a curious expression. He could only shake his head and hiss. He knew the answers to all of his questions were summed up in one name.

"Dragonblade," he snarled.

CHAPTER EIGHTEEN

TOBY HAD NEVER met a queen before. As she gazed at the woman she had heard about her entire life, she could hardly believe that the woman had come to Wigmore and thanked God for her good fortune. Now Mortimer's attention was directed elsewhere and it was like an intervention from heaven.

Isabella was short, with big dark eyes and dark hair and a face that looked as if it had seen better days. Roger was absolutely beside himself; he took the woman's hand and held it to his lips sweetly. He was quite loving towards her, something that both disgusted and fascinated Toby considering that not an hour before he had been propositioning her.

She'd not left the hall since the announcement of the queen's approach. Roger had made her sit down and wait, along with him and his retainers, for the queen's arrival. Kenneth had also remained in the hall, standing behind the dais and watching Toby like a hawk while Timothy sat near the hearth to watch the scene unfold with trepidation. Kenneth ignored the physic for the most part; all he was concerned with was the fact that since Toby had complied with Roger's demands, Mortimer had left her alone. His preoccupation with the queen's arrival was obvious and Kenneth was thankful.

So Kenneth skirted the hall as the queen and her retinue arrived, watching the group filter into Wigmore's large and warm hall. Kenneth knew the queen and she knew him, and when she caught sight of the big blond knight she nodded faintly. He bowed slightly in reply. They had a long history of association, dating back to her husband's early reign. Soldiers were trickling in after the queen, men dressed in mail and the queen's colors. They took position near the door.

Kenneth looked at a few of the faces, recognizing some but not others. As he neared the entry to the hall, one of the queen's soldiers, standing in the recesses by the entry, suddenly reached out to grab him. Kenneth immediately went on the defensive until he saw the face. Even then, he could hardly believe his eyes. It took him a moment to realize what he was looking at.

Tate gazed steadily at him from beneath the hauberk and helm. Kenneth struggled not to react, but his eyes did widen briefly as Tate swiftly motioned him to silence. Kenneth immediately turned around to face the room with Tate slightly behind him, hoping to protect the man from Mortimer's knowing gaze. Suddenly, the dynamics of the situation had changed dramatically in more ways than he could comprehend and Kenneth was both relieved and on edge. His heart was pounding.

"Where is Toby?" Tate whispered behind him.

Kenneth turned slightly to speak, trying not to be obvious about it. "On the dais," he muttered. "See her? Behind Mortimer?"

Tate was silent for a moment. "Aye," he murmured, incredible gentleness suddenly in his tone. "I see her. Is she well?"

"Well enough."

"Thank God."

For a man whose entire nature revolved around an unflappable manner, Kenneth was very close to jumping out of his skin. He simply could not believe that Tate was here, disguised as the queen's guard. Yet he should not have expected less; it was a cunning and logical plan. Kenneth's gaze began to move around the room and he noticed Stephen on the opposite side of the hall; he should have recognized his tall frame right away. Familiar cornflower blue eyes gazed warmly at him. Nearer to the queen was Wallace, although he hardly recognized the man for he had cut his wild gray hair off. Kenneth was stunned.

"Get Toby out of here," Tate whispered again behind him. "I do not care how you do it, but get her out of this room. Take her to the stables and I will meet you there."

"That may not be so simple," Kenneth muttered. "Mortimer keeps her close."

"Now is the perfect time with his attention distracted by Isabella."

Kenneth nodded once and moved away from Tate, skirting the room and paralleling the dais. He could see Toby sitting there, looking rather bored, and his heart began to pound harder. He moved closer, trying not to be conspicuous about it, as he finally slipped up behind her.

Toby was facing forward, watching Mortimer slobber all over Isabella's hand as he told her how much he had missed her. The sight of it made her rather ill but it also emphasized her longing for Tate. She imagined that it was Tate holding her hand, telling her how much he missed her. Her heart began to ache with the thought and her mood turned dour, so much so that she was startled when she felt a tug on her skirt. She looked down to see a big hand tugging at it, turning slightly to realize that it was Kenneth.

"You are ill," he whispered. "I must remove you from this hall immediately."

She wasn't following him. "I am fine."

He lifted his blond eyebrows at her in a manner that suggested she not refute him. "You are *ill*. I must take you out of here."

Her brow furrowed. "I am...?"

"You are seriously ill. You cannot stay conscious any longer. You are dying, for Christ's sake. Fall down already."

Toby looked at him as if he had lost his mind but she understood his message. She wasn't sure why she needed to leave but in reflection, it didn't matter. Kenneth surely had a good reason. She did as she was told and, with dramatic flourish, went limp in the chair and toppled over.

Kenneth wasn't prepared for her the swiftness of her act but caught her before she could strike her head on the chair next to her. He scooped her up into his arms, hoping he could get her free of the hall before anyone noticed. But Mortimer, in spite of his attentions on the queen, noticed almost immediately. All attention turned to Kenneth and Toby as the knight was thwarted from slipping out unaware.

"What is wrong with Lady de Lara?" Mortimer asked with great concern.

Kenneth shifted her in his arms so that her head wasn't hanging upside down. "I do not know, my lord," he replied honestly. "Perhaps she is simply overwrought."

Isabella gaze was intense on Toby as she moved past Roger, studying the lovely women passed out in Kenneth's arms. All eyes were on the queen as she observed Toby's face, her hands, her body. She was inspecting her, secretly satisfying herself on this woman who had managed to capture Tate's heart. What she saw did not disappoint her.

"So this is Lady de Lara," she murmured, reaching out as if to touch Toby's hair but stopping just short of it. She glanced at Kenneth as she drew her hand away in an almost embarrassed gesture. "She is lovely. You must take her to rest immediately, of course."

"Perhaps she needs a physic," Roger said, suspicion in his eyes. He didn't trust St. Héver not to run off with Lady de Lara but he could not do anything about it at the moment. "Perhaps I should send Timothy with you."

"Or perhaps she simply needs to be left alone," Isabella looked at Roger. "I suspect she has had more than enough company for the duration of her stay with you."

It was a direct rebuke and Roger shut his mouth to any further protest. Kenneth didn't wait for further debate and whisked Toby out of the hall, moving faster than he should have and praying that Roger did not become overly suspicious. Just as he neared the stairs, Timothy suddenly appeared.

"'Tis the excitement," the physic was trying to get a look at the lady but Kenneth was being most evasive. "Mortimer has given her more than she can handle."

Kenneth shifted Toby so that her head was against his shoulder, trying to keep the physic from getting too close. "She will be fine. She simply needs to rest."

Timothy cocked an eyebrow at him. "I am the one who will determine her health, if you do not mind."

Kenneth's gaze didn't waver. "Trust me; the lady is fine."

Timothy ignored him, managing to put his fingers against Toby's neck to feel a pulse. "Her heart feels strong enough."

"It is," Toby's eyes opened but her head didn't move; she looked at the startled physic. "Did you not hear Kenneth? I am fine."

Momentary surprise was replaced by confusion. "But…?"

"Please do not ask questions."

The physic stood with his mouth gaping. "But… what will I tell Mortimer?"

Toby hissed at him. "Tell him that you put me to bed and that I should sleep for hours. Tell him not to disturb me, no matter what."

"Are you going to rest?"

"Nay."

"Then where are you going?"

Toby dared to lift her head, looking at Kenneth. "I do not know. But I trust Kenneth."

Timothy was perplexed but refrained from arguing. Kenneth left him standing in the entry hall as he took Toby out into the muddy bailey. By the time they hit the ward, Toby's head came up again.

"Is it safe?" she asked.

"Not yet," he shoved her head back down.

They walked for several more paces before she spoke again. "Now?"

"I believe so."

Her head came up once more. "Then put me down."

He set her to her feet and she noticed immediately that her pale surcoat was in danger of getting mud all over it. She froze where he had set her.

"Pick me up!" she commanded.

Dutifully, Kenneth picked her up again and began his trek over to the stables. Toby looked around the ward at the remnants of the queen's entourage; a carriage, a few men, and a lot of horses. It was a big gathering.

"Now," she looked at Kenneth. "Would you care to tell me what this is all about?"

He remained silent as they entered the stable yards. "Can I put you down yet? She looked at the soupy, muddy ground. "Nay," she told him. "You will have to carry me so my skirt will not become soiled. Answer my question; why did you bring me out here?"

Kenneth veered into the stables. It was cold and dark inside, although it was dry. It smelled strongly of horses and hay and he set her to her feet.

"I was ordered to bring you here," he told her as they faced each other in the dim stable light.

She scowled at him. "Who on earth ordered you to bring me out here?" she demanded, rubbing at her arms. "I am cold. The least you can do is go and get my cloak if you are going to make me wait outside."

"You will survive. That dress is warm enough."

She growled. "Go get my cloak, I say. And bring me some warmed wine as well. I shall catch my death of chill out here and it will be your fault."

"Good lord; have you been ordering Kenneth about like that all along?"

It was a familiar voice that didn't register with Toby right away. Tate abruptly swung around the corner and into the stalls, almost plowing into his wife because she was standing so close to the door. Toby screamed at the suddenness of his appearance, tripping over her own feet. She would have fallen had Tate not reached out to grab her. She screamed again, startled by his grip, startled by the face, but only for a moment; when she realized her husband was standing before her, she threw her arms around his neck so tightly that she hit him in the throat with her rush.

Tate coughed a joyous cough from his bruised Adam's apple as he wrapped his mailed arms around Toby tightly enough to crush her.

"My God," Toby couldn't catch her breath. "My God, my God, *my God!*"

She seemed incapable of saying anything else at the moment. Tate laughed softly, his face in her hair, feeling tears sting his eyes. He was so emotional he could hardly control it. He took a moment to breath in her scent; she smelled like roses. Then the kisses started and he kissed her face furiously, listening to her gasp with delight.

"What...," she asked, interrupted when he kissed her soft mouth, "are you doing here? How did you get here?"

He didn't want to answer any foolish questions at the moment; he just wanted to taste her, hold her, and convince himself that she was real. His hands moved to cup her face, swallowing up her entire head with his enormous grip. He just stared at her, drinking her in.

"Are you well, sweetheart?" he asked, his voice trembling. "The missive I received from Mortimer said that you had been injured."

There were tears in Toby's eyes as she gazed back at him. "I fell off the horse and broke three ribs," she told him. "But I am as good as new."

He sighed heavily, one hand moving to touch her torso as if to convince himself that she was indeed in one piece. It brought him more relief than he could have imagined.

"Thank God," he murmured. Then he took her by the arms and looked her in the eye. "You foolish woman; you could have been killed with what you did. What in the world possessed you to lure those soldiers out of Harbottle?"

The tears in her eyes spilled over. "I could not let them find you. I was terrified they were going to kill you."

"Oh, sweetheart," he kissed her forehead, her temple, listening to her sniffle. "It was very brave of you but very foolish. I was so... well, it does not matter. All that matters is that you are well. And Mortimer...

he has been a respectful to you? He has not harmed or touched you?"

She wiped at her eyes. "Not yet," she didn't know why she suddenly felt so weak and frightened. "But he has been using Kenneth to ensure my behavior. I refused to do his bidding once and he beat Kenneth. He has not done it again so far, but he has threatened."

Tate tore his eyes off her long enough to look at St. Héver; the big blond knight's gaze was steady, as if there was nothing amiss. But Tate knew Kenneth well enough to know that the man would never react or complain about any personal offense against him.

"Is this true?" he asked Kenneth, pulling Toby tightly against him once more.

Kenneth cleared his throat softly, glancing at Toby before replying. "It was not that bad," he said, wanting the focus off of him. "He did, however, make a pact with your wife shortly before your arrival. He told Lady de Lara that he would kill me if she did not spend one night with him in the conjugal sense."

Tate's nostrils flared as he looked at his wife. Toby nodded emphatically. "The queen's arrival interrupted his plans, thank God. But he seemed to know that you had sent her."

"How did he know that?"

"I do not know. But when he was told the queen was approaching, he looked at me and said 'Dragonblade'".

Tate fell silent a moment, his arms around his wife, his cheek against the top of her head. It felt so good just to hold her again even though he knew they were not out of danger yet. He could not relax. After a pensive moment, he sighed heavily.

"It was Isabella's idea to disguise me as one of her own guard to gain access to the castle," he said softly. "Stephen and Wallace are here also."

"I know," Kenneth replied. "I saw them both. Where is the king?"

Tate lifted an eyebrow. "Safe," he replied vaguely. "More importantly, there is a ten-thousand-man army a mile to the south, awaiting my command to unleash on Wigmore."

Toby looked at him with shock. "Ten thousand men?" she repeated. "Why are they here?"

Tate rubbed her arms affectionately. "When I received Mortimer's message, my first thought was to raise an army bigger than anything England has ever seen. I was prepared to raze Wigmore and destroy everything, and everyone, in my path in order to gain you back." He sighed, watching the fear in her eyes. "But when my fury cooled, I knew that the one person who had the best chance of securing your release was Isabella. She holds much power over Mortimer. So I went to see her in London."

"That is why you did not come for me right away?" Toby was beginning to understand.

"Exactly. As much as I wanted to rush to Wigmore, I knew I had to lay my plans well against Mortimer. The man is no fool."

She gazed up at him, feeling foolish for ever doubting him. "So what now?"

He shrugged. "Isabella will order him to let you go."

"It is that simple?"

"If he wants to retain his life it is."

"What if he does not?"

"Then I raze Wigmore and him with it. I will destroy him."

His voice had taken on a deadly tone. Toby held him tightly, not wanting to let him go. "Take me from here now," she begged. "Why can you not take me out this moment?"

In truth, Tate hadn't anticipated seeing her the moment they arrived and he surely did not anticipate having her in his arms in the privacy of the stables. Now that he had her, he had absolutely no intention of letting her out of his sight. He had what he came for.

"Perhaps I can," he smiled warmly at her. "Perhaps it is as easy as that."

"If you are going to do it, you had better do it now," Kenneth told him seriously. "Mortimer is quite fond of your wife. Queen or no, he will be looking for her eventually. You will need time to get clear of this place before he realizes she is gone."

Tate's smoky eyes glittered. "I will take her back to the army but then I plan to return," he said. "I intend to have a serious discussion with Mortimer about his abduction of my wife."

Toby tugged on him. "It does not matter." She didn't want Tate engaging Mortimer in any manner of conflict; not now when they were so close to freedom. "You do not need to confront him. I am whole and sound and he has not touched me. Please, Tate, let us leave this place and never look back."

As he gazed into her frightened face, he realized that his vengeance, at the moment, was the most important thing on his mind. He realized that it had always been the most important thing on his mind save his wife's reclamation. He wanted to punish Mortimer for taking Toby. He very much wanted to make the man pay for his sins. It wasn't even about king or crown any longer; Mortimer had attacked him personally and Tate would not stand for it. His pride, his family, was at stake.

But as he held Toby in his arms, he realized that vengeance was futile. It was a waste of his strength and attention. He had his wife and that was all that truly mattered, but it was difficult to fight off the lingering need for justice. He struggled to refocus on the task of getting her out of Wigmore; his mind raced through the queen's escort in the ward, the strength of the men he saw upon the battlements and the state of the main gates the last time he saw them. If they were closed, it would make his escape far more difficult. But the last he saw, they were open. Reaching behind him, he grabbed a horse blanket that was laying over one of the stall partitions.

Tate swung the blanket around Toby's shoulders for both protection and a disguise. She stood out brilliantly in her pale gown and he needed to make her less conspicuous. He smiled at her when she looked puzzled by the action.

"Kenneth," he said as he secured the blanket around her shoulders. "Return to the hall and locate Stephen and Wallace. Have them meet us in the bailey. We are taking Elizabetha home."

Kenneth nodded shortly, feeling a tremendous sense of relief. He turned on his heel and quit the stable, his mind focused on finding Stephen and Wallace. But just as he exited the door, heading into the stable yard, a body was waiting for him. And that body drove a broadsword into Kenneth's torso.

Kenneth fell to his knees as de Roche removed the blade, bringing it up for Tate, who was just emerging from the stable. Toby screamed as she saw the flash of the blade a split second before Tate pushed her out of the way. Tate jumped back as well but not far enough; the tip of the broadsword sliced him across the collarbone and down his chest. It was a nasty gash but not deadly. Giving Toby a shove back into the stables, Tate unsheathed the broadsword at his side and launched into a full offensive against de Roche.

"So you think...," de Roche dodged a heavy blow and answered with one of his own, "to take your wife away unseen? I will give you credit for a clever disguise, Dragonblade. I would not have guessed you to come as the queen's own guard."

Tate thrust and chopped skillfully at de Roche, rewarded with nicking the man on the forearm enough to tear a good portion of the mail away. He was without his custom broadsword because it was too recognizable; he was using young Edward's instead. It was a good blade, but it was not the fearsome dragon-hilted blade. He wished fervently that he had it against an opponent as strong as de Roche.

"That was always the trouble with you," Tate said as he ducked a rather sloppy chop by de Roche. "You do not think for yourself. You only do as you are told and that is why you have never been able to outsmart me."

De Roche was on the defensive, backing away from Tate and nearly tripped over a stone in the muddy earth. "That is where you are wrong," he said, bringing his blade about. "I found you in the stable, did I not? How fortunate for me that Mortimer ordered me to saddle St. Héver's charger. Had I not been occupied with the beast, I would have never seen St. Héver bring the lady to the stables. And I would have never seen you enter shortly after him. The right place at the right time, as it were."

Tate understood a great deal in that halting sentence and he also understood that de Roche was more than likely alone. He and de Roche seemed to be quite alone as they battled in the stable yard, which was fortunate; Tate was terrified that someone, seeing the fight, was going to notify the entire castle. He had to do away with de Roche quickly or the element of an unnoticed escape would vanish.

"It matters not," he grunted as he managed to shove de Roche back against the yard wall. "In a few moments I will rid myself of you forever. I should have done it a long time ago."

De Roche tripped and fell back. When he came up, it was with a handful of mud, which he slung into Tate's face. Mud filled Tate's vision and he spun away, struggling to clear his eyes, knowing that de Roche would be upon him for the killing stroke. With Kenneth incapacitated, he could not expect any help. He wiped furiously at his eyes, only managing to clear one as he saw de Roche bearing down on him.

"It is over, my friend," Hamlin hissed, sword in an offensive position preparing to strike. "Once and for all, this will be over."

Tate lifted his blade to deflect the blow but the blow never came. He watched, through one muddy eye, as Hamlin suddenly lurched heavily and toppled over. The sword fell to the ground. Astonished, Tate looked up to see Toby standing where de Roche once stood with an enormous pitchfork in her hands.

She looked terrified and ill. The pitchfork prongs were dripping blood. De Roche was not dead but he was in a great deal of pain with three very deep puncture wounds in his back. One of them had gone into his spine. Though his head was moving, his legs lay completely still. When he realized that he could not feel or move his legs, he began to howl. It was an unearthly, harrowing sound that echoed against the cold stone of Wigmore.

Tate rushed to his wife, grabbing the pitchfork and tossing it away.

Together, they raced to where Kenneth lay on his back, now struggling to sit up. They went down on their knees beside him.

"Ken," Tate's voice was full of concern. "How bad is it?"

Kenneth's hand was covering the deep wound on the left side of his torso, below the rib cage. "Help me get to my feet," his voice was weak and gritty. "Get me on a horse and I can ride."

"You are bleeding all over the damn place."

"Just get me on my feet."

Tate lifted while Toby tried to pull; Tate ended up doing most of the work while Toby realized she could be more help if she found something to stop the bleeding with. He was oozing buckets. Ripping a portion of the long hem of her gown, she wadded up the wool and pressed it up against Kenneth's torso.

"Hold this tightly," she instructed him. "Press it against the wound."

"Thank you," Kenneth said weakly, eyeing her as he put a big arm around Tate's shoulders for support. "I am sorry to have ruined your gown, my lady."

She gave him an impatient look. "Are you mad? Stopping the bleeding is far more important."

Tate began half-carrying him back towards the bailey. "You will get the bottom of your garment muddy," Kenneth told her.

"It is of no consequence."

"Do you want me to carry you?"

"Oh, shut up."

Kenneth's lips twitched while Tate just shook his head at the two of them. "If this is any indication of how the two of you got on while you were incarcerated together, it is a wonder you did not kill each other." They were clearing the kitchen yards; horses were directly ahead and Tate went in that direction. "Can you make it back to camp?" he asked his knight.

Kenneth was supporting his own weight rather well for a man who had just been gored. He even removed his arm from Tate's supporting shoulders as they made their way to the horses.

"I can make it," he said, gathering the reins of the first horse they came to.

Tate helped him mount, but in truth, Kenneth remained relatively strong. Tate went to help Toby, lifting her up onto the very next horse. He was about to say something to her when small man in dark robes emerged from the keep, waving his arms wildly. Toby recognized Timothy immediately.

"My God," she gasped. "It is Timothy. What is wrong?"

Tate saw the young man as he descended the steps leading from the keep and almost tripped. "Who is that?" he asked.

"A physic," Toby told him. "A friend. What is he doing?"

They both watched as Timothy raced towards them, still waving his arms crazily. He was shouting something they could not quite hear.

"What is he saying?" Toby wondered aloud.

Tate shook his head. "I do not know. It sounds like...."

He never got a chance to finish his sentence; Timothy came close enough so that they were able to hear him. "*Run!*"

Startled, Tate and Toby watched as the keep suddenly came alive with dozens of soldiers pouring through the open door. Upon the walls, shouts could be heard and the portcullis, still in its raised position, began to crank closed. Timothy was still waving his arms, still shouting, until a soldier caught him from behind and knocked him to the ground. After that, they could no longer see him. Toby shouted his name, fearful for the man. He had come to warn them; she was terrified that he had paid the ultimate price for that kindness.

As for Tate, he was faced with a very harrowing reality; as he had feared, an alarm had been raised. Somehow, some way, they had been alerted to his presence and Toby's physic friend had been attempting to warn them off. The element of secrecy was no longer on their side and he knew their time had run out.

He turned to Kenneth. "Get her out of here," he told him. "I will do what I can to keep Mortimer from following. Go!"

It took Toby a moment to realize that he was not going to ride out with them. He was already unsheathing his borrowed blade, preparing to face the incoming enemy. Realizing that he intended to hold off the horde as they escaped, panic surged through her.

"Nay!" she cried, reaching for him even as Kenneth tried to turn her horse around. "Tate, I will not leave you, not again!"

He turned to look at her as the chaos around them increased. "I will find you," he said calmly, though the pain in his eyes was powerful. "Go with Kenneth. You will need to tend him. I will catch up."

She burst into tears, pulling her horse to a halt even as Kenneth tried to get the animal moving.

"Tate, please," she wept. "Please come with me now. I cannot leave you here to die."

"I will not die, sweetheart," he said softly, noting with increased panic that the portcullis was about a third of the way down. "Go with Kenneth and do not argue with me. I need to see that you are safe. I will see you soon."

"Nay!" she screamed.

Tate's emotions were on the surface as he looked to Kenneth. He couldn't bear to look at the agony in Toby's eyes. "Take her home, Ken," he pleaded quietly. "Just… take her home."

Toby reached out for Tate, straining, even as Kenneth took hold of her horse's reins. Tate reached also, like a last desperate effort, and their fingertips brushed. He could feel her warmth but he couldn't quite touch her. Kenneth was pulling her along and she was quickly out of his reach. Heart aching with sorrow, with fear for them both, he managed to smack the horse's rear with the broad side of the blade, like a swatter, and the beast took off. The last Tate saw, Kenneth and Toby had barely cleared the portcullis. But it was enough. They had escaped.

Knowing his wife was now free, Tate turned to face his duty as the soldiers began to swarm. He could see Mortimer at the top of the stairs and smiled at the man. It was a smile of victory.

The last Toby saw of her husband was of him standing in a circle of well-armed men. As she and Kenneth cleared the gatehouse, she lost sight of him altogether. As she had once sacrificed herself to save him, he was now doing the same for her. God help her; she realized he was now doing the same for her and the knowledge of it was as emotionally crippling as anything she had ever known.

All she could do was pray.

CHAPTER NINETEEN

I T WAS A dark and cold night. A few weeks ago, Toby had spent the night lying on her back with aching ribs, with Kenneth sitting next to her vigilantly. Tonight, it was different; it was she who was sitting next to Kenneth vigilantly. The man was sleeping soundly thanks to a potion given to him by one of the barber-surgeons belonging to Liam de Lara. She'd not yet met Tate's adoptive brother but she was sure she would at some point. At this moment, however, she frankly did not care. She only wanted to see her husband, safe and sound, and no one else.

The tears had been falling most of the night. Every time she thought of Tate standing strong against the horde of Mortimer's men, she dissolved into quiet tears again. She prayed continuously that it would not be her last glimpse of her husband alive. As she listened to Kenneth's heavy breathing, she wiped the silent tears that fell, scared and feeling very much alone.

They were all waiting for Tate; all ten thousand men. Toby had never seen so many people in her life as she and Kenneth had ridden into camp. They had been taken right away to an empty tent where Kenneth's wound had been tended. Men had brought food and drink, and several knights she had never seen before had come to talk to Kenneth about Tate's whereabouts and the current status of Wigmore. The men had ignored her until Kenneth had introduced her as Lady de Lara. Then, it was as if they could not do enough for her; food, furs, and warm things were sent to her in droves. She had piles of it. But all she wanted was her husband and he was nowhere, as of yet, to be found. As the minutes of the dark night ticked away, Toby slipped deeper and deeper into anguish.

It has been a long night with her turbulent thoughts. As she sat next to Kenneth, she noticed that the eastern horizon was beginning to turn shades of pink. She could see it through a crack in the tent opening. The new day was dawning and still no Tate. She finally lost her battle against despair and she lowered her head, weeping softly as dawn began to break. The next thing she realized, a warm hand was grasping her fingers gently. Toby looked up to see that Kenneth was holding on to her, a warm grip the only comfort he could give. She squeezed his fingers tightly and wept louder.

"Do not despair, my lady," he murmured thickly; the physic's sleeping potion was still at work. "He shall return. You must have faith."

She wiped at her eyes, unable to give up the tears completely. "But I am so frightened. There were so many soldiers...."

"I know," he squeezed her fingers. "But he always finds a way to survive. He has since I have known him. But he has more of a reason to survive than ever before; he has you now. Have faith that he will find his way back to you."

She nodded although the tears still fell. As she wiped her cheeks again, the tent flap opened and a tall figure entered. Startled, Toby wiped at her face quickly, turning to see who it was.

An older man in well used armor came into the weak light of vizier, a timid smile on his face. He was a big man with dark blond hair that was graying at the temples. His clear blue eyes found Toby where she sat next to Kenneth. When he saw that she was looking at him, he nodded his head at her.

"My lady," he had a soft, deep voice. "I am Liam de Lara. I apologize that I have not had the chance to introduce myself before now. It would seem that you and I are family."

Toby gazed up at the man; he was handsome and square-jawed. He was also one of the more powerful marcher lords with his family going back before the time of the Conqueror.

"My lord," she greeted.

By this time, Kenneth had opened his eyes and focused on the baron. Liam went to Kenneth's other side, taking a knee beside the injured knight.

"St. Héver," he patted the man's shoulder. "I have no idea why you lay here. You could have both arms and legs cut off and still ride into battle. Surely a stronger man has never lived."

Kenneth grunted. "I am not really injured."

"No?"

"'Tis all a ploy to gain sympathy."

Liam laughed softly, displaying nice white teeth and slightly prominent canines. "I have absolutely none to give you," he replied, glancing up at the very lovely lady sitting next to him. "And this lady is married to my brother, so you are wasting your time if you are trying to gain her favor."

Kenneth actually grinned, looking at Toby. "Your brother has her attention quite captivated," he replied. "Moreover, her only interest in me is ordering me about. Perhaps I feign injury so she will leave me alone."

In spite of her emotional state, Toby could not help but grin. She smacked him gently on the shoulder. "You are a lout," she scolded softly, looking at Liam. "Just so you are aware, if I were to order him up at this moment to do my bidding, he would rise from his deathbed in order to see my wishes fulfilled. The man is as loyal as a dog."

Liam laughed softly again. "I know this to be true," he looked back to Kenneth. "My physic tells me that you will survive. He says the puncture is deep but that it did not hit anything vital."

Kenneth nodded wearily. "I should be fine by tomorrow."

Liam just shook his head; the man meant every word. He had known St. Héver for years and the man was virtually immortal. Nothing could get him down for long. But he could feel Toby's gaze on him and he looked over at her, seeing the red-rimmed eyes. He knew how frightened she was and he wished he had better news to offer her.

"Have you heard anything of my husband?" Toby asked him before he could speak.

Liam could see the strength within the woman with just that question. She had an unwavering manner about her, besides the fact that she was enormously beautiful. It was his first exposure to her and he could see what his brother found attractive in the lady right away. He shook his head to her question.

"Not a word, my lady," he said quietly. "Perhaps we will very soon. Mortimer cannot keep quiet for long."

She nodded slowly, absorbing the information. "Where is Edward?"

"I am told that the king is asleep."

"He has not yet come to see me."

"I know," Liam nodded faintly. "In truth, I have not seen him, either. He has made himself scarce as of late. But I am sure he feels some guilt for what has happened. He gave his mother the approval for this venture, I am told. You and St. Héver returned, but Tate and Pembury are now trapped. Surely he is beside himself."

Toby pursed her lips in sorrow. "He need not feel that way. It was not his fault."

"I know. But he is young. He has not yet learned to deal with the weight of responsibility."

"Are there any plans for my husband's rescue?"

"Not yet. We must see what this day brings and go from there."

"You are not going to go after him right away?"

"I do not believe that would be prudent. But have no doubt that we will act when the time is right."

Toby let the conversation die, her gaze returning to Kenneth once more. He was looking at her, trying to gauge her reaction to all of this. Liam's attention lingered on the two of them before he politely excused himself, exiting the tent into the day that was growing lighter by the moment. He had much to do and was pleased at Lady de Lara's brave attitude. It made his life easier.

But Toby wasn't being brave at all; she was reflecting on the conversation and growing increasingly distressed. *We must see what this day brings and go from there.* She didn't like the inaction or the waiting. Her husband was in trouble and just as he sought to save her, she knew that she must seek to save him also. She had to; she simply couldn't sit around and wait for others to act. When the situation had been reversed and she had been held captive, Tate's plan had been to involve Isabella. As Toby sat and pondered, she suspected that might be her best option also.

And why not? Toby remembered how Mortimer fawned over Isabella the moment she arrived at Wigmore. She remembered the sickening flattery, watching as the queen soaked it up. The woman wallowed in the adoration. She wondered what the queen would say if she knew that her lover had indecently propositioned another woman. And what if that woman were to expose Mortimer's lustful intentions? Toby wondered... an exchange... *me for Tate.* But she would make sure that Isabella knew the details of the exchange; chances were that both she and Tate would see freedom were Isabella sufficiently jealous and angered at Mortimer. God help her, she had to try. If these men weren't going to act, then she had to.

Abruptly, she stood up. Kenneth was dozing off, startled when she moved suddenly.

"What is wrong?" he asked sleepily. "Where do you go?"

"Nowhere," she lied. "Go back to sleep. I am simply going to stand by the door. I... I just want to observe the morning."

Kenneth was weakened and exhausted and took her for her word. He could never have imagined what she really had in mind; if he had, he would have latched on to her leg and never let go. But he drifted off to sleep again, unaware that Lady de Lara was about to take her life into her hands again. In hindsight, he should have guessed it knowing her as he did.

Toby stood by the tent flap, watching Kenneth and waiting for him to drift off again. She wanted to make sure he was asleep before planning her next move. She was about to steal a horse again and try to leave the camp unseen, both of which would be tricky. But she was determined.

Tate and Kenneth had once called her brave; she had never thought on herself as being brave until this very moment. With what she had in mind, she was about to find out just how brave she truly was.

☙

THANK GOD FOR *Isabella*.

That was the thought foremost on Tate's mind as he sat in the great hall of Wigmore, watching Isabella and Mortimer interact. It had been Isabella who had saved him from a quick death in the bailey and Isabella who insisted he be given the respect of the royal family. When Toby and Kenneth had fled the gates, no one had touched him. There had been enough noise and saber rattling to believe he had been taken apart limb by limb, but no one actually came close enough to do it. Several angry soldiers had brought him into the great hall and planted him in a chair while a good deal of arguing went on around him. That had been several hours ago.

So he sat in the great hall all night and well into the morning. He was also thankful that Stephen and Wallace had not yet been discovered. They maintained their disguises as guards of the queen's household although Stephen had managed to position himself very close to Tate. The two of them were able to speak briefly. So far, none of the other guards had given Stephen or Wallace away. Tate did not expect them to; they were the king's troops and loyal to the monarchy. It was Tate, in fact, who commanded them, so in a sense he had his own contingent of troops in the room. But they were insignificant compared to Mortimer's hundreds.

De Roche had been brought back into the keep, moaning and groaning from the injuries that Toby had inflicted on him. As Tate had learned, it was their epic battle that had roused attention in the keep, leading to his capture. The physic had been killed trying to warn them.

Even though de Roche was in another room, they could still hear him in the great hall, bellowing his agony. The man was paralyzed and doomed. Every time de Roche screamed, Tate was reminded just how brave Toby was. He was incredibly proud of her. He was also incredibly grateful that she had escaped.

But there was another lady on his mind at the moment; Isabella had not let him out of her sight since his capture. She had remained in the great hall all night, arguing with Roger, and her stress showed. At first, the argument had been about Tate. Hours later, it wasn't even about him any longer; they were arguing over a lordship in Yorkshire. The entire night and into the morning had been a mass argument about almost everything other than Tate. Oddly, Edward's name had never even come up. Tate wasn't even concerned for his own life any longer; it was clear that he was not to be killed. Now, he was just bored.

It was close to the nooning meal when the keep began to stir once again; Isabella and Roger were still in the hall, now at separate ends of the room in their mutual exhaustion. The Earl of Suffolk had joined them at some point and stood with Roger in the corner, quietly conversing. Tate wondered why the man had two black eyes and a swollen nose. It never occurred to him that the injuries had anything to do with Toby, but had he known, he surely would have laughed about it.

As he pondered the stark tedium his life had become over the past few hours, servants began dashing into the hall, scattering like chickens in the wake of several soldiers entering from the bailey. There was much activity that had Tate curious. Whispers seemed to be floating about the hall but he could not discern what they were about. It was apparent that something big was happening, big enough that it had everyone's attention, and he was soon to find out what it was. His curiosity fled the moment he saw a familiar figure emerge into the stale warmth of the great hall.

Toby strolled into the room as if nothing was amiss. She walked in as easily as if she would have walked into her own home. Soldiers skirted her and servants fled from her; in their distant corners, Isabella and Mortimer suddenly emerged from their exhaustion. All eyes were on the lovely lady as she lit up the room like a thousand candles. They were so focused on her beautiful golden-brown head that no one thought to look at Tate. It was their undoing.

At this point unguarded, Tate shot to his feet, vaulted over the table, and made it to his wife before several soldiers tackled him. He grabbed Toby, the soldiers grabbed him, Stephen and Wallace grabbed the soldiers, and everyone went down in a pile.

Screaming erupted from various women in the hall, including Isabella, as chaos ensued. Suddenly, the queen was scampering to the struggling mound of men. Somewhere at the bottom was a small woman who was surely, by this time, crushed.

"*Se lever!*" Isabella hollered, smacking the soldiers on the top of the heap. "Get up and release them!"

There were at least a dozen soldiers she had to weed through, slapping and yanking at them. Roger was on the opposite side of the pile, his dark eyes wide with surprise. As Isabella commanded the men to release Tate, Roger was far more interested in Toby's arrival. He was strangely thrilled by it. But he suspected, as he watched the uproar, that her reappearance could not be a good thing. In fact, he had a deeply unsettling feeling about it. But he waited, apprehensively, to see what would transpire.

It wasn't long in coming. As the soldiers removed themselves from the mound, including Stephen and Wallace, Tate finally appeared at the bottom with his arms around his wife. She hadn't been hurt in the crush, thanks to Tate's strength, but she was furious at having been shoved to the ground. Tate stood up and pulled her to her feet, his arms around her protectively.

"Back away," he bellowed at Mortimer's men. "Touch her and you die."

It was not a threat; it was a promise. Tate's tone was full of power and hazard. Toby, in fact, had never heard that inflection in his voice and it was frightening. Stephen and Wallace had placed themselves close to him, unfortunately revealing their loyalties as they did so. Stephen even pulled off his soldier's helm, revealing his face to Mortimer and his men. He heard the name *Pembury* whispered through the room but, at this point, he didn't care that he had revealed himself. As Mortimer's men knew Dragonblade, they knew his ally Pembury also. And his duty was to protect Tate and Toby.

"You heard him," Stephen growled as he unsheathed his sword. "Back away or feel my wrath."

The men backed off. Isabella was still slapping soldiers away, widening the circle of wolves that were surrounding Tate and Toby. Tate, however, was not paying much attention to the ring of doom all around him; his focus was on his wife as he took her by the arms and shook her gently, beseechingly.

"What are you doing here?" he demanded quietly.

Toby's reply was to throw her arms around his neck and squeeze tightly. He held her close, inhaling her scent, his shock fading and being replaced but a fierce sense of protectiveness. She had returned to the lion's den and he would know why.

"I do not understand," he rasped into her hair. "Why are you here? What has happened?"

Her mouth was on his ear. "I had to come," she murmured. "I had to save you."

Tate felt as if he had been hit in the stomach. "Save me?" he repeated, incredulous. "Sweetheart, you were safe. You were free. What are you...?"

She cut him off abruptly by releasing him. Tate gazed into her beloved hazel eyes, never more in love with her nor more terrified for her. His control, so carefully held when it was only himself to worry about, was in danger of shattering.

"Whatever I say, do not fight me," she whispered. "You must let me do this."

"Do what?" he was becoming increasingly agitated. "What are you doing?"

She smiled bravely at him and he nearly came apart. He just knew it was something awful. Toby squeezed his hand and released him, turning for Roger.

Mortimer was gazing at her with suspicion and delight, an odd combination. Toby's heart was pounding in her chest as she summoned the courage to do as she must. She had reviewed her plan as she had ridden to Wigmore and was convinced that the only way to gain Tate's freedom would be to play on Isabella's jealousies. More than that, it was the only plan she had. She could not think of anything else. She prayed that it was enough.

"My lord," she addressed Roger steadily. "I have returned to offer myself to you in return for my husband's life. You once offered a proposition to me; one night for St. Héver's life. I have returned to offer you the same proposition with one change; one night for my husband's life. I will spend a night of passion with you if you will release him. Will you accept?"

Roger visibly blanched, his gaze darting to Isabella as she stood near Tate. But he could not wait for her reaction. He looked back at Toby, his nerves evident as he spoke.

"You must have misunderstood, Lady de Lara," he replied. "I never made such an offer to you."

Toby cocked an eyebrow. "I believe we have several witnesses to your proposition who will swear that I did not misunderstand you," she said. "I have returned to make you the same offer with the mentioned changes provided that the Queen approves."

The mood of the room suddenly turned dark and brittle; all eyes turned to Isabella, whose cheeks were turning a dull shade of pink. She gazed back at Toby with the stark jealousy that all women have when facing a younger, more beautiful rival. But instead of focusing her venom on Toby, she looked at Roger.

"Did you ask this of this woman?" she demanded, her voice low and shaky.

Roger shook his head. "Of course I did not."

Isabella sighed sharply, her jaw ticking and her dark eyes burning. Toby, watching the interaction, knew it was time to act. If she was going to succeed as planned, then she needed to be strong and dramatic. Bursting into loud sobs, she suddenly buried her face in her hands.

"It is true," she wept loudly. "He tried to force himself on me again and again. He told me that he would kill St. Hével if I did not spend a night of passion with him. He was most descriptive in his desires, how he wished to taste my flesh and gorge himself on my delicacies. I… I did not know what to do. Now that he has my husband, I felt that I had to offer myself in order to gain his freedom. I had to come back!"

It was an overwrought performance at best. Tate stared at her, torn between the urge to tear Mortimer apart with his bare hands and his curiosity on how Isabella was going to react. He could see what Toby was doing; God bless her, he knew exactly what she was doing and had to admit that it was brilliant. He had tried to do the same thing but Toby was playing upon the queen's jealousies far better than he ever could. So he held his tongue, and his fists, to wait for the queen's reaction.

It wasn't long in coming. Isabella's face darkened with fury and she clenched her little fists, pushing her way past Stephen and standing next to Toby. She stood for a moment, watching the woman's lowered head as she sobbed. Her lips pressed into an angry, flat line.

"Did he touch you while you were his guest at Wigmore?" she demanded.

Toby bawled. "He touched my… my…."

She appeared too distraught to continue. Even Tate was on edge. Isabella reached out and shook her.

"Where did he touch you?"

Toby took one hand away from her face and put it on her inner right thigh, very close to the junction where her legs joined. "Here!"

The location could have been interpreted many ways. Isabella's nostrils flared and the grip on Toby's arms turned gentler. It was evident that the queen was struggling.

"Did he do anything else?" she asked, quieter.

Toby shook her head, still weeping. "He did not," she sobbed. "But the fact that he would want to… after all, I am pregnant with my husband's child but it made no difference to him. He wanted to bed me regardless. It is a disgusting and unholy desire."

Tate went from coolly observant to wildly shocked all in a split second. He leaned in Mortimer's direction, or perhaps he swayed; in either case, Stephen was there to grab him. Or steady him. Together the two of them stared at Toby, stunned, as Isabella seemed to morph into something rarely seen. She became enraged, like an avenging angel, and swung on Mortimer viciously. Roger barely had time to draw a breath before she was plowing into him with the fury of a woman betrayed.

"Is this true?" she roared.

Roger was taken aback; he had never heard that tone from her. But the man stood his ground. "It is not true!"

Isabella's jaw flexed dangerously. "You… you foul beast," she hissed. "I have known of your desires for other women all of these years but I have ignored your tastes because… because…."

She growled, sweeping her arm across the table directly to her right and scattering the cups and utensils to the floor. Everything crashed with a clamoring noise but she wasn't done yet; she clenched her fists and howled angrily. As the room stood in stunned silence, including Roger, Isabella turned to Tate.

"Take your wife and go," she commanded, whirling to Roger with an extended arm. "If you refute my order, I will take all you hold dear and destroy it. Do you understand? *I will destroy you.*"

Tate didn't wait to be told twice. He grabbed Toby, nodding quickly to Stephen and Wallace. The two knights fell in behind him, Stephen facing the crowd to challenge anyone who might try to stop them. Wallace leveled his broadsword against the room as they made their way to the exit. Suddenly, they had the upper hand. Trapped inside the

Mortimer stronghold, they were now stronger than those who held them.

Roger watched the group head towards the cavernous threshold, his attention split between furious Isabella and his captives. Isabella's anger finally won out and he focused on her completely.

"You are making a mistake," he told her softly. "I did none of those things. I am ever faithful to you, my love. You *know* this."

Isabella raised a dark eyebrow. "You are faithful so long as my power holds true," she said. "You are faithful so long as it means that England is under your control."

Roger stood before her but refrained from touching her; now was not the time. He had to wait until she cooled.

"If you let de Lara go, you are continuing to fuel the rebellion," he said gently. "It is not wise to let him leave."

Isabella's jaw flexed. "You will not stop them," her anger was rising again. "You have more important issues to deal with at the moment. For as I gave you power, Roger, I can easily take away. And you are very close to losing everything."

Roger did the only thing he could do; he smiled at her. "You would not do that," he purred. "Not to the man who saved you from your husband. You would not destroy me."

Neither one of them noticed the lone queen's guard that was suddenly standing very close to them. It was a solitary figure, covered with mail and draped in the queen's colors. As Tate and Toby reached the giant doorway of Wigmore's great hall, the tall, slender figure standing next to Mortimer leaned close to the earl and removed his soldier's helm.

"Perhaps she would not destroy you. But I will."

Startled, Mortimer turned to gaze into the eyes of young Edward. The lad was taller and stronger than he had remembered, a young man of considerable presence in just those few words. In fact, he looked very much like his grandsire, Longshanks. Roger's eyes widened when he realized that Edward had been in the hall since the queen's arrival; he had been there all along and no one had been the wiser. But there was nothing that Mortimer, or anyone, could do about it at the moment. He had no choice but to let the lad slip from his grasp, one more time in a world that had been full of a thousand such times.

And Edward was well aware of it. His presence was a statement, a promise of things to come. With a lingering glare at the man who had usurped his power for the moment, Edward strolled away, snapping his fingers at the rest of the queen's escort who immediately unsheathed their weapons to the room full of Mortimer supporters. As Roger watched with shock and Isabella with pride, Edward joined Tate, Toby, Stephen and Wallace at the door. There was no mistaking the triumphant grin on Tate's face.

With the queen's escort as protection, the five of them made their way from Wigmore's enormous keep and out into the snowy bailey. When they rode away, it was on Mortimer's fine horses, disappearing into the wintery afternoon. As quickly as the king had appeared, he had vanished just as he always had for the past two years; without a trace and escaping Mortimer once again.

On the wings, as they would say in later years, of the dragon.

EPILOGUE

December, 1330
Forestburn Castle, Northumbria

"KILL HIM, BOY," Wallace encouraged. "If you do not kill him first, he will kill you."

A young boy of four years stood with a wooden sword in his hand. He was dressed in a little suit of mail that Wallace had made for him, complete with a tiny helm. The old knight had even built the dummy from straw that the child was doing mock battle with. At the old man's latest command, the child came to a halt and pulled off his little helm.

Big hazel eyes gazed at the old man questioningly. "If I get good enough, can I fight with Papa?"

Wallace's ancient eyes glimmered warmly. "Your father will be proud to have you," he told him, going to the child and putting an enormous hand on his shoulder. "In fact, with a little more practice, you can probably fight with him now."

Roman de Lara scratched his dark head. "Is he still fighting?"

"More than likely, boy."

"But when will he come home?"

Wallace's warm expression faded, thinking of Tate leading the coup against Mortimer. It had been the culmination of the rebellion building to the final capture of the man who had ruled the country *de facto* for four years. Lady de Lara had received word three weeks ago that her husband and his forces had captured Mortimer at Nottingham. Mortimer was slated to be executed while Isabella had been banished to

Castle Rising in Norfolk. Things were finally at an end.

Tate had been gone since August, leaving his four children and pregnant wife. It had been a sad parting, for Lord and Lady de Lara were quite attached to each other. After four years of marriage, they were more in love than ever. Pembury and St. Héver had accompanied their liege while Wallace, too old to do any good, remained behind with Lady de Lara. As Wallace pondered the battles he had missed, a little hand tugging on his sleeve brought him back from his reflection. He looked down to see Roman pulling at him.

"When will my father come home?" the child repeated.

Wallace put a big hand on the boy's dark hair. "I have no way of knowing, lad. As soon as he can, I am sure. He misses you a great deal."

Roman smiled happily; at four years old, he was a big boy with his father's good looks and his mother's almond-shaped eyes. As he turned back to his hay-stuffed opponent, the door to the new keep at Forest-burn opened and a little girl emerged. The child was no more than three years of age and on her heels came two little boys, almost as tall as she was. The blond-headed twins were faster than their dark-haired sister and made their way down the wooden stairs more quickly than she did. The children gripped the banisters as they took the steps with their tiny feet; their mother was fanatical about the children being careful when they descended stairs. But when the twins came to the bottom of the steps, one boy tripped and the other one fell on top of him. As they began punching each other, the little girl slipped by untouched and headed in Wallace's direction.

Wallace smiled at the beautiful little girl with the curly dark hair and storm-cloud eyes. She looked exactly like her father. He held out a hand to her.

"Come along, Cate," he called to her. "Come sit with me and away from your boisterous brothers."

Catherine Ailsa de Lara would turn three years old in February. She had been called Cate since the day she had been born because it rhymed with her father's name and her mother liked it very much. Moreover, it had been Toby's idea to name her after Tate's dead first wife, a gesture that touched Tate deeply with its graciousness and compassion. Little Cate toddled over to the old man she loved as a grandfather just as her mother emerged from the keep to find the twins rolling around in the mud.

Toby sighed heavily at the sight of her youngest children. At fifteen months, they were big, strapping boys with a good deal of coordination and a vocabulary that grew by the day. They were particularly loud and physical, fighting with each other one moment and hugging each other the next. They also tried to engage their eldest brother, Roman, who barely held his own against them. Dylan and Alexander de Lara, she could already tell, were going to be trouble. Since Tate had been gone the last four months, he'd not yet had a chance to see how his twins had grown. The man was in for a surprise.

"Dylan," she snapped. "Alex, get out of the dirt this instant. Go on; get up."

The boys began wailing because one of them had jabbed the other one in the eye with a dirty finger. The one who did the jabbing knew he was in trouble, hence the dual wailing. Toby sighed again and made her way down the steps, carefully; at seven months pregnant, she wasn't moving very swiftly these days.

"Dylan," she held out her hand to the whining child. "You are alright, sweetheart. Get up now."

With a pouting face, much like his mother displayed when she was upset, Dylan took his mother's hand. Alexander rose shortly thereafter and took his mother's other hand. Toby walked the boys over to where Roman was jabbing at his hay dummy with Wallace and Catherine looking on.

Wallace was calling encouragement to Roman when Toby walked up with the twins. He eyed the youngest de Lara children sternly, but in truth, he loved them to death. They were incorrigible little hooligans already and he was taking great delight in their antics.

"Soon I will make them their own swords," he told Toby. "I can already tell they will be excellent knights. Dragonblade will have many fine progeny."

"Not too soon," Toby let go of Dylan's hand as he rushed to his eldest brother, clamoring to play with the toy sword. "They are already difficult to handle. I fear they will have us completely overwhelmed by the time they are five years old."

"Then you will send them away to foster," Wallace told her firmly. "Better the knights of Kenilworth or Alnwick to temper their wild streak than you."

Toby frowned at him, rubbing at her aching back. "Why not me? I have done well enough with Roman."

Wallace looked at the eldest de Lara child, now bombarded by both younger brothers as each wanted to play with the sword. "Ah, Roman," he said in a satisfied tone. "He will be the greatest knight of all. He is already showing his father's skill and intelligence."

Raised voices caught Toby's attention and she turned in time to see the twins attempting to tackle Roman and steal his sword. But Roman was cunning like his father and took off running. She watched as the boys ran a circle around Forestburn's new bailey; Tate had kept good on his promise and set to rebuilding Forestburn from a fortified manor into a castle. The burned-out shell of the manor was now the great hall and a new stone keep had been built to the east of it. The *garçonnaire* and outbuildings were now incorporated into the massive structure, including a newly built chapel that, as of six months ago, contained the crypts of Balin, Judith and Ailsa. And with that, Toby was finally at peace. Forestburn was once again a prosperous place and she had her entire family with her.

Except for the fact that Tate had been gone these long four months. She thought of him for the hundredth time that day as she watched her sons wrestle for the toy sword. She missed her husband so much that her heart hurt and she wait with every sunrise and sunset for news of his return. She knew that he had survived Mortimer's capture but she had not heard anything from him in three weeks. It was three weeks of torture, waiting and wondering. Every night she slept with one of his tunics, unwashed, smelling of his scent. She would lay there and breathe its strength, praying that he would return to her whole.

Catherine eventually grew tired of sitting with Wallace and went to her mother, who picked her up and kissed her. Toby brushed the stray hair from her daughter's eyes, remembering the little sister she raised so long ago and wishing Ailsa was here to see the children. Dylan and Alexander reminded Toby a good deal of her baby sister; aggressive and bright and inquisitive. She had to grin when she thought of her sister arguing with her young nephews. She had a feeling it was one argument Ailsa would not win.

Lost in thought, she did not hear the guards lift the creaking port-cullis, nor did she hear the horses crossing the new drawbridge over the newly-dug moat. Her back was to the gatehouse. Only when her sons began shouting and Roman took off running did she turn around to see what had them all so excited.

Knights bearing the blue and silver dragon pennant of the Earl of Carlisle were beginning to fill the bailey. Men on foot were spilling in, congregating near the entry. Wallace was already on his feet, calling for the boys who were now in danger of getting trampled by the war horses. But he was not fast enough; three of the knights that were intermingled in the crowd suddenly dismounted, each going for an errant boy.

The Earl of Carlisle was the first one off his horse. The last time Tate had been home, the twins had not been walking. Now they were running. He tossed off his helm with a laugh of delight as Alexander ran within arm's length. He grabbed the boy, swinging him up in the air and kissing his little face furiously. Alexander screamed as if he were being stabbed.

It made Tate laugh all the more. He was thrilled to hear his children yell. Stephen, by this time, had Dylan and was holding the boy upside-down. Dylan was screaming, but mostly in delight. Kenneth was fortunate and had the calm child; his big hand was on Roman's head as he and the boy made their way over to Tate.

"My God," Tate gasped as he set Alexander to his feet. "I cannot believe the babies are walking. I feel as if I have been gone one hundred years."

"As do I." Toby was smiling broadly as she came upon her husband and children, her face rosy with joy as she drank in his handsome face. She looked to the faithful men at her husband's side; she was glad to see that they were alive and well, too. She embraced Kenneth, the closest one to her. "Kenneth, welcome home. You also, Stephen."

Kenneth nodded his thanks as Stephen smiled his. Tate's gaze softened as it fell upon his wife; everything around him ceased to exist for a moment as he beheld the woman that he loved. Although he had at least three more children clamoring for his attention, he gently pushed through them and went straight for Toby. Taking her in his arms, he hugged her, and Catherine, tightly.

Toby held on to him fiercely, struggling not to cry in front of her children. But her joy was on the surface. It was difficult to hold back. Tate kissed her cheeks, her lips, before pulling back to look at her.

"You are more beautiful than I remembered," he murmured, kissing her again. Then he turned to his daughter and kissed her sweetly on the cheek. "My God, you are a lovely creature, Cate. Look how beautiful you have grown."

Catherine grinned and chewed her fingers. With a hand still on his wife, Tate finally turned to Roman, who was standing patiently beside his father.

"Roman, you have been growing behind my back," he said seriously. "If your mother does not stop feeding you, you will be taller than me by next week."

Roman grinned and fell into his father's embrace; Tate picked him up, cherishing the feel of his first born in his arms. He could not have been happier. But next to him, Dylan was still screaming in Stephen's arms and Tate looked at the red, upside-down face.

"Greetings, Dylan," he said.

Stephen grinned and the set the boy to his feet, at which time Dylan punched Stephen in the armored shin and ended up smacking his hand. He began to wail as the knights laughed. Tate put Roman down and picked up his injured son, rubbing his little hand.

"Well," he said casually, "I will commend him for his bravery. It is not every child who would take on a man four times his height."

"He will be a fearsome warrior," Wallace announced.

"He will be just like his mother," Kenneth put in drolly.

As the men snorted, Toby rolled her eyes, handing Catherine over to Stephen and taking Dylan from his father.

"You will not rush these boys into battle yet," she told them sternly, comforting her son. They were still snickering when she looked seriously at her husband. "And speaking of battle; am I to hopefully assume that yours are concluded? Are you finally home to stay?"

Tate exhaled slowly and put his arm around her shoulders, pulling her head against his lips for a gentle kiss. It was Kenneth, Stephen and Wallace's signal to give them their privacy and the three of them pretended to go about their business. But neither Tate nor Toby noticed, lost in each other's eyes. They began to walk towards the keep.

"Edward has assumed his full authority as king," Tate told her softly. "Mortimer is no longer a threat."

"What happened?"

Tate was gazing up at the four-story keep as he spoke, his exhaustion evident. But it was more than his expression; it was in his manner. As if everything he had been fighting for over many years had finally caught up to him. He had the look of a very weary man.

"Mortimer was taken to the Tower shortly after we captured him," he said quietly. "He was executed two weeks ago in London."

Toby looked at him, shocked yet relieved. "On Edward's orders?"

"Aye," he replied softly. "Edward is of age now and already a powerful king. When I left, he was convening Parliament and preparing his agenda." His thoughts drifted to the fair-haired boy, now a fair-haired man. "He is strong and intelligent. He will do well."

"And what about you?" Toby wanted to know. "Will you do well now that you are not fighting his cause?"

He looked at her and smiled. "I will always fight his cause," he said as they reached the steps leading into the keep. "But for now, I believe I am entitled to my own life. I deserve it."

"Is it over with Mortimer, then?"

"It is over."

She smiled in return, setting Dylan to his feet when the boy squirmed to be put down. Tate drew her into his arms, watching as his twins resumed their attempt to steal their older brother's wooden sword. He relished their screaming, delighted in the chase. Their voices were like music to his ears.

"We have missed you," Toby laid her head on his chest as they watched the boys scramble. "I was so fearful that you would not return in time for the birth of this child."

Tate put his hand on her belly, feeling the firmness. He caressed her tummy gently, savoring the results of their deep and committed love to each other. He kissed her deeply as he continued to rub her belly, a profoundly intimate moment between the two of them.

"I would not have missed it, not for anything," he murmured. "And you know that I will always return to you, no matter what."

The tears that she had kept at bay finally found their way to the surface. "Will you promise me something, then?" she whispered.

"Of course, sweetheart," he wiped the tears streaming down her cheek. "Anything you wish."

"Will you promise me that we shall never again be apart?"

He paused a moment. "If it is within my power, I swear we will never be parted. I have missed you as much as you have missed me. More, even."

"Can you promise me that these wars for Edward's throne are finished?"

In truth, he could not. There were stirrings in France that Edward had already made mention of. Tate knew that, at some point, he would find himself in France fighting for the king. But he would not tell Toby that, not now when she was so emotionally brittle.

He held her at arm's length, gazing into her sweet face. "I can promise you that I will remain here for the birth of my fourth son and that we will live happily together for the rest of our lives."

She wiped at her eyes. "It will be a girl."

"I could only be more blessed. What name did we decide on again?"

"Arabella Mary."

He nodded in recollection. "Ah, yes. Arabella Mary. And if it is a boy?"

"It will not be a boy."

He grinned at her, knowing she had probably had her fill of little boys for the moment. "As you say, madam."

She cocked her head, staring up into his handsome face. "It was a good attempt at changing the subject, but you will answer my question now."

"About what?"

"Whether or not you are going to put away your dragonblade for good."

He smiled at her and pulled her against him, feeling her big belly against his mail. "Do we have to talk about this now?"

Before she could retort, a scream went up as Dylan managed to steal Roman's wooden sword. He toddled off as fast as his tubby legs would carry him but Roman was faster and grabbed hold of his brother, trying to wrest the toy from him. Alexander joined in the ruckus and between the two brothers, they managed to shove Roman to the ground. Like any small boy, Roman began to cry as his brothers fought over who would be the first to play with the toy.

At some point, Stephen had set Catherine down and she walked over to where her brothers were fighting; while Roman wiped the tears from his eyes, the twins started slapping at each other and the sword fell to the ground. Catherine calmly picked it up and walked away.

Tate and Toby watched with varied degrees of amusement and, in

Toby's case, exhaustion. Tate finally turned to his wife.

"Have they been like this since I left?" he asked.

She began nodding before he finished his sentence. "Since Dylan and Alex learned to walk about two months ago. This is constant."

Tate put his hand on her belly again. "And another one on the way."

Toby sighed wearily. "I can hardly stand the anticipation."

He laughed softly and kissed his wife on the temple. "Perhaps one of these days we will finally take that trip to Rome I promised you so long ago," he murmured. "That should give you respite from the chaos of our children."

She shrugged as she watched the boys wrestle. "They are too young to be without their mother. As weary as I am, I would not want to leave them for any length of time."

"Not even for Rome?"

"Perhaps someday."

He smiled gently at her before moving to the writhing hoard of children with the intention of settling them down. Toby appeared as if she couldn't take the squabbling another minute. Crouching on his haunches, he tried to reason with the twins. They responded by jumping on him, causing him to lose his balance and end up on his buttocks. As he fell back, Roman jumped into the melee and pounced on him. Tate laughed as he ended up lying on his back with three little boys atop him. Not to be left out, Catherine stood over them and swatted her brothers with the sword.

As Tate allowed himself to be pummeled by his toddlers, he couldn't remember a time in his life when he was so completely happy. From the horrors of eight years ago to the delight of the day, every pain, every effort, had been worth the price. The road that had led him to Cartingdon those years ago had been the best path he had ever taken and he could have never imagined that the aggressive, rude woman with the strange name would become his very reason for living.

He eventually pushed himself up from the mass of boys. Toby was standing with Kenneth and Stephen in conversation a few feet away but Tate noticed that he was not alone. Catherine was standing next to him, the sword still in her hand, as she gazed up adoringly at her father.

Tate smiled and picked her up, his little angel, so sweet that all she had to do was look at him and he would melt away. She had that effect on all of the knights, particularly Stephen. The man positively adored her. Tate kissed her cheek as she wrapped her little baby arms around his neck. He took the sword from her so she would not put his eye out with it.

"Papa?" she put her little face in front of his so that she could look him in the eye. "Where did you go?"

He smoothed her curly dark hair out of her eyes. "I went to help someone."

It was as much of an explanation as she could understand. "Did you help them?" she wanted to know.

"I did, angel."

Catherine thought on that a moment. "Will you stay home now?"

He smiled gently. "I will stay home now."

"Papa?"

"Aye, angel?"

"Will you sing the baby song?"

Tate's grin broadened. He had dreamed of this moment his entire life. When Arabella Mary was born in January, he had two little angels to sing the baby song to.

To the sky, my sweet babe;

The night is alive, my sweet babe.

Your dreams are filled with raindrops from heaven;

Sleep, my sweet babe, and cry no more.

Seven years and three more children later, Tate finally took his wife to Rome. It was everything she knew it would be.

Cß THE END ßO

The Draogonblade Trilogy Series contains the following novels:

Island of Glass

The Savage Curtain

Fragments of Grace

The Fallen One

The Dragonblade novel is also grouped in the Marcher Lords of de Lara. Tate's brother, Sean de Lara, is the main character in Lord of the Shadows.

Lord of the Shadows

For more information on other series and family groups, as well as a list of all of Kathryn's novels, please visit her website at www.kathrynleveque. com.

Bonus Chapters of the exciting Medieval Romance ISLAND OF GLASS, BOOK 2 IN THE DRAGONBLADE TRILOGY to follow.

1333 A.D. – The lovely and educated Lady Aubrielle Grace di Witney is what is kindly termed an unmanageable woman. Her uncle, the Earl of Wrexham, has been awarded custody of his niece because her mother can no longer handle the head-strong beauty. Like a coward, the earl abdicates his duties to his most powerful knight, Sir Kenneth St. Héver with the instructions to transform her into a submissive lady. Aubrielle and Kenneth are at odds from the onset; Kenneth expects obedience and Aubrielle is less than compliant. When the battles die down and a strange, wonderful comfort settles, Kenneth comes to discover that Aubrielle is a lady with a secret. Because of this secret, her mother is murdered and Kenneth finds himself protecting Aubrielle because he wants to, not because he has been ordered to. Mysterious sects and a crazed warrior want the lady dead for different reasons. It soon becomes a test to Kenneth's cunning and knightly skills to keep his beloved Aubrielle alive.

CHAPTER ONE

Kirk Castle
The Welsh Marches
October, 1333 A.D.

"YOU CANNOT KNOW my pain," the woman wept. "I do not understand where I went wrong in raising my only child. She has had the best education that my husband and I could provide for her. She has wanted for nothing. I do not understand why she rebels against me."

The man seated opposite the woman had heard this tale before. It was difficult not to yawn in the face of her agony. He had stopped offering his advice long ago, mostly because he had no children and was therefore not an expert on their rearing. But he knew where his sister had gone wrong, experience or not. A fool could have realized it.

"You have spoiled her," he said simply.

The woman's weeping grew louder. She muffled it in her expensive kerchief, held tightly to her nose. "What have I done that you would not have in my place?"

Garson Mortimer, cousin to Roger Mortimer and the First Earl of Wrexham, was not a normally patient man. His only sister was trying him sorely to the point where he wanted to rip out what was left of his thinning hair. She never listened to him as it was, only using him to vent her frustrations.

He leaned back against his chair, a sturdy piece of furniture built by Welsh craftsmen. So close to the border of Wales, English and Welsh cultures seemed to blend together in a calliope of disciplines ranging from food to architecture. His opinions on women and childrearing, however, were strictly English.

"Do we truly need to revisit this subject?"

"We do!"

"Then I would not have sent her to receive her education at a monastery," he said flatly. "I told you that was a mistake. St. Wenburgh is far too unconventional."

"But her father…!"

"God rest his soul, he wanted the best for Aubrielle, but she does not have the countenance to gracefully accept the privilege that has been given her. The more she is given, the more she wants."

Graciela Mortimer de Witney sniffled into her kerchief again, the tears in her dark eyes lessening as she thought on her brother's words. "Aubrielle is merely curious for knowledge, Garson. Since the monks taught her to read…"

"A sin!" Garson slapped his hand on the arm of the chair. "Tevor should never have allowed it. Imagine, a woman knowing how to read!"

"My husband was only doing what he thought best for her. He believed that a lady with education would be an attractive asset to a potential husband."

"An asset, pah," Garson snorted. "Education has only put ideas into that inherently fertile mind she possesses. And what has it reaped? Only grief."

Graciela was feeling like a scolded child, not at all receiving the sympathy she had hoped for. "She has been a joy at times."

"Then why are you here?" When his sister faltered in her reply, Garson stood up and began to pace the rough wooden floor of his solar. The joists creaked beneath his weight. "You are here because you cannot handle her. She has become unruly and unless something is done, she will shame the entire family with this wild dream she pursues."

Graciela's tears had faded. "She is spirited and intelligent."

"She is out of control. Any young lady that would set off from her home on a journey, without escort or thought to her care and safety, is idiotic."

"I would not call her idiotic."

Garson emitted a grunt of frustration. "Graciela, do you hear your-self? Your daughter set off from Highwood House en route to Glastonbury because the monks at St. Wenburgh told her that the Holy Grail of Christ was buried there."

"She simply wanted to prove them right."

He threw up his hands. "Not to glorify God, but to prove a myth."

The woman fidgeted with her hands, the golden tassels of her belted dress. "She has always had a fascination to verify the legend. She believes the discovery of the Grail would be a boon for the entire country, especially with its war against Wales and Scotland."

Garson stared at her a moment before running his hand over his face. Why his sister attempted to justify her daughter's psychosis was beyond him. "Of all the wonderful things she learned, out of everything she had been told, the only item that sticks in her mind is the Quest for the Holy Grail. Where Arthur failed, the Lady Aubrielle Grace de Witney will succeed? How arrogant."

"She would try."

He couldn't continue with the conversation. It was making him crazy. "If you have not come for my help with Aubrielle, then why are you here? To lament your woes and aggravation with a daughter who is headstrong without compare?"

Graciela lifted her pale face. Soft gray light from the lancet windows fell upon her fine, pretty features. "I am afraid, Garson."

"Of course you are. So am I."

"I cannot manage my own daughter. I am afraid tragedy will befall her if she continues on this quest."

"What do you want me to do about it?"

"She needs someone stronger than she is. Since the death of her father, that duty must fall to you. You are all that I have that stands between me and the destruction of my child."

Garson exhaled heavily. "I am not a nursemaid," he said. "Moreover, I have enough battles on my hands. As we speak, half of my army is in Wales at Dinas Bran Castle in retaliation for the raid against one of my villages six days ago. People were killed and the food stores raided."

"I am sorry for your troubles, brother, truly, but there is much at stake with Aubrielle," she pleaded. "Please, Garson. You are my only hope."

He knew he shouldn't. But he could not stomach her pleading. "If I agree, then it will be done my way. I want no interference from you."

"Of course."

"If she so much as sets foot outside this castle, I will lock her in the vault and throw away the key."

"Whatever you feel necessary."

He cast her a condescending look. "You do not mean any of it."

"But I do! Perhaps you can convince Aubrielle of the error of her ways. She respects you."

"She does not. And she fears nothing, either." Garson shook his head with regret. "Not even her dazzling beauty will overcome her character flaws. There is no man on earth that will want a wife he has to do battle with on a daily basis."

Graciela toyed with the fine kerchief in her hand. "Will you… will you perhaps consider finding a husband for her? She brings an attractive dowry of the Lordship of Tenbury. And then there is Highwood House…."

Garson waved his hands irritably. "I know very well what my own niece brings to a husband and if I die without an heir, she will also inherit Wrexham."

"Do you intend to remarry soon, Garson?"

His flustered manner fell dramatically. "My widower status is not at issue," he muttered. "We were discussing Aubrielle."

"Of course, Brother."

Garson tried not to linger on thoughts that his sister's question provoked. Five years after the death of his beloved wife in childbirth, the pain was still fresh.

"I will do what I can for Aubrielle," he struggled to shift focus. "But I can promise nothing."

Graciela rose from her chair and went to her brother. "My thanks," she put her cold hands on his fingers. "I know she will be in good hands. Pray be understanding with her."

He cocked an eyebrow. "You swore not to interfere."

Graciela smiled. "That is not interfering, simply a mother's request."

Garson knew even as he agreed that he was going to regret it. He kissed his sister on the cheek all the same, resigned to the fact that he was a fool for her troubles. The door to the solar creaked opened and a small man with gray hair appeared, bowing profusely in the presence of his lord.

"My lord," he said. "I beg pardon, but we have a... problem."

Garson knew he shouldn't ask; he probably already knew the answer. "What is it, Arbosa?"

The Majordomo of Kirk looked between the earl and his sister. "The Lady Aubrielle has gone missing."

"What?" Graciela exclaimed softly. "I left orders that she be watched!"

"We did watch her, my lady," the man assured her. "She said she wanted to gain some fresh air and wandered into the bailey. We've not seen her for some time."

Garson left Graciela in the musty solar. If he was to be in charge of his niece's redemption, then it would start at this moment.

CHAPTER TWO

Dinas Bran Castle
Powys, Wales

F OR EARLY JUNE, the weather was typical. The rain had fallen so heavily that it had been like walking through sheets of crystalline silver. Spoiling the effect was the mud that it created, churning like black rivers as it rolled down the sides of the motte. Men in chain mail, bearing the seal of Wrexham, had struggled up the slick, sloping sides en route to the keep at the top to do battle. From beginning to end, the entire deed had been a nightmare.

The clash had lasted nearly two days, not particularly long where battles were concerned. Dinas Bran Castle had been held by Dafydd ap Gruffydd, brother of Llewellyn the Last, though no one had actually seen the man leading his men to battle. Mostly, it seemed to be held by raiders disguised as Welsh soldiers. It hadn't taken tremendous effort to breach the wooden gate and penetrate the castle. Rather than fight, most of the Welsh had fled. Kirk's army had come away with little more than exhaustion and minimal satisfaction.

On the way back to Kirk Castle, the rain had washed away the layers of mud accumulated from mounting the enormous Welsh motte. The men-at-arms were on foot, tired, marching on muddy roads that had them sloshing up to their ankles. The chargers were wet, filthy beasts with bad tempers, handled by knights that were equally filthy and bad tempered. Armor rusted in the rain, creating problems with comfort and movement. The closer they drew to Kirk Castle, the more evident their misery.

Kenneth St. Héver was one of those knights with the filth and bad temperament engrained into his skin. Wet and exhaustion were nothing new to him, as he had been in the knighthood since his twentieth year. Eighteen years later, it had completely taken over his nature. He had a reputation for being exceptionally unfriendly though never unfair. He commanded one hundred and twenty five retainers, men personally given to him by King Edward for Kenneth's service against Roger Mortimer.

Kenneth's relationship with his fellow knights was an agreeable one but he was very reluctant to form friendships; he only had two true friends, men he had served with since he had been knighted, and both of them were tied up in wars with the Scots. Kenneth, in fact, had only recently returned to the Marches after helping Tate de Lara, Earl of Carlisle, and Stephen of Pembury, Guardian Protector of Berwick, subdue the Scots at Berwick-upon-Tweed. He was back on the Welsh Marches now because the king wanted him here and was not particularly happy about it. He wanted to be back at Berwick with his friends. Yet he had no choice; he had a job to do on the Marches.

So his mood was consistently clouded these days. Kenneth paid little attention to the men marching in distress beside him; his focus was diverted to the countryside in search of threats. Over the years, scanning his surroundings had become habit. Somehow the landscape was always threatening, rain or shine, and he was not one to be caught unaware. As he scrutinized the trees, a knight on a large bay steed rode up beside him, lifting his visor to reveal brown eyes set within an unshaven, dirty face.

"We'll be seeing the turrets of Kirk over the crest of this hill," the knight commented. "I can already taste the cool ale and a knuckle of beef."

Kenneth's visor was down, but not to shield his face from the rain. He simply didn't like others looking at him, studying his face, perhaps reading his thoughts.

"Had these lazy fools moved faster, we would be seeing those turrets sooner," he growled.

"The men are tired."

"Then they are women. To be exhausted after a small skirmish is an insult."

The brown-eyed knight grinned. Everett l'Breaux was a congenial man and hardly offended by Kenneth's brusque manner.

"If you'd lift that visor, I am sure I would see exhaustion written all over your face as well," he commented. "There is no shame in that."

Kenneth flipped up his three-point visor, of the latest style for ease and protection. Eyes of the palest blue, like a sea of ice, gazed steadily at Everett. "All you will see on my face is boredom."

"You are a hard man, Ken."

A massive gray stallion jogged up between them, shoving Everett's horse aside. Kenneth's animal, muzzled after the battle, snapped its teeth and swung its big head at the intrusion. Only Kenneth's phenomenal strength kept the beast at bay.

Lucius de Cor was the captain of Wrexham's army. He was an older man that had seen many battles for a succession of English kings. Close to retirement, he was nonetheless fully in charge of the men under his command. But he looked to Kenneth, his second, to make sure his orders were enforced. St. Héver was the only man in the corps who inspired that kind of fear and respect. Only an idiot would argue with him.

"Have the men pick up the pace, Ken," he ordered. "I want to be cleaned and seated by sup."

Kenneth moved into action before the command left Lucius' lips. He spurred his beast back along the lines of marching men. His armored arm was lifted, commands bellowing from his throat. Immediately, the block of three hundred men picked up into a steady trot. Somewhere in the back of the lines, a few of the men seemed to be exchanging an inordinate amount of conversation. Kenneth spurred his charger around the rear of the column and came upon them.

"What goes on?" he demanded.

When St. Héver demanded, men listened. These soldiers were not

Kenneth's retainers; they belonged to another knight who had stayed behind at Kirk, Sir Reid de Bowland. But they responded with more attention to Kenneth than they would have to their own liege.

"A soldier's disagreement, m'lord," one man replied. "We didn't mean to disrupt the march."

Kenneth's gaze was so piercing it could have cut steel. "What kind of disagreement?"

The two men arguing looked at each other, fearful to speak. The second man finally spoke. "I lost my crossbow on the slopes of Dinas Bran Castle, my lord," he said. "Malf found it and will not give it back."

"So he has stolen from you."

Malf's eyes widened. "No, my lord, I didn't steal it."

"Then return it to him."

"But this isn't his weapon," the soldier was almost pleading, afraid of what was coming. "I know of Sheen's weapon. This is not it."

Kenneth continued to look between the two men, a heavy silence filling the air. By this time, Lucius had come upon them.

"What is the issue, St. Hever?" he demanded.

"Sheen lost his weapon on the slopes and tells me that Malf found it. Malf insists it is not the lost weapon but another."

Lucius frowned impatiently. "There is no time for this foolery. Perhaps you both need to be reminded on the value of weapons and camaraderie." He glanced at Kenneth. "Ten lashes each when we return. Perhaps next time, Sheen will be more careful about his weapon and Malf will be more apt to share his found one if he sees that his comrade has none."

It was swift justice designed to send a message to all of the soldiers. Kenneth nodded, knowing it was expected that he would deliver the blows. That was his position, as second in command of the army. He followed Lucius back to the front of the column just as they crested the hill.

Kirk loomed ahead, a massive fortress with her green, gold and scarlet Wrexham banners waving in the wind. But something else caught their attention: a lone figure moving off of the road and into the trees. It was at some distance, a black little spot with legs. Kenneth focused in on it, as did Lucius and Everett. As they drew closer, it appeared to be a figure on a small palfrey or donkey. The little beast's legs were moving furiously, making haste for the shelter of the forest.

Lucius frowned. "Go see what that is," he told Kenneth.

Kenneth spurred his unruly animal into a gallop. He knew it would be no time before he overtook the figure on the palfrey. He entered the border of trees nearly the same time as the figure did.

"Halt," he ordered.

The figure kept going. Kenneth rode up beside it and gave a shove to the shoulder, sending it tumbling to the wet ground. He heard a high-pitched cry, indicating to him that the figure was a woman. As he brought his horse around, the lady came to her feet and took off through the bramble at a dead run.

Kenneth spurred his charger after her. His prevailing emotion was irritation; the woman was small, dodging through some bushes that he couldn't get through on his big horse. A savage game of cat and mouse was afoot as the two of them plowed deeper into the forest.

He followed her, closer at some times, further away at others. She was fast and she was clever. The more she ran, the angrier he became. At one point, he fell in directly behind her and she ducked into a cluster of close-knit trees. He should have known better; he was too close and going too fast when she led him through some heavy branches. Unable to respond fast enough, a big branch caught him and knocked him off his charger.

Rising from a supine position in full armor was no easy task, but Kenneth managed to do so quite ably. Aggravated, he suspected the woman was somewhere out of the trees, well ahead of him and well rid of him. He couldn't remember the last time someone, especially a woman, had bested him. In fact, there had never been a time to his recollection. His anger grew, but more at himself. As he considered which direction to take, something heavy struck him on the back of the head.

The blow pitched him forward onto his knees. Dazed but not sense-less, he rolled onto his back, away from the follow up strike he knew was coming. It also brought him face to face with his attacker and, for a moment, he could not believe his eyes. The woman he had chased all over Creation had a large piece of wood in her hand, swinging it at him with the intent to kill him.

But she made a mistake that would cost her. She was too close as she came in for another hit. Kenneth lashed out with a massive leg and took her feet out from under her, reaching out to disarm her as she fell. He tossed the wood far off into the trees, pinning the woman to the ground in the same motion. She was small and no match for his strength.

"Get off me!" she fought and grunted. "Let me go!"

Kenneth's vision was still muddled from the blow, but it wasn't so muddled that he couldn't see what lay beneath him. A woman with the most astoundingly beautiful face he had ever seen lay there, her sea-colored eyes blazing and her rich brown hair spread over the ground like angel's wings. Before he could utter a word, she thrust her head forward and smashed him in the nose with the top of her head. It was a brutal move. Blood spurted but he didn't let go; he let it drip down onto her soft white neck.

"Oh!" she shrieked. "You are bleeding on me!"

"That is your misfortune."

She stopped squirming and glared at him. "If you do not release me, I swear I shall do more than bloody your nose. I shall wring your neck!"

He had no idea why that statement made him want to smile. It was a struggle not to react. He leapt off of her with the agility of a cat and grabbed her by the wrist, pulling her up with him in the same motion. "I would sincerely like to see you try," he said.

The woman twisted and pulled. "Let me go, you brute."

"What is your name?"

She pounded at the hand that held her. "That is none of your business!"

"I beg to differ."

She flew at him, all fists and feet, but he caught her, turned her around, and trapped her against him. It was dangerous to have her head near his face where she might head-butt him again. As it was, the blood from his nose was dripping down onto her hair. She struggled ferociously as he leaned down.

"Now," he growled in her ear. "You will tell me who you are."

"Never!"

He tightened his grip, squeezing the air from her. "Name, woman."

"N-no!"

His response was to pick her up, legs dangling, and carry her in the direction of his charger. The muzzled animal was attempting to graze a patch of wet grass several feet away. The woman kicked and struggled. As he passed by a birch tree, she thrust her legs out, kicked off against the tree, and sent him off balance. Kenneth recovered and made a mental note not to get close to any more trees.

They were at the horse and Kenneth was trying to decide how, exactly, he could maintain his hold on her and mount the horse at the same time. Pounding thunder in the distance signaled catching his attention.

He turned to see Everett approach. The knight's brown eyes widened when he saw the woman, the blood. "Jesus," he breathed, focused on the struggling woman. "Lady Aubrielle...."

Somewhere in the back of Kenneth's mind, the name sounded familiar. Everett dismounted his steed.

"Lady Aubrielle, are you all right?" he asked.

Kenneth wasn't sure what to say. But he knew he was not going to release the woman lest she attack him again. "You know this wildcat?" he asked Everett.

Everett looked rather pale. "I have forgotten you've only been at Kirk a couple of years," he said. "You've not yet met the earl's niece, the Lady Aubrielle Grace de Witney."

The information sank in. The earl's niece. Kenneth released his grip and, true to his fear, the lady swung around with a fist. He put his hand up, catching her wrist before she could strike his face. They glared at each other, each one completely unwilling to bend to the other.

"Brute," she hissed at him. "Fiend!"

Everett was making a fool out of himself in his effort to ease the situation. "Can I assist you, my lady? What are you doing out on the open road?"

"That is none of your affair, Everett l'Breaux," she snapped. "Give me your horse so that I may be on my way."

Everett shook his head. "Alas, I cannot, my lady. My horse responds only to me. He is far too much for you to handle."

The woman seemed to back off somewhat, but only by necessity. Kenneth could see it was temporary; she was simply re-thinking her strategy. Aubrielle Grace de Witney. He had heard the name before, several times. As Everett mentioned, however, he had never seen the earl's only niece. He knew that her father, the earl's brother-in-law, had passed away about the time Kenneth had come into the earl's service and it was up to the earl to help manage his widowed sister's estates. Other than that, he knew little about her. He'd certainly never heard she was such a spitfire.

He would not take his eyes from her, but there was more to it than the fear that another fist would come flying at him. As he had observed before, she was unquestionably beautiful; her wide sea-colored eyes and long lashes were set against a sweet oval face of porcelain skin and rosebud lips. Her dark hair fell straight and silken to her waist. When she reached up to smooth the strands in her face and tuck them back, he could see that her delicate little ears stuck out ever so slightly. In truth, it was a delightful feature. He could see nothing unappealing about the woman other than the fact that she behaved like a wild animal.

"Then I shall find my mount and be on my way," she was trying desperately to stay in control of the situation.

Everett and Kenneth looked at each other.

"I am afraid we cannot allow you to go," Everett was reluctant to deny her but sensibilities dictated he should. "Perhaps we should return to Kirk and see about procuring you an escort for your journey."

Her pretty face darkened. "I am not going back," she growled. "You cannot force me."

"But...."

"No!"

By this time, Lucius had come upon his missing knights. Wondering what had befallen them, he set out to discover for himself. He saw the lovely young woman, immediately recognizing her. Being closer to the earl than the others, he had heard stories of the Lady Aubrielle Grace and he had met her on a few occasions. He knew what a burden she had been to her mother. Whatever she was doing out here, in the middle of the wild country, could not be good. He did not relish the confrontation that was undoubtedly to come.

"My lady," he greeted her evenly.

Aubrielle looked at the captain with little tolerance. "Ah, the fearless Captain de Cor," she said with a hint of sarcasm. "Three knights against one small lady? That hardly seems fair."

"What are you doing out here, my lady?"

She lifted a well-shaped eyebrow defiantly. "As I have told your henchmen, it is none of your affair."

Lucius scratched his chin. He knew the earl would be angry if he simply left her out here, alone. He already suspected they were well beyond the negotiating stage. He looked at Kenneth, his nose bloodied, and sighed with resignation.

"Take her."

Kenneth grabbed her again before she could run. She screamed and yelled, struggling as Kenneth mounted his charger with Everett's assistance. At one point she tried to flip herself off the horse, kicking Kenneth in the side of his helmed head in the process. Stoically, Kenneth maintained both his temper and his grip on her. She kept fighting, and he kept holding.

It was thus the entire way back to the castle.

ః

THE DOOR WAS locked and there was little chance escaping. Aubrielle had spent a long time pouting, alternately sitting in the only chair the chamber had to offer and stomping about the floor. When she would grow weary of one, she would do the other.

Night was falling and still, her mother had not come to tell her farewell. She knew that it had been her mother's intention all along to leave her with her uncle, though the woman had camouflaged the truth in the guise of a family visit. Soon her anger gave way to disappointment, and then sadness. As the sun set, she knew that her mother was never coming. Disappointment gave way to tears.

Aubrielle's tears eventually faded and she wiped her eyes, trying to be callous to the fact that her weakling mother had abandoned her. She consoled herself with the knowledge that she would have escaped Kirk also had it not been for the big blond beast that had caught her. Her mind wandered to the knight they called Kenneth; all she had been able to see of him was his eyes, so blue that they were nearly silver. He had thick blond lashes, too. His body was enormous, much larger than any man she had ever seen, and he had easily used that strength against her. The more she had struggled against him, the easier it seemed to become for him. He'd never raised a sweat or uttered a word of pain in all of the struggles they had been through.

She was singling out a particular hate for him at the moment. Mostly, she was feeling hurt and abandoned and needed someone other than herself to blame. Rising from the chair, she paced over to the hearth, watching the embers burn low. The night would be cold; she could feel the breeze passing through the lancet windows. Glancing around her chamber, she noted that it was a large room with a big bed. It was then she noticed her trunks in the corner. Her tears sprang fresh, realizing this place was to be her prison.

Her foot was sore where she had kicked the big knight. She sat on the bed and removed her slipper, rubbing her sore toes. It had been stupid to kick armor, but she had done it anyway. As she was rubbing, the door to her chamber rattled and her heart leapt, startled by the sound. The panel finally opened and the earl entered, followed by a serving woman with a tray in her arms. Behind the woman came Lucius.

Aubrielle hadn't seen Lucius in a few years. He was a tall man, nice looking, his dark brown hair now tinged with gray at the temples. His dark beard was neat and trimmed. When he smiled apprehensively, she gave him a hateful look and focused on her uncle.

"So you bring food to the prisoner," she said. "I suppose I should thank you for your humane treatment."

The earl's pleasant expression faded. "You are as lovely as ever, Aubrielle. A pity I cannot say the same for your manner."

She lifted an eyebrow at him. "What would you know of my manner? You make it a point of not being around me whenever my mother and I visit. In fact, I would say this is the first time in years you have addressed me civilly."

The earl rubbed a hand over his face, glancing at Lucius, wishing to God he had never agreed to his sister's plea. The serving girl set the tray down before Aubrielle and quickly vacated the chamber. As the woman left, another figure entered the room.

Aubrielle knew it was the knight who had captured her simply by his eyes. The rest of the man meant nothing to her, even though he was without his armor. His enormous size gave him away as well, arms the size of tree limbs and legs as thick as a horse's neck. His hair was a pale shade of blond, the thick curls close cropped against his scalp. He met her gaze, feeling her hatred clear across the room. His only reaction was to plant his thick legs and cross those massive arms across his chest. If she were hoping to intimidate him, she would be sorely disappointed.

Aubrielle felt as if she was being ambushed. She pointed at Kenneth. "So you bring him to fight with me again?" she looked at her uncle. "Why have you brought them both? To punish me?"

"No one is going to punish you, Aubrielle," the earl sat in a chair, slowly. "Everything in your life does not have to be a battle. If you would only stop your belligerence, you would see that."

She didn't know what to think. "Then why have you come? Why are they here?"

"Can I not come and visit my own niece?" the earl asked. "You are a guest in my home. Am I not allowed to visit with my guests?"

She fixed him in the eye. "Where is my mother?"

"She has gone home."

Aubrielle knew that, but still, the truth hurt. She felt like an orphan. For the first time, her aggressiveness slipped.

"So she has left her burden with you," she murmured.

Garson could see she was wavering and he welcomed the opportunity for rational conversation.

"She had hoped that a change would do you good," he said. "Your mother is not a strong woman. She is weary."

"Weary of me," Aubrielle said. "I know the truth, uncle. You need not spare me."

The earl tried not to validate her too much. "I wasn't aware I was sparing you anything," he said casually. "Aubrielle, your mother is tired. The death of your father has taxed her sorely and she needs time to rest and recover. At this moment, your headstrong manner and determination is simply too much for her to bear. She hopes that...."

"She hopes that you will somehow conquer the shrew that has made her life miserable and drove her husband to an early grave," Aubrielle stood up from the bed. "Do not assume that I am oblivious of the truth, uncle. I know that she has left me here for you to put some sense into my head. She cannot control me and bears the hope that somehow you can."

Garson crossed his arms, formulating his words. "You have had an unconventional upbringing, Aubrielle. Though you are as beautiful as a new morning, you are without a doubt the most unusual woman I have ever known. Your father permitted you to read and write, and the liberal monks at St. Wenburgh filled your head with such nonsense as I cannot comprehend. Do you not understand how odd you are, child? Do you not understand our frustration?"

Aubrielle looked at him, hurt on her face. "I am sorry if my learned mind is considered an oddity. I am not ashamed of my upbringing."

"I know you are not. But the time has come for a more conventional education."

"What do you mean?"

The earl rose wearily from his chair. "I mean that your mother has asked me to domesticate you. She would like you to learn to behave more as a proper woman should."

"You mean she wants me to become another stupid sheep in fine silks and lace."

"I mean that you are to put foolish ideas like searching for the Holy Grail out of your mind," Garson wagged a finger at her. "It means that you learn to act like a lady so that a potential husband will approve of you."

Aubrielle cast a long glance at Lucius, then Kenneth. "And you have brought my trainers, is that it?"

"They will help," he admitted. "Between the three of us, I think we can handle you. Perhaps we can teach you something from a male perspective."

Aubrielle focused on Lucius. "How noble, being reduced to a nursemaid."

Lucius merely smiled. "I can think of a worse task, my lady."

It was meant as flattery, but she mocked him. "Really? Perhaps you'll be assigned to cleaning the stables next."

Lucius did not let the comment bother him. He maintained his smile and his composure. The earl, knowing nothing would be settled in one night, decided to end the conversation at this juncture. Aubrielle was still too brittle to rationally handle. He indicated Kenneth as he moved for the door.

"I am told you have already met, but allow me to formally introduce Sir Kenneth St. Héver, second in command of Wrexham's army," he pronounced the last name "Saint Hay-ver". "Get used to him. He seems to be the only one strong enough to deal with you."

"What about dear Lucius?" she asked, contemptuously sweet.

Lucius and the earl were heading out the door. "You shall see enough of him," the earl said. "Try not to eat Sir Kenneth alive, Aubrielle. I need him."

The door slammed with grim finality. Aubrielle stood there a moment, thinking on the entire conversation, aware that the massive blond knight was still standing there. She looked at him, more closely this time. He really was a big brute, though not unhandsome. In fact, if she thought on it, he was really quite pleasant to behold if one liked that type. She couldn't have cared one way or the other.

"So," she turned away, moving back to the food that was cooling on the tray. "You lost the wager, I take it."

Kenneth hadn't moved since he had first entered the room. He watched her inspect a piece of white bread. "What wager would that be, my lady?"

She picked at the crust. "You drew straws to see who would have to tend me this first night. I assume you lost."

"I won."

She looked at him, a piece of crust halfway to her lips. Much to his surprise, she laughed softly. "Of course you did. You won a sleepless night, wondering if I am going to kill you as you sleep."

Kenneth wondered why he suddenly felt so strange. The very instant she laughed, he felt as if all of the wind had been knocked out of him. She had a delicious smile that curved delicately over her straight white teeth, changing the entire countenance of her face. He'd never seen anything so lovely.

He shifted on his thick legs, unwinding his arms. "I believe I can defend myself."

"You barely held your own this afternoon."

"Fortunately for you I did not fight back."

She put the bread in her mouth, cocking her head as she chewed. "I have never seen you before. You are new to Kirk."

"I came into the earl's service two years ago, my lady."

"I see. Whom did you serve before?"

"The king."

Her eyebrows lifted. "You left the king's service to swear fealty to a mere earl?"

"I was a gift from the king to the earl for his support during the battle for the crown."

No matter how unconventional Aubrielle was, she knew that St. Hèver must be a great knight to warrant such respect from young King Edward. The gifting of a knight was a great honor. Her respect, and fear, for the man took root.

"Are you going to stand there all night or are you going to sit?"

Kenneth took the chair the earl had been seated in. Aubrielle picked at her bread, eyeing him as she did so.

"Are you married?"

"Nay, my lady."

"Why not?"

"Because I am not."

She puckered her lips. "You are not the friendly type, are you?"

He would not dignify her question with a response. She returned to her meal in silence. Kenneth watched her, thinking he might have been able to warm to her had she not been so disagreeable. Their first meeting earlier in the day had fairly negated that possibility. He did, however, admire her cunning and fighting ability. She was a surprisingly tough woman and he respected that.

Aubrielle was bored with her meal after only a few bites. She pushed the tray aside and went to stand before the fire. She yawned and stretched, peering out of the corner of her eye to see if Kenneth was watching her. He was, but pretended he wasn't.

"I think I should like a walk before retiring for the night," she said.

Kenneth shook his head. "The rules have been established, my lady. The earl has dictated that you may not leave this chamber, for any reason, without his permission. Any attempt to do so will result in imprisonment in the vault."

She stopped mid-yawn. "He wouldn't dare!"

"I am afraid he would, my lady"

She marched over to him, her little fists resting angrily on her hips. "And just who are you? The enforcer of this ridiculous rule?"

"One of them."

"Is that so? How do you intend to stop me? I can slip out and you'll never know it. I invite you to try."

"I wish you wouldn't."

She scowled at him, torn between the undeniable attraction to prove her point and the undeniable knowledge that he would be forced to prove his. Bullying hadn't worked with the man. Perhaps another tactic would.

"Fine." She turned on her heel, stomping towards the bed. Clothes and all, she lay down upon it. "I would retire now."

"As you wish."

She rolled over on her side, her mind racing in a hundred different directions. Her ears were painfully attuned to St. Héver's movement, but there was none. He was apparently still seated, as silent as a ghost. Her determination grew that she should out-last the man, wait for him to fall asleep, and then slip from the room. She had no doubt that she could accomplish this.

What Aubrielle didn't anticipate was how exhausted she was. The strain of emotions and the physical exertions of the day took their toll. She awoke with a start, unaware of how long she had been asleep, or even when she had fallen asleep. She only knew that she had that heavy groggy feeling, as one does when one does not sleep nearly enough. But no matter; she had a plan and needed to act on it. She listened for any sounds in the room but heard nothing. If St. Héver was still there, he was asleep. Perhaps her falling asleep hadn't been a bad thing after all.

She debated a moment as to whether or not she should roll over and take a look. Curiosity won over. Slowly, she turned onto her back.

The fire in the room was dim. St. Héver was still in his chair, sitting like stone, his ice-blue eyes staring into the dying embers. Not strangely, fury swept Aubrielle. She had waited for the man to weaken, had fallen asleep over the turmoil of it, only to awaken and see that he hadn't moved a muscle. Was the man not human? In a huff, she put her feet on the ground and stood up.

Kenneth turned his attention away from the fire, watching her as she took the coverlet and the linen covering the down mattress and tied the ends together. He remained silent as she ripped one of the canopies off the bed and tied it on the other end of the coverlet. He knew quite clearly what she was doing. He also knew that he was going to let her waste all of her effort and then tie her up with her own creation. If she wanted to push him, then he would push back.

It was past midnight as she pulled her makeshift rope off the bed and marched to the lancet window, ignoring Kenneth altogether. He hadn't tried to stop her so far. The cold air blew in from the north, running icy fingers through her silken hair; she shivered. A support post stood near the door, several feet from the window, and she tied the end of her rope to it. Still, St. Héver hadn't said a word. Aubrielle's first test of her rope unraveled the end; slightly chagrinned, not to mention concerned, she retied the end, more firmly this time. Testing it again, it held. She took the other end and tossed it out of the window. Peering from the sill, she could see that her rope fell several feet short of the bailey below. In fact, she would be dropping about twelve feet before hitting the ground. The odds weren't good.

She took the second and last canopy off the bed, reeled in her rope, and tied the canopy to it. It was amazing and methodical to watch her work, so dedicated and well processed in her endeavor. Tossing it out of the window again, the drop to the ground was now down to five feet. Much better odds. Without a word, Aubrielle gathered her skirt and prepared to leap onto the windowsill. She'd almost forgotten that St.

Héver was in the room until his powerful arms suddenly grabbed her. It was an instant fight.

"Let me go!"

Aubrielle kicked as he pulled her away from the window. Because of their first bloody encounter, Kenneth was aware of her skills and took no chances. He had her around the torso, her arms pinned, her body dangling as he took her over to the bed. As they reached the stripped mattress, Aubrielle somehow got a foot in behind his knee and tripped him. They crashed onto the bed.

Aubrielle grunted as his weight came down on her. Because she was struggling so much, Kenneth had landed half on her, half on the mattress. She tried to kick him so he clamped an enormous leg over her thighs, trapping her in a human vise.

Aubrielle shrieked in frustration, realizing she was effectively corralled. Kenneth's mouth was by her ear.

"Time to sleep, my lady," he said as casually as if he was talking about the weather. "Relax and go to sleep."

Aubrielle was grinding her teeth. "Let go of me, you beast," she growled. "Let me go or I swear you'll regret it."

"I have heard those threats before," he said steadily. "Go to sleep, now. 'Tis late."

She was more than frustrated that he had let her go through the motions of rigging an escape route, only to thwart her efforts. Deep down, she knew that he would stop her eventually, but it had been cruel of him to let her get her hopes up. She wasn't used to being impeded, but she had experienced an entire day and night full of St. Héver's preventative presence. She hated everyone, as they hated her.

Her fury dissolved into hot tears. Her struggles came to a halt and huge, painful sobs shook her small body. The more embarrassed she became, the deeper the sobs. Kenneth felt the weeping that shook her body, wondering if it was another ploy, yet instinctively knowing that it was not. Her sorrow was real. Her body was limp, a warm soft mass against him, and he loosened his grip on her. It was difficult to be so severe with her in her moment of weakness.

Kenneth had never been good with words or emotions. His mother had died when he was still an infant, leaving him to be raised by his father, a knight, who had been crushed by his wife's death and buried himself in alcohol to avoid the pain. Consequently, Kenneth had hardly known a compassionate or loving touch. Being sent to foster at age five, raised by the knights of Warwick Castle, had left him little concept of what emotion was. Years of being forced to repress any feeling he had left him numb to anything other than what his sworn duty dictated; if it dictated compassion, then he would mechanically give it. If it dictated mercy, then he grasped the concept well enough to deliver it. But he'd forced himself long ago to stop truly feeling anything. In his experience, it had always been too painful.

Which was why he was genuinely surprised to feel a strange tugging in his chest as Aubrielle wept. She was crying and it was his doing. But he had only been doing his duty. Could she not understand that?

"Why do you weep?" his voice was husky, commanding.

Aubrielle wept softly. "Leave me alone."

"As you wish."

She sobbed, sniffled, wiping her nose on her hand. "Why am I treated as if I am a mindless animal, meant to be caged?" she apparently wished to tell him in spite of her earlier retort. "God has given me a sharp mind, eager to learn, yet no one understands my needs. I have been educated but unable to further my knowledge."

Kenneth put a hand up, smoothing the brown strands of hair that had drifted across his cheek. The softness of her hair didn't escape his notice.

"Is that why you are attempting escape?"

"Of course. Why else did you think I was trying to leave?"

"A lover."

"I do not have a lover. Only a love of knowledge."

He fell silent a moment, contemplating. "What is it that you must discover?"

She sniffled again. Her sobs were lessening. "Something Man has been seeking for a thousand years."

"What is that?"

"The Grail."

Kenneth fell strangely silent. When he finally released her, Aubrielle realized she was sorry to see him go. She had enjoyed the warmth of his arms, even if he had been subduing her. She sat up on the bed, watching him as he went to the window to remove the make-shift rope.

His manner was stiff and cold. She sensed something more than his usual demeanor.

"So you are shocked by my answer?" she ventured.

He untied the knot on the column. "You speak blasphemy, lady."

She had heard that before. "Why?" she demanded. "Why must everyone that knows of my quest say that? Do you know that the only people who did not call it blasphemous were the monks of St. Wenburgh, the only men who would truly have the right to say so? If they do not believe it, why should you?"

He reeled in the rope. "Suffice it to say that now I know of your reasons for attempting escape, I shall do more than my diligence in ensuring that you do not."

Her brow furrowed. "Why do you have such bias and determination against me?"

Kenneth paused, rope in hand. He looked at her, stricken above all other thoughts with those of her beauty. He was a knight of the realm and all of the rigid requirements that went with it. Weakness of any kind had never been part of his nature. Now was not the time to start.

"I am a knight and I have a duty," he said simply. "Moreover, when I swore my oath of fealty, I vowed to God to protect the Faith, and that includes holy relics like the Grail. They are not meant to be sought like common treasure. They are not meant for mortals to touch, but to be revered and protected always."

She cocked her head. "Protect it from me?" He didn't say anything and she continued. "But you do not understand. It is my intention to bolster the Faith by the discovery of this most precious relic of Christ. I will do this for God's glory, and for England's."

He began to untie the knots of the linens so he could put them back on the bed. "I will not argue this point with you, lady. I have no interest in your logic or explanations, so you can save them for those who would listen."

Aubrielle could see that he would not be convinced. He was the coldest man she had ever met.

"Are you always so indifferent?" she asked softly.

His eyes were like ice. "If you will rise from the bed, I will replace these linens. 'Tis late and you should be asleep."

The softness in Aubrielle's voice was quickly replaced by hardness. "I do not require a nursemaid, knight. Other than your orders from my uncle, you'll do nothing else for me and you'll certainly not issue commands. Is that clear?"

"Aye, my lady."

She yanked the linens from him, placing them on the mattress as the monks at St. Wenburgh had taught her. Her lines were straight, her corners tight and perfect. Resigned to the fact that she would not be escaping this night, she removed her shoes and silently slipped under the coverlet.

As she lay there, facing the wall, she wondered what thoughts ran through St. Héver's mind. There was something to his coldness that ran beyond mere knightly training. All knights were supposed to be even tempered, chivalrous, and deadly to the enemy. It was as if St. Héver was somehow dead inside. She wondered why.

For the first time in weeks, she slept the entire night and well into the dawn.

CHAPTER THREE

KENNETH HAD WATCHED her sleep until Everett came to relieve him after sunrise. He relinquished his post with some reluctance, unsure if Everett could handle the lady. He would never have admitted that he did not want to relinquish guard duty because he had found watching the lady sleep a pleasant experience. But he left Everett with Lady Aubrielle and went down to the great hall where the earl was having his morning meal.

There were dogs everywhere fighting for the scraps. The hearth wasn't working correctly and smoke billowed up into the rafters as the steward and a couple of servants tried to clear the blockage. Garson sat at the long table, chewing on his bread with rotted teeth and wondering if he would ever find a meal pleasant again. His dour expression lifted when he saw Kenneth.

"Ah," he motioned the knight to the table. "And how is my niece this morning? She didn't give you too much trouble, I trust?"

Kenneth shook his head. "None at all, my lord."

The earl cocked an eyebrow. "I am sure you are being generous, Kenneth. Do you mean to tell me that she behaved like a princess and went right to bed without incident?"

Kenneth couldn't lie to him; he shrugged his big shoulders. "She was determined to escape at one point, but I was able to convince her that lowering herself four stories to the bailey on a rope of bed linen would not be the wisest decision."

"A rope of linen?" the earl almost spit his bread onto the table. "Surely you jest?"

"Hardly, my lord. She would have broken her neck had I not intervened."

Garson shook his head, taking a large gulp of watered wine. "Not only is she determined, she is reckless. A dangerous combination."

Kenneth didn't reply; his silence was agreement enough. He stood there a moment, waiting patiently as the earl swirled his wine. It seemed as if there was much on his mind.

"I am sure you are exhausted," he finally said, without elaborating on his thoughts. "Take your leave. I do not require your services the rest of the day, as I am sure you could use the rest. And do not lie to me and tell me that you do not need to sleep."

Kenneth fought off a grin; it was a joke between them that Kenneth never slept. The earl accused him of being a nocturnal beast, ever watchful, always vigilant. Dipping his head respectfully to his liege, he quit the hall and made his way to the knight's quarters.

The two structures that serviced the upper class warriors were built against the outer wall. As he traversed the bailey, he crossed paths with Reid de Bowland and Sir Bradley Trevalyn. The two knights rounded out the earl's five-man knight corps, seasoned men with retainers and power of their own. Reid was a tall, congenial knight with copper-colored hair, while Bradley was shorter, stockier, and more rugged in appearance. They saluted Kenneth as their paths merged.

"My lord," Reid greeted him. "I see you've returned from both battles unscathed."

"Both battles?"

Reid grinned as Bradley spoke up. "Everett told us about Lady Aubrielle. If Dinas Bran wasn't enough, you had to take it on the chin from her as well."

Kenneth grunted. "Hardly a battle, I assure you. Properly handled, she's quite manageable."

"It helps when you employ ropes and shackles, Ken," Bradley muttered.

"I did nothing of the sort." He cocked an eyebrow. "The weight of my body and brute strength were sufficient."

"Aye, but barely," Reid offered.

"Barely."

He left Reid and Bradley with snorts of humor as he completed his trip to the knight's quarters. Entering the larger of the two buildings, he made his way to the room at the end of a long, narrow hall. It was a dingy room with a small slit window for light and ventilation. If he stopped to think about it, it was a depressing little room, but it was something he was used to. There was comfort in the dreariness. Removing his armor, he arranged it carefully on the rack in the corner. When he finally lay upon the hard bed, he found that he could not sleep at all.

For a man whose only physical contact with women had been an occasional whore, his thoughts lingered around the soft sweetness of Aubrielle in his arms. She hadn't been like any other woman he'd ever had contact with. She smelled sweet, and her hair was silken and clean. Her skin, from what he had touched whilst grabbing her wrists, had been baby-soft. No, she certainly wasn't like any woman he'd ever been with. It was like comparing a priceless wine against rancid ale.

She was a beautiful, fine woman, no doubt. But it was her mind that he questioned. Her quest had him puzzled; the search for the chalice of Christ was the root of her attempts to escape. There was no lover, which strangely relieved him, and her only reason in wanting to flee Kirk was to travel to Glastonbury. That's why she had run from him in the forest, and why she had made her foolish attempt to escape her chamber. But to seek what Arthur and his knights could not find was not only arrogant, it was sacrilegious. He couldn't believe she had such a lofty goal. If God had meant it to be discovered, He would have arranged for such an event by those far more worthy than Aubrielle Grace de Witney.

He somehow managed to fall into a fitful sleep. As a trained warrior, he always slept lightly, but the noise from the bailey didn't bother him in his exhausted state. He slept through all of it.

The scuffling of feet in the late afternoon awakened him, however. He was just sitting up as a knock fell upon his door. He grunted a word of entry and the panel opened. Kenneth's squire, a lad of nineteen years, stuck his head into the room. His dark, handsome features were wrought with concern.

"My lord," he said. "Captain le Cor says you should come."

Kenneth passed a weary hand over his face before reaching for his boots. "What is it, Max?"

"The earl's niece, my lord," the boy said. "She is in the vault."

Kenneth wasn't surprised. "What happened?"

"She hit Sir Everett across the head with a fire poker."

He didn't let the lad see the smile that tugged at his lips. He didn't know why he found it so humorous. He simply nodded his head and pulled on his other boot. The lad preceded him from the knight's quarters, leading him across the busy bailey. Kenneth plowed a straight path while Max dodged soldiers and animals; he had yet to acquire the commanding presence that his liege had. Eventually they reached the vault that was lodged on the two lower levels of Kirk's enormous gatehouse.

Kenneth descended the narrow spiral steps into the dungeon, his bulk barely fitting down the passage. Widely spaced torches lit the way. On the first level below the main ground level, they found the earl, Lucius, Reid, Bradley and Everett. One look at Everett with a huge welt across his forehead and a cut lip, and Kenneth cocked an eyebrow.

"I told you to watch your back."

Everett gave him an intolerant look. "It wasn't my back she struck."

"What happened?"

"You wouldn't believe it; she simply walked to the fireplace, picked up the brass poker, walked right up to me and slugged me across the face."

"What did you say to upset her?"

"I told her that she could not leave."

"Even when she cried and pleaded?"

Everett rolled his eyes. "That woman is incapable of crying. She sat like a stone, all day, hardly moving and not speaking a word. Then, she asks if she may leave. I told her, regretfully, that she may not, so she smacks me on the face with the poker."

"That's it?"

"That's enough."

Kenneth looked at the earl; he was curious how the man would react to the latest incident. Garson was leaning against the wall, his expression weary. His focus was on Kenneth.

"It would seem that you are the only one able to control her," he said.

Kenneth shrugged modestly. "I am not sure if you would call it control, my lord. I literally had to sit on her. And I didn't let her get near the fire poker."

Reid and Bradley fought off varying degrees of smirks. Everett looked disgusted. Lucius held no discernible expression. The earl, however, cast Kenneth a penetrating look. "I cannot have her attacking my knights."

"Understood, my lord."

"Then consider her your problem until the problem is solved."

Kenneth didn't like the sound of that. "My problem, my lord?"

It was apparent that the earl was tired of dealing with his niece. She had only been at Kirk one day and, already, he was done with her. He should have never consented to having her in the first place.

"Since you are the only one who can handle her, I henceforth leave her to you. But if you come to the conclusion that she cannot be controlled, you have my permission to commit her to a convent, or a prison, or whatever else you deem necessary." Garson pushed himself off the wall, heading for the narrow steps. "I am finished with this. I wash my hands of the girl. Do what you will with her, but I do not want to hear any more about her. Is that clear?"

Kenneth knew he could not protest the decision, much as he wanted to. He was, frankly, stunned. "It is, my lord."

Lucius gave him a long look as he followed the earl up the steps. Everett, not wanting to be sucked into being a party to Kenneth's task, followed shortly and took Max with him. Reid and Bradley were the last to leave, offering some semblance of assistance that was politely refused. They felt sorry for Kenneth, but were nonetheless glad it wasn't their problem.

When everyone had fled, Kenneth stood there a moment, thinking the earl most cowardly for his actions. As an obedient knight, however, he prepared to fulfill his requirements. He had no choice.

It was dark in the dungeon, smelling of mold and rot. It was a hellish place for a man much less a woman. There was a cell several feet in front of him and a second cell off to his right. He peered into the second cell; it was empty. Looking into the first, he could see Aubrielle seated against the far wall, a heavy iron shackle around her ankle. Her arms were scratched and bleeding, and her gown was torn.

She caught movement and looked up, meeting Kenneth's icy gaze. She was trying very hard to be brave. Slowly, he entered the cell, looking down at her cuts and bruises. Knowing Everett, there was no possibility that the man had beaten her. Whatever was on her had happened in the ensuing struggle to get her into the cell. He could have only imagined the battle.

He didn't quite know what to say. He crouched down, several feet away. Aubrielle met his gaze steadily.

"So," she said quietly. "I see that they have called for you. And how are you to punish me for my actions this time?"

As he continued to gaze at her, his most prevailing thought was how beautiful she was. He'd spent all last night gazing at her beauty and it had managed to disrupt his normally steady mind. Now, looking at her, he realized to his horror that the feelings of fascination were growing stronger. But he had no time to indulge his foolishness.

"You will listen to me carefully, lady, for I will only explain this one time," he said in a low voice. "The earl wants nothing more to do with you. For all intents and purposes, you are no longer a consideration or a burden to him. He has entrusted your welfare to me entirely, to see to and to do with as I see fit and necessary. In simple terms, you are now my ward. Do you understand what I have said so far?"

Aubrielle stared at him, confused. "Your ward?"

"Aye."

"What does that mean, exactly?"

"That you belong to me."

Her look of confusion grew into one of outrage. "So the term 'ward' is a kind word for a concubine?" She rattled her chains violently. "I shall have none of it, do you hear me? I shall not be your whore!"

He remained cool. "You misunderstand. Our agreement does not entail physical or emotional terms. The earl has ordered me to either subdue you or commit you. Your choices are to either learn to conduct yourself as a proper lady, with all of the behavior modifications related thereto, or to be committed to a convent where you'll never again know freedom or leisure. The earl is unwilling to indulge your current behavior a moment longer. You have pushed him to the limit of endurance and a decision must be made."

She stared at him before turning away. "Are you asking me to make that choice now?"

"You have no alternative."

It was clear she was attempting to hold back hot, angry tears. The shackle around her ankle had rubbed a bloody welt and she touched it distractedly as if trying to ease the pain. "Do you think a convent can hold me?" she murmured. "I can escape far easier there."

"If that is your intent, then I have your uncle's permission to throw you in prison."

Her head snapped up. "You wouldn't dare!"

"If there is no other choice."

"On what charge? I have done nothing!"

"I am sure your uncle would swear that you've done something. Stealing, perhaps. Or perhaps you owe him money and refuse to pay. Believe me when I tell you that it doesn't matter what charge. You will go to prison if that is the decision."

Her mouth was hanging open in disbelief. "All of this simply to keep me from following my dream?" she whispered. "I am not a criminal, sir knight. I am a lady of noble birth, highly educated and worthy of respect. I have never done anything even remotely evil or subversive in my entire life. Why is there such a set against me?"

Kenneth could feel her pain; it was radiating from her eyes, reaching out to touch him. He had a strange sensation, suspecting it was weakness but unsure how to react to it.

"It was evil to hit Everett," he said simply.

She averted her gaze. "I do not like the way he looks at me."

"What do you mean?"

"He stares at me. Strangely. I do not like it."

"Is that why you hit him?"

She shrugged. "I hit him because he touched me."

Kenneth stood up from his crouch, so fast that the movement startled Aubrielle. He was standing over her, his eyes like shards of glass. "You will tell me now. How did he touch you?"

Aubrielle had found herself in many confrontational situations with St. Héver, but she had never been truly frightened of him until now. There was something in his voice that was inherently terrifying.

"When I tried to leave," she hated the quiver in her voice. "He put his hand on my arm to try and force me to stop. So I hit him."

Kenneth's mercurial fury abated. In fact, when he thought on it, he was surprised at how venomous he had felt at the thought of someone other than himself laying a hand on her. Of course, it was perfectly all right for him to physically restrain her, even lay on her if necessary in order to control her, but in his mind he was apparently the only one allowed to do so. He realized he would have killed Everett had the man's intentions been anything other than chivalrous. He looked down at the frightened woman as his anger cooled, feeling like an idiot.

"He should have spanked you," he muttered.

"What was that?"

"I said that he should have spanked you," he repeated, loudly. "No, you are not evil or subversive in the conventional sense, but I have never in my life seen such a headstrong female. A good spanking would do you a world of good."

Her expression hardened. A hand drifted up to her shoulder, fingering the material of her gown. "If you are thinking of beating obedience into me, do not bother." She yanked the top of her sleeve down, exposing a good portion of the top of her left shoulder blade. "The monks of St. Wenburgh already tried."

Kenneth could see the montage of faded scars on her back. Someone had obviously taken a branch to her. He'd seen flogging many a time; he'd delivered more than his share. As a child, he'd been the recipient of one or two rounds. It was a painful, ugly act. He didn't know why he was suddenly coming to regret being so harsh with her.

"How old were you?" his voice was husky.

She pulled her garment back up on to her shoulder, torn between embarrassment and indifference. "I was nine years of age the first time."

"The first time? There were more?"

"Three."

For the first time since they'd met, his icy façade faltered. He exhaled slowly as he reclaimed his crouched position. He'd never before seen such stubbornness, yet he found himself admiring her for her determination.

"And still you dream," he murmured. "Will nothing short of death convince you to change your path?"

A smile spread across her lips. "Have you never had anything that meant so much to you that you would brave fire and brimstone to attain it? We are mere mortals, Sir Kenneth. Our lives are finite. All we have are our dreams before our lives are quickly ended. If I must endure tribulation in the pursuit of my dream, it is of little consequence. I could never live with myself had I not tried."

He understood, somewhat. But the concepts of dreams did not come easily to him. He'd never been allowed to have them. "Whatever you feel you must pursue and however you feel you must achieve it, you must understand that your ideas are unconventional."

"I understand that. But unconventional does not necessarily mean wrong."

"Agreed. But it has taken many hundreds of years to achieve the civility and society that we have now. Unconventional ideas threaten the order of our world."

She thought a moment, seeing an open door for debate. "But did we not achieve such civility by pursuing thoughts and dreams that, perhaps at one time, would seem unconventional? Did we not learn by trying and by making mistakes?"

He could see where she was leading. "Aye."

"But still we forged on, with bizarre notions and half-witted schemes that, perhaps when the time was right, blossomed into fruition." She smiled at him, sensing that he was open to her logic. "All I ask is to be a part of that discovery process, to advance our ideals of religion and the heights of our knowledge. I know that going to Glastonbury to find the chalice of Christ must seem strange, but perhaps believing in a man who preached the love of his enemy seemed strange a thousand years ago to those people who eventually formed the basis of Christianity. But it doesn't seem strange now."

Kenneth didn't care that he was actually listening to what she had to say. She was passionate and articulate, and made a great deal of sense. But his inner demons began to fight him and it was difficult to resist.

"Your reasoning is sound, lady," he said softly. "But there were also those crucified for those unconventional beliefs. Even now, heresy is punishable by death. No matter what your dreams or beliefs, you must tread carefully."

"I know," she said bravely. "Those marks you see on my back tell the tale. But it did not stop me."

"What would?"

"Finding the Grail or die trying."

He sighed. "What makes you believe that you can find this Grail that the great Arthur and his knights could not?"

She seemed to back off. He could see she was hiding something. "I simply believe that I can, that's all."

He lifted an eyebrow. "That's not all. Tell me why you believe you can find it."

"I just do," she leaned back against the stone wall, coated with green growth. "May I ask you a question, sir knight?"

"Perhaps."

"Do you intend to leave me in this place all night?"

He thought a night in the vault might help her see the error of her ways. But then again, maybe not. No matter his indecision, she had to be punished for striking Everett.

"I do," he replied steadily. "Do you require anything to make your stay more palatable?"

It was a foolish question; the woman had absolutely nothing but the clothes on her back. She wasn't even wearing shoes.

"No. I am quite content."

She was lying, but it was a commendable lie. Without a word, Kenneth quit the cell. He returned shortly with a lit torch; night was falling and the weak light that strayed down the stairwell was fading rapidly. Soon it would be pitch black. He propped the torch in the iron wall sconce.

"I shall return with your supper."

"Do not bother." She shifted, laying down in an attempt to get comfortable. "I am not hungry. I simply want to sleep. It's been a busy day of thrashing knights."

It was a humorous statement. Kenneth looked at her as if she was mad, but inside, he was grinning. There was no possible way that he was going to allow her to see him crack a smile.

He left the cell and returned a nominal amount of time later carrying bread, a knuckle of beef, and a cup of ale. Aubrielle still lay on the ground, her eyes closed, presumably asleep. He stood there a moment, watching her quiver. It occurred to him that it must be terribly cold on the hard stone. He simply couldn't stand by and observe her discomfort. If she would not allow him to bring her anything to see to her comfort in her time of punishment, perhaps she wouldn't object to what comfort he could offer her.

He set the tray down and went to sit against the wall, next to her head. Carefully, he put his hands underneath her shoulders and gently lifted. She was limp, like a sleeping cat, as if she had no bones at all. She became lucid as he settled her head atop his right thigh.

"What...?" she muttered.

"Shh, quiet," he put his hand on her head to silence her. "Be still now. Go back to sleep."

The trauma of the day must have been exhausting, for she fell back asleep without another word. Kenneth settled back against the stone, his hand still on her head, wondering if he was going above and beyond the call of his knightly duties. Was he overstepping his bounds? Perhaps he wasn't doing enough? She was his charge, after all. He'd never had a charge in his life, especially not a woman. He didn't want one, even now, but he was strangely pleased by it. It was a peculiar situation.

Aubrielle shivered again and he moved his hand from her head and put it on her arm; it was cold. In fact, the whole dungeon was cold. He moved his hand back and forth, rubbing some warmth back into her slender arm. Damn her for not allowing him to bring her a coverlet. Now he would have to spend all night rubbing her flesh to make sure she didn't freeze. It would be a very long night.

The dawn came too soon as far as he was concerned.

Read the rest of **ISLAND OF GLASS, BOOK 2, DRAGONBLADE TRILOGY** in eBook or in paperback.

ABOUT KATHRYN LE VEQUE

Medieval Just Got Real.

KATHRYN LE VEQUE is a USA TODAY Bestselling author, an Amazon All-Star author, and a #1 bestselling, award-winning, multi-published author in Medieval Historical Romance and Historical Fiction. She has been featured in the NEW YORK TIMES and on USA TODAY's HEA blog. In March 2015, Kathryn was the featured cover story for the March issue of InD'Tale Magazine, the premier Indie author magazine. She was also a quadruple nominee (a record!) for the prestigious RONE awards for 2015.

Kathryn's Medieval Romance novels have been called 'detailed', 'highly romantic', and 'character-rich'. She crafts great adventures of love, battles, passion, and romance in the High Middle Ages. More than that, she writes for both women AND men – an unusual crossover for a romance author – and Kathryn has many male readers who enjoy her stories because of the male perspective, the action, and the adventure.

On October 29, 2015, Amazon launched Kathryn's Kindle Worlds Fan Fiction site WORLD OF DE WOLFE PACK. Please visit Kindle Worlds for Kathryn Le Veque's World of de Wolfe Pack and find many action-packed adventures written by some of the top authors in their genre using Kathryn's characters from the de Wolfe Pack series. As Kindle World's FIRST Historical Romance fan fiction world, Kathryn Le Veque's World of de Wolfe Pack will contain all of the great story-telling you have come to expect.

Kathryn loves to hear from her readers. Please find Kathryn on Facebook at Kathryn Le Veque, Author, or join her on Twitter @kathrynleveque, and don't forget to visit her website at www. kathrynleveque.com.

CPSIA information can be obtained at www.ICGtesting.com
Printed in the USA
BVOW06s0144040516

446594BV00020B/112/P

9 781494 229597